The Pharaoh's Amulet

Andrew Clawson

This book is a work of fiction. The characters, incidents, and dialogue are drawn from the author's imagination and are not to be construed as real. Any resemblance to actual events or persons, living or dead, is entirely coincidental.

Get Your FREE Copy of the Harry Fox story *THE NAPOLEON CIPHER*.

Sign up for my VIP reader mailing list, and I'll send you the novel for free.

Details can be found at the end of this book.

Chapter 1

Brooklyn

A water bottle nearly killed Harry Fox.

It lay in wait for him as he moved silently through the darkness of an old candy factory in a quiet corner of Brooklyn. A factory permanently under construction thanks to the machinations of Altin Cana. Plastic sheets hung from the ceiling. Temporary railings guarded open stairwells. The elevator door hung slightly open. And a plastic water bottle lay on the scuffed concrete floor, invisible in the darkness.

Harry slid past a window and moved with purpose down the hall to a turn ahead. Frigid night air gusted through an opening in the exterior wall, thinly covered with black plastic sheeting that snapped in the breeze. Clouds covered the moon, leaving Harry moving blind. He picked up his pace, reaching for the flapping sheet to pull it back and let in a sliver of light.

Plastic crunched underfoot.

His shoe slipped across the water bottle and sent him hurtling forward, arms flailing for balance as he crashed into something in the darkness, something solid that sent him toward a gaping hole in the wall where a window should have been. A gaping hole three stories above hard concrete. Harry grabbed at the black sheeting as his momentum carried him forward into the hole. He grabbed at the thick plastic with two hands, but a gust of wind sent it whipping between his legs, tripping him up as he twisted and fell backward through the hole, plummeting into the night's cold embrace.

As he fell, the sheeting tore away bit by bit, popping free from the nails holding it. Harry plunged toward the sidewalk in a jerky, halting fall, each nail holding his weight for an instant before giving way. One, two, three *pops* and at last he plummeted sideways until an invisible fist punched him in the kidney, stopping him cold.

His body went numb. Harry gasped for air. He'd have screamed if he could have made a sound. He threw an arm out to grab whatever had hit him, and connected with an unlit floodlight bolted to the brickwork of the exterior wall. He latched onto it in a death grip and took his weight off the black sheeting now torn halfway off the wall. Harry closed his eyes and went still. *Maybe they didn't see me.*

Seconds passed. No shouts, no pounding footsteps. And no gunshots. Harry opened one eye, then the other. His nose was pressed against the brick wall. One arm was wrapped around the massive floodlight; the other kept the bunched sheeting under an elbow. He leaned back from the brickwork. The opening he'd fallen through was only a few feet above him. If he could get a hand on it, maybe he could haul himself back into the building and avoid becoming a greasy spot on the concrete over thirty feet below.

The *smack* of a heavy steel door banging open sounded beneath him as a man walked out of the building to stand on a lower landing. A lighter flashed, his cigarette caught, and the guard Harry desperately hoped to avoid leaned against the railing directly beneath him and drew down on a cigarette.

The floodlight casing jabbed into Harry's side. He clenched his jaw and tried to hug the wall. *Don't move.* The guard might not look up. That's all it would take for Harry to find himself in the clutches of Altin Cana, the last person in the world Harry wanted to see. Albanian gangsters like Altin didn't like people breaking into their buildings. They liked it even less when they did so planning to steal a valuable cultural artifact.

A newspaper delivery truck rumbled past on the street below. Harry watched the guard turn his head to follow it, puffing as he stared, smoke clouds rising above him. Finally, a swirling ember twirled in the night air as the guard flicked his cigarette butt toward the street and went back inside, the steel door banging closed behind him.

Air burst from Harry's lungs. How long he'd been holding his breath he had no idea. A few more gulps of frigid air got his nerve up. While one hand kept a tenuous grip on the plastic sheeting, his other arm hugged the floodlight like a new best friend. He reached up for the window opening as his armpit threatened to rip in half on the floodlight. The window opening waited just out of reach.

Harry grabbed the sheeting and shifted his weight to give his other arm a break. Another *pop* as another nail tore loose, and the plastic shifted, plunging him a few inches further downward. A second try to reach the opening cost him two more nails. Harry pressed his forehead against the brick wall and cursed the woman who'd put him in this mess. *Last time I ever help you.* Nora Doyle was in for an earful if he survived the night.

Harry frowned. The sheet was ready to come down if he pulled too hard, and the few remaining nails couldn't hold his weight long enough for him to push off the wall and swing back to the opening. Harry adjusted his grip on the floodlight casing, the only sturdy handhold available. He paused. The plastic sheeting couldn't hold his weight. But the floodlight could.

It might work. Harry leaned away from the wall, judging angles and distance. Yes, it might. If he played it just right. Before common sense could intervene he pushed his toes into tiny grooves in the brickwork and scrambled up, the tips of his boots catching just enough to get him moving vertically. At the same time, he pulled on the sheeting, using it to execute an awkward one-armed pull-up. His stomach sank as one of the last nails popped loose under his weight, feet churning wildly against the bricks and as the sheet ripped free, Harry flung his torso over the floodlight to safety.

Torn black sheeting fluttered to the sidewalk as Harry lay across the metal casing, chest heaving. The bolts holding the floodlight groaned ominously. It wasn't built to hold a grown man's weight. With nothing to grab but the brick wall, he eased his legs gently up and got one knee and then his foot atop the light fixture, balancing with the skill of a doomed man. Slowly, carefully, he placed his other foot beside the first and then, like an acrobat, he was crouching low on the casing, arms splayed to either side.

The window opening was only a few feet away. If he could push off the casing and it held long enough, he should be able to grab the frame and pull himself up to safety. Unless he bounced off the wall as he jumped, or lost his grip trying to haul himself inside. He shook his head. No time to think like that. Harry laughed without humor. *I've made it out of tougher spots.*

A bolt sprang loose from the floodlight casing and his foot slipped. One hand shot out and left a trail of blood across the brickwork, his fingers shredding as he barely kept his balance. The floodlight screeched and another bolt clanged as he lowered himself, aimed at the opening and jumped.

The floodlight casing snapped in half to steal much of his momentum. Gravity reached for him, not quite grabbing hold as he half-flew, half-fell toward the opening, his arms out and fingers reaching for the concrete edge. One hand caught the lip and he latched on. His other hand grabbed for purchase. And missed.

He crashed into the wall. His face smacked into the bricks right below the opening, brain rattling as he skidded along it, hanging by one hand to swing pendulum-like across the wall. His free hand scrabbled for a hold on the sill, and he nearly got one finger on, but then his hand slipped across it and his weight kept moving. His legs splayed out as he tried frantically to slow the deadly swinging and then, gritting his teeth, he heaved himself back toward the opening and clamped his second hand onto the sill. He pulled up, chin and nose and who knew what else grinding over the rough brick until he flipped himself into the building and rolled onto his back.

Harry gulped air until his arms stopped shaking. *Nothing to it.* After a few moments, he sat up, rubbed a hand over his sweaty face, and had to bite off a scream as the salty sweat hit his cuts and scrapes. A minute passed before he could stand and look down the shadowed hallway. No guards in sight, no footsteps sounding down the hall. Harry was still in the game.

He retrieved the small crowbar he'd brought with him and began to move, hugging what would have been the inside wall if this place had walls, keeping close to standing studs and as far away from the windowless frames as he could get. Harry had entered the building from the very top and needed to work his way to the basement, a path that required passing at least a few of Altin Cana's guards. The Albanian crime boss kept his stolen artifacts in the basement of this permanently under-construction building. According to the city, this old factory would eventually become an apartment building, though in truth Altin had other plans. Every year he moved the building's ownership from one shell company to another, each time selling it to himself at a profit and artificially increasing the value. Each sale required new paperwork, delaying any further construction and letting Altin use the building for his true purpose: a safe house for storing whatever Altin wanted to keep hidden.

Including a marble bust depicting Philip of Macedon. A bust commissioned by Philip's son, Alexander the Great. It was the only known surviving image of Philip in the world. A bust recently acquired by Altin Cana's right-hand man, Stefan Rudovic. Stefan wanted fewer things more in life than to see Harry Fox dead. Stealing the bust from Altin's safehouse would cut Stefan deeply. However, Harry had other reasons for risking his life to get to this particular hunk of marble. Reasons that didn't matter one bit if Altin's guards captured Harry tonight.

He made it to a stairwell entrance, easing the heavy metal door open and moving down to the second level where the walls were thankfully intact, concealing him from view and keeping the cold night air at bay. Harry moved down to the next landing, opened a door and snuck in. It looked much like the upper floor, with plastic sheets, open windows and construction debris lying around. These upper floors were construction zones meant to hide the true wealth below, tucked behind a false wall in a corner of the basement where the occasional inspectors never cared to look.

Harry knew all of this because his own boss had a man working inside Altin's operation. This inside man had told Harry about the building and about the guards on the first floor and in the basement. He had also told Harry it was a fool's errand to try to get in; the only access route involved sliding down the empty elevator shaft to the basement level, then climbing back up the open shaft before jumping across rooftops to escape. Harry had wanted nothing to do with it. Until he realized it was the only way to save his oldest friend in the world.

Harry gritted his teeth. *Joey had better appreciate this.*

The elevator shaft ran down the building's center. A wooden barricade was erected in front of the closed doors, so Harry used the crowbar to lever a board loose. That allowed him to lean through and use the crowbar to pull the doors open. They clanged and banged. Harry went still. Silence. Nobody had heard him. At least he hoped not.

Braided steel cables dangled in front of him. The elevator car had been removed, leaving the cables to sway gently when he touched them. He leaned out over the shaft, looking up and down to find two empty black holes, one above and one below. A small headlamp came out of his other pocket. The headlamp went on his head and Harry selected the red-light setting before feeling around the corner of the door, his aching fingers finding and latching on to a metal ladder running the length of the shaft. It held steady when he stepped onto a rung with one foot, then the other. Slowly, he began to descend.

The red light let him keep some of his night vision while also emitting a low light signature. Halfway down the shaft he stopped, turning an ear toward the blackness below and hearing nothing. He wiped the sweat from his brow and flicked it off. His hand brushed against something. *What the heck is that?*

He turned to find a rope dangling behind him. Two ropes, actually, strung tight next to the braided metal cords. Why were those ropes in here? Harry tugged on one. It barely moved. Why they'd be in here he had no idea. He turned back to the ladder and kept descending until he reached the basement. On the floor sat a wooden box with two ropes tied to it. Ropes that disappeared into the darkness above. He pulled on one and the box moved. It appeared that workers had rigged this box to carry tools or other small objects up and down the shaft using a pulley system with the two ropes. Harry stepped over the box to the closed doors in front of him.

This would be tricky. The inside man had said this door faced away from where the guards usually sat, so if Harry opened it quietly he could most likely get into the main part of the basement undetected. A *chance*. Pry open the elevator door, get to the false wall and make his way out with the marble bust in tow. Easy. Harry stuck his crowbar between the elevator doors and slowly levered them open. *Easy*. He flicked his headlamp off.

The doors separated several inches, enough to allow him to peer through. Nothing moved outside; there were no footsteps, no cries of alarm. Another few inches, then several more, and Harry could stick his head out. The basement was shrouded in darkness, the only light coming through several street-level windows near the ceiling. Harry opened the doors fully as he stepped out of the shaft. If any guards happened past he'd have to chance it they didn't realize those doors should be closed, not open. He didn't plan on staying there long enough to test that chance.

The false wall was off to his right, next to a massive tool chest called a job box. Sheeting, boards and construction material were strewn everywhere. A furnace hummed somewhere in the distance, while pipes ran across the ceiling in every direction before disappearing into the walls. He moved around the central elevator shaft toward the front exit. Light snuck through a partially open door, along with the sounds of a television. It seemed a soccer game was on, the announcers shouting in rapid-fire Spanish.

He moved back to put the shaft between him and the open door before turning on his headlamp. The job box was right where Harry had been told it would be. Harry stood to one side of the box and ran his hands over what looked like damp stones along a specific section of wall. Felt like them, too, except some of the stones weren't quite damp. They were cool, but dry, because they weren't real stones. His fingernail found an almost invisible crack in a specific stone, one with a barely noticeable cut on it. The stone his informant had told him to look for. Harry leaned on it, pushing against the wall with his entire weight. It held. He pushed harder, and with a *click* the stone slid into the wall.

A section of the wall swung inward, a door made to look like part of the basement wall opening. Harry stepped forward, then stopped abruptly with his foot inches off the ground. No need to walk into a booby trap. He'd done that before and it had never ended well. The light on his headlamp switched from red to white when he pressed a button, washing out in front of him to light up the hidden room. Harry did a double take.

A Roman shield.

A towering rectangular shield stood in front of him. He'd seen shields like this before in museums, a few in private collections. A Roman soldier had once carried this shield as he marched with his legion a thousand years ago. The shield should never have been in a basement like this. It shouldn't, but here it was, and Harry knew who was responsible. The same man who had brought the exquisite Chinese vase here, the one sitting beside the Roman shield. And the pair of samurai swords on a table. They looked authentic—and sharp enough to slice through limbs.

The man responsible was Stefan Rudovic. A man Harry had last seen in Greece, limping away after attacking Harry inside an ancient Greek temple. Stefan had clearly recovered from his injuries and was back in the black-market antiquities trade. Harry's jaw tightened. Stefan would be after Harry with a vengeance when he realized Harry had stolen the marble bust from this hiding place.

He pushed that worry aside and focused on the reason he'd come. Philip was the father of the most successful general in history, and the only accepted portrait of him sat right in front of Harry now, concealed in a dark Brooklyn basement. Harry studied the fine-grained marble carving. It stood a foot high, its aristocratic nose and tight lips forming a stern expression that seemed to warn Harry as he reached out his hand. The bust of Alexander the Great's father went into a bag Harry had brought with him, a specially designed one with straps he put over his shoulders and cinched tight. Now he could run if need be and the awkward bust wouldn't slow him down. Much.

He ignored the other tables in the room as he headed back for the hidden door. Ancient Roman coins and what looked like gold ingots were left behind as Harry flicked his light back to red and stepped through the open door, closing it behind him. With luck, Altin Cana and his goons wouldn't know the bust was missing before Harry used it to end the Canas' war on his employer.

The small but weighty carving pressed tight against his back. Harry touched the knuckledusters tucked into one pocket, then moved quickly back to the elevator shaft. Climb back to the third floor, head out onto the fire escape, then up to the roof where he could retrace his path across several buildings. Quickly, quietly, and without anyone knowing he had even been here.

Harry stepped around the elevator shaft toward the doors. A man stood in front of them.

"Hey, Albi." The man's back was to Harry as he spoke. "Did you open this?"

Harry didn't move. The man hadn't heard him yet. The man kept staring at the open elevator doors, reaching out a hesitant hand out to touch them.

"Albi." The man raised his voice, this time yelling toward the sound of the soccer match. "Who opened this door?"

"Be quiet, Rudi. The match is on," Albi shouted from the room. "I cannot hear over your loud mouth."

Rudi mumbled something under his breath about Albi's mother. "Who opened this door?" he asked more softly, as though the door would explain itself.

Harry spoke from the darkness. "I opened it."

Rudi spun around. Harry balled his reinforced fist and blasted Rudi directly on the chin. Rudi never saw it coming, and with a resounding *crack* he dropped in a heap. So much for Harry slipping away unnoticed.

Harry knelt beside the unconscious man. The pistol he found in Rudi's waistband was tossed in one direction, the magazine with its bullets in the other. Harry stood, stepped into the elevator shaft and hauled himself up the ladder, nearly reaching the first floor before Albi's voice filtered up the shaft.

"Rudi?"

Harry passed the first-floor elevator doors. Now Albi was really shouting.

"Rudi, where are you?"

The closed second-floor doors were in front of him when Albi found his friend.

"Rudi, wake up."

Harry accelerated, the sound of each step banging in the hollow elevator shaft like hammers striking. Albi didn't miss it.

"What is that noise?"

Harry went still, suspended halfway between the second and third floors. Albi's voice sounded. Light filled the shaft and Harry flew up the ladder. Too late.

"There he is!"

Harry's feet sounded like thunder. The second-floor doors were just out of reach as the two Albanians shouted below him.

"He took my gun," Rudi yelled. His voice sounded groggy.

Albi didn't have that problem, however. The flashlight beam waved crazily an instant before a gunshot roared. Sparks flew to Harry's side as the bullet pinged off the shaft inches away. Another blast, and sparks erupted on his other side.

"Keep shooting up the ladder," Rudi yelled. Albi responded with a barrage of fire, each shot more inaccurate than the last.

He won't miss forever. The second-floor doors were just ahead.

"Take the light," Albi yelled. The swaying flashlight beam locked on Harry. Albi wouldn't miss now. In the half-second it took Albi to aim, Harry jumped.

He flew backward, twisting in midair as Albi fired, reaching for the ropes hanging behind him. One hand got hold, the other missed, and he swung across the void to smack against the far wall. He bounced off, and as he began swinging back toward the other wall, his other hand found a grip on the ropes. Back he swung—into the flashlight beam. Albi fired, the shot whizzing past Harry's backside.

Harry pulled himself up the rope like a spider as he flew back toward the first wall, then kicked off it to propel himself toward the third-floor doors. As the flashlight beam came back, he let go of the rope and flew straight through the open doors, boards cracking and flying as he punched through them a beat before more gunfire boomed below. Harry crashed to the floor as more shouting came from the shaft's bottom.

Harry scrambled to his feet. Albi was shouting again.

"Intruder on the third floor. Jon, Lou—get him." Static crackled before more voices responded. *Albi's on a radio.*

Harry ran for the fire escape. If he could just make it to the third-floor landing, he could get back up to the roof, where the board he'd used earlier to cross from a neighboring building to this one was tucked carefully against the edge. It was a quick tightrope-walk back across, high over the alleyway, and then he could escape over the rooftops to safety. As he rounded a corner, however, he collided with a sawhorse, juking into a toolbox to send the contents flying with a deafening clatter. If the bad guys didn't know where to find him before, they did now. He scooped up a wrench and bolted toward the fire door.

When he reached it, he skidded to a halt and eased the door open rather than bursting through. Frigid air snaked down his sweaty neck as he stretched a leg out and placed one foot on the fire escape landing.

Gunfire filled the air. Harry jumped back as bullets whined past him, some banging off the metal grating. Another voice rang out from below.

"He is on the fire escape."

Harry froze, listening. Someone was racing up the escape toward him, footsteps clanging on the metal steps. Harry waited until the man reached a landing, then threw the fire door open fully and jumped out. The guy looked up as the door banged open, and Harry looked down at him in turn. He was on the second-floor landing, leaning out to get a clear shot at Harry. Harry cranked back his arm and chucked the wrench directly at the man's chest. The heavy tool sent him down and knocked the gun from his hands, the weapon clattering onto the pavement in the alleyway below.

Still got it. Harry ducked back through the door. His primary escape route was blown now. Time for the backup plan. Harry's father had taught him always to have a backup plan. Back inside, Harry stooped to grab a discarded cut of wood from the floor. If anyone showed up he could throw it to the other side of the room as a distraction while he ran in the opposite direction. He could still escape—if he made it to the elevator shaft.

He raced back to the elevator, sliding around a corner as the main entrance door banged open and a single gangster rushed through. Harry skidded to a stop. The man aimed his pistol at Harry and fired, his shot going wide as Harry threw the wood missile at him. The shooter ducked aside at the last second, so it missed by an inch. He barked out a harsh laugh.

Or tried to. The board hit the now-closed door behind him and bounced back to whack him in the head. He stumbled, Harry jumped at him, and a reinforced right hook sent the gangster down for the count. Harry grabbed the man's pistol, ripped the entrance door open and fired a volley of shots down the staircase. Shouted curses told him the man coming up that staircase next wasn't in such a hurry any longer.

Harry ducked into the elevator shaft, dropped the gun into the abyss—he wasn't here to shoot anyone—and clambered up the ladder. Up he went until it ended at a platform hardly big enough for him to stand on. The ceiling was close enough that he could reach up and touch it. He glanced down. His headlamp was long gone, so nothing but blackness loomed beneath the steel grating underfoot. Above, however, was his way out: the elevator access hatch, which was secured with an industrial-grade lock to keep it inaccessible. From the inside, that is. The only way to open it from here was with a key. A key Harry Fox happened to have. He'd opened the lock earlier, when he first arrived on the roof, just in case his initial escape plan was compromised.

The night wind whipped into his eyes as he unlocked the hatch, pushed it open, and hoisted himself onto the roof. The bust on his back made it a tight squeeze, but he got through and re-locked the hatch before moving to the roof's edge. The board he'd used to cross the alleyway earlier was tucked against the edge. He reached for it, thought better of it, and instead peered over the edge, down onto the fire escape.

A gangster stood ten feet below. The one Harry had whacked with a wrench. A new pistol was clenched in one hand as the man stood to one side of the third-floor door, peering around, clearly looking for Harry. After a moment, he opened the door and darted inside, pulling the door shut behind him. *About time I caught a break.*

Harry lifted the board by one end, shifting his grip so it rose into the air above him, high enough so that when he let it drop the end would land on the roof across from him. The board swung down and crashed against the far roof, bouncing in his grip as a gust of wind kicked up out of nowhere. Harry scrambled to regain his grip, but the board skewed awkwardly and then spun away into the darkness, landing with a bang in the alleyway below.

Harry didn't have a backup board, of course. He looked around, but found nothing useful. The only other way out was down through a bunch of armed mobsters with quick trigger fingers. The gap between buildings looked larger the longer he stared at it. *I can make it.*

Shouting voices came from inside the building, moving closer. That made the choice easy. He looked down at the alley. Yes, he could make the leap. Just not with the marble bust on his back.

The bag came off his back. Harry pulled his shirt off next, then his undershirt, and stuffed both inside the bag to protect Philip before zipping the bag shut and grabbing the straps. He pulled his arm back, then took a step and slung the bag across the alley onto the far rooftop. It cleared the gap, landed with a thump, and skidded across the flat surface. Damaged or not, he had no idea.

Harry jogged back to the elevator access shaft as the sound of shouting grew louder. He didn't stop to think, just stood straight and closed his eyes. *I can make it.*

His breath was smoke in the cold air. Harry leaned back, got low, and ran. The edge came up faster than he expected. He accelerated and took the gap at speed, leaping into the void, arms flailing as he flew through the night air. He never looked down as the far roof raced up to meet him.

He almost made it.

His chest crashed into the far wall and his arms flew instinctively upward. His lungs burned and his shoulder muscles screamed as he grabbed hold of the roof's edge and pulled, kicking at the wall until, finally, he stopped sliding and hauled himself over the edge to collapse in a heap.

Salty blood coated his tongue. His fingers, scraped raw twice over, found the bag, which he slung over his bare torso. He stumbled, took two awkward steps, then righted himself and raced to the far edge where another fire escape waited. He stepped onto the ladder and turned to descend, looking back toward the candy factory. The last thing he saw before dropping out of sight was the elevator access door popping open. A pistol came out, with a gangster's head following behind.

Harry ducked out of sight, a grin on his lips. His father's face came to mind. *I hope you're watching.*

Chapter 2

Brooklyn

Harry stared at the coffee maker, willing it to work faster. His entire body ached, he had cuts everywhere, and he could still hear the whine of bullets zipping past, just inches from his head. He'd got home early this morning and crashed onto the couch, never even making it to a bed. Sara had tiptoed around him until noon, when he cracked one eye and understood what Mike Tyson's sparring partner must have felt like. A shower did little but make him yelp when scalding water hit his flesh. Caffeine was the only answer.

Gray skies loomed outside the windows as Harry filled his cup and sat at the table in his living room. Sara was in another chair, staring out the window. She wasn't looking at the two objects on the table, two golden amulets with differing Egyptian hieroglyphs inscribed on them. One amulet had belonged to Harry's father. An amulet Harry had rarely taken off, until last week.

"Any luck?" Harry asked.

Sara looked at Harry, her gaze unfocused. He nodded at the amulets. "Oh," she said. "No, not yet." She looked away. "I spoke with people at the museum this morning."

Harry's coffee cup stopped halfway to his lips. "What did they say?"

"They asked if I'd reconsidered."

The aches and pains vanished. "Did you?"

"No."

He kept his shoulders from slumping. "Does that mean you're leaving?"

A week ago Harry and Sara had returned from a relic hunt that had gone terribly wrong. While searching for a long-lost artifact from Viking lore, a pair of Norse fanatics had captured Sara to try to force Harry's hand. She eventually escaped, but the confinement had changed her, casting a cloud over her usually upbeat disposition. A month ago she'd been set on moving to New York, leaving her academic career in Germany behind for a job as an Egyptologist at the American Museum of Natural History. Now, things had changed.

"Yes," Sara said. "I'm leaving."

"Back to Trier University?"

"Perhaps. Perhaps not. My sabbatical runs through the end of the semester."

That's all she offered. "What about the amulets?"

Sara bit her lip. A good sign, the first one of the day. "I was working on them last night. While you were out." She frowned at his appearance. "Did you have trouble?"

Sara knew everything. That Harry worked for the mob. That he also worked undercover for the New York district attorney's Anti-Trafficking Unit, a team of law enforcement officers dedicated to stopping illegal artifacts trafficking in New York. Now his gut told him it was all too much for her. "I got it."

She perked up a bit. "Where is it?"

He inclined his head toward a bag beside the couch. "In there."

Sara didn't ask permission as she grabbed it. "Was your source right about the bust?"

"Yes. Among other things." He detailed what else had been in the building, from the Roman shield to the samurai swords to the gold.

Philip's bust came out of the bag. "It's incredible." She set the piece down on the table. "The only known image in the world. Hidden in a basement."

"They would have moved it quickly."

"I'm glad you saved it." Again she looked at his wounds. "How are you?"

The last thing he would tell her was how close he'd been to not coming back. "I'm fine."

She chose to accept that. "Are you taking it to Nora?"

"She wants to come and get it herself." His phone vibrated on the table and he grabbed it. A text. "She'll be here in a few minutes."

Sara's voice was again distant when she responded. "It will be nice to see her."

"Nora and I need to talk about her amulet today. I did her this favor. Now it's time to get back to our search." He watched closely. She didn't react to *our*.

"It's strange." She leaned forward and a flash of the old Sara surfaced. "Both amulets have glyphs on them, along with faience decorations." She tapped the bluish glaze accenting each solid gold disc. "Your amulet has obscure hieroglyphs. Very rare, but I could read them because I'd seen the scarab medallions of Antony and Cleopatra."

Harry had worn his amulet every day since his father was killed nearly a year ago. He had never found a way to read the glyphs inscribed on it until a chance meeting with Sara in Germany, when she became intrigued by the amulet and revealed she understood the message on it. A message from Mark Antony and Cleopatra.

"The message led us here," he reminded her. A lot had happened in between. The most important part? Finding Sara.

"The message led us to this second amulet." She touched the other piece. "Nora's. The glyphs are different. They aren't just obscure. They're impossible."

She had told him as much a few days ago, the last time she was willing to talk about it. "Because they shouldn't exist."

"They're unlike any I've ever seen," Sara said. "I'm an Egyptologist. I thought I'd seen them all."

"Do you think it's because this one belonged to Cleopatra Selene?"

Their winding search revealed that Harry's amulet had been made by

Antony and Cleopatra for one of their children, a boy named Alexander Helios. He had a twin sister named Cleopatra Selene II. A hidden message inscribed on a statue of Ptolemy Soter—who founded Cleopatra's Ptolemaic dynasty—confirmed this. The statue was now in the Grand Egyptian Museum in Cairo.

"Possibly," Sara said.

"The glyphs could be in code."

"I thought of that. I tried several encoding systems from Cleopatra's time," she said. "None worked. She spoke up to nine languages and I have no idea which one to base my work on. Perhaps it's a combination of several systems."

"Do the glyphs look familiar at all?"

"Yes. They're common, which makes this even more frustrating. The problem is the message makes no sense."

This was more than she'd ever told him about the second amulet. "What does it say?"

"That's just it. Nothing." She turned the amulet so he could see it. "It's a random series of words."

Harry could barely read any hieroglyphs. This collection left him mystified. "Looks like a couple of birds, a bug, a god or two and some kind of jackal."

"Correct, and also completely wrong." One side of her mouth turned up a fraction. "It's a jumble of words, as though someone picked them randomly and threw them together. It says '*Anubis seat tongue disappear reed soul flamingo beautiful young people wine Amon-ra.*' Gibberish."

Harry tried and failed to make any sense out of the jumble. "It must be a code. We've run across those before."

"True, but where to start? I'd need someone who speaks most or all of the nine languages Cleopatra did, and who also understands contemporary clues that may be needed to decipher the message."

Harry winked. "Sounds like we need a world-class Egyptologist."

She did not wink back. "Someone other than me." The clouds seemed to roll across her face again. "I'm stumped."

Harry reached out and laid his hand atop hers. She flinched, but didn't pull back. "You've been the right person every time so far," he said. "We'll figure it out."

Someone pounded on his front door as though they wanted to knock it down. Harry stood. "Nora's here."

Nora Doyle was the only person he knew who knocked like that. Every single time. He moved as fast as his aching muscles would let him to open the door before her fist came through it. "Hello, Nora." Harry stood back to allow her inside. "I see you've had your coffee today."

She glared at him. "You look terrible."

"Nice to see you too," he said as she barged past and headed for Sara.

The two women embraced. "How are you?" Nora asked. All the feeling she never offered Harry was in her voice now.

"Fine." Sara shrugged. "Harry had a successful night."

Nora looked to the bust. "I'll say." She reached to touch it, then stopped. "Tell me what happened."

Harry's eyes narrowed. "I'm fine. Thanks for asking."

"You're resilient," Nora said. "Now tell me what happened."

He offered a sanitized version of the events, skipping the guns and him nearly becoming a smear on the pavement. Even so, Sara visibly started several times. "This should do it," he concluded, ignoring the twinge in his gut. "It's proof the Canas are trafficking artifacts. Your father can get the D.A. to go after them now."

Nora's father was an assistant district attorney in Manhattan whose purview included prosecuting organized crime. Nora crossed her arms. "The guards saw you."

The knot in his stomach tightened. "Which means you have to move fast. Get there before they can react. Altin Cana won't give up on that safe house easily."

"He also won't leave any other artifacts there for long," Nora said. "I bet they're already gone."

Harry clenched his fists. "You don't know that."

Nora pointed a thumb at herself. "Yes, I do." Now she aimed a finger at him. "And so do you."

She was right. He'd say the same thing in her shoes. Altin Cana's hideout wouldn't go anywhere, but the stolen relics would.

"I can testify where I got it," Harry said. "That will prove the Cana family is responsible."

"It will only prove men you can't identify were in a building Altin Cana doesn't technically own that contained one stolen bust."

He didn't even bother arguing. "That won't stop the war."

Her face softened. "No. It won't."

Harry may have been technically working for Nora Doyle's anti-trafficking team last night, but in truth he was working for his real boss. Joey Morello, head of the Morello crime family and the biggest mobster in New York. Or at least he would be if Harry succeeded. "The Canas won't stop," he said. "You know it. They want war with the Morellos. You want to see that happen?"

"No. That's why I need better proof."

"Then I risked my life for nothing."

Sara shook her head. "You saved this artifact," she said. "Part of Greek history that would have been lost forever."

To Sara, that mattered. Harry glowered at the bust as though it were at fault. "That doesn't stop the war. Altin Cana is still going after Joey."

Nora came to his rescue. "I'll talk to my father." She turned back to Sara. "What did you learn about the amulet?"

Sara relayed her assessment to Nora, namely that she wasn't the right person to unravel the amulet mystery. "It would help if we knew where Jennifer Doyle obtained her amulet. That may give me leads on how to interpret it."

"She'll be back in town in a few days," Nora said. "Her trip was planned a long time ago."

A few days earlier, after Harry and Sara returned from their ill-fated Viking quest, Nora Doyle had walked into Harry's house wearing a piece of her mother's jewelry. Not just any jewelry, but the second amulet Harry and Sara had been seeking since learning about its existence at the

Grand Egyptian Museum. How Sara's mother Jennifer came to get it was a question they couldn't answer just yet, as Jennifer was out of town and Harry insisted on asking that question in person. Not after all he'd been through trying to figure out what his own amulet meant. An amulet that was the only connection he had to his father.

"I need to ask her where she got it," Harry said. "In person. It's too important to just call her." He hoped her answers to his questions would pull the curtain back on his personal mystery.

"She's had it for years," Nora said. "Waiting another few days to ask her won't hurt. It'll give you time to think." She directed that at Harry, pointedly failing to mention what exactly he should think about.

Nora sat down beside Sara. "What are your plans?"

The distant voice again, Sara not looking at Nora as she spoke. "I turned down the museum job." Nora merely nodded. "I'm going back to Germany."

"What about the amulet?" Nora asked.

"I'll stay a few more days to work on it," Sara said. "I need to speak with a colleague. I think this puzzle is beyond me."

Nora glanced over at Harry, then flicked her eyes toward the front door. "You'll solve it," she said. She stood from her chair. "I need to speak with Harry about something. Work-related."

Sara turned her eyes to the amulets as Nora followed Harry out the front door. They stopped on the sidewalk, Harry pulling on the coat he'd grabbed against winter's coming chill.

"She's still in a funk," he said.

"Sara isn't like you. She's a professor. Not a treasure hunter."

Harry didn't dispute it. "I thought she'd snap out of it by now."

"She was *kidnapped*, Harry. By two men with no qualms about killing her to get what they wanted. The reason she survived is you."

"And she's the reason I'm alive," he said. "I wouldn't have made it without her." The memory of a massive Viking longboat and an incredible relic came hurtling back. "We got through it together."

"You both nearly died. That sticks with people. Some more than others."

Hard to argue with her, even if he didn't really understand it. "I think she's really going back to Germany," Harry said glumly.

"*After* she helps with the amulet." Nora tucked her hands into her coat pockets. "I chatted with Sara yesterday. Reminded her you're not such a bad guy."

High praise from Nora Doyle. "Thanks."

"I know you want her to stay. I do too. She's good for you."

"That doesn't stop you from sending me into harm's way."

"Don't start with that. Your working with my team is the only reason she agreed to stay in the first place."

Again he couldn't argue. Nora had saved him with that little white lie. "Sorry. I'm frustrated."

"Channel it into figuring out how to stop the Canas and Morellos from killing each other." Nora turned away. "I'll talk to Sara. See what I can do." She took a step, stopped, and turned back to him. "Have you talked to Detective Barnes lately?"

A hollow pit materialized in Harry's stomach. "Yes."

"Is she certain about the voice?"

Harry regretted ever telling Nora about it. "Yes. My father was the man she overheard at the crime scene." By crime scene he meant the desolate spot on the banks of the Hudson River where, over twenty years ago, a body had been found. A woman the police identified as Harry's mother.

"No progress on why your father would bribe the cops to misidentify the body as that of his wife?"

"No."

Nora didn't know when to let it go. "What about the coroner's office? Any idea who misidentified it for that report?"

"A man who claimed to be her brother." Harry's mother had been an only child. "The coroner couldn't say if it was my father or not when I showed him a photo. Too long ago."

Jessica Barnes had been a newly minted detective working the murder. Harry's father, it seemed, had paid Jessica's partner to misidentify the body as his wife. Logic suggested Fred Fox also had been the one to mislead the coroner, claiming to be Dani Fox's non-existent brother and confirming a false identification. Harry had no idea why his father might have done such a thing. He could barely stand to think about it.

"I'm handling it," he said briskly. "Thanks for asking."

Nora left without another word. Harry watched her go, wondering how it had all come to this. Was Nora Doyle truly his best hope of keeping Sara around? If so, his budding relationship with Sara was in trouble.

Chapter 3

Brooklyn

A full winter moon hung in the night sky when Sara at last moved from the living room table.

"I need a break," she said.

Harry sat across the table from her. He watched as she stood and went to the window, not looking at him as she spoke.

"Any luck?" she asked.

"None." They'd been studying the amulets for hours, twisting and turning the hieroglyphs in every imaginable direction, looking for a pattern, a starting point to help unravel the mystery. Between them they were fluent in a half-dozen languages, yet their efforts had yielded nothing. The odd imagery on Cleopatra Selene II's amulet may as well have been written in Martian. "Any word from your colleague?"

Sara had reached out to a fellow Egyptologist several hours ago, sharing the odd assortment of hieroglyphs from the second amulet to see if her fellow scholar could make sense of them. So far the woman had come up empty, as puzzled by the strange collection as Sara and Harry were. "She has the same impression as us."

"That it makes no sense." Harry rubbed at the stubble on his chin.

Sara leaned closer to the window and looked up at the sky. "It's a full moon tonight. Maybe it'll bring us luck."

He frowned. "It was a full sun today and we didn't get anywhere. Luck has nothing to do with it."

"Egyptians believed a full moon indicated good fortune. The opposite of what we've had…" Her voice trailed off.

Harry half-rose from his chair. "You okay?" he asked.

"The opposite." Sara twisted on a heel to face him. "What if it's backwards?"

"If what is?"

"The message." Her voice picked up steam. "We may need to read it backwards. Start at the end and go back to the beginning."

"We tried that. The words don't make sense that way either."

"Not the words." Sara walked back to her chair, pulled it around next to his and sat down. "Give me that notepad." She grabbed the legal pad before he could touch it, snatching a pen as well. "Hieroglyphics can be interpreted in different ways. Each image can indicate a word or idea, which is how I interpreted them."

Harry's rudimentary understanding of the language ended there. "You said they can represent individual letters as well."

"In certain situations, yes." The pen scribbled madly. "But the way these images are arranged doesn't suggest letters. This style is meant to tell a story through ideas, not to spell words."

Harry leaned closer. "What do they spell?"

She finished writing. "Gibberish. *A-B-M-U-T-C-I-T-R-O-H*."

"Is that an Egyptian word?"

Sara turned to him, and for the first time in over a week, her face was alive. "No. Which is why we need to read it backwards."

"And somehow this involves the moon and sun?"

"Perhaps." Sara wrote on the notepad. "Your talking about luck made me think of it. We've had nothing but bad luck so far, the opposite of what we want." She paused. He didn't react. "*Opposite*. I think that's the key. We're not supposed to read this front to back. It's a code, Harry. A message hidden in plain sight."

"I'm listening."

She tapped the pad with her pen. "Read back to front, it spells *H-O-R-T-I-C-T-U-M-B-A*."

"What's *hortictumba*?" Harry asked.

"It's not a word I know."

Harry grabbed her computer and searched for that sequence of letters. "It's not a word in any language."

She tapped his forearm with one finger. The touch of her skin on his shot electricity through his body. "You're correct. It's not a word. It's a *place*. Written with an abbreviation. *Hortictumba* is *Horti C Tumba*."

"Three words?"

"It stands for *Horti Caesaris*. The name of a villa owned by Julius Caesar in Rome."

"That's only two words. And *tumba* is Latin for *tomb*."

"Correct," Sara said. "Which means we may need to find a tomb."

"Are there any at this villa?"

"I don't know." She drummed her pen on the table. "Horti Caesaris is where Caesar and Cleopatra spent enough time together that Caesarion was born."

"Julius Caesar's only son. Who was alive when Antony and Cleopatra created the amulets." Harry considered the timeline. "Caesarion outlived Cleopatra. If this is telling us to find his tomb, she wouldn't have known where it was when she made these."

"He did outlive her," Sara said. "Though by only a year. After she committed suicide, her son was killed by Emperor Octavian within a month."

"What I mean is Cleopatra wouldn't have known where his tomb is."

"Not true. Pharaohs in Cleopatra's time were buried in one location—the Valley of the Kings."

"Where they found King Tut's tomb."

"And dozens of others. It's arguably the richest archaeological site in Egypt."

That sounded promising. "So is Caesarion buried there?"

Sara let out a long sigh. "His tomb has never been found. If it even exists. Octavian likely wasn't concerned with giving Caesarion a burial worthy of a pharaoh since he murdered him. Doing so would only help people remember Cleopatra and the Ptolemaic dynasty."

"Octavian saw himself as the first true emperor," Harry said. "He'd want people to forget about Cleopatra and her kids."

He opened a new browsing tab and searched for anything on Cleopatra and her children. One link caught his eye. "The Donations of Alexandria," Harry said. "Ever heard of those?"

Sara gave him a look. "Antony and Cleopatra distributed their various kingdoms among their children as a way to keep a grip on power. It looks like they gave them out to each child according to the first letter of their name," Harry said. "Every kid received at least one country matching their first initial." He scrolled further. "Ha, what a power play. Antony had just gotten his butt kicked in a war with the Parthians. He was trying to make people forget about it."

"How does any of this relate to finding a tomb?"

"It doesn't." Harry refocused—he wasn't giving up yet. "What about the villa? There could be tombs of some kind there. Julius Caesar ruled Rome. His villa must have been massive." Sara confirmed it was. Which led to the most important question. "Does it still exist?" Harry asked.

"The villa eventually went to one of Caesar's friends, a historian named Sallust. Later owners expanded it until, like all of Rome, it fell into disrepair as the empire fell. It was eventually absorbed by the city. Parts of it still stand, though I'm not aware of any tombs."

"That doesn't mean they don't exist." He pointed to the amulet. "If you're correct about this message, at least one tomb existed. If there's anything left of it, we'll find it."

He waited to see if she took the bait. Sara kept her eyes on the notepad. "Perhaps. I need to do more research."

Harry gave it a second. "I have a better idea. Why don't we go see for ourselves?"

It was as though a charge went through her. Not in a good way. "No." She hesitated, then spoke quickly. "Not yet. I need to learn more first. We can't run to Italy based on a hunch."

"We've done it before."

She shook her head. "Not this time. I need more information before doing anything that crazy." Now her voice dropped. "If I go at all."

There were times to push and times to pull back. "Makes sense," Harry said. "Let's keep digging. The answer will be out there if we look hard enough."

"It usually is."

Sara went back to her computer. Harry breathed a silent sigh of relief. Close call. Sara was on the fence about everything. New York. Relic chasing. *Him*. Even if he didn't fully get it, understanding her position was the best way to support her. Remind Sara of the excitement, the thrill of what he did. And show her he was changing. If Harry wanted to help Sara and see her decide to stay in America longer, he needed to meet her where she was comfortable.

A gust of wind hit the window, making the panes rattle. Bare tree limbs shook in the darkness beyond the glass as Harry looked outside, up at the moon, which had inspired him to make a comment which may have helped Sara unlock this next step on Cleopatra's journey, one possibly leading to Rome. As much as he wanted to pack up and leave at once, there was no way he could fly out until Nora's mother returned. She held the key to his personal mystery. Namely, where had she acquired the second amulet? Even thinking about this made his chest tighten. What if Jennifer could tell Harry where to go next, not on Cleopatra's journey, but his own? She might have the answer to what had happened to Harry's mother and not even realize it. A name, a receipt, anything to tell him how his mother's amulet had ended up around Nora Doyle's neck.

Harry shook his head. Nora's mother would be back soon. Right now, though, there was an Egyptian puzzle to solve. He reached for the keyboard just as his phone buzzed. A familiar number popped up. "It's Joey," Harry said as he stood and made for the door. "I'll be right back."

Sara barely acknowledged him as he went outside and sat on the front steps. There was still a part of his life she didn't ask questions about. At least, not many. Harry connected the call. "Hey, Joey."

"I have a problem."

Chapter 4

Brooklyn

The wine glass on Joey's desk sat empty. He'd filled it only moments ago. Then his informant in the Cana family had called. Now he had Harry Fox on the line, and a real problem on his hands.

"There was a fire at the old candy factory," Joey said. "A small one in the basement."

"I didn't set it," Harry said.

"I know you didn't. Altin set it after someone stole his Greek bust."

"To cover his tracks." Harry fired off a choice word. "It's not going to work. My plan backfired."

It had. And on Harry's plan hung all Joey's hopes. To keep the Canas in their place. To maintain the Morello image. To take his father's place as the *capo dei capi*, the boss of the bosses. Joey had to prove to the other family leaders he was worthy of the throne by avenging his father's murder. A murder he knew—but couldn't prove—Altin Cana had ordered. The catch? Do it without starting a war between Cana and Morello. And do it this week.

"It would have helped if your district attorney friend acted on the evidence you provided."

"I know," Harry said. "She's working on it. Her father is pushing back."

Joey kneaded his forehead. "You have any other ideas?"

Nothing but silence for a long while. "No," Harry finally said. "Not right now. But have faith. We'll get him."

"We'd better."

Harry caught the unspoken message. "Has something happened?"

"My man inside the Cana family told me about the basement fire. He also said Altin isn't stopping. He has another attack planned."

"At a counting house?"

"I don't know." Memories of the burning buildings where the Morello family laundered and stored cash made Joey grit his teeth. The last incident like this, barely a week ago, had cost him five million dollars. "Altin thinks I'm weak. He knows that I know he hit our pizza shop and the laundromat."

"And the dancing club," Harry reminded him. "But you can't hit back yet. Gio Sabella wouldn't like it."

"I'd like to tell Gio Sabella a thing or two." He'd do more than that, except the head of the Sabella family was the key to Joey replacing his father as the leader of New York's families. Gio was old school, had risen to the top at the same time as Joey's father. Vincent Morello and Gio Sabella were the men other families listened to, and with Vincent in his grave, Gio was the man in charge. Temporarily, at least. Gio wanted Joey to take the leadership role. Once Gio was on board, the other families would fall into line. But Gio would only give his blessing if Joey did one thing: avenge his father's murder without throwing the city into chaos.

"We still have a few days," Harry said. "I won't let you down."

"I know you won't. Problem is I have to go to a meeting tonight with Gio and the other family leaders. Altin Cana is still on the streets and my father is dead. I have no vengeance, and I have no plan."

"They don't know that," Harry said. "Tell them it's under control. Make them believe, Joey. Because it is. We'll get him."

The man who would be New York's mob king had pinned his hopes on a relic hunter. A Pakistani-American without a drop of Italian blood in his veins. Joey nearly laughed. "Let me know what I can do to help."

"The best thing you can do is lay low," Harry said. "Don't get any ideas about going after him again. That won't end well."

A few days ago Joey had his men assembled for a full-on attack. They planned on overrunning the Cana headquarters, taking out anyone inside and putting Altin Cana in the past forever. Only Harry's insistence that this would never work had stopped Joey. Gio Sabella forbade Joey from taking the throne through bloodshed. Joey's anger had nearly gotten the best of him.

"You're right," Joey said. "It's tough to think like my father."

"What would he do?" Harry asked. "He'd use his head. Be smarter than Altin Cana. Hit him once, hit him hard, and do it in a way that keeps people out of the morgue. Your men follow you, Joey. Don't lead them to an early grave."

Harry was right. Vincent Morello hadn't been averse to violence, but he'd been smart about it. Never use a fist when your brain could do better. A lesson both their fathers had preached. "Can't get away from our old men, can we?" Joey chuckled. "Sometimes I think you're the only guy who understands what it's like."

"We're both works in progress," Harry said. "We learned from the best. We'll do this. The right way."

"All right. I'll lay low until I hear from you."

Joey clicked off as a knock sounded on his door. A mountain of a man peered inside. "You'se ready to go, boss?"

Joey stood and took his suit jacket off the hanger. "After you, Mack." He followed his bodyguard out to the waiting vehicle, which zipped across town to a Sabella warehouse in Queens. They stopped outside of a building that had seen better days. Only a closer inspection revealed steel-reinforced doors, surveillance cameras on every corner, and a number of well-dressed men waiting in parked cars outside. Mack parked and led Joey through one of the doors, which opened to reveal two guys who could have been Mack's twins. The big men let Mack and Joey pass without checking for weapons, a sign of respect for the Morello leader.

Shipping containers and forklifts surrounded a large round table in the middle of the warehouse, well away from any walls so every man had clean lines of sight. Gio Sabella had also left plenty of room between each of the five chairs. Four seats were filled. Joey took the fifth. Mack joined the other oversized bodyguards leaning against the closest container, watchful.

"Welcome, Joey." The man sporting a full head of coiffed silver hair lifted his hand and the room fell silent. Gio Sabella's words came to Joey through the twirling ghosts of smoke flowing from the end of a cigar. "Thank you for joining us."

The other men murmured greetings as Joey unbuttoned his suit coat. "It's good to see you, Mr. Sabella."

Gio Sabella took a moment to re-light his cigar. "Thank you all for coming, gentlemen. I invited you here to discuss our shared future. This is the first time we have all sat together since Vincent was lost." Gio crossed himself. "May he rest in peace."

The other men followed suit. A man who had been handsome twenty years and two hundred pounds ago spoke up. "What about our future, Gio?"

Joey clenched and unclenched his fist under the table. Of course Albert Zurilli would speak up.

"One thing of which I am certain," Gio said, "is that if we do not work together, we will all suffer for it. For thirty years we have existed together peacefully. It is my wish we continue for another thirty years, and then many more after that. Peace brings prosperity, in my view."

"It does," Al said. "I have no issues with my friends at this table."

A shadow flew across Gio's face, there and gone. "I hope not. Our success comes because we find ways to co-exist."

"In an alliance forged by Vincent Morello," Al said.

Gio almost suppressed his frown. "Yes. By Vincent."

"Taken from us far too soon." Albert Zurilli didn't look at Joey as he continued. "I hope his death is avenged."

Joey leaned forward. "It will be."

Albert Zurilli finally turned to face him. "When?"

"Soon," Joey said. "I'm handling this the way my father would want."

"Do you require any assistance from us?"

Joey could have wrung his neck. Instead, he straightened his tie. "No.

Thank you for the offer."

Albert lifted his hands, palms up. *As you wish.*

"Joey Morello will handle his business," Gio said, his words hard. "When he does, I will recommend him as our *capo.*"

Albert put his elbows on the table. "From where I sit, vengeance has been delayed too long already."

"Filling the streets with bodies is not how we operate," Joey said. "Not any longer. That time is past."

"Some would say it's past time to handle Altin Cana," Albert shot back. He quickly lifted his hands. "Though I do not. Your business is just that—your business."

"We work together," Gio said. "The families respect each other." He narrowed his eyes at Albert. "Correct?"

"Yes," Albert said. "I meant no disrespect."

Albert meant a whole lot of it, but if Joey snapped back he was only rising to the bait. A leader didn't do that. "I'm doing it my way," Joey said. "The way that's best for all of us. Bodies are bad for business."

General agreement sounded from the four other leaders. Louis Esposito cleared his throat. "A ship needs a captain," he said. "Perhaps it would be wise to name someone temporarily, until we agree on our new leader."

Joey had played this scene out in his head on the way over. Who would say what, and how to react. The Esposito head was no pushover, but he'd grown comfortable in old age. He didn't have his eyes on the throne. Not like Albert, who saw a chance to install his own son as the next *capo.*

"We have an agreement and a deadline in place." Joey spoke slowly, clearly, so that even the bodyguards were sure to hear. "Two weeks. I will avenge my father's murder. Once it's done, we move ahead with an election." One he would win if Gio Saballa cast his lot with Joey.

"We do," Louis said. "And I mean no disrespect, Joey."

Joey dipped his head. "None taken."

"I only suggest it in the interest of us all," Louis said. "Less than a week remains in our agreement. I must consider that your task may not be completed by then."

"It will be," Joey said. Albert Zurilli opened his mouth. Joey cut him off. "I could shoot up Altin Cana's headquarters. Kill a bunch of my men. Maybe I get all of his, maybe I don't. The problem is you never know what will happen when you start a war. Do I want to take him out tonight? Yes. But out of respect for my father"—and now Joey waved a hand at the gathered mobsters—"and for all of you, I don't. My father dedicated his life to building a new world where we don't kill each other. One where we all thrive. I won't throw that all away. I'll do this the right way."

"As a leader should," Gio Sabella said into the ensuing silence. He looked at Albert, daring him to contradict. "Our agreement stands. The full two weeks. After that time we will review the terms if necessary. Does anyone disagree?"

Albert Zurilli sat back in his chair. "No, Mr. Sabella."

The other men quickly offered their agreement as well. "Good." Gio puffed on his cigar. "Thank you for coming, gentlemen."

With those words Mack materialized behind Joey's chair, leading his boss out to the car with a look on his face that even these hardened gangsters shied away from. As Joey settled into the back of his car, one thought shouted down everything else in his head. *I'm counting on you, Harry Fox.*

Chapter 5

Brooklyn

Harry woke to the sound of a fist abusing his bedroom door. For one terrifying instant between sleeping and waking he had a vision of Nora Doyle banging on the door, ready to gang-press him into service for another relic recovery.

He didn't open his eyes to look. "Go away," he yelled.

"No chance."

Both eyelids shot open as his fortunes changed. Not Nora Doyle. "Sara?" he asked groggily.

"What other woman would it be?" She stepped into the room, her lips pursed. "Don't answer that. Now get up. We have a mystery to solve."

She turned and left him lying there, wide-eyed and mystified. Could it be? Sara, who hadn't displayed anything approaching excitement since returning from Norway, was now banging down his door with the sun barely up? He couldn't get out of bed fast enough. Which, for Harry, meant moving at more than a shuffle. Joints popped, knees ached, his back mounted a full-throated protest, but the fact Sara had told him to get his butt in gear made him push though until he was down the stairs and sipping coffee in record time.

Early light fell through a window onto the table as he stood behind Sara's chair. "Find something?" he asked.

Her eyes were on the laptop in front of her. "Not yet, and we won't if you sleep the day away again."

Not everyone woke at the crack of dawn like Sara. Harry wisely didn't comment. "Easy, boss. I'm up and moving."

"Find a link between Caesarion's tomb and Julius Caesar's villa. Then I'll be impressed. We're not going anywhere without more evidence."

Harry hid a smile behind his coffee mug. Things were looking up. "I'm on it," he said.

A half-hour passed, the only sound their fingers hitting the keys. Harry learned more than he cared to know about the Roman city district called Sallustiano, the modern name for where the villa ruins stood. The city had grown and changed over the past two thousand years, slowly eating away at the once-grand ancient estates until the ruins now occupied only a few blocks at most, some of that underground. Cities didn't just grow *out* over time, though; they grew *up*. If you were asked what any city with a storied past was built on, the correct answer was always itself.

The cracking of Sara's neck grabbed his attention. She stood and rolled it back and forth to the sound of fireworks.

"Sitting in front of a computer is hard on your body," he said.

"Not as hard as getting shot, stabbed or set on fire in the field."

He shrugged. His aches and pains proved it. "True."

"I cannot find any reference to a grave or tomb in the villa." Sara sat back down and looked past him, her gaze on the open window as she pulled a strand of lavender-scented hair off her face. "Graves are often the last parts of historic sites to vanish," she said. "Though Rome was eventually sacked by the Visigoths—"

"Please don't bring up King Alaric again." That was the Visigothic king whose conquest of Rome had set them on the path that led to Sara's kidnapping.

"—was eventually sacked by the Visigoths," she continued without looking at him. "They didn't stay in Rome, which suggests they had little reason to remove or build over a gravesite. Neither would the Byzantines or any subsequent rulers." She pulled at another wayward strand of hair. "Any graves should still be there."

Harry often faced roadblocks in his relic hunts. Physical ones, which occasionally tried to kill him, or intangible ones such as lack of information, like now. You could pound your head against challenges like that all day without getting anywhere. He knew from experience that a better way was to look at the problem from a new angle. One of his favorites was flipping the problem on its head. "What if we're not looking for Caesarion's tomb?" he asked. "What if it's something else?"

"The message seems straightforward," Sara said. "Why do you say that?"

Harry shrugged. "Because we've been at this all day and night with no luck. The villa isn't large. I've seen enough tourist photos that I could give a tour of the place." He raised a hand. "Which means nothing if what we're looking for is hidden."

"Or doesn't even exist anymore." Sara was a realist. "That's one possibility."

"I believe it's there. Chances are there's a marker or indicator of some sort to help guide us."

"A guide for Antony and Cleopatra's children."

"Cleopatra *wanted* her kids to succeed. Which is why I'm wondering what we're missing." He glared at the image on his monitor. "The only connection I can find related to death is a painting on the dome of one building. It has nothing to do with Caesarion."

"Why do you think it relates to death?" Sara looked at the ceiling and blew air through her lips. "It's a compilation of mythological creatures alongside Caesar, indicating his place among the gods."

Harry hadn't made that connection. "The dog by his feet has three heads. That's Cerberus, isn't it? Hades' dog who guards the underworld." Harry flipped his laptop around so she could see the image. "Here."

"Yes, that's Cerberus. Quite the brute. Hercules captured him as part of his twelve labors."

Harry vaguely recalled that from a long-ago history lesson. Likely given by his father. "I forgot that," he said. "What if this painting isn't about Caesar's greatness? What if it's about his *death*?"

Sara bolted out of her chair. "Impossible."

"It's not that bad of an idea."

"No. It's impossible I could be so dense." She ran around the table to his side and grabbed the laptop. "I didn't make the connection."

Harry tried to keep up. "You think I'm right?"

"No. This connection. Look." She zoomed in on the image of Caesar and Cerberus, to a point below Caesar's foot. "See those?"

Harry squinted. A series of letters were inscribed beneath the man. "It's Greek."

"Koine Greek," Sara said. "Cleopatra's first language. I assumed the painter who created this was Greek and these were his initials. But what if this is what we're looking for?"

"Then those aren't initials. They're Cleopatra's *directions*." He looked up at her. "What does it say?"

"*A-D-I.* They appear to be initials, because that's what anyone looking at this painting would expect to find. A mark from the painter. Only a person expecting to find something else would see it."

"Like Cleopatra's children—"

"—who would know to look for a message hidden in plain sight," Sara said. "And more importantly, who could read both Kione Greek and Latin. That matters because *A-D-I* isn't a Greek or Latin word. I believe it's an abbreviation. For *Aedes Divi Iuli.*"

Harry sent out a silent apology to his dad for hating all those Latin lessons. "*Temple of Divus Iulius.* The Temple of Caesar."

"Julius Caesar's burial place." Sara bodily hauled him from the chair and did her best to crush him. "That's it. That must be it. Harry, you are a genius."

He let her hold him until his lungs threatened to burst. "Thanks," he croaked, extricating himself. "Nothing to it."

He blinked, and her face dropped. "Oh, no." Sara leaned over the computer. "The temple is in Rome. It's nothing but ruins."

"That's not necessarily a problem."

He looked at her face, blinked, then looked closer. She was almost smiling now. Clearly, Sara had taken a step back from whatever darkness had consumed her after being kidnapped. A step back to being the woman he knew. He couldn't let her falter now. "Ruins are a specialty of ours," he reminded her.

"Not these ruins. The entire temple was torn down centuries ago for building materials. Only a few exterior walls remain. And those were restorations from when the temple burned down two hundred years after Caesar died."

A cloud covered the sun outside. "There's nothing left of the original temple," Harry said.

"Nothing but the floor." Sara shook her head. "Which would almost certainly be solid stone."

Zest he didn't truly feel filled his words. "There must be a painting or portrait of the building. A written description, at least. Whatever Cleopatra left to guide her children could be there." He laid a hand on her shoulder. "Where we can find it."

She didn't shy away from his touch. But she didn't move closer, either. Harry slid around her to sit. "I'll bet I can find it."

Her hand grabbed his arm so hard he nearly shouted. "What's wrong?" he asked.

"I am." She pulled him up and took his place in the chair. "I've been so wrong. I'm sorry, Harry. My focus is off."

"I haven't noticed."

"You're a terrible liar." Moments later a new image popped up on the screen. "You are correct again. Here's a record of Caesar's tomb. Far better than any painting or story."

An elegant marble building with pillars fronting the towering entrance filled the screen. "Nice place," he said. "What is it?"

"Julius Caesar's tomb."

His forehead wrinkled. "Come again?"

"This is Caesar's tomb."

"You just showed me his tomb a second ago. The big mess of ruins?"

"Yes. And no." Sara pointed at the screen. "This is what Caesar's tomb looked like when it was built. The tomb is nothing but ruins now. This is a replica."

The hair on his arms stood up. "Who built it?"

"Julius Caesar's closest friend. And his former lover."

"Mark Antony and Cleopatra."

"They built this replica beside Cleopatra's palace in Alexandria."

He looked at the picture again. "That looks like a digital re-creation."

"It is." She touched his arm again, gently this time. "The original existed. To honor Caesar. It stood for three centuries until an earthquake sent a tsunami crashing into Alexandria."

His arm hair went down. "It's gone."

"Not gone." Her teeth flashed. "Underwater. Cleopatra's palace is now ten feet underwater in Alexandria's harbor. It was discovered not thirty years ago, and is one of the richest sources of Egyptian artifacts ever found."

"Did they also find Caesar's palace?"

"Every last stone. Want to know the best part? You can explore it on a guided scuba diving tour."

Another silent thank you went out to his dad. Fred Fox had never taken his son on a relic hunt that required going underwater for longer than they could hold their breaths. He had, however, taken Harry scuba diving during an island vacation, during which Harry obtained his certification. Underwater relics weren't ideal, but they also weren't out of reach.

"Her entire palace sank into the harbor," Harry said. "It must be spread across a massive area. Where do we start?"

"Others have already helped us." Sara was back at her keyboard again. "Divers and archaeologists have been inspecting the site for three decades. Look at what they already found." She moved aside so he could see her screen.

"That's Cerberus." She pointed to a statue of the three-headed beast in blue-tinged water, resting on a sandy floor. "It's bigger than the diver beside it."

"Which suggests it was meant to last. As were the other markers Antony and Cleopatra left behind. They couldn't have known a tsunami would destroy the palace, but we're still able to follow the path." The last thing he wanted to do was dampen her enthusiasm, but still. "We won't know if this is the marker until we get down there."

"I can't think of another reason why Cerberus would be in Julius Caesar's palace. Caesar was a Roman dictator. A warrior whom the people loved. He didn't need to curry favor, so there's no reason for him to pretend to worship Greek gods. What other reason would he have to include this statue in his tomb?"

A year ago Harry would have accepted this conclusion at face value. That was before Sara, though, before he realized there could be merit to stopping and thinking instead of diving in. At times. "What if the people who built it—not Antony—wanted to reach out to any Greek-loving citizens?"

"Good question. Those builders were senators honoring Caesar. Basking in his reflected glory was a welcome side effect. Roman citizens revered Caesar, so honoring him on his own was enough to achieve their goals. Plus"—here Sara lifted a finger—"Antony was the first advocate for building Caesar's tomb. It was constructed during his rise to power, while he and Cleopatra were together. They had access, means and a reason to include a marker for their children. That's convincing enough evidence for me."

"As if I ever doubted you." He winked. "I'll get us two tickets to Alexandria. This is our trip. Not Nora's." He paused. *Joey.* "We'll need a few days to get ready." What he really meant was he needed a few days to save Joey Morello's backside.

Sara spoke softly. "I won't need a ticket."

Harry stayed bent over, fingers on the keyboard, unmoving. "What?"

"I don't want to go underwater."

"You can take a certification course—I already have mine. I'm sure they offer them."

"I didn't say I *can't* go. I said I *don't want to.*"

He stood up. "Scuba diving isn't that bad. I'll be there with you."

"That's not it." Sara bit her lip. She kept looking out the window. "I don't want to go. Not now."

"You want to wait a few weeks? Cerberus isn't going anywhere." Plus, that would give him a chance to talk with Jennifer Doyle about her amulet.

She looked at the floor, arms hugging herself. "The thought of going underwater terrifies me. Not because I'm afraid of diving," she said quickly. "I'm certified to scuba dive. It's that I don't think I can."

Harry Fox had many skills. Reading between the lines was not always one of them, though even he knew enough to keep his mouth shut now.

"You know I'm still thinking about what happened." Being kidnapped. "I've changed since we met." A sad smile. "Quite a bit. I used to think Egyptology was all dust, sand and books. You showed me that it can be exciting, thrilling. Dangerous. All of those, but most of all what it can be is out of control."

"We'll minimize risk," he said. "Like we always do. Together."

She didn't seem to hear him. "It's out of *my* control. I don't like that. I carved my place in the world, a purposeful place. My doctorate let me control where I worked, what I did. My home in Germany let me control what laws I lived under, the society I existed in. Even kickboxing, the reason we met. Personal defense skills give me a measure of control where one otherwise wouldn't exist. Control is important to me."

"I'll be there."

"You were with me in Norway."

The accusation made him wince. He couldn't refute it. Did it matter that he'd been half-conscious, trapped in a wrecked car when they took her? That he'd risked his life to get her back, nearly drowned, been crushed, burned and shot to save her? No. None of that mattered right now. It didn't matter how he saw it. All that mattered was what Sara believed. Right now, she didn't believe in him. "I'm sorry."

A raindrop hit the window across from them. "I don't blame you," she said. "You saved me. But that doesn't change how I feel. I can't do it right now, Harry."

"I'll wait."

"I don't know if I'll ever be ready." Her head shook once. "Go without me. You're close to finding the truth." He had to lean closer to catch her next words. "I wish I could go with you."

He tried to tell her she could. That he wouldn't let it happen again, that the world was unpredictable and could never be completely controlled. Or that he'd never have made it this far without her. This wasn't only his quest now. It was theirs.

He opened his mouth to say all that as the doorbell rang. Sara flinched. "I'll get it," Harry said.

She turned to look out the window. Harry went to the front door, cursing the world in general, but three dead Norsemen in particular. And himself, for letting them steal the Sara he knew. He opened it to find Joey Morello on the front porch.

"You have a second?" Joey asked. He looked over Harry's shoulder. "Hey, Sara. Good to see you."

She didn't walk to the door. "You too, Joey."

"Mind if I steal this bum for a second?"

Sara said it was no problem, so Harry closed the door behind him. Joey inclined his head to the car parked at the curb. "Hop in," he said.

Mack was behind the wheel as Harry slid into the rear seat beside Joey. "We going for a ride?" Harry asked. "Good to see you, Mack."

"You too, Aladdin." Mack rumbled at his oft-used joke.

"I wanted to talk where it's private," Joey said. He watched a mother and two young children walk by the window. "I met with the other family heads last night. Took a bit of talking, but they agreed I have until the end of the week."

"To make things right."

"Yes." Joey turned to him, and Harry was dismayed to realize he was no longer the guy Harry had grown up with. One hand rubbed a bloodshot eye. Dark stubble covered his face. Joey's hair didn't look perfect. "I'm in trouble, Harry."

"The week isn't over."

"I can't shoot Altin Cana. Can't burn his place down. I do that and there's no chance of taking my father's place. Albert Zurilli is itching to get his son as the next *capo*. I kill Altin and I'm handing it to him."

"We knew you had to do it like this. Gio Sabella said so." Harry bunched one hand into a fist. "Don't worry, Joey. I'll get the A.D.A. to go after the Canas." How, he had no idea. He'd figure it out. "I owe you. And your father."

"You don't owe me anything." Joey looked at the floor. "I'm counting on you, Harry. We all are."

Alexandria would have to wait. Harry opened his door. "I'll take care of it."

Joey didn't say anything as the car pulled away. Harry sent Sara a quick text, then turned from his front door and started walking, one wary eye cast up to a dark sky. The cold rain had skirted his neighborhood for the moment. Good thing, because he needed privacy and a chance to talk to the one person he knew could help him. Joey was down to his last hope. Harry couldn't count on Nora to fix this, not now. Which meant Harry was on his last chance as well. At least he'd kept his biggest bullet in reserve. He dialed a phone number. She answered almost at once.

"Harry Fox." A glass clinked. A martini glass, Harry knew. It was never too early for Rose Leroux. "How are you?"

Chapter 6

Manhattan

Rose Leroux gazed out her window. Central Park looked dreary in the rain. Rose set her martini down and looked around her Upper East Side home. Sharp angles, minimal fuss, elegantly appointed. A home to mirror its owner.

"I'm fine." Harry Fox's voice came through the phone. "How are you?"

"Harry, I've been alive far too long to believe everything I'm told." She picked up a lighter from the bar, put a fresh cigarette into the black-stemmed holder, and a flame flashed to life. "Tell me the truth," she said. A thin stream of smoke trickled from her mouth.

"I'm not fine." Harry seemed to wrestle with the next sentence. "Neither is Joey."

"His deadline draws near. I imagine he is anxious."

In New York, as in most of the world, it wasn't what you knew, but rather who. And Rose Leroux knew everybody who mattered in her city. She didn't need Harry to tell her what she already knew. She needed to know why he was calling her, and she suspected Joey Morello needed her help.

"Right, as usual." Harry recapped how his plan to implicate Altin Cana in artifacts trafficking had fallen to pieces. "Altin had a fire in the candy factory basement," Harry told her. "Any evidence is gone."

"So I heard." She waved her cigarette as though he could see, leaving a smoke trail in the air. "A valiant effort on your part for naught. Though perhaps you wish to sell the bust?"

"Maybe later."

Rose Leroux fenced black-market antiquities for New York's most discerning clientele. She always had an eye open for profit. Even when it came to one of the very few people she trusted in this city. "You know I'll handle it quietly." She flicked ash into a crystal ashtray. "What is on your mind?"

"Vincent Morello. Everything Joey worked for."

"Quite the list." Rose sat on a bar seat that looked designed to be anything but. The white marble floor beneath her heels turned a vibrant shade of red, reflecting the sole of her shoe. "I hope Joey knows his father would be proud of him even if he does not lead the families."

Rose had fenced antiquities for all five crime families over the past decades. The work earned her a fortune, but more importantly, it earned her respect. From the most dangerous men in the city. No amount of money could purchase that. It also brought her as close as she was willing to get to such men. But of all the men in all the five families who utilized her services, a Morello man was the only one she allowed into her life. Harry Fox, son of Fred Fox. Her lips tightened. Only one other such person had been welcomed into her inner circle. That had proved to be a mistake.

Harry agreed. "You're right, but Joey is beside himself. We all know Altin Cana ordered the hit on Vincent. We just can't prove it."

"Gio Sabella will not support Joey without peaceful vengeance. As Vincent would have done."

"That was the plan," Harry said. "Give the cops enough proof to arrest Altin. We take him out, his organization falls apart. The only guy who might try to step up is Stefan Rudovic." Harry's voice darkened. "And I plan to take him down as well."

Rose closed her eyes. She opened them again, reached for a crystal decanter and poured fresh vodka. Ice followed. "Stefan is dangerous," Rose said. "I understand he has returned."

"Yes," Harry said. "Unfortunately."

She knew about Harry and Stefan's battle in Greece. "He will not forget his defeat at your hands."

"Stefan came after me."

She didn't bother warning him to be careful. Harry possessed his father's adventurous spirit while lacking his caution. It was the one thing she would change about him if she could. "We live in a dangerous world. Your father knew that. He prepared you as best he could."

"I'll be fine," Harry said. "I need your advice. If I don't find a way to take Altin down, Albert's son will likely be the next *capo*."

"Unless Gio Sabella is installed as a placeholder."

"Do you eavesdrop on their meetings?" he joked.

"I have my sources."

"You're right," Harry said. "Either Gio warms the seat or Albert Zurilli's son takes it. Either way, the Morello name takes a hit and Joey feels like he let Vincent down. True or not, he'll feel that way."

Harry was correct. "Which does not bode well for the future," Rose said. "Joey will feel pressured to act. To reclaim his family's place at the top. Which will require conflict."

"Joey's men will follow him anywhere, including head-on into a war with the Canas. Altin's already goading him."

The counting houses, the laundering fronts, the gentlemen's clubs. Rose knew of them all, each incident handled so Joey couldn't prove Altin was behind it. "I know," she said. In truth, she knew much more.

"What would you do in Joey's shoes?" Harry asked. "Altin tried to kill Joey earlier this year and nearly succeeded. Then he tried again and he killed Vincent. Joey barely escaped."

Her cigarette had burned to nothing. Rose replaced it with a fresh one and fired the lighter. The hot smoke in her abused lungs did not help. *There is so much you do not know.* Rose took a sip of her drink and kept silent.

"I have to stop it," Harry said. "I promised Joey I'd find a way to beat Altin."

Rose knew about his relationship with Nora Doyle on the Antiquities Anti-Trafficking Unit. Given Nora's father was an assistant D.A. in

Manhattan, he was the logical choice for help bringing Altin down, but Joey didn't have time to wait while Nora convinced her father to act. In short, Harry's plan had failed. He was stuck.

"A predicament," Rose said. Joey Morello faced an impossible choice if he missed Gio Sabella's deadline. Accept his reduced status, or take drastic action before the deadline. The first choice would undo decades of work by Vincent Morello to cement his family's status as first among equals. Joey's pride wouldn't let that happen. He'd choose action, and it would be the same risky strategy. Starting a war with Altin Cana meant men would die, alliances would be destroyed. The world might never be the same. All due to one man's reckless ambition. Rose would have laughed if it weren't so predictable or sad. Predictable because all powerful men were the same. Sad because some of the men who would die in such a war were close to her heart. Two, to be exact. Harry Fox was one. The other? Stefan Rudovic, who wanted to kill Harry Fox and see this war come to fruition. Rose had known Stefan his whole life. Rose and Stefan's mother had shared experiences no one should have to suffer, and in the end Rose gave Stefan's mother a promise. She would watch out for Stefan. Rose had fulfilled her promise until Stefan committed an unforgiveable sin: he had betrayed Rose.

She had to decide if she would shield him one more time. When a much younger Rose had been held by a Balkan gang, forced to help them traffic humans across international borders, one of those women had a small child. She was trying to escape the Kosovo War, escape from Yugoslavians intent on slaughtering any Albanian they found, even one with a child. A child named Stefan.

Rose made her decision. *It is time to act.* "Harry, you can still succeed. With my help."

"What are you talking about?"

"I will help you," Rose said. "If you speak of this to anyone, I will forget our relationship. Do you understand?"

"I swear I'll never tell anyone."

She knew he meant it. "Good. I know who killed Vincent Morello."

"Altin Cana." Harry's voice was wary. "Who else would have done it? He tried to kill Joey and missed, so he went after Vincent."

"No. Altin had nothing to do with Vincent's murder. He is being used as a scapegoat."

Silence ensued. Rose freshened her drink and waited until Harry finally spoke. "You wouldn't lie to me."

Not any longer.

"If Altin didn't order it, who did? Only those Albanians are crazy enough to take on the Morello family."

"You are correct, Harry."

"You just said Altin didn't kill Vincent."

"Also correct."

Harry's voice was breathless. "Someone in the Cana gang did this without permission? Who would…" His voice trailed off.

"Who indeed," Rose said. "An ambitious man. One who does not respect the old ways."

"Stefan Rudovic."

"Yes. Stefan killed Vincent Morello without Altin Cana's permission. He orchestrated the restaurant bombing. He wants the Cana family to take over Vincent's territory, for one day he intends to run the Cana family."

"How do you know?"

"He told me."

Harry could barely get the words out. "You *knew* Stefan did it, and didn't tell anyone?"

"Stefan contrived to be with me when the bomb exploded. I became his alibi. Admitting I knew he set the bomb would implicate me as an accomplice. After the explosion."

"He told you?"

"A slip of the tongue."

"Who actually set the bomb?" Harry asked. "Was it the two waiters we can't find?"

"Yes. They were given jobs in Sanna at Stefan's request. After he invested in the failing restaurant. A business failing due to its location."

"Directly between Morello and Cana turf."

"I understand you and the owner are close."

"Ahmed and I have been friends for years." Sanna hadn't had any trouble until tensions rose between the Morello and Cana families. "He asked me for help around the same time I went to Vincent with the request. He said no."

"You cannot change what happened."

"I could have loaned him the money myself."

"You could not give it to him after Vincent declined to assist," Rose said. "He would not have permitted that."

"I know. But this all happened before Stefan invested with Ahmed. It was his way of getting close to Ahmed." His words sharpened. "That's why Stefan forgave the loan. Once he had his two men in place, he told Ahmed not to worry about paying him back. Then Stefan must have warned the Cana crew to stay away from Sanna."

"So that the Morello associates would return." Rose had to admire the shrewdness of it. "Vincent walked into a trap."

"I appreciate knowing the truth, Rose. If you have an idea of how I can expose Stefan, tell me."

"I cannot do it alone. Nor can you. I can provide proof Stefan crafted this scheme on his own. You must take it from there."

"You have proof?"

She closed her eyes. "A recording of Stefan admitting his actions. That will be your proof. Which may not be enough to convince Gio Sabella that a direct move against Altin Cana is justified. Or enough to save Joey."

"Albert Zurilli will say we forced Stefan to say it so Joey can justify taking Altin down. Gio Sabella has been adamant this be done the smart way. Without too many bodies."

"An interesting stance for a lifelong mobster to take."

"Who knows why he's saying it? Maybe he's under pressure from the other families. Maybe he really wants Joey to show he can follow his father's example. It doesn't matter."

The finely tuned gears in Rose's head spun rapidly. "Your plan was to steal the bust from Altin's safehouse and prompt the authorities to arrest him. Why would the police move on Altin with just your word? You stole the bust yourself. They are just as likely to arrest you."

"My credibility comes from being part of Nora Doyle's anti-trafficking team. Nominally."

"How far is Nora Doyle willing to bend the rules to bring Altin down?"

"I only need to convince Nora to say she has another confidential informant on her team. One very close to the Canas."

"I will help you if you do not use my name. But you must promise me two more things. First, you will pin this on Altin Cana. Second, you will not go after Stefan if he leaves town before Altin Cana is arrested.

"I can guide Stefan to say the proper things," Rose continued. "And he will never know he is being recorded."

"Why do you want to let Stefan get away?" Harry asked.

Rose waited until enough time had passed with no response. "Do we have an agreement?"

Her silence told Harry volumes. "Yes," he said quietly. "We do."

"I will have the proof to you within two days. Prepare Nora Doyle. Do whatever it takes to make certain this works. Do not let me down."

Chapter 7

Brooklyn

It took Rose twelve hours to deliver on her promise.

Streetlights burned above him when Harry's phone buzzed with an incoming message. Rose Leroux, telling him she'd be at his house in thirty minutes. Harry said he would meet her, put his head down and walked faster. Even though his house was ten minutes away, no need to risk being late.

A knocking sounded on Harry's front door precisely thirty minutes after he spoke with Rose. A freshly-made martini was in Harry's hand. Harry had needed to look up the recipe on his phone.

Sara watched from the couch as Harry opened the door to find a man standing on his front porch.

"Mr. Fox." It was one of Rose's hired guards, a man Harry knew. The man looked at the glass in Harry's hand. He did not blink. "Ms. Leroux is waiting in the car."

The *car* was a blood-red Rolls Royce Ghost. The hired guard opened the rear passenger door. The scent of money poured out on a cloud of cigarette smoke. Harry slipped into a seat that cradled him with exquisite care. He couldn't imagine what Rose paid for this overpriced spaceship, but it was worth every penny.

"Good evening, Harry." Rose Leroux put her cigarette holder to her lips and inhaled. Smoke streamed from her nostrils.

"I brought you a martini." Harry held out the glass. "With olives."

Rose set her cigarette down. "Wonderful." She held the glass in front

52

of her, not moving to drink. "I did not think you knew my type of vodka."

Uh-oh. "I don't."

Rose blinked. "What did you use?"

"I think it was Absolut."

Rose turned, lowered her window, and poured the martini out. She returned the empty glass to him. "The thought is what counts."

Harry didn't speak.

"We will take a short ride." The privacy window was closed, so Rose pushed a button that likely notified her driver and the car slid forward, its turbo-charged engine growling softly. "I spoke with Stefan."

So the Albanian menace was back. "Is he in the city?" Rose said he was. "Should I worry?"

"Always."

The faint hope in Harry's chest that Stefan's injuries would have somehow proved fatal extinguished. "I appreciate the warning."

"You may speak freely in here." Rose indicated the plush interior. "No one can hear us."

"Did Stefan confess?"

"This should suffice." Rose removed a digital recording device from her pocket, pressed a button, and the voice of the man Harry last saw in Greece filled the car. A man who had been trying to kill him with an ancient Grecian trident.

"What is it?" Stefan's gravelly voice was just as Harry remembered it.

"We need to speak," Rose said on the recording. "Right now."

"I'm busy."

"Make time."

Grumbling in Albanian, a language Harry didn't speak, then, "I am listening."

"Your reckless action has put my business at risk," Rose said. "Altin Cana's push to claim Morello family territory is impacting my livelihood. My revenues are down thirty percent."

"I doubt you are running out of money."

"You caused this situation. You are responsible for my losses."

"You will make more money when Altin runs the show."

"I would not have a problem if you had not killed Vincent Morello."

"I did not kill him. I was with you."

Rose let out a theatrical sigh. "You used me as your alibi. If anyone finds out you hired the two workers to bomb Vincent's table, it will come out that we were together, and then I am implicated." Rose's voice lowered a fraction. "And after all I have done for you."

"I hired those men to change the future," Stefan fired back. "To create one where you still make money. Why do you care who controls the city?"

"I care because our city is becoming unstable. Because of you, we all suffer. Your superior would agree with me."

"Is that a threat?"

"Altin Cana does not know who killed Vincent Morello. He knows he is being blamed for it, so he has little choice but to move on the Morello territory. It is an opportunity he cannot pass up. I expect Altin would be displeased if he knew you killed Vincent and he is being blamed."

"Altin will thank me one day," Stefan said. "Even if he does not see it, this had to happen."

"So you can one day run the Cana family."

"We all make our own way in the world. You showed me that."

"I never blackmailed those who cared for me."

"I did what I had to. The Morellos' time is over. Now it is Altin's, and soon it will be mine."

"I hope you treat your future employees better than you treated the two men who set the bomb for you."

"You think I killed them."

"They have disappeared."

Stefan laughed without humor. "I helped them. Sent them back to Albania with enough money that they never need to leave again. They went to the airport after the explosion and flew to Germany. I have not spoken with them."

Rose's voice went silent for a breath. "I understand you may not have artifacts to sell right now. A fire at Altin's safehouse?"

"How do you—forget it. There will be more relics."

"I hope so."

A pause. "Remember, we are in this together. Do not do anything stupid."

"You have that covered for both of us."

Rose Leroux pressed a button and the recording stopped. She didn't look at Harry, her gaze focused on the rowhomes rolling past outside her window. "Will this suffice?"

Now it was Harry's turn to think. The truth was it wouldn't right now, not if he wanted to convince Nora Doyle to go after Altin Cana's crew. Rose had persuaded Stefan to admit his role in the killings. Too bad it didn't implicate Altin in any way. Lucky for Harry, he knew a guy who could fix that. "It's perfect," he said.

Rose pushed the button again, and at the next intersection the rolling mansion turned back in the direction of Harry's home. "My name will not be publicly associated with that recording. Agreed?"

"Yes. I'll make certain the D.A.'s office does not jeopardize a highly placed source close to Altin's operations."

Rose removed a memory stick from her pocket. "This is surveillance footage from JFK the night of the bombing. You may recognize two men entering the international terminal one hour after the bomb exploded." She held the stick out to Harry, who took it.

"The police couldn't find them?"

"The NYPD is overworked and understaffed," Rose said. "They do not have time to watch hours of footage searching for two men who may have killed a mobster."

"How did you get this?" he asked, turning the device over in his palm. Lines creased her forehead and Harry lifted a hand. "Forget I asked."

Her vehicle slowed to a stop outside his home. "This is an unusual position for me," Rose said as Harry opened his door. "Counting on someone else to protect my interests."

"It's not just you. The whole Morello crew is counting on me."

"And the other families as well, even if they do not know it."

Nothing like a little pressure. Harry put one foot on the street and paused. "What did you mean when you told Stefan *After all I have done for you?*"

Rose did not look at him when she responded. "I knew his mother." She did not elaborate.

The engine rumbled as the car rolled away. Harry went back inside his house, locking the front door behind him. Sara had apparently called it a night, leaving the amulets and an open book on the table. Perhaps that was a good thing, for what Harry needed to do was best carried out in private.

He walked into the kitchen and grabbed a beer, then pulled out his phone and dialed a number. Several long rings passed before someone picked up.

"As I live and breathe. Harry Fox?"

"Hey, Dustin." A guitar solo played in the background. "Can you turn that down? I can't hear you."

"Hang on." The music faded and Dustin came back on the line. "What's up? Haven't heard from you in ages."

Dustin Wood had been Harry's buddy since high school, a guy who loved music, theater, pretty much anything to do with performance. He ran a recording studio in New Jersey and was a wizard at audio production. Dustin and Harry had had their fair share of questionable fun back in the day. Dustin was the kind of guy who could keep his mouth shut.

"It's been a while," Harry said. "You have a second?" Dustin said he did. "Hypothetical question," Harry said. "Between old friends."

"Between old friends."

"Say I have a recording of a conversation. And say I want to change the conversation a little. Is that possible?"

"How much change are we talking about here?"

"A few names switched around. Edit out a section."

"Any chance all the names you want to change are already mentioned somewhere in the conversation, or do you need to create them out of thin air?"

"I need to switch one name with another, and both are mentioned in the call." Harry wanted to make the conversation indicate that Altin, not Stefan, had ordered Vincent Morello's death. Then the tape would pin the blame squarely on the Cana leader and give Nora Doyle's father what he needed to go after the Albanian gangster.

"That's easy, my man. We'll listen to the file together. You tell me what you want it to say, and I'll make it happen."

Harry sipped his beer. "Dustin, do you know what I do?"

"Only if I'm supposed to."

Harry smiled. "Good man."

"Your old man, may he rest peacefully, had a crazy job. From what I understand you've inherited it."

"Then you know who I work for."

"Depends on who's asking. I trust you, man. We go back a long way. If you're getting me in over my head, you'll be honest about it."

"The honest answer is it depends."

"On what?"

"On how good you are at your job."

He could hear the grin in Dustin's voice. "I'm the best."

"Will this new recording fool a district attorney's office?"

Dustin actually laughed. "A civil servant? You're joking. I can throw it past him so fast he'll never know what happened. I have the best equipment money can buy. How else do you think I get Rock & Roll Hall of Famers into my studio?"

Dustin had never lacked confidence. "I'm impressed."

"Metadata and HEX analysis, LTAS, recording parameters, spectrographic analysis. I know all the tricks. This recording will be the smoothest, cleanest, most authentic one they've ever heard."

Harry didn't even pretend to know what any of that meant. "How long will it take?"

"For you? An hour."

"Tomorrow morning?"

"If by morning you mean noon, then sure."

"Come on, Dustin."

Dustin grumbled a bit. "Fine. Be here at ten. But just because it's you."

"I'll pay double your rates if you make it nine."

"Deal. Bring coffee."

Harry clicked off and immediately called Nora. She picked up at once.

"What is it?"

"I figured out how to stop the Canas and Morellos from killing each other."

A pause. "I'm listening."

"Hear me out." He pushed on before Nora could argue. "You now have a confidential informant who recorded a conversation implicating Altin Cana in Vincent Morello's murder."

"No, I don't."

"Yes, you do."

"Cut the crap, Harry."

Harry found it easier to be entirely straight with Nora than with Sara. Something to do with the fact that Sara could change his life forever, while Nora could only make it a lot harder right now. "I have a recording of Stefan Rudovic admitting he ordered the hit on Vincent."

"How did you get that?"

"I know people."

"Okay, Harry. Does it show Altin ordered Stefan to arrange the hit?"

"No."

"Then how does this get me to Altin Cana?"

"It doesn't. But it will."

"Stop right there. I play by the rules."

"You can bend them, not break them. This is a little bending, that's all."

Colorful language came through the phone. "Tell me *exactly* what you have."

Harry did, leaving nothing out. Nora listened in silence. "Stefan works for Altin," she eventually said. "That doesn't mean we can charge Altin for something Stefan does on his own. Altin will say Stefan went rogue."

"Not yet. I know a guy."

"This is not a gangster movie, Harry. It will eventually play out in a court of law, and there are rules in a courtroom, with judges to make you follow them."

"My guy," Harry went on, undeterred, "is the best. He can tweak the confession so it says Altin ordered the hit, not Stefan. You'll have proof to arrest Altin and stop this war before it really starts."

"I won't have proof. I'll have a lie."

"It's your foot in the door. Once your father's people dig into Altin's world, he's done. I can't even tell you how many crimes he's committed, and I know these things."

"It's still a lie. I can't take a lie to my father."

"Do you want to stop a bunch of people from killing each other or not?" He lifted his beer bottle to find it empty. "The world is messy, Nora. You can't always have a perfect solution."

"I don't need perfect. I need legal."

He ran a hand through his hair. "Look, I know it's not exactly true."

"It's an outright lie."

"Which is the right thing to do. You know it and I know it. Altin is a bad guy. Heck, lots of people would say we're all bad guys, but my point is not all bad guys are the same. Joey Morello is going to keep the city operating how it was. No gang wars, no bodies, just business."

"Illegal business that harms innocents and destroys cultural heritage."

"People choose to do those things."

"By that you mean gamble, solicit and use?"

"It's not going away," Harry said. "But Joey makes it safe. And, if you can still hear me up there in your ivory tower, Joey's looking to pivot. He's getting away from those revenue streams, moving into other ventures. Ones you might not be so judgmental about."

"I'll believe it when I see it."

"I'm serious, Nora. The mob families aren't going anywhere. You want to make a difference? Stop them from killing each other. Put Altin Cana behind bars."

He steeled himself to argue further. In a most surprising development, he didn't need to. Nora didn't respond. Harry let the silence linger. He also grabbed another beer.

"The world isn't black and white." Nora sounded like a much older woman now. A woman who had seen glimpses of the future. A future she couldn't stop, like it or not. "It's often gray. My mother reminded me of that not long ago."

"Is she back in town?"

"No, no. I was only thinking."

"That I'm telling you the truth?"

"I know you're telling me the truth. But it's not that simple. Altin Cana belongs in jail. So, technically, does Joey Morello." He started to speak but she cut him off. "I'm an officer of the law, but that doesn't mean I ignore facts. If I let Altin stay on the streets, men will die and neighborhoods will be terrorized. The Morello and Cana turfs will be war zones where innocent people will be in danger. If I do what you suggest—which, let's be clear, is against everything my job stands for—then that's all avoided."

"And Altin's crew is eliminated."

"Which looks an awful lot like I'm playing favorites. Why not fabricate evidence against Joey Morello and put his crew in jail as well? Then Altin can take over the Morello turf without a fight."

"You know he won't stop there. If Altin doesn't make a move to be the next *capo dei capi*, Stefan will. Which means another war, because the Italian families won't let him have it without a fight."

"Which leaves me where? Uphold the law, or become no better than a criminal."

Harry spoke softly. "I'm one of those criminals. Look how our partnership turned out."

Nora may have smiled. "It's working so far."

"You're a person, Nora. Not just a cop. People have feelings. They're complex. They do the best they can. You want to make New York a better city? It's Altin or Joey. Take your pick." Now he fell silent, and she didn't fill the air. An unexpected feeling warmed his chest. "Your decision will change quite a few lives. Mine included."

"You won't be out of a job if Joey goes to jail," Nora said. "You're still on my team, remember? Our agreement still stands."

Nora meant the immunity agreement he had signed when she twisted his arm to work with her. "That's not what I mean. It's not just a job. The Morellos are my family. They're all I have left."

"I don't do emotional," Nora snapped. "But I see your point. I still have my parents. You never really did." A beat passed. "Not to mention Sara won't stick around if you get dragged through the mud with Joey Morello. I can tell."

"She already knows what I've done. Well, mostly." He didn't add that Sara's decision had already been made. Nevertheless, Harry wouldn't give up on her yet.

"She's good for you, Harry." Nora sighed, not too loud or long. "Do it."

"What?"

"I said do it. Get the evidence ready and send it to me."

Harry's tongue momentarily failed him. "Okay, sure. I'm on it. But I can't reveal my source."

"I'll tell my father I cultivated a source inside Altin Cana's operation. No names."

Harry's kitchen became a vacuum without sound. He forced himself to blink. "I'll have it to you tomorrow morning."

"I'll call my father now. This better be spotless, Harry. Unimpeachable."

Harry's lip curled up on one side. "It's better than that. It's perfect."

Chapter 8

Brooklyn

Sara walked out of Harry's spare bedroom to the sounds of a man rushing about the house. She tensed, rooted to the floor, until Harry's voice rang out from downstairs. "Want coffee?"

Sara exhaled. "Strong," she called out as she headed downstairs. Her steps felt lighter today. The morning sunlight was brighter, the wintry sky sharper. It had been getting better the past few days. Sara knew why. The clouds covering her world had parted when she uncovered the message hidden on Nora's amulet. She understood the next step could lead to Alexandria.

"How did you sleep?" Harry asked as he offered her a steaming mug.

"Quite well." That got a second look from him. "I have a good feeling about today."

Now he was clearly lost. "Why's that?"

"I'm not certain," she said honestly. "Other than we're making progress on Cleopatra's trail. Perhaps today is the day." For what, she didn't say, but it didn't matter. They were making progress, and each step brought her closer to her old self.

Sara opened her laptop and navigated to a diving enthusiast site where people shared photos and stories of their experiences, grouped by location. The page for Alexandria's harbor provided a wealth of information for Harry's next trip. What it had not provided as of yet was a clear answer of where he should dive. As Jennifer Doyle was not yet back from her trip, this was their only option for progress until Harry could meet with her. Sara didn't have the heart to ask him again about Detective Jessica Barnes. That was off limits.

The submerged statue of Cerberus filled her screen. A dozen different shots allowed her to study it in detail while also showing other ruins that surrounded it. She and Harry believed Antony had deliberately placed a statue of the mythical Greek watchdog in Caesar's replica tomb. Determining *where* it had been located in that tomb was the key.

She stopped typing. This was Harry's search, not hers. She'd made the mistake before of getting too close, ignoring the obvious red flags. It had nearly killed her. She would help him with Alexandria. Then take a step back.

"Any luck?" Harry asked. "I assume Cerberus is near the remains of whatever room it was in."

She pushed her thoughts aside. "A fair assumption. The challenge is that objects originally in the room, as well as debris from the room itself, are all in the water due to earthquakes and tidal waves. There's no guarantee what you seek is anywhere near the statue."

"There's no guarantee it's not."

"Also true. The site is in only twenty-five feet of water and is concentrated due to being in the protected harbor. You should be able to investigate most of it in a day."

"I'd rather narrow the search area down before I get wet."

"Then you're lucky I'm here. Look." She pointed to a series of images on-screen, snapshots posted by an amateur diver. "You already caught a break. See this plinth? The wear pattern suggests it's what Cerberus stood on before the building collapsed. The bottom of the base still has the floor attached."

"Looks like marble."

"Marble with a unique color pattern. White with red lines." He pointed to the lines, which ran through the chunk of marble floor like veins in a body. "Here is a large piece of flooring not far from the plinth, which has that same color pattern." Sara flipped open a notebook. "I drew a map. Cerberus is here, the plinth is next to it, and I've marked each section of similarly colored floor."

Harry leaned over the rough map. "They're all near each other. That means most of the room where Cerberus stood is probably still intact."

"Which also means anything Cerberus was meant to show you is likely still nearby. Such as this." She indicated another mark on her map. "It's a statue of Cleopatra." Now she turned to the monitor. "This photo depicts Cleopatra as a goddess, and it has red-veined marble flooring around the base."

"It's in incredible shape," Harry said. "Why's it still in the water?"

"Likely due to the sheer number of artifacts down there. Also, lifting a several-ton statue to the surface is challenging and expensive."

"Anywhere else grab your eye?"

"I saved the best for last." She indicated a large X on the map. "A section of wall with writing on it. Not Egyptian writing. *Greek.*"

The screen's light reflected in Harry's eyes as she enlarged the artifact in question. Ten feet tall, the dun-colored wall had inscriptions running up and down its surface, along with several engravings of a woman he recognized. "That's Cleopatra." He squinted. "I can only make out a few symbols."

"This is the best image I could find." The wall fragment was partially buried, and with the lighting meager at best, deciphering the writing was impossible. "You'd better brush up on your ancient Greek. You'll have to decipher it there."

He didn't look at her when she spoke. "Or I could bring a translator with me."

A second passed before she shook her head. "I'm not going, Harry."

"Worth a shot." His phone dinged. "I have to take this."

He walked to the front door and went outside, the phone pressed to his ear. Sara looked at the images on the screen, twisting her map to be certain it showed the proper locations of each artifact, turning it this way and that so it made sense. Or at least she tried. The problem was her mind wouldn't cooperate. Harry needed this map, needed to know as much as he could before going underwater. He was counting on her, because he would do this alone.

The same thought ran through her head again and again, one that had surfaced only after they realized the second amulet pointed to Caesar's tomb. *What if I'm wrong about this?*

Not about the trail. She was confident in her analysis, positive that Harry would find what Cleopatra intended for her children to discover. Her doubts were tied to a different question. *Should I go with him?*

She'd been certain. So certain. She shouldn't go, not after Greece. Even now, her stomach clenched in a knot at the memory of it. Harry behind the wheel, Sara in the passenger seat. A car appearing out of nowhere, smashing into them. Hazy memories of strong hands ripping her from the ruined vehicle, of being dragged into another car, her hands bound. She had caught a glimpse of Harry as the car roared off, saw his blood-stained face through the broken window.

Before she met Harry Fox, Sara Hamed had been a respected Egyptologist who plied her craft in the classroom and on dig sites. Now she was a respected Egyptologist who had nearly been killed several times, a woman who rewrote the past, often in ways a respected Egyptologist should not. It was terrifying, exhilarating, sometimes illegal and—if she were being honest—addictive. Which was why she couldn't go to Alexandria. Why this might be the last trip she made to Brooklyn.

She looked up at Harry gesturing animatedly outside the front door. *What if I'm wrong?*

Her phone buzzed with an incoming call. The name on-screen warmed her heart. "Good morning, Jane."

"Still in the States, I see. Dare I ask where?" Jane White chuckled at her own joke. "Is now a bad time?"

"It's never a bad time for an old friend. To what do I owe the pleasure?"

"Curiosity. We haven't spoken in a while. I wanted to see how you are."

Sara and Jane White were colleagues, academics whose paths had crossed enough that they had formed a close bond. "I've been better."

"What's the matter?"

With Jane it was no shallow question. The scion of a wealthy Scottish family, Jane was a relic of the past in many ways, all of them good. Jane didn't open up easily. It must be hard to make serious friends, Sara suspected, when you lived in an actual centuries-old castle on a loch. The property was spectacular, though from what Jane had revealed about herself, the stone walls—and the old money behind them—were as effective at keeping people out today as they had been long ago.

"You wouldn't believe me."

"I insist."

Sara bit her lip. "I was kidnapped while helping Harry decode a riddle on an ancient Egyptian amulet. The one you saw around his neck. I escaped and my captors were killed, but it's had an effect on me. Not a positive one."

Jane stood still. "I'm so sorry." She paused. "That is the most incredible story I've ever heard."

"It was a bit of a test."

Jane must have picked up on her unease. "About Harry. How is your slightly short, dark and handsome man?"

Sara burst out laughing, the sort of laugh only a dear and deliciously wicked friend could inspire. "It isn't Harry's fault you run around with a muscle-bound banker."

"I do not *run around* with Parker Chase." Sara let her silence do the talking. "Again," Jane continued. "How is Harry?"

"The same as ever. Which is the problem." Sara retreated to the kitchen, putting more distance between her and Harry. "He lives in a different world than I do. You and I are academics, Jane. We study the past. We shape narratives. We do not create history. Or at least I thought we didn't, until Harry came along. Now I have an impossibly wonderful chance to do just that."

"Believe me when I say I understand."

Jane had never fully explained her dealings with Parker. Sara knew only that they had cost Parker's fiancé her life. "It's a challenge for me.

A balancing act."

"Harry is unique," Jane said. "From what I know, he had a challenging life. Losing your mother at a young age changes you."

Sara wasn't going to get into that issue right now. "True, but not everyone resorts to chasing relics for a living."

"Perhaps that is because not everyone is capable of it."

"It almost sounds as though you're defending him."

"Harry Fox is a good guy in some ways. He's a simple choice in a complicated world. Is he a safe choice? Not at all. Is he the *right* choice? Only you can answer that."

Sara's entire life had been played by the rules. Her studies, her teaching, her research. All of it fulfilling, and all of it by the book. Never once had she seen it as merely scratching the surface. Then Harry landed in her life, rewriting what was possible and showing her an entirely different world. One unconstrained by the normal rules. Dangerous, yes, but also fantastic. She had been far to one side, Harry far to the other. Could they find a way to meet in the middle?

"Harry listens to me," Sara said, mostly to herself. "He causes trouble for the right reasons, but it's still trouble. The kind that sometimes gets people killed."

"Use that brilliant mind of yours to help him."

"Help him how?"

"Live the life you imagine. He can change, the same as you. You can help each other. I saw it work with Parker and Erika."

That jolted Sara. "She died in a car bombing."

They were both quiet for a moment. Finally, Jane spoke again.

"You can't be afraid to reach for what you truly want while you still have the chance." Jane paused for a beat, then laughed. "Listen to me, lecturing you on relationships. It's not my place."

"Your advice is always welcome," Sara replied truthfully.

"I suggest you stop listening to me prattle and find Harry. Talk to him. See if it's real."

Sara knew it was real. Dangerous, enthralling, and most certainly real.

As was the chance to unearth a part of history no one had ever seen before. In the waters of Alexandria's harbor. "Thank you, Jane. For everything."

"Tell Harry hello."

Sara ended the call and walked through the kitchen, past the table with her open laptop and notebook, directly to the closed front door. Harry was still outside with his phone pressed to his ear. She knocked on the inside of the door. He looked up, his eyes narrowed, and she motioned with her forefinger. *Come here.*

He ended the call, shoved the phone in his pocket and opened the door. "Are you okay?" he asked.

"Yes." Sara drew herself up to her full height. "I've changed my mind. I'm coming to Alexandria."

His mouth formed a little circle. She forced herself not to grin. "Stop standing there and make yourself useful. Reserve two plane tickets and a private diving tour in the harbor. I'll pack." She turned on a heel and marched off, and was halfway to the steps when it hit her. "Oh my." She spun around to find Harry hadn't moved. "All of that after you speak with Nora's mother, of course. Forgive me. I was excited. We'll leave once you talk to Jennifer Doyle."

Harry found his voice. "Who were you on the phone with just now?"

"Jane White."

"Tell her she's my new favorite person in the world." Harry marched over, wrapped his arms around Sara and lifted her clean off the floor. "I'll take care of everything," he said, his breath warm on her neck. "As soon as I talk to Jennifer, we're out of here." He set her down and stepped back, studying her face. "Why?"

"Why what?"

"Why the change of heart?"

She lifted a finger. "Just accept it."

"Fair enough."

He was grinning like a fool. "Wise man," she said. "Sorry for interrupting your call."

"No worries. It was an old friend."

"Is everything all right?"

Harry crossed his arms on his chest. He uncrossed them, then took a breath. "We're in this together, right?"

"In what together?"

A wave indicated the room at large. "This. The amulet hunt, Alexandria, my problems, all of it."

One hand went to her hip. "Harry, I just agreed to accompany you on another reckless artifact chase despite having been kidnapped. So, yes, we are in this together. All of it."

"Then I have to tell you something. About Nora, Rose Leroux and an old friend." Now his face lit up, a look that should have scared her away. A look that changed everything. "To answer your question, nothing is wrong. In fact, things are about to get much better."

Chapter 9

Brooklyn

The well-used rocks glass on Joey Morello's desk was empty again. He glared at it. Maybe that was enough for tonight. He looked to the well-stocked bar in his father's office. Maybe just one more.

He stood and shook his head. *My* office. This was his office now. Joey stood and took a step toward the bar, his eyes on the bourbon.

"Hey, boss?"

Joey looked over at his open office door. Mack's head had appeared. "Are they here?" Joey asked.

"All o' them," Mack said.

Joey cast a sad eye at the bourbon. It could wait. "Then let's go."

He followed Mack down the hall to his conference room, where his crew leaders had gathered after an evening summons from the boss. Joey walked to the center of the room. "Listen up." He met every pair of eyes before continuing. "I know it's tough to sit back right now, but we're in a tight spot. The Canas are trying to prove they belong with the real families who run this city. It's not right, and they went too far."

One of his longest-serving men spoke up. "They killed Gabe and Dom in the pizza place explosion. We know it was them."

"They did," Joey said evenly. "And I won't stand for it. We can't let them win." He lifted a hand, one finger raised. "They're cockroaches. And what do you do to a cockroach?" He paused, then dropped the finger and made a quick grinding motion. "Crush it."

70

Murmured agreement, most of his men joining in. One voice rang out. "How, boss?"

"I can't say how, not yet, but I need you to trust this is under control and that Altin Cana will get what's coming to him."

"A dip in the Hudson," one man said.

Fists thumped their approval and hard men cheered. Joey raised his voice. "If I just put Altin Cana in the river—and believe me, I want to— one of his punk men will take his place. So I'm going to do better than just getting rid of Altin." Joey paused, metal creaking and leather rustling as his crew leaned in. "We'll take down his whole crew. Every last one. That organization will no longer exist."

Several men called out the same question. "How?"

Joey tapped the side of his head. "By being smarter than them. Stay with me, fellas. It's coming soon. Very soon, so hang tight and don't do anything stupid."

Fists pounded tables and men shouted their approval along with heartfelt wishes to destroy the Cana crew. Joey raised his voice.

"Stay focused, men. Don't lose faith."

He didn't take a breath until he exited the room, his men still railing against the Canas. Two steps down the hallway and he paused, his chest rising and falling, eyes closed. The men were behind him. For one dark moment he had worried they had lost confidence in him. But no. So Joey would take the fight to Altin Cana, sure, but do it the smart way. Save his own men's lives. No need to get any more of them killed if he could outmaneuver that Albanian chump.

His phone buzzed. Joey pulled it out. He read the message. Read it again. His stomach dropped. He turned around and realized the room behind him had fallen silent. He took one step back toward the open door just as Mack stepped through it, holding his phone.

"Someone hit your restaurant."

Joey moved past Mack into the conference room. Every man had his eyes locked on a phone as the text messages flew. One looked up at him, then another, until the weight of every eye pressed on him. "Stay here,"

Joey said. He turned and left the room, phone to his ear. He called Matteo, the manager of Linda's Ristorante, Joey's Italian restaurant that was named for his aunt.

Matteo answered breathlessly. "Boss."

"What happened?" Joey asked. "Who did it?"

"I don't know who," Matteo said. "The dining room was nearly full. Four guys in ski masks pushed through the front door, waving guns in the air. Four more came in the back way, through the kitchen. They were all shouting, aiming their weapons at customers."

"Did they shoot anyone?"

"No," Matteo said. "They forced the customers to hand over their wallets and purses. They took them and left."

"A *robbery*?" Joey said incredulously. "Who carries cash anymore? They wouldn't get much." Unless that wasn't the goal. "They didn't want money," he said, as the realization hit him. "They wanted to insult me."

Matteo agreed. "I believe so."

"Did the gunmen have any accents?"

"I didn't hear any."

"Where are the cops?"

"The first cars just arrived," Matteo said. "What do you want me to do?"

"Tell them the truth." Joey wracked his brain. The Italian restaurant was a rare type of Morello business: legitimate. "Then call me if you learn anything."

Matteo said he would and clicked off. Joey squared his shoulders, put his chin up and walked back into the conference room, where he told his men this was nothing but a robbery. The quiet following his pronouncement told Joey nobody believed him. He didn't believe it himself.

One of his *capos* spoke up. "What do we do now, boss?"

"Stay the course. A few more days. Then the world goes back to the way it should be."

The *capo* didn't argue. He also didn't stop asking questions. "Only the

Albanians would be stupid enough to hit our restaurant. We don't respond?"

Joey wanted nothing more in the world. "No." The single word landed with the force of a sledgehammer. "Anybody goes after the Albanians, they answer to me. Understood?" He did not like what he saw on their faces. His hands clenched into fists. "Understood?"

His crew muttered agreement. Joey's phone buzzed again. He checked the screen. *Damn.*

"Wait until you hear from me," Joey said. He connected the call, putting the phone to an ear as he headed back to his office. "Good evening, Mr. Sabella."

Gio Sabella did not mince words. "Not from what I understand."

His jaw tightened. "Everything is under control. This is an unfortunate incident. Robberies happen."

"I wish that were true," Gio said. His next words were measured, precise. "This is a delicate time, Joseph. Your days are running short. I will not be able to grant you an extension."

Joey walked into his office and leaned against the edge of his father's—*his*—desk. "Are the other families concerned?" Joey meant the ones who would decide if Joey was worthy of sitting on his father's throne or not.

"Their concerns are not mine," Gio said. "Yet."

Which meant they were beating Gio's door down to end Joey's hopes. "Nothing has changed," Joey said. He channeled a strength he didn't feel. "Even if Altin Cana did do this, his day is coming. Sooner than my deadline."

"I hope that is true. Albert Zurilli senses weakness."

Albert had better be careful about what he hopes for. "Do you?" Joey asked.

"What matters is that I can ensure you receive every minute of the days left to prove your worth. Beyond that, it is out of my control. The agreement will be honored."

"Thank you, Mr. Sabella. I have a plan that my father would approve of."

A pause. "A plan you have not shared."

"Plans can unravel when too many people know of them."

"Joseph, now you sound like your father."

High praise. "Thank you," Joey said, then clicked off. He grabbed his empty rocks glass and headed for the bar, where he poured himself another generous measure of bourbon. That done, he strode to the chair behind his desk, sank into it gratefully, and sipped. Cool fire arced down his throat. Joey closed his eyes as he leaned back. *Harry had better come through.*

A few drops remained in Joey's glass when a commotion sounded in the hallway. Joey stood and walked out into the corridor. He turned a corner and found Mack headed straight for him. The big man held an open box in his hands.

"What's going on?" Joey asked.

"You gotta see this, boss." Mack lowered the box so Joey could see inside.

"Wallets." Dozens of them, small metal ones and larger leather ones of all colors, men's and women's, an entire box of them. Joey grabbed one at random and flipped it open. He pulled out a fistful of hundreds. He reached for another one, then a third. Each one he opened had cash, credit cards and identification in it, apparently untouched. "These are from the restaurant."

Mack balanced the box on one hand. With the other, he handed Joey a sheet of paper. "This was inside the box."

Two lines were hand-scrawled across it. His eyes narrowed as he read the inscription. "Where was the box?"

"On the front step," Mack said. "Someone rang the doorbell. I open the door, see this box and nobody around. Kicked it a few times and one of the wallets fell out, so I open it, find this letter on top." He shrugged. "Then I brought it to you."

Security cameras monitored every inch of the Morello compound, inside and out. Whoever had delivered this would be captured on camera. Not that it mattered. Joey knew who had sent the note. "Check the footage," Joey told Mack. "See which way he went, then have someone take the box to the restaurant."

Mack rumbled off to dispense orders. Joey stared at the single sheet of paper. At two lines heralding the end of an era. One way or the other.

Dear neighbor—see you soon.

Joey didn't crumple the paper, didn't rip it to pieces. He went into his office and laid it on his desk. Not his father's desk. *His* desk. He looked out of a bulletproof window.

Altin Cana's men had robbed his restaurant. They had dropped the box of wallets on his front step. Joey knew this in his bones because Altin Cana's territory ran up against Joey Morello's, on the street where Vincent Morello had been killed in another restaurant called Sanna. The Cana and Morello families were neighbors. Now Altin Cana had made Joey a promise. He was coming for him. Coming soon.

His phone buzzed again. Joey scooped it up when he saw who was calling.

"Harry. Tell me you have good news." Joey listened for a moment, and then his grip on the phone tightened. "Say that again."

Chapter 10

Brooklyn

Twenty-four hours after Altin's men robbed Joey Morello's restaurant, Stefan Rudovic found himself in an uncomfortable situation. Not because of the lingering pain in his surgically repaired ankle, though that dull ache often reminded him of a debt to be repaid. Not because he hadn't slept last night and was running on caffeine. That wasn't unusual. No, the reason for his discomfort was the gruff Albanian mobster with bags the size of zeppelins under his eyes. The man who had given him everything in life.

Altin Cana stared across his desk at Stefan. "You will have this great honor."

Honor was not the way Stefan would describe it. "Your faith is appreciated. What is the plan?"

"To take the Morello territory as our own. By force."

Stefan gripped the arms of his chair. "I am to lead the men."

"Yes. The men must see that you are ready. That you are the one who will show them the way."

A way guarded by men with guns and murderous intent. "I see." Stefan didn't trust himself to say anything further. He knew Altin could sense his reluctance. "We move on them tonight?"

"Yes. The men are readying now." Altin shifted his considerable bulk. "The other families now see Joey Morello is weak. We attack his counting houses, his gambling operation, his restaurant. What does he do?

Nothing. Now we finish the job. If we hit his headquarters, his safest place, the world will see that the Morello family is finished. Their territory becomes mine." Altin took a cigar from the box on his desk. He touched a lighter to the end, puffing until it caught. "And you." He pointed the smoldering tip at Stefan. "Prove yourself."

"I have not already done that?"

"Yes. Now do it again."

Stefan searched for a way out. "Some of our men will die."

Altin puffed at his cigar. "Their families will be compensated."

Stefan phrased his next words carefully. "I may be one of those men."

The cigar burned. Smoke poured from Altin's mouth, his gravelly words sliding through the haze. "I hope you are more careful than that."

So much for talking his way out. "I am honored to finish the Italian scum," Stefan said. "Is Joey Morello at his headquarters?"

This time Altin pointed his cigar toward his office window. The Morello compound lay only a few miles distant. "He is there. So are some of his men. They are unprepared. My delivery last night made them nervous. Yet Joey Morello has done nothing today."

"You have people watching."

"Two women. You know them."

Stefan did. Iris and Cici, both contractors Stefan had himself used before. "I will speak with them before we go in."

"They are still there," Altin said. "Do it tonight. Take enough men to make sure this settles the matter. Tomorrow morning, the Morello territory is mine." Altin inclined his head toward Stefan. "You will run it for me. All of it."

A jolt went up Stefan's back. Control of what used to be the Morello territory? A clear sign Altin had plans for Stefan Rudovic. Plans that likely included taking over the family when Altin retired. The very plan Stefan so desperately wished to see come true. Plans that required him to be alive tomorrow morning. "I will not let you down."

The big man waved at the door and Stefan stood and took his leave. He passed a number of men on his way outside, nodding quickly and moving on before they could say anything. Once the early evening moonlight cast Stefan's shadow on the sidewalk, he pulled out his phone and dial Iris's number. It took her a few rings to answer.

"Hello?"

Iris spoke in English, not Albanian. Smart, considering she was in enemy territory. "Are you watching the compound?" Stefan asked.

"From a car down the street."

"Is Joey inside?" Iris said he was. "How many are with him?"

"No more than a dozen."

Which was about eleven more than he wanted. "Any sign they are waiting for us?"

"No."

"Good. What did Altin tell you to do?"

"Watch the house until I am told to stop."

"Keep watching it. I am running the operation tonight."

"Operation?"

Not exactly the one Altin hoped for, but close. "We move on the Morellos. Tonight." Iris said nothing. "I need your help."

"I am here already." Iris didn't realize it, but she would play a pivotal role, one that Stefan had just created for her.

"Stay there. I need you to provide a distraction."

"How?"

Stefan stopped at a red light, waiting for traffic to pass. "By knocking on their front door."

"They will shoot me."

"They will not. You will be with one of our men. He will have a package, like a delivery man. You will tell the guard the package is for Joseph Morello. A signature is required. When the guard signs for it, our man will pull his gun and go inside. That is when you leave. Quickly. The rest of our men will be coming through."

"How are they all going to get close enough without being seen? There are cameras outside."

"In two vans." Ones Altin Cana had in a garage, along with a dozen different decals for fictitious plumbing or electrical companies. Sometimes the old tricks worked best. "Get the door open and then get out of the way."

"That's dangerous, Stefan. You'd better pay me for it."

"Tomorrow. It will be a new world and you will have plenty of money."

Iris was no fool. "Pay me tonight."

"A thousand dollars when I see you." Which wouldn't be until after the fireworks ended, but she didn't know that.

"Fine."

Altin wanted him to move late enough that the Morello men would be off their guard, but not so late that a routine delivery would cause suspicion. The dinner hour seemed about right. "We move in two hours," Stefan said. "Call me if you see Joey Morello leave." He clicked off without waiting for an answer.

Iris was the first part of his plan. The part that kept him out of harm's way until the shooting was over. Plenty of foot soldiers among the Cana men would leap at the chance to go through the door first. Good for them. Stefan would be at the rear, keeping his head down until enough Cana men were inside to overwhelm the Morellos. The Italians would put up a serious fight, which was why Stefan planned to bring nineteen men. Twenty, if you counted him, which he did not. Bring Joey Morello's turf to Altin Cana and Stefan's path to the top would be confirmed.

Stefan paused beneath a streetlamp. The tall window of a bar behind him offered his reflection, which he turned to study. No longer was he looking at an immigrant who had washed up on American shores without money, hope or a future. The boy who had arrived in the company of a mother who would soon leave him had become something. A force that would shape the future of Brooklyn, perhaps even New York. Altin Cana had started this Albanian family. Stefan Rudovic would lead it into the future. A rich, rewarding future. Where he called the shots.

Stefan admired his reflection a moment longer, then turned and headed back to Altin's headquarters. More men had arrived, twenty in all, gathered in a smoky basement. Metal clinked and pistol slides snicked as Stefan walked downstairs. Several men had already donned body armor. He raised his voice.

"Quiet."

The men fell silent. They all looked to Stefan. A jolt of electricity shot down his chest. He lifted his chin and spoke. "Here is the plan."

The men listened as he outlined how they'd arrive in vans, parking outside Joey's headquarters. One man needed to accompany Iris to the Morello door. Theirs would be the hardest part of the mission, for that man had to convince the guard, Mack, to open the door. Jamming a pistol between his eyes should do the trick. Any volunteers?

Nearly every hand shot up. Stefan chose a man whom Altin had seemed to favor recently. A man with ambitions. Stefan hoped Mack decided to fight back tonight.

"Any questions?" Stefan asked. None. "We leave in one hour. Be outside and in the vans by then. I have to get a package for our friends."

Harsh laughter followed him up the basement stairs. His apartment wasn't far, close enough that he could grab a cardboard box, put on his bulletproof vest and return to Cana headquarters in time to depart. He would drive one of the vans. The first one, so he could park farthest from the front door. Stefan winced when he bent down to tie his boots, a familiar pain arcing through his wounded leg. If Harry Fox wasn't in the Morello house, Stefan's first order of business would be to hunt him down. Their confrontation in Greece had only been the start—this personal battle was far from finished.

He maneuvered a shirt over his vest, slipped a pistol into his waistband, and checked his watch. Thirty minutes until departure. Stefan headed for the door, reaching for the empty cardboard box, which had been taped shut to look full. His phone buzzed. The name on-screen brought lines to his forehead. What did she want? He almost declined the call, then thought better of it. Perhaps now was as good a time as any to share his news.

"Hello, Rose."

"Where are you?" Rose Leroux spoke quickly, her words clipped. "Exactly."

A strange question. "Why?"

"Answer me."

He spoke without thinking. "My apartment."

"Do you have a suitcase?"

"*What?*"

"A suitcase. Focus, Stefan. Time is short."

"Yes, I have a suitcase." Now his mind caught up with her question. "Why are you bothering me? I do not have time."

"Less than you realize."

"Stop talking in circles."

"Then *listen carefully*." Her words made him go still. "You must leave the city. Tonight."

He almost laughed. Almost. "Tonight is important. You will understand what I mean tomorrow."

"Tomorrow morning you will be in a jail cell if you do not listen."

The first long, cold finger of doubt touched his soul. "Jail?"

"Altin Cana's time is over. The district attorney has issued a warrant for his arrest. It is being executed tonight."

Time slowed. "Tonight?" Stefan asked weakly.

"In thirty minutes Altin's headquarters will be raided." A pause. "Make that twenty. Get out of the city. Now."

"Why would I run? I didn't do anything wrong."

"Do not lie to me, Stefan. You do not deserve this chance, yet here it is. I cannot help you if you fail to take it."

"How do you know the police are coming tonight?"

"They told me."

Stefan barked a laugh. "Why would the police tell you?"

"Because I gave them the evidence to arrest Altin."

Now time stopped. No noise, no movement. Stefan could only manage a single word. "You?"

"You provided it. When you blackmailed me into being your alibi for

Vincent's murder. Placing yourself in my home when the bomb went off tied our fates together. You betrayed my trust. I cannot forgive that."

"I never gave the cops anything."

"No, but you told me everything about the bombing. How you planned it, who was involved, and why. I recorded one of our conversations. The recording was altered to implicate Altin instead of you."

"Altin will have you killed."

"Altin will do no such thing, for he will never know the identity of the confidential informant who recorded the conversation. He will, however, learn that you were one of the people speaking on the tape. Which is why I am warning you. Leave, and never come back."

Stefan leaned against the wall lest he fall over.

"I am your savior despite what you did," Rose said. "For your entire life I have offered protection, as I promised your mother I would. That promise is the reason I warn you now."

"What do you mean, protected me?" Stefan spat. "I made my own way. You did nothing."

"You lived with other Albanians in this city," Rose countered truthfully. "People who only had money because I gave it to them. For your entire life I provided the means for you to survive. You repaid my kindness with treachery."

Stefan rubbed a hand over his face. The old Albanian couple he'd gone to live with after his mother died had cared for him while he struggled through everything that came with losing your mother as a child. A mother who had sold herself to escape from the Kosovo War, bringing her little boy with her. The price? She had agreed to smuggle drugs into America.

"You made a promise to my mother. Now you break it."

"No." Rose's words sliced into him. "I am keeping it one final time. Altin Cana will know you ordered the explosion that killed Vincent Morello, and that you said it was on his orders. How long do you think you will last then?"

"I will warn him. He can escape."

"It is too late." Her words softened. "Take this final gift. Leave, and never come back. You have one chance. Do not miss it. For your mother's sake."

Stefan closed his eyes. Rose wouldn't lie about this, for the simple reason there was nothing to be gained from it. Rose had turned his iron-clad alibi into a trap. His life expectancy would be measured in hours once Altin learned of his involvement, regardless of whatever else happened.

"One more item," Rose said. "You will not seek revenge against anyone in the Morello family. Leave it all behind. The outcome should you fail to do this will be disaster."

Leave the Morello family out of it? Why would she care? His eyelids flashed open. *Because they were involved.* "You had help." It wasn't a question.

"Heed my warning, Stefan."

He wasn't listening any longer. "You worked with the Morellos." It all came together as he spoke. "With Harry Fox. He is working with Nora Doyle." A slight intake of breath came through the phone. "I used to work with Nora, and you knew that. Then Harry Fox took my place, offered Nora Doyle a better deal. You have a soft spot for Harry Fox, and you used him to frame Altin."

"You framed Altin."

Harry Fox. The half-raghead upstart who had been handed everything when his father died. Stefan sneered in his empty apartment. "You are smart, Rose. I have no other options."

"I force your hand to save your life."

It was time to retreat until another day. A day that would surely come. "I will leave the city," he said grudgingly.

"Do not come back. Start a new life."

"I will not forget this. You betrayed me."

A weariness he had never heard in Rose seasoned her voice. "As you betrayed me. The cycle must end. Go."

"I have a gift for you. It is in a bank vault. The bank opens at eight o'clock tomorrow morning, by which time I will be gone." The sneer curled up at the edge of his lips. "Write this down." He rattled off the bank's name, a safe deposit box number and the security password. "The password will grant you access. Take what is in the box and give it to Harry Fox. A gift for both of you."

"I will do no such thing."

"You will," Stefan said. "Because it will answer a question."

"This is a trick."

"It is not a trick." His words quickened. "Open the box. What you will find has great value. Keep it to remember me."

"I am sorry for this," Rose said. "I wish our paths did not have to diverge."

He hesitated for a beat at the pain in her words. Stefan frowned, shook his head and hung up without another word, then ripped off his body armor and went back to his room. A suitcase came out of his closet and clothes were shoved in as his mind raced. Everything Rose said had been true. About his mother. About what would happen when Altin discovered Stefan had killed Vincent Morello without permission, then allowed himself to be taped implicating Altin in the crime. It didn't matter if the tape had been altered. Altin would seek revenge, even from inside prison, which was where Stefan would be as well because he was the best-known of Altin's associates. Disappearing was his only option.

A dead man's passport went into his pocket, along with a driver's license and credit card in the same name. All of it obtained from the body of a Cana soldier. Stefan had liked the man, felt a tinge of sorrow even as he had taken a small fishing boat far offshore and heaved the man's corpse overboard. Stefan would raise a glass to the man's memory when he made it somewhere far from New York, far from the reach of Altin Cana. And then he would wait.

A false board in the floor came up. Stefan removed a velvet bag filled with emeralds, rubies and diamonds. Over a quarter million dollars in value. One final check of his room and Stefan headed for the door. He didn't look back as it closed for the final time. This life was over. Down the street, Stefan hailed a cab, telling the driver to take him to the airport on a route that passed near Altin Cana's headquarters.

Even from blocks away, he could see the flashing lights that painted the surrounding buildings red and blue. The driver slowed as they passed a block down, both of them peering at the police cars and armored vehicles surrounding the Cana headquarters. A man came out the front door, his hands cuffed behind his back, two burly police officers pushing him along. Nearly every Cana man was a felon. Both federal and New York state law prohibited felons from possessing firearms, and there were enough weapons in that building to put most of the Cana men behind bars for a long time. Rose was right, Stefan knew—at least one of them would turn on Altin in exchange for a lighter sentence.

His cabbie accelerated onto the expressway. First step, get on a plane and get off American soil. Greece sounded like a good place to hide, despite what happened during his last visit. He knew people in Athens. Not friends, but people he could pay enough to not turn him in. Greece bordered Albania, where he would regroup. Stefan's jaw tightened. Not immediately. First, he would wait for Rose to collect his gift. It was an invitation. One Harry Fox would never refuse. And when Harry crossed Stefan's path again, Stefan would finish what he'd started years ago. Stefan had never expected to part with the items in the safe deposit box, but now he had no choice. He pulled out his phone, then composed and sent a carefully worded text message. That done, he turned and looked out the window at the city he had called home since childhood, a city he might never see again. And for that alone, he would soon settle his differences with the Fox family in permanent fashion.

Chapter 11

Manhattan

The news made the morning edition's front page.

Towering bold type proclaimed the district attorney had dealt organized crime a massive blow, taking down the head of a powerful Albanian family along with nearly his entire organization. A snapshot of the district attorney standing beside the chief of police as Altin Cana was led out of his headquarters sat beneath the headline, all of it above the fold and almost big enough to satisfy the D.A.'s towering ego.

Rose scanned the article. No mention of her or Harry Fox. The police chief attributed Altin's arrest to work by the Manhattan Anti-Trafficking Unit in partnership with Assistant D.A. Gary Doyle. More than twenty names of those taken into custody were listed in the report. No mention of Stefan Rudovic. Apparently he had taken her advice and fled. Hopefully across an international border.

Sunlight made the white marble floor come to life as she set the paper down. Rose reached for a cigarette. Her hand moved past the filled vodka decanter. It paused momentarily. Private business required her attention first. A business she would not consider too closely, for the edges of this puzzle might become too clear if she did. She could not say with certainty what Stefan had left in the bank vault. She could only say his request to involve Harry Fox did not bode well for either of them.

Her lighter flared and Rose drew a lungful of hot smoke through her long, black cigarette holder. She squinted against the morning light, stood and closed the shades.

The pointed soles of her high-heeled shoes clicked against the floor. Rose picked up her phone and sent a text message to the bodyguard downstairs, one of the men who rotated at her front door.

Rose almost never slept poorly, but last night she had suddenly sat bolt upright, heart racing. The clock on her desk said the day was barely three hours old. A buried memory had pulled her from a dreamless sleep, a phone call from a year ago. A call from a man she had dealt with only a handful of times. A bank employee who handled safe deposit boxes and was well-versed in the regulations surrounding said boxes. This man had called her with an offer. A safe deposit box had recently been opened at his bank, and he knew it contained cultural artifacts. Perhaps Ms. Leroux would be interested in obtaining the contents? For a fee, of course.

One problem. Rose didn't steal relics. She sold them. Her transactions required three participants: owner, buyer and facilitator. Rose's expertise lay in connecting the first two parties. She didn't want artifacts for herself—they ended up being more trouble than they were worth. However, she had called a man who might be interested. Harry Fox.

Harry decided he wasn't interested in the offer. Rose told the banking man she would pass and that was the end of it. Until last night, when the memory ripped her from a deep slumber. The connection had blared through her head. The name of the bank where Stefan's deposit box waited was the same bank where her contact had said a deposit box containing cultural relics was located.

It couldn't be a coincidence. Her cigarette burned down to nothing as she forced the thoughts from her mind once more. Her doorbell rang. "Come in," she shouted. Her bodyguard opened the door, a takeaway coffee cup in his hands. "Wait," she said, her voice only slightly lower. "Get the car ready. We are going to the bank."

The guard took her to Stefan's bank, which sat on a street corner in a nondescript commercial part of Brooklyn. Two stories, light brick exterior, easily forgettable. Which was why Stefan had chosen it. No one would think this bank held anything special. Safety in anonymity. It also offered a unique safety measure for its safe deposit boxes, designed to maintain the box owner's anonymity to a degree often associated with Swiss banks.

Several employees glanced up as Rose walked through the front door. She went straight to the youngest teller. He leaned back and peered at her through his glasses. "May I help you?"

"I require access to a deposit box."

"Yes, ma'am."

Rose blinked and all that remained of him was an empty swivel chair. Seconds later a suited man appeared from an inside office, his hand extended as he approached. "Good morning. I'm the manager. How may I assist you?"

Rose repeated her desire to access a box, and the manager led her through a door and down a set of steps into the basement. "Do you have the key, madam?"

"I have the password."

The man opened another door. His back seemed to stiffen. "I see. Follow me." The door led to a long hallway, at the end of which was an open vault. They walked to the front of the vault and stopped, the manager turning to a steel door adjacent to the vault, which held a biometric pad at waist level. He placed his hand on the screen, which blinked and hummed for several seconds before flashing green. Then he leaned over and spoke his name. "Lloyd Demchak." More lights flashed before he stepped back. "Please enter your box number and password, madam."

Lloyd turned away to afford her privacy. Rose entered the box number and password. The screen hummed for several more seconds, flashed green again, and with a *snick* the steel door released. Lloyd pulled it open. "After you."

He had not asked Rose for identification or even her name. Clearly this bank was used to a discriminating clientele. Rose could use services such as these.

Steel drawers of all shapes and sizes lined the walls, with a long table and two chairs placed in the center of the room. Tiny lights dotted the front of each deposit box. All of them glowed red. Except one. Lloyd led her to that box, the front of which was no more than a foot square. He slid the steel box out of the wall and put it on the table.

"The room is yours," Lloyd said. "Please return the box to its slot when you are finished. I will be outside, should you require any assistance, and to ensure you are not disturbed."

Rose waited until the door clicked shut behind him before turning to the box. Bright, sterile light filled the room. The air cooled as she waited, tiny drafts sneaking down her back to raise the hair on her neck. She touched the box. Cold metal, hinges, a tiny green light. She studied it, then squared her shoulders and lifted the lid. Her eyes narrowed.

A worn leather binder filled the box. Although dark and aged, the binder was obviously no more than a decade old. Several dark spots stained the surface. She lifted the binder, grunting at its weight. When she set it on the table, it clinked. The sound two drinking glasses made when tapped for a toast. There was something made of glass inside. Rose undid the metal clasp and lifted the cover. She gasped, one hand going halfway to her mouth.

Thick glass plates held a sheet of paper between them. She leaned close, studying the rough fibers, the curved script of a language she couldn't read. It looked like papyrus. Writing covered the surface in dense scribbles, the words bunched together as though whoever wrote them couldn't get them down fast enough.

Another sheet between glass plates lay below the top one, and another after that. She laid them out on the table, five in total, each papyrus sheet filled with writing. Whatever these were, Stefan thought them valuable enough to store in a bank vault. These would come with her to be properly evaluated. Perhaps then she would share their existence with Harry Fox. Why Stefan thought these would deliver a message to Harry was not clear. But she had no intention of taking them to Harry before she knew more.

As she placed the glass protectors back into the binder her gaze passed over the open box. She stopped stacking the plates. What was that? A flash of metal, tucked into the corner. She reached in and her fingers brushed the worn leather strap of a wristwatch, which she lifted into the light. A well-used brown leather strap attached to a metal watch. Gold dots marked the hours on a black face. A red mark at the top marked high noon. She held the watch closer, turning it so the light caught the writing on the front.

"A Rolex Submariner," Rose said to the room. Classic, at least fifty years old. The arms did not move. She angled it, trying to read the smaller text across the bottom. A smudge on the protective glass cover blurred the words, so she used her nail to scrape it off. Only after a fleck came free did she realize it was a red smudge. Rose nearly dropped the timepiece.

The smudges were drops of dried blood.

The watch clattered back into the box. She removed one silk glove from her pocket and maneuvered the watch into it. Had it not been a Rolex, she would have left it behind. Rose slipped the glove and its cargo back inside her pocket, then opened the door. "I require assistance."

Lloyd stood at attention. "How may I help?"

Rose pointed to the leather binder, now closed. "Please carry that and follow me. Be careful. There is glass inside."

Lloyd may have frowned slightly, but Rose took no notice. She swept past and headed for the stairs. Lloyd finally caught up to her as she pushed through the front door and walked into the sunlight. Her car idled at the curb, her driver popping out to open Rose's door.

"The manager has my package," she told him. "Put it on the back seat with care."

When the binder was safely tucked into the rear seat beside hers and she was safely underway, she pulled out her phone and placed the call. Not to Harry Fox, but to a document specialist employed by the Metropolitan Museum of Art. He could tell her when the papyrus was made, along with the general time period of the writing. The expert answered at once, requested a photograph and then asked Rose to stop by the museum. Yes, today. In one hour? No problem, not for Rose.

"We are going to the Metropolitan Museum of Art," she told her driver. They arrived in under an hour. Her expert was waiting at the curb, and he carried the binder in for her, using his credentials to get them through a side entrance and directly to his office.

Thirty minutes later Rose had a preliminary report in hand. She thanked the expert, strode back out to her car, settled into her seat once more and told her driver to head home. She made one call en route, inviting a man to visit her home. He did not refuse. Slightly more than an hour later Rose was mixing the first afternoon martini when the doorbell buzzed. She watched on her phone as the bodyguard let the man in, a short, dark and handsome man. He knew the way upstairs from experience.

"Hello, Rose." Harry Fox knocked on the open door before entering. "I could have updated you over the phone."

"This is not about the Cana family." Rose sat on a tall stool beside her bar. The leather binder lay on a table next to her, closed. "Though I would like to know what I missed."

Harry's teeth flashed as he walked over. "A lot." She raised an eyebrow. "Did you read the paper?" Harry asked. Rose said she had. "What they didn't say was that all of the men were found waiting inside two vans. Every man had at least one weapon, and every single one had a record. Those guys are facing serious jail time. Which is probably why they've started turning on Altin Cana. Nora texted me not long ago saying the police called in extra detectives to help with the statements and requests for plea deals. The Cana family is finished."

Rose did not smile. She sipped her drink. "What about Altin?"

"He had a safe full of illegal drugs in his place. He's facing a long sentence even *before* they talk about any murder charges."

"There were no issues with the recording?"

Harry shook his head. "None. Nora Doyle took it to her father, who had the NYPD's best electronics guys check it out. Every one of them said it's authentic."

"In that case, I may need to use your audio specialist in the future." A shadow darkened her floor as a lone cloud zipped past the sun. "I did not see my name in the paper."

"You never will. Gary Doyle signed off that the tape came from a confidential informant who infiltrated the Cana organization. Revealing the informant's name would put that person in grave danger. Your voice will never be heard in court."

"Which means the only person besides you who knows of my role is Stefan. I did not see his name on the list of those arrested."

"He's disappeared," Harry said. "Lucky break for him."

Rose grinned without humor. "I assume he left the city as I warned him to do. But do not assume he is gone forever."

"I'll watch my back," Harry said. "Besides, I have friends to look out for me. Can't say the same for him."

"A man without options is the most dangerous kind."

"I'll be careful." Harry still hadn't noticed the binder. "Speaking of friends, Joey is meeting with the other family heads tonight."

"On the last day of his window to handle the Cana problem without destroying the city."

"Gio Sabella told Joey he will move to have Joey elected the *capo dei capi*. Tonight."

"Albert Zurilli will not be pleased." A thousand sparkles filled the room as Rose touched the diamond necklace around her neck. "He will also be pragmatic. The other family heads will follow Gio's lead. Joey's election is assured."

"Then all appears to be well." The tip of her cigarette glowed orange before Rose continued. "Or not."

Lines creased Harry's forehead. "What do you mean?"

"I warned Stefan to leave the city. The country, preferably." She detailed her conversation with Stefan. "I did this to protect you. To protect all of us."

"Stefan can't tell Altin the truth. It doesn't matter if Stefan betrayed him or not. None of this would have happened if Stefan didn't kill Vincent Morello."

"How is Joey now?"

Harry shrugged. "He has an empire to run. He's looking ahead."

"Wise. Nothing will bring Vincent back."

Harry looked at the floor. "No. Nothing will. Nothing we can do about it now."

She knew he meant Fred Fox as much as Vincent Morello. "Stefan did not leave without a parting shot." Harry's face came back up. "Though I am not certain as to the meaning."

"What?" She had no time to answer. Harry had spotted the leather binder. "What's this?"

She reached over and released the metal clasp. "Look for yourself."

He opened the cover to reveal the first glass-protected sheet. "Papyrus," he said without hesitation. "Ancient Greek writing, likely from classical antiquity. A few centuries B.C. is my guess." He looked up. "I'd need an expert to confirm it."

"I already did." She produced the preliminary report. "My expert believes it is from several hundred years before Christ arrived. The papyrus and ink are consistent with the time period."

"My ancient Greek is terrible." He lifted out each protected sheet in turn and lined them up on the table in a row. "Did he translate any of it?"

"No."

"Sara Hamed reads ancient Greek. I could ask her." Rose gestured for him to do so. His head snapped up. "What aren't you telling me?" He quickly stepped back from the table as though it were electrified. "You got these from Stefan. They're old, certainly valuable. He wouldn't just give them away."

"He did not give them out of kindness." Rose stood and walked to the window, where she stood with her back to him, looking out over Manhattan. Clouds loomed on the horizon. A storm was coming. "Stefan told me it was a gift for both of us." She turned back and waved her smoldering cigarette at the Greek sheets. "His purpose is a mystery. I do know this is not the first time we have heard of these sheets."

"I've never seen these in my life."

"Neither had I until today, though a year ago we came quite close to doing so." She took a puff. "These were in a safe deposit box." The blank look remained on Harry's face. "A year ago I was offered the chance to access a safe deposit box in a specific bank. Do you remember that offer?"

Harry leaned back, eyes closed and face to the heavens. "Yes. You offered it to me." Harry looked at her sharply. "I said no. Another relic had my eye."

"A wise decision, given what you found. Fate chose to put these artifacts in our path once more."

"How would Stefan get them, and why give them to you?"

"Not to me. To *us*. He specifically mentioned both our names. Which I suspect means it is truly a message to you. I suggest we speak with Sara Hamed."

Harry reached into his pocket. "Maybe this is her." He pulled out a vibrating phone. "It's Nora."

Rose crossed to her bar refrigerator and opened it as Harry connected the call and stepped away. She wanted fresh olives for her drink. They often constituted the entirety of her lunch, and today she was hungrier than usual. She had just set the olive jar on her bar when Harry's voice filled the room.

"She's back?" Rose looked up to see Harry holding the phone to his ear. His other hand had formed a fist. "Can I talk to her? Where? I'll see you there."

He stuffed the phone in his pocket and turned around. "I can take the documents to Sara if that's okay with you."

Rose lifted a hand to show her approval. "Is anything wrong?" she asked.

"No." Harry darted over and picked up the sheets, putting them back inside the protective covers. "Nora Doyle's mother is back in town early.

I've been waiting to speak with her." His voice faltered. "About another matter."

"We are all entitled to our secrets." The steel toothpick between her fingers speared an olive. "Be cautious with those papers, Harry. The past can be deadly."

Chapter 12

Manhattan

Harry and Sara pushed through the towering building that housed the Manhattan district attorney's offices and spotted Nora Doyle by the elevator banks. A silent ride up to the twenty-seventh floor brought them into a hubbub of activity.

"It's a little crazy around here right now," Nora said. "Let's use my father's office."

Harry recalled the office, which was more like a hotel suite. The large desk beside the windows was empty. "Where is the big man?" Harry asked as Sara went to the windows and looked out toward the river.

"Sorting through confessions and accusations from professional criminals."

Harry chuckled. Gary Doyle could have it. "How did you avoid that job?"

"There's already plenty on my plate." She crossed her arms. "My mother is stopping by as a favor. She typically avoids the city unless it's to meet me or my father."

"Doesn't like the traffic?"

"Something like that. She's more of a suburb person. Always has been."

Harry reached into his shirt. For the first time he could recall, his amulet appeared in public as he took it from around his neck and held it out. The gold Egyptian piece shone dully in the light, while the decorative faience glowed a lustrous blue-green. Sara turned from the window and removed a nearly identical amulet from her pocket, wrapped in soft cloth. One that belonged to Nora's mother.

The two amulets were a pair, one belonging to each of Mark Antony and Cleopatra's twin children. The initials *AH* on one, *CSII* on the other. Alexander Helios and Cleopatra Selene II. The trail Harry now followed had been meant for them, though what purpose it served or what awaited at the end remained a mystery. If Nora's mother could shed light on where the amulet came from, he and Sara would have a new avenue to pursue about not *what* this path led to, but *why* it existed.

Sara laid her amulet on a conference table. "Is there a coffee machine?"

"Down the hall, then take a right."

Sara thanked her and walked away. Harry couldn't help but notice Nora shuffle a step closer. "You want to see it?" He held out the amulet in his hands.

Nora shook her head. "No, thanks. Do you and Sara have plans?"

Harry made her ask for it. "What sort of plans?"

Her eyes narrowed. "International travel."

"You talked to Sara."

"I tried to do you a favor."

He lifted a hand. "We're going to Alexandria as soon as possible. Depends on what your mom says about this amulet. There's a promising location in the harbor to investigate." Nora didn't respond. "In the harbor as in *underwater*. We'll be diving."

"I know."

"Then why are you asking me?"

"Because I did you a favor, and I want to see if it worked."

He frowned back at her. "What is the favor?"

She walked over, her finger aimed at his sternum. "I mentioned to Sara that you're not as bad as you seem to be. I'm starting to think I was wrong."

He blinked. "You did?"

"She told me about her plans to return to Egypt. I didn't want her to make an emotional decision." Nora pulled her finger back. She did not holster it. "I've never been kidnapped, so I can't help her with that. What I can do is provide perspective. She came here for a reason. She took a sabbatical, considered taking a new position in this country. Mostly because of you."

The world had accelerated while Harry wasn't yet strapped in. "Wait. You and Sara talk about me?"

Nora did not blink. "Yes, and it isn't always positive. I thought she could use someone to talk to. Someone who wasn't you."

"She's coming to Alexandria."

"I know, Harry."

"When did she tell you?"

"Listen for a moment. You're falling behind. Sara and I talk quite a bit. About more than just you, but when necessary, you come up. I reminded her that, contrary to most evidence, you are in fact a decent man. You've made questionable choices, but you've also done the right thing lately."

Harry's frown deepened. "Did you tell her you blackmailed me into working with you?"

Nora lifted her chin. "I did no such thing. I presented you with an opportunity. You accepted it." Now the finger came back out. "I definitely did not tell her I stretched the truth about our professional relationship last year."

Harry had nothing. One reason Sara hadn't packed her bags back then was that Nora had intimated Harry was working undercover for her team. Stretching the truth was putting it mildly. Harry could never repay her. "Thanks. But it can be true now."

"It's already true."

"No, I mean it really can be true." Harry spread his arms out wide. He paused. "Is this place bugged?"

"No."

"Good. I just took down the Cana family and put Joey on the throne. I can do anything I want to now."

Her eyes widened. "Hold on. Joey Morello is replacing his father? I thought that wasn't a sure thing."

"It wasn't until Altin Cana was arrested. Now Joey has the support of the other family leaders. It will be official shortly."

"You're telling me you made him the mob boss of New York."

Harry sighed. "I thought we were past this."

"*We* are. I think I even managed to get Sara past it, though she doesn't know the full details and isn't asking too much." Nora took a step closer. "What I would appreciate is an acknowledgment that I stuck my neck out for you with Sara."

"You really don't think I'm a good guy?"

"I do. But some days you make it hard to be sure."

They glowered at each other like only close teammates can. Voices coming from outside Gary Doyle's office reached his ears. Sara, talking to someone else. A woman.

"I appreciate what you did," Harry said quickly.

Nora replied through gritted teeth. "Don't mention it."

Nora looked over his shoulder toward the door. Sara was talking as she came through with a coffee cup in hand. A woman followed behind her, laughing at something Sara said. Harry looked out the window and bit his lip. Nora could get under his skin even when she was trying to help. They were on the same team, but sometimes he wanted to give her a piece of his mind. It's what teammates did. *Now forget about it and figure out where this amulet came from.*

He squinted against sunlight reflecting off the harbor and turned around. Nora's mother had her back to him as she embraced her daughter. She had radiant black hair cut to shoulder length. Jennifer Doyle hugged her daughter, hanging on for a long while before Nora slipped free and leaned her head in Harry's direction.

"This is the man I want you to speak with," Nora said. "An associate of mine. Harry actually made possible the headlines you read today." She looked pointedly at him. "Harry, this is my mother, Jennifer. Mom, Harry Fox."

Jennifer Doyle stopped moving. One hand shot out and grabbed Nora's arm.

"Mom, are you okay?" Nora asked.

Jennifer did not respond. Her black hair swirled as she turned to Harry, letting him get a clear look at her face. He blinked, and Jennifer Doyle screamed.

Nora tried to hold her mom. "What is it?" she asked. "Mom, talk to me."

Jennifer reached lightly for her throat, her mouth an oval as she stared at Harry. A beat passed. Jennifer pushed Nora aside. Harry flinched as she launched herself at him, bracing an instant before she slammed into his chest, flung her arms around him and squeezed the air from his lungs. Her head pulled back. She looked at him, her eyes glistening. "It's you."

He twisted in her grasp. "Yes, ma'am. I'm Harry."

She reached up with one hand and touched his face. "Harry. You're here."

A place deep inside Harry's soul sparked. A place that had been buried so far inside that he'd forgotten it existed. A place he hadn't visited since he was a little boy.

"Don't you recognize me?" She touched his cheek. "I'm your mother."

Chapter 13

Manhattan

"Mother?" The words barely escaped his dry throat. He pulled away. "You're not my mother. She left me years ago."

"We had no choice."

His voice was scarcely a whisper. "You can't be."

He stumbled backwards into Sara Hamed's arms. Jennifer Doyle remained rooted to the ground. "It's me, Harry."

Nora Doyle shattered the silence. "What the hell are you talking about, Mom?"

Jennifer Doyle found her voice. "I'm telling you the truth." She turned quickly to Nora. "You never told me his name."

Nora threw her hands up. "What does it matter? What's gotten into you?"

Jennifer bypassed her daughter and went straight for Harry again. She put an arm on his as he leaned against the desk. "It is me, Harry."

Cold fire scorched him where her skin touched his. "My mom disappeared two decades ago."

"Yes. She didn't die. She disappeared." Jennifer Doyle touched her chest. "It's me, Harry. Truly."

"You can't be my mom." His jaw clenched. "She would never have left me if she was alive."

A sound of pure anguish escaped Jennifer's throat. "It was the hardest thing I've ever done. But we had no choice. Your father and I—"

"—No!" He didn't mean to shout. Now he couldn't stop. "You. Are.

Not. Her. You live in New York. My mom would never stay in the same city for *twenty years* and never find me. No one could do that."

Jennifer Doyle did not flinch. "I did. I had no choice. And I am sorrier than you will ever know." She pointed to the conference table. "Sit. And listen. I will explain."

Harry's legs didn't seem to want to help him, so Sara helped him into the closest chair. Jennifer Doyle pulled up a chair, placed it inches away and sat facing him.

"Mom, enough of this." Nora tried to raise her voice and failed. "This is cruel."

"Sit down, Nora. You both need to listen."

That was the voice of a mother. Harry felt his back stiffen as Nora took a seat.

"Why are you doing this?" Nora asked.

"Because I am your mother." She turned to Harry, her back erect, eyes open wide. "I am also *your* mother. My real name is Dani Fox. Over thirty years ago I married Fred Fox, and we had a son." She touched Harry's knee and didn't let go. "You."

Harry fought to get any words out and failed.

"The world is giving me a second chance. The lies stop now. I am Dani Fox, and I am your mother."

He stared at her. Impossible, his mind told him. Harry tilted his head. The pictures Fred Fox had kept on his dresser came to mind. Harry tried to swallow and failed. "Why?" It was all he could manage.

Sara stood from her chair beside Harry. "I should go."

Harry grabbed her arm. "Stay." She quickly sat down, and he gripped her hand once, hard. "Thanks," he said.

Dani looked to Sara for an instant, back to Harry and then at Sara again. "This will not be easy to hear."

"I don't believe you," Harry said.

Dani Fox's lip twitched. "I would not either. Unless I had lived through it."

She folded her hands on her lap and took a breath. "It all began when your father accepted a job to authenticate two artifacts."

Harry flinched despite himself. "What artifacts?"

Dani Fox, and it was the first time he'd called her that in his head, smoothed her hair. "A forged notebook and an authentic Greek statue of Zeus."

Nora wasn't having any of it. "Hang on." She pointed at Harry. "You're telling me that I'm his half-sister?"

"Yes. I realize this is challenging. However, I am still your mother, and I am having a very hard time right now. Let me talk through this with Harry."

"Does Dad know?"

Dani Fox averted her gaze. "Please, listen." She looked to the ceiling as though searching for strength. "Fred was contracted to authenticate the artifacts by an intermediary, who was supposedly working on behalf of a wealthy collector."

"That part was true," Harry said.

Dani raised an eyebrow. "How could you possibly know?"

He tried and failed to keep the bitter taste from his mouth. "I didn't sit back and accept everything. I didn't give up."

"Neither did I. Even if it doesn't seem that way. As for the artifacts, your father inspected them and found the Zeus statue to be authentic. The Greek notebook was a forgery. Your father indicated as such and went to meet with the buyer to show his findings." A darkness came across her face. "He was arrested at the meeting."

"Right before you...disappeared." Harry tilted his head. "I know some of it."

Dani almost smiled. "You were never one to take no for an answer. Perhaps you should tell me what you learned and I will try to fill in the rest."

He didn't sugarcoat anything. "A woman's body was found by the Hudson. My dad paid a retiring cop to misidentify that body as you. I suspect he also went to the morgue and misidentified you to the coroner, claiming to be a brother you don't have."

Dani's mouth was slightly open. "How did you learn all that?"

"The other detective on the case," Harry said. "The honest one. I never would have known for sure that it wasn't you except for a note in the autopsy report. The coroner noted the woman he autopsied had never given birth."

Dani no longer looked at Harry. She looked beyond him, into the past. "Fred had to move quickly," she said.

Harry shot out of his chair. "Why would you do this to me? You and Dad? Pretending you're dead my whole life."

"I will apologize every day for the rest of my life. We only did it to keep you safe."

He threw his arms out. "Tell me why."

"The men trafficking in stolen artifacts said they would kill me unless your father took the blame."

Harry had guessed as much. He sat back down again, still uneasy. "They worked for a man named Magnus Dahl. Sara and I met him. He's dead now. He didn't know his men threatened you."

"We knew the men who framed him were small-time," Dani said. "If they had been the only ones making threats against our lives and yours, none of this would have been necessary."

Harry jerked his head around. "Magnus Dahl's men weren't the only ones involved?"

"Men like that are contractors, hiring themselves out to any disreputable collector in need of a search team. There was a second employer. A man who took pains to remind your father he was always being watched, even long after the arrest."

"You're saying someone other than those crooks who framed Dad threatened him?"

Dani nodded. "The initial threat came through the attorney for the men who framed him. A letter, left out so your father could read it, then taken from the interrogation room. The attorney who delivered it didn't even read it—all he did was ask your father if he understood the message."

Nora jumped in. "What did it say?"

"That if Fred didn't admit to stealing the artifacts and trying to sell them on his own, the men he'd been arrested with would make sure that both Harry and I were never seen again." Her face tightened. "I received a package the day after your father was arrested. It contained a snapshot of you, Harry, with me walking in the city. That picture could only have been taken a few days earlier. There was a bull's-eye drawn around each of our heads. A note on the photo said Fred would always be watched, and if he ever recanted his confession, we would disappear." Dani stood, reached across the table and retrieved a pitcher of water. Only after pouring a glass and drinking did she continue. "A pair of my earrings was also inside the package, along with one of Harry's toys. I had worn the earrings a day earlier."

"They broke into our house," Harry said. "To show you they could get to us any time they wanted." Dani confirmed he was correct. "Who else wanted Dad to keep quiet so badly they would kill us?"

"Fred never knew for certain," Dani said. "He suspected another collector who wanted to control him in some way, to use his skills." She took another drink.

"You were scared enough to abandon me and fake your own death?"

This time Dani didn't flinch as much. "Yes. We could not take the chance. Not when your life was at stake. The threats were real."

"Sorry to interrupt," Nora said. "How in the world did you and Harry's dad manage to turn Dani Fox into Jennifer Doyle?"

"Jennifer is my mom's middle name," Harry said. "Or at least it used to be. That's where it came from."

"The answer is money," Dani said. "Your father knew a police officer with a reputation for skirting the rules, and Fred paid him."

"Detective Connor O'Sullivan," Harry said. "His partner was a young woman named Jessica Barnes. She helped me figure out what happened at the scene by the river and with the coroner. She also overheard a man talking to O'Sullivan about a bribe."

"Your father convinced Detective O'Sullivan that nobody would be hurt," Dani said. "That, in fact, he would be helping to save two lives. Not to mention the money he received. O'Sullivan agreed to call your father when a body resembling me was found. It wasn't long before he found a match."

"That's all it took?" Harry asked. "Seems like someone would have asked a few questions."

"Thirty years ago if a detective attested a body was a certain person, and the coroner confirmed the family identification, other authorities had no reason not to believe them."

Nora crossed her arms. "How did you just disappear?"

"Acquiring sufficient documentation to fly to Pakistan was not challenging."

"At which point you took a whole new identity," Nora said.

"Yes. I still had family there. After six months in Pakistan, I returned to the U.S. as Jennifer Shah. Which is who I was when I met Gary."

"Why did you come back?" Harry asked. "And why didn't you ever try to contact us?"

"This is my home." Dani Fox indicated the buildings and the harbor beyond. "Pakistan was nothing more to me than a place in stories."

"You mean you're not from Saudi Arabia?" Nora glared at her mother.

"No. That part of my cover story was intended to mislead anyone looking for me."

Harry plowed ahead. "You came back here, eventually met Gary Doyle, started a new family. But you didn't forget about us completely. You recruited imam Abdul Jalali to forward messages to Dad." Dani confirmed it was true. "How do you know this dangerous collector is still around after all this time?" Harry asked. "He could have died twenty years ago."

The water in Dani's glass trembled as she lifted it. It did the same when she set it down. "Your father would have contacted me if he ever confirmed it was safe for me to come out of hiding. I stayed away to keep you safe."

"Which means Dad never confirmed it was safe. That doesn't mean he was right."

"I know your father," Dani said. "He would have done anything to learn the truth, much like you. In fact, I can prove it. Do you still have your father's travel case?"

Dani meant Fred's battered leather suitcase. "Yes."

"Fred hid important documents in it. That is where the proof will be."

"I'll check when I get home," Harry said.

A quasi-silence possible only in cities like New York filled the room. Muted traffic sounds came from far below. A government-funded ventilation system whirred none too softly, sending stale air past Harry's face.

"I am sorry," Dani said. "I know you can't forgive me now. Leaving you was the hardest decision I ever made."

Harry looked out the window. "You seem to have managed."

Dani continued, undeterred. "I made my choices. Now I choose to stop hiding, and to count on you."

He turned to face her. "What do you mean?"

"We must keep our family safe." Dani glanced at Nora. "Check your father's suitcase. Tell me what you find. We will deal with it together."

An idea flashed in his head. "Do you think Dad's murder had something to do with your disappearance?"

"I don't know. I suspect the answers we need are in that suitcase."

"There's another challenge to keeping everyone safe." Harry reached into his shirt and lifted his amulet into view. "Dad gave me his amulet before he went to Rome," he said. "I knew it held a mystery, but I never understood it until I met Sara."

Dani appraised Sara with renewed interest. Sara ran a hand through her hair and lifted her chin a fraction. "What caught your eye?" Dani asked.

"Besides me?" Harry said. Nobody laughed. "She understood the markings on it," he said quickly. "It's a long story from there, but the gist of it is these amulets belonged to the twin children of Mark Antony and

Cleopatra. My amulet was the starting point on a quest Cleopatra created for them. We made it as far as a statue of Ptolemy Soter. From there we need the second amulet to keep going."

Dani lifted an eyebrow. "A statue of Ptolemy?"

Sara jumped in. "In the Great Egyptian Museum in Cairo."

"Which is where we are stuck," Harry said. "I knew we needed the second amulet to keep moving, but had no idea where to find it. Then Nora wore it right in front of us and said it was yours."

"I can imagine your shock."

"They keep coming."

Dani ignored him. "How can I help?"

Sara spoke up. "We used your amulet to pinpoint a location in Alexandria where we believe Antony or Cleopatra left a marker for their children. Harry and I were planning to inspect the site."

Dani had moved to the edge of her chair. "What sort of marker?"

"A replica of Julius Caesar's tomb in Rome," Sara said. "It's called the Temple of Caesar. Antony and Cleopatra built it. We suspect they hid a message meant for their children."

"Do you have any idea why they created this path?"

"Nothing certain," Harry said. "We suspect Antony and Cleopatra left the trail for only their children to follow. For whatever reason, that never happened."

"Likely because Cleopatra Selene II was married off after their deaths and Alexander Helios disappeared from history," Dani said. "They had no opportunity to follow it."

"Which left it for us to follow now." Harry inclined his head toward Sara. "Thanks to her."

Sara cleared her throat. "Dani, may I ask you a question?"

"Of course."

"How did Fred find these amulets? Fred never told Harry their history."

"Fred acquired them. Money was tight when we first married, so Fred took on freelance work as a historical expert. This was before Harry, of course. A man brought the two amulets to Fred and asked him to determine where they might have come from and what they could be worth."

"Did Fred buy them?"

Her answer was a while in coming. "No," Dani finally said. "The man never returned to collect his property, and Fred had no way to contact him."

Harry touched the amulet around his neck. "Who would abandon these? They're authentic Egyptian relics."

Dani took nearly as long to answer this time. "I suspect the man was unable to retrieve them." Every eyebrow in the room went up. "He said his name was Walt Glover. He was polite, though a bit intense. I only saw him once, when he brought the amulets to our apartment. He claimed to have read one of your father's articles in an academic journal and offered him the job. Glover wanted his professional opinion. That's all. Your father confirmed the pieces were authentic. That's when Walt Glover vanished. He never tried to contact Fred again. Fred tried to find anyone who knew the man, but nobody in his circle of contacts had ever heard of Walt Glover. Your father had a partial photograph of him, though. When Fred took initial shots of the amulets, one of them happened to have Walt's face in the frame. Fred showed that photo to a contact in law enforcement who handled antiquities trafficking cases, with the same result. Walt Glover could not be found. Your father kept asking, quietly, but never learned anything more. Glover vanished and left the amulets behind."

Harry looked up to find every eye on him. "Nobody ever came looking for them, right?"

"Correct," Dani said. "The older I get, the more I believe there are sometimes forces at play we cannot understand. We can only try our best and be cautious."

"Then think good thoughts for Sara and me. We're headed to Alexandria. We'll find the message when we dive into the harbor."

Dani tilted her head. "Dive?"

One corner of Harry's mouth turned up in a faint smile. "Sara and I will be diving to inspect the sunken ruins."

"You will do no such thing." Dani's sharp, biting words took the air from the room. "I cannot risk losing you again."

"Get ready," Nora said into her hand. "You're in for it now."

A heat lit up Dani's eyes, one Harry didn't know existed. "I forbid you to go."

"Worried about losing me?" Harry asked. "We both already know how that feels."

Dani winced. Harry immediately moved toward her, a biological response he couldn't stop. "I'm sorry. I didn't mean it."

"No." Dani lifted a hand. "You're right. It's not my place to tell you what to do."

Harry felt more than saw Sara looking at him. He glanced over. Her face told him exactly what he needed to do. "You did what you thought was right. I'm still your son. Dad started this search. Sara and I are going to finish it. We'll be careful, and we need to pack," Harry said. "I want to check Dad's suitcase. Will we see you before we leave?"

Dani had found her voice by now. "Of course. Any time."

Harry stood. He sat back down. "Where do you live? Nora never invited us over."

"I don't live with my parents," Nora said.

A man's voice boomed from the open doorway. "We have plenty of room." Gary Doyle walked into his office with an armload of files, which he dropped on his desk with a resounding *thump* before turning to face the group. "Quite the crowd. Mr. Fox. Good to see you. Dr. Hamed, you as well." Gary rubbed his hands together. "Lots of work to be done." He looked closely at his wife. "What brings you here?"

Dani Fox, formerly known as Jennifer Doyle, stood and put her arm through Harry's. "A miracle," she said. "I'll explain, but perhaps you should sit down first."

Chapter 14

Brooklyn

Two young women sat on a park bench in a quiet section of Brooklyn with a stroller in front of them. Both women had scarves covering their lower faces, with hats to ward off the chill. A brisk wind blew, yes, but the scarf and hat combination also served as an excellent disguise. Once in a while one of them would lean forward to adjust the piled blankets in the stroller. If anyone happened to walk by, they might think the baby inside was asleep. They would be wrong. The baby inside this stroller was made of plastic.

One woman slowly rocked the stroller back and forth as she spoke through the scarf covering her mouth. "Do you hear anything?" Her companion reached to touch her own ear. "Stop it," Iris said. "Do not draw attention to your earpiece."

"Relax." Cici worked a piece of gum. "Everybody listens to music. That's what I'm doing."

Iris bit her tongue. Cici was right. Anyone looking at her would think she had an earbud with music playing. Unless the person looking was Harry Fox, who lived across the street. Iris didn't like this assignment. Not after what had happened this morning.

"We don't have backup," Iris said. "All we have is Stefan's promise. Follow Harry Fox, keep Stefan in the loop, and we pocket ten grand." She hugged her arms tighter around her chest. "Looks like this is the last paycheck we'll get from the Canas."

"What are you going to do now?" Cici said. Her jaw worked behind the scarf.

"Lay off the gum."

"What, I can't chew gum? We're supposed to fit in. People chew gum."

"The whole park knows you're chewing it."

Cici didn't argue. She never did with Iris. "Maybe Harry needs a couple of girls like us," Cici said. "We could help watch his back."

"Work with a Morello man? No chance. He'd be more likely to shoot us." Iris looked at Harry's front door and leaned closer to Cici. "If he ever finds out we were the ones who ran surveillance on Joey Morello, he'll have us thrown in the river."

"We didn't kill Vincent Morello," Cici said.

Iris was nearly whispering. "We're on Morello turf. There is no more Cana turf, which means we're not safe."

"Stefan is still around."

He was, and that bothered Iris. How had the heir apparent to Altin's empire escaped arrest when nobody else had? Last night she'd received a text from Stefan, a common enough occurrence. Iris and Cici went where the Cana men couldn't. In the process, they made a nice living, nice enough that they lived well and never had to take real jobs.

His text had said it was all over. Altin and the entire crew were in jail and probably never getting out. Stefan had escaped, he hadn't explained how, but he had one last job for her. One he couldn't do himself, and he'd pay them ten grand each. Then he told her the target.

"Harry Fox?" Iris had shaken her head as though Stefan could see. "He's Joey's guy. He catches me watching him and I'm dead."

"Go find a real job, then."

Iris had cursed Stefan in a language he didn't understand.

"You are my only option right now," Stefan said. "And I am yours. Will you do it?"

Iris had been around too long to let this chance slip by. Stefan needed her. Needed her bad. "I need Cici's help. She gets ten grand too. Take it or leave it."

"Agreed."

That was too easy, she'd thought. "What do we do?"

Stefan explained what he needed, which was why Iris and Cici had dusted off their trusty stroller and parked their backsides on a park bench across from Harry Fox's home. They had arrived in the late morning, a time when plenty of young mothers were pushing strollers or watching children in the neighborhood park. There was no sign of Harry Fox, so the girls did what they were well-suited to do: they blended in and waited. Right after they planted a listening device on Harry Fox's front window as they passed by on their way to the bench.

A piece of clear adhesive, no bigger than a postage stamp. Invisible unless you knew to look for it. The tiny transmitter sensed vibrations inside the window and picked up even the softest of sounds from inside. The ingenious piece of plastic turned those vibrations and whispers into a clear record of any conversation on the first floor of Harry's house and transmitted it to the women's earbuds. So far all they'd heard was an annoying ticking clock.

Cici's puffy coat rustled as she shifted. "I'm cold. I need coffee. You want one?" she asked as she stood.

Iris grabbed her wrist. "No."

"Come on." Cici tried to pull her wrist free. She failed. "I'm frozen."

"Sit down."

Cici stuck her lower lip out. "Why?"

"Because Harry Fox just got here."

Cici's yoga pants smacked back onto the bench as they both watched the swarthy man walk up his front steps. "I still think he's cute," Cici said.

"I imagine his girlfriend does as well." Sara Hamed came into view and followed Harry up the steps, a thick book in one hand. "That's her. She's a professor."

"She looks like no fun."

Iris turned her head away from Harry's front door as the transmitter picked up fragments of conversation. The door closing in her ear sounded as though she were on the front step. "Listen. And rock the baby."

A basketball thudded on the nearby park court. The wind carried children's shouts past their bench as Iris burrowed down into her coat-and-scarf cocoon and listened to a conversation so clear she might as well have been on the couch in Harry's home.

Harry's voice came first. "I need a drink." The sound of footsteps, a bottle opening.

"Sit down." A female speaking: Sara Hamed. "That was a traumatic situation. Nobody should have to go through a shock like that."

Harry made a sound somewhere between laughing and choking. "I was right all along. She wasn't dead. But why would my dad help her vanish?"

Iris reached into her purse and removed a small pad. The pen in her hand struggled to keep up. *Mom not dead, Dad helped her, Alexandria, scuba diving…amulets.*

Three pages of notes later she set the pen down. Harry walked out the front door a minute later, alone. He set off down the street, while the sound of fingers clicking rapidly on a computer keyboard came through Iris's earbud. She waited another minute before turning to Cici. "Did you hear that?" she asked.

"It's crazy," Cici said too loudly. "Sorry." She lowered her voice. "A dead mom and some kind of gold in Alexandretta?"

"Alexandria," Iris said. "It's in Egypt." She pulled out her phone. "Keep an eye on the door. I'll text Stefan." She composed a brief message and sent it off. A minute had not yet passed when her phone buzzed with an incoming call. "It's Stefan," Iris said. "Take the baby for a walk."

She connected the call as Cici stood and pushed the stroller away. "Yes?"

"What you sent is impossible." Stefan's voice came to her through a background of blaring horns and rumbling engines. "Harry Fox's mother died twenty years ago."

"It's what I heard. Where are you, the Indy 500?"

"Are you certain?"

"I'm certain. Harry Fox said his mother is alive and he was with her today."

"Impossible."

"You keep saying that. I can ask him myself when he gets back if you want."

"Where is he?"

"Out walking. By himself. Sara Hamed is inside."

"Follow him."

"No. I watch people. I don't follow them."

"I will pay you more."

"That won't help when one of those Morello guys shoots me." Iris's jaw tightened. "The fight is over, Stefan. Your side lost and I'm on my own. If the Morellos figure out I helped you, I'm dead. No way am I following Harry Fox."

"Will Cici do it?"

"You must be joking."

Stefan grumbled a colorful Albanian curse. "I have to know where he goes."

Iris didn't miss much. "What's so important about his mom being alive?"

"That is not your concern. Did they mention any locations other than Alexandria?"

"No. Sounds like they're leaving soon. You want to find Harry Fox? Head to Alexandria."

Only the sounds of traffic came through the phone for several breaths before Stefan spoke up. "You have a new assignment. Continue to watch and listen to Harry Fox and tell me anything he says about the amulet or his travel plans."

"I can't sit in this park all night."

"The range on the listening device is several hundred meters. Work in shifts with Cici. Park a car down the street. A small one, so he does not notice. Listen and report back."

"This will cost you. Want my help? You pay for it."

Stefan befouled the airwaves with another string of colorful expletives, but eventually realized he had no ground to stand on. "Fine," he said. "Another five hundred each."

"Another five *thousand* each."

"No."

"Right now I'm your only friend in the city."

"We are not friends."

"Then too bad you need me."

He didn't grumble as long this time. "Five thousand if you help me find the right man."

"What man?"

"I need a man for a very specific job. The kind of job Cana men used to handle for me."

Iris crossed her legs. "I may know the right man. I will connect you on one condition. I want to know why you are so interested in his mother. This could be dangerous for me." Anything Stefan wanted so desperately must be valuable to him. Considering Iris's only revenue stream was now in jail, she needed a rainy day fund.

"It is none of your business."

"Good luck finding someone else to handle your dirty work."

Malice tinged his words. "I will not forget this."

"The world has changed. You don't control me."

He didn't bother arguing this time. "Harry Fox's amulet leads to a treasure. I do not know what it is, but it is valuable and I want it."

"You have nowhere to go." There was a pause while she waited for her words to hit home. "Find the treasure and you can disappear forever."

"I will get Cici to help me," he said stubbornly.

"I can go get her if you want." Stefan didn't reply. "What about the mother? What does she matter?"

"Knowing about Harry's mother gives me leverage. I have a score to settle with Harry Fox. His mother is how it will happen."

Iris pulled her coat tighter around her. One blessing in this mess was she'd never have to see Stefan Rudovic again. "It's a deal."

"One more thing. You must find out where Harry's mother is."

"That's not part of this deal."

"I will pay you another five thousand for the information. Twenty thousand dollars in total."

"What about Cici?"

"She gets fifteen, no more."

Iris closed her eyes. "Deal."

"Now, who is this man you know?"

Chapter 15

Brooklyn

The familiar thunderous knocking on Harry's front door made Sara jump from her seat. Harry rolled his eyes. "Who do you think that could be?" he asked. He noticed that Sara edged closer to the shotgun leaning against the wall. At least she wasn't glued to the couch any longer.

Sara consulted her watch. "I lost track of time. Do you want me to leave?"

"No way." Harry paused, one hand stretched toward the front door. "This is *our* quest, not mine." He couldn't be sure, but she might have nodded. Just a smidge. He unlocked the front door, opened it and was nearly run over.

"It's freezing out here." Nora Doyle barged in as though he weren't there. "Evening, Sara." She went straight to the only person in Harry's house she seemed to like and hugged her.

Another person lingered on the front porch. "Come on in." Harry stepped back. "It's cold."

Dani Fox walked in and embraced him. "Hello, Harry. Thank you for having me over."

He took her coat. "Thanks for coming. I know today was a lot for you, too."

She stepped back and looked toward an exposed brick wall. "I've waited twenty years for this day," she said. "A day I wasn't sure would ever come." He didn't answer because he didn't know how. Dani angled her head to look past him. "What is that on the brickwork?"

He started when he realized what she was looking at. He wrestled with his thoughts for an instant. He lost. "They're bullet holes." Dani gasped and he touched her shoulder. "Don't worry, I'm fine. Can't say the same for the other guy."

Dani recovered quickly. "I see. Well, perhaps you'll tell me the story one day."

"Not tonight." Harry guided her to the table, to a seat beside Sara. Several items sat on top of the table, along with Sara's computer and notes. "You were right about the letters in Dad's case. I found them exactly where you said they'd be." Harry picked Fred's travel bag off the floor and set it down in front of her. "The bottom didn't seem thick enough to hide anything until I pulled it out. You'd never notice the latch on the end unless you knew to look for it. Even then it took me a minute."

"Your father was a man of habit." Dani ran a finger across the bag's worn leather. "Once he found a process that worked, he rarely deviated. He would conceal sensitive material in the bottom of his bag to mask them from airport x-ray machines."

"I found ten letters." Harry tapped the stack in front of Dani. "One came every other year. Postmarked up and down the east coast, printed on generic computer paper with a normal printer. They could be from anywhere, written by anyone who knows English."

"You think they tell you nothing."

Harry's eyebrows came together. "If there's anything to find, I will."

"What do the letters say?" Dani asked.

"It's the same warning to Dad over and over, saying if he ever followed up on what happened with the artifacts bust, it wouldn't go well for him, or us."

Dani put her hands together in front of her. "Did this person suspect I was still alive?"

"Hard to say. He, if it is a he, never mentions you by name. Each letter references something Dad did recently to prove the writer has been watching Dad. Some of them talk about me and school. They wanted him to know I was always vulnerable."

Dani was quiet for a moment, looking at her hands. "Perhaps it's best to let this go. Fred is gone. Whoever wrote these has no reason to hurt you now."

"You really think I'm going to drop this?"

Dani looked up at her son. "No."

"Glad we're on the same page." He picked the top letter. "One thing caught my eye. This last letter included the phrase *the night brings advice*. It stuck out because it's so odd. I checked, and guess what? It's how French people say *sleep on it*. I think the person who wrote this letter is a native French speaker."

Dani seemed intrigued. "Did your father ever mention anything regarding France?"

Harry shook his head. "Not that I recall. Maybe it'll come to me later."

Dani looked to Sara's computer, to the image of an Egyptian statue underwater. "I realize I cannot change your mind about going," she said. "Before you tell me your plan"—here she looked right at him—"which you *will* do, I have a question about your father."

Harry took a seat across from her. "Fire away."

"Why did Fred go to Rome?" Dani asked.

Harry leaned back and searched the ceiling. *No avoiding it now.* "He would invite me on some of his trips. Other times he wouldn't. He didn't say this trip was different from any other, so I assumed he wanted to let me get on with my work."

"Collecting artifacts for a mobster."

Harry shrugged. "I wanted to be like Dad." Dani looked away. "I didn't think anything of him going without me," Harry said quickly. "I knew he was looking for a piece tied to Archimedes. I don't know if it was tied in some way to the fake artifact from when he was arrested."

"Archimedes did not limit himself to mathematical writings," Sara said. "He also wrote about engineering and other scientific topics."

"Either way, Dad eventually made his way to an area around Rome's largest soccer stadium, the Stadio Olimpico. An international match between Italy and Russia was going on. Russia is notorious for hooligan elements in their fanbase. They travel to away matches looking for a fight."

"Did Fred have reason to be there?" Dani asked.

"Not that I know of," Harry said. "The official police record is that Dad was in the wrong place at the wrong time. They found him holding a blood-stained shirt with Cyrillic lettering on it. He'd been stabbed once in the heart."

Dani already knew this, yet the words still seemed to hit her like a physical blow. She slumped in her chair, her eyes closed.

"I've been hunting for answers since he died."

That put some air back into his mother. She opened her eyes again and looked at him. "Have you learned anything?"

"My only lead was the relic. If I can find that, maybe I can work backwards and figure it all out."

"That sounds hopeful at best," Dani said. "Futile at worst."

"I work with what I have. But you're right, I haven't found anything useful." He glanced at Sara and Nora. "There have been other matters demanding my attention besides the amulet search, but I was able to clear Dad's name without finding out who murdered him." Harry stood. "On that front, I might have something." He walked to a closet, retrieved a box and returned to the table. He set it down and put a hand on either side of it. "Before I show you, you need to understand I'm serious when I say this is dangerous. I received this from a woman who knew Dad. Rose Leroux."

"She is unaffiliated with any crime families?" Dani asked.

"Think independent contractor. A very successful one, for a very long time. She's the reason Nora's task force brought down the Albanian mob." He tapped the box. "And that's also how she came to have this. A man named Stefan Rudovic left it for her. And me.

"I'm nervous because Stefan has it out for me, for lots of reasons. The main one being I'm better at my job than he is. Stefan was Altin Cana's right-hand man, so he's always been dangerous, but even more so now that the Canas are ruined.

"Rose spoke with Stefan." Harry paused. "He told her to give me a message. A message that was in this box." Harry detailed how Rose had accessed Stefan's safe deposit box, and then he opened the box and removed the protected sheets. "For some reason, Stefan described these as a *gift* for me."

"Not the sort of man you wish to receive a gift from," Dani said. She leaned forward in her chair and peered at the sheets. "What is it?"

"One second." Harry's jaw tightened. "Stefan would give me something for only two reasons: to taunt me, or to draw me out. Maybe both." He looked at Sara. "You want to explain these?"

"These documents are written in ancient Greek," Sara said. "Before I go on, understand this is an educated guess on my part. Rose confirmed that these sheets are papyrus, from the time of classical antiquity. The ink is also correct for the period." Another pause. "The documents may have been written by Archimedes."

Nora and Dani both drew in sharp breaths. "They must be valuable," Nora said.

"Incredibly, if they are authentic."

"Which is what worries me," Harry interjected. "Stefan wouldn't give these away without a good reason."

Sara cleared her throat. "The documents outline two of Archimedes' inventions. One is thought to be myth, and the other has never been shown to actually work." She indicated the top protected sheet. "This describes a weapon called the Claw of Archimedes, which is a type of crane combined with a grappling hook, which defenders used to catch and sink enemy ships. Archimedes lived in the Sicilian city of Syracuse, which has a large harbor. The city was well-defended against any land attack, leaving invaders with the unenviable option of attacking from the sea."

"Hold on." Nora peered at the cramped Greek writing for a moment, then gave up. "You said this claw may not have even worked. Then what's so scary about it?"

"We have no accounts of it being used. There are vague references from the history books, though there are no first-hand reports or specific information about how the device worked." She tapped the sheet. "These sheets are the instruction manual. And this"—she touched a different sheet—"is a different manual. For a heat ray."

"A what?" Nora asked.

"A device for concentrating the sun's rays. It supposedly turned them into a beam of heat that burned enemy ships."

"An ancient laser gun."

"Which may never have been built. This may be more of a proposal than a blueprint."

"How much are these papers worth if Archimedes wrote them?" Nora asked.

"Easily ten million dollars. Even if they are copies made from an original, still quite a bit."

"And Stefan left this for Harry?" Nora shook her head. "I don't like it."

"Neither do I," Harry said.

"It makes your plans seem far more dangerous," Dani said. "Who knows what Stefan has in mind?"

"Right now he's beaten and he knows it. He left the country because he can't be here, not after the evidence Rose provided." Dani raised an eyebrow. "Trust me," Harry said. "Stefan isn't on U.S. soil, and he won't be back."

"All the more reason for you to stay here."

"No. It's reason for *you* to lay low." He pointed at his mother. "Until Sara and I get back and figure this out."

"I appreciate your concern. I have hidden long enough. What cause do I have to worry about him when he can't come back?"

"He still has friends here," Harry said. "Not many, but a few. Promise me you'll lay low until we're back from Alexandria." He turned to Sara. "Or wherever else we have to go."

"Fine." Dani pointed at herself. "*I* will stay out of sight"—now her finger turned on Harry—"if *you* cancel your trip to Alexandria."

"I can't."

"Why not?"

"Because this is the only connection I have to Dad." He touched the amulet around his neck.

Dani put her hands together in front of her face, looking at him over the tips of her fingers.

"What?" he asked.

"You are exactly like your father," Dani said. "The commitment." She lowered her hands. "The obstinate nature. Every bit of it is Fred." Now she stood from her chair. "So be it. I will not stay in the shadows, and you will not stay in New York."

Harry opened his mouth to argue.

Nora cut him off. "Don't waste your breath."

Harry paused. "Okay, I won't." He looked back to the Greek sheets. "There's one other angle to all this. I said Stefan may be taunting me. I think these may be the documents Dad went to Rome for. If these are what Dad was after, figuring out who had them might tell me what really happened to him." He raised a shoulder. "Or it might not." He tried and failed to stifle a yawn. "I'm beat. We leave for Egypt in less than two days and I have nothing ready. I'm going to bed."

Dani walked over and put her arms around him. "May I stop by tomorrow?"

Harry hugged her back, holding on tight. "Any time, Mom. We have a lot to make up for after we get back from Egypt."

His mother didn't see him glance at Sara when he said it. Nora Doyle did.

"Good night," Dani said.

Harry saw her out, then came back to find Sara and Nora still at the table. "Mom drove herself," Nora said. "I'm headed out soon. But I want to chat with Sara first."

He couldn't have stayed up if he tried. "Keep the racket down," he said, and headed upstairs, a fog descending on his brain with every step, one not even the thoughts of Alexandria's harbor could clear.

Nora waited until the sound of Harry's footsteps faded away. Then she waited a bit longer.

"I assume you're not staying to help me with my research," Sara said. She closed the laptop and turned to Nora.

"I do want to talk to you," Nora said. She took a seat at the table across from Sara. "A few minutes, that's all."

"Ladies only?"

"Yes, because I actually want to get something done." Nora smiled to herself when Sara started laughing. "Seriously, though, it's not for Harry or my mom to hear."

"I'm intrigued."

Nora lived with making decisions. At work and at home, decisiveness propelled her forward. Which made this conversation a challenge. She searched for the right words. "It's about Harry."

Nora didn't miss much. Sara missed even less. "Yes?"

Nora crunched her eyebrows together. The right words weren't coming. Might as well let it all out and hope Sara understood. "Today's been tough."

"To put it lightly."

"First, I find out my mom's been holding out on me my entire life. Then my dad walks in and we go through the whole process again. You didn't have to stay through all that, by the way."

"Harry seemed to need the support."

Nora perked up. "Yes, he did. I'm also dealing with Harry Fox being my half-brother." The words tasted funny in her mouth. Not bad. Odd. "Which is what we need to talk about."

"Should I get a glass of wine?"

"No, I'll make it quick. Harry's family now. I don't know him well yet, but I can tell you one thing. He's upset. About you."

"I noticed."

"Which is why I need to know how you're really doing."

Nora did it without thinking. Her blunt approach to life cut out a lot of superficial crap and, for whatever reason, it made people talk. Even Sara wasn't immune to it.

"I'm better," Sara said. "Not great. Being kidnapped…affected me."

Nora nodded. "I won't pretend to know what it's like. Having a badge means I deal with bad guys, but they don't get to come after me very much. Most of them don't, at least. The ones that do get handled. You're in a different boat, one with more freedom and more risk. If I get in trouble the cavalry is already there. When you're in trouble the cavalry probably never comes, so you have to figure it out. Which you seem to be good at."

"Harry is the one who is adept at surviving."

"Baloney. He'd be long gone if it weren't for Sara Hamed. You two are a team, a good one." She aimed a thumb at her own chest. "*We're* a team. All three of us."

Sara touched her hair, though nothing was out of place. "I've tried to adapt to his world, Nora. I truly have. It's so different from my own. Thrilling, frightening, utterly exhilarating, yes. But also terrifying. Accepting that is a challenge."

"Harry needs someone to watch his back. He also needs a partner. A person to lean on. Nobody can do it alone."

"Harry can be a challenge to manage at times," Sara said. "He also is the most amazing man I've ever met. Which is not the same thing as being the right man to uproot my life for."

"I'm the last person to give relationship advice. What I do know, though, is he needs both of us. And we need him."

"You mean *you* need him."

"I do. He can go places and do things I can't. You want to be an archaeologist who makes a difference? This is how you do it."

"I'm an Egyptologist."

"Then we'll help expand your horizons so you can help preserve other cultures as well. My point is you matter. What you do matters. And Harry can't do what he does without you. He needs you."

Sara didn't blink. "Perhaps he should tell me that."

"Some people aren't good at that sort of thing."

"Perhaps they should learn." A wry smile appeared on her face.

"Good luck with that." Nora blinked, looked away. "There's one more thing. Harry doesn't know this yet, so don't let it slip. After today, my stock went up with the district attorney. My team can have anything it wants for the foreseeable future."

"All well deserved."

Nora waved a hand. "I don't forget my friends." She touched the tabletop, making a circle with one finger, over and over. "The first request I'm making is for a new position on my team. An undercover position reporting directly to me. Not even the D.A. will have a line on their assignments."

Sara chewed her lip for a moment. "Do you have someone in mind for the position?"

"Applications will be by invitation only."

"Do you think he'll accept?"

Nora shrugged. "No idea. But I'm going to try." She stopped making circles and pointed at Sara. "It's not only about Harry. He's my in to his world. The problem is antiquities trafficking doesn't only happen underground. Many stolen artifacts pass through museums or are held in them. Our team could use a person with access to that world."

Nora had to lean forward to catch Sara's response. "I turned down the New York museum job. I'm going back to Europe after Harry and I inspect the site in Alexandria."

"I had no idea."

"It's the correct decision for me right now." Now Sara looked up. "At least I believe it is. Harry needs time to focus on his family. I cannot imagine what he's feeling. Or you. Sorting through your emotions will take time."

"It's here, and I'll deal with it. The work isn't going to stop." Nora wanted to say more, but a voice inside her cautioned her to hold her tongue. "I won't see you before you leave." She stood, offered Sara her hand. "Stay in touch."

Sara rose and took Nora's hand. She gripped it lightly. Nora never saw the embrace coming until it was too late. "Thank you, Nora. You're a good friend. To both of us."

Nora said her goodbyes and headed for the door. She didn't look back. If she had, Sara might have seen the hope on her face. *This isn't over yet. Not at all.*

A biting wind whipped down the street as Nora walked outside. She pulled her collar up against the chill, put her chin down and marched into the night. Her shadow ran ahead on the sidewalk as she hurried beneath the streetlights, her elbow nearly brushing against the mirrors of cars hugging the curbside. She didn't turn to look inside one parked vehicle she passed, one with the engine running and smoky exhaust trickling from the tailpipe to fog the air. The tinted windows reflected a porchlight and made it impossible to see inside, where a woman with an earbud in one ear watched Nora Doyle stride past.

Chapter 16

Harry rubbed sleep from his eyes as he fell into a chair beside Sara. The past few days had brought a change in her, moved her a step closer to the Sara she used to be. A good change, except the part where she got up early and went from zero to sixty when her feet hit the floor. That part he could live without.

"What do you want me to look at?" He yawned. "I didn't even have coffee yet."

"This is important." She pointed to one of a series of images on her laptop screen. "I had a thought last night after Nora left."

"What did she want to talk to you about?"

Sara's finger twitched. "Nothing. Last night I couldn't get this picture out of my head." She indicated the underwater snapshot of Cerberus, the three-headed underworld watchdog. "This statue has pieces of a white marble floor attached to the plinth it was on. Marble with red veins running through it. The flooring is unique enough that we can use it to identify other items from the same room, if they have the same marble attached to or near them."

It came to him through the fog of sleep. "That's how we identified the statue of Cleopatra and the wall with Greek writing on it."

"The wall is the key." Sara flicked through images as she spoke.

"It has Greek writing on it. Cleopatra spoke Greek."

"Which means her children would have as well. Unlike many of the Egyptians who visited Caesar's replica tomb."

"Greek is a way for Antony and Cleopatra to hide their message in plain sight." He squinted at the screen. "Most of the writing is too small to read in these photos." Another yawn overtook him. "I'm getting caffeine." He started to rise from his chair.

"One second. I'm almost there." She tapped an image of blurry Greek writing. "We can make out the word *Cleopatra* on the wall and not much else. That's not important."

He plunked himself back down. "I thought the writing was the whole reason for our trip."

"It is, but the writing isn't what woke me up this morning. It's the *wall.*" She pointed between the blurred letters, touching the dun-colored wall on which they had been inscribed. "This color and the distinct pattern of swirls in it. It stuck in my head all night. I didn't figure out why until early this morning."

He waited. So did she. "You're going to make me ask, aren't you?"

Sara did little to hide her grin. "Yes."

The stubble on his face rustled when he rubbed it. "Okay. Sara, what did you find?"

"Glad you asked. I found this."

She pulled up what resembled two half-buried slabs of rock. They came together at right angles, the jagged top edges sticking perhaps six feet out of the dirt. A scuba diver floated above them, waving at the camera. "What is that?" Harry asked. "Looks like a couple of flat rocks leaning against each other."

"That's what I thought. Then I saw this." She clicked and a new image appeared. It resembled the first, though in this one the camera was much closer and the scuba diver had turned, looking over their shoulder at the photographer. "Look at the diver's breathing tanks."

He tilted his head. "They're shiny. Either that or the camera has a really bright flash."

"Both are correct. Except I wouldn't call the tanks shiny. I'd say they're reflective. And the camera? It's high quality." She zoomed in on the tanks. "High quality enough that it captured a reflection of these objects on the metal. Look familiar?"

"Holy smokes." It was clear as day now. "Those aren't rocks. They're pieces of walls. With *Greek writing* on them." He grabbed her arm. "Those walls are the same color as the other ones you found with Greek lettering on them. They're from—"

"—the same room," Sara finished for him. "There's more writing down there from the Cerberus room. More writing means more chances of finding a message. We need to inspect both locations." Now she gripped his hand. "That's where we'll find Cleopatra's message. I'm certain of it."

The energy, the steel grip, the excitement. It was all here again. "Welcome back," he said.

"Excuse me?"

"You're back. It's you again."

She dropped his hand and stood. "I've been holding that in all morning. Forgive me."

"Are you kidding?" She wasn't getting off that easily. "Come here." He jumped to his feet and grabbed her before she could get away, holding her tight. "You're awesome."

She didn't grab him back. But she didn't try to slip away, either. He'd count it as a good sign. "Two sites means we need a longer dive," he said. "I'll let the guide know he's in for a full day, not just a couple of hours. We're serious divers now."

"Don't tell him anything you shouldn't."

One side of Harry's mouth turned up. "Come on. You think this is my first chase? You know me better than that."

"That's what worries me." She finally grinned. "Get to work. We leave in less than twenty-four hours."

He stood and stretched. The reservations could wait a minute. Meandering to a window, he looked out at the ever-busy park across the street. Children zipped back and forth, their shouts muted through his window. Two women sat on a bench with a stroller in front of them, one chomping gum while the other rocked the stroller. A pair of enterprising youths had set up a hot chocolate stand nearby and were doing a brisk business.

About as pleasant an early winter's morning as a person could hope for. Which did nothing to explain the unease in his gut. Everything seemed to have come together. A promising destination in Alexandria harbor. The Cana family's demise. Joey's ascension to *capo*. His newfound family. All of it wonderful, yet here he stood, staring out a window with a hollow pit in his stomach. Dani Fox was supposed to come see him today. Right now that didn't seem like such a good idea.

A flash of light caught his eye. A scratch on the window. He looked down and frowned. *The window had better not be cracked. We just put these in a few years ago.* The sunlight glinted off an imperfection in the glass. He tilted his head. Not a scratch or a break. He peered at it more closely. A clear sticker with some sort of line running through it. He reached down and picked at it. *I thought I took all the stickers off.* Actually, he was certain he had. The darn things had been a pain, leaving adhesive all over the glass. It had taken him forever to clean. He scratched at the sticker without result.

"It's on the outside," he muttered to himself.

Sara called out from the table. "What?"

"Nothing." He knelt to get a better look. The sticker was nearly invisible, with a translucent line running through it, like a plastic string, that had glinted in the sunlight and caught his eye. Otherwise he'd never know it was there. "This wasn't on the window before," he said to himself. "I'm sure of it." The hours spent cleaning the windows down here after they'd been installed came back to him. He'd cursed the manufacturer and their incredibly sticky adhesive. "I would have taken this off."

Which meant someone else had put it there. Someone *outside* his home. The temperature in his gut dropped. Harry pulled out his phone and dialed a number. Nora Doyle answered on the first ring. "I need a favor," he said before she could get a word out.

"What?"

"Is anyone on your team savvy with electronics?"

"Why?"

"Do you have anyone?"

"I know a guy."

"I'm sending you a picture." He snapped an image of the odd sticker and fired it off. "This sticker wasn't on my window before. And it's not a random sticker. There's a weird wire or string of some sort inside it. It may be a transmitter of some sort."

"I got it," Nora said. "Yes, that's strange. Any idea when it was put on your window?"

"No," he admitted. "It could have been yesterday, could have been a year ago. All I know is it shouldn't be there."

"I'll have my guy check it out and call you. And one more thing."

His guard went up. Mainly because it was Nora. "What's that?"

"I'll tell you about it when I call back."

"Or you could tell me now. I'll be overseas starting tomorrow. It could be tough to have a quick chat."

"That's why I'm warning you now. Don't do anything stupid."

"Be more specific."

"Stupid as in land yourself in jail, get killed. The usual stuff. I need you free and uninjured."

Sounds like I'm about to be useful again. Finding lost relics wasn't only a talent. With Nora around, it felt like a curse as well. "You know me. Safety first."

"Right. Keep your phone on. I'll be in touch."

He rang off, then pulled up the travel website and set about extending their diving trip in Alexandria. His phone buzzed moments after confirming their trip was now for the entire day. Harry pulled it out of his pocket and found a message from his mother. She was on her way over.

Something's wrong. Maybe he was crazy and that little sticker was only that. Or maybe one too many close calls had him exactly where he needed to be. He dialed Dani's number. No answer. Same result when he called again. "She's not picking up," he said.

Sara did not look away from her monitor. "Who isn't?"

"My mom. She's coming over now." Harry's eyebrows came together. "Is this a bad idea?"

"Why would it be? I know this is hard, but relax. Your emotions are running high." Now she did look up. "Who knows when you'll see her again."

His words barely made it to her ears. "Something's wrong." His chair squeaked on the floor. "I'll be right back."

He was out the door before she could respond.

The two women on the park bench watched Harry Fox race out his front door with purpose. One of them put a phone to her ear. The other kept rocking the empty baby stroller.

Iris waited while her call connected. "You might have a problem," Iris said when Stefan answered. "I think Harry Fox is suspicious." Iris recapped what they'd caught of the conversation between Harry and Sara, including the red-veined marble floors. "He's nervous," Iris said. "I could not hear why he left. His voice was too low." She lowered hers as well and made a guess. "He may be on to us."

"He is not. Stop worrying."

She bit off a caustic reply. "Then good luck doing this yourself." She ended the call and jammed the phone in her pocket. It buzzed instantly. She yanked it out again. "What?" she nearly shouted.

"Wait." Stefan sounded like he wanted to say a whole lot more. "Listen. You might be correct."

Which was as close as she'd ever get to an apology from Stefan. "I *know*. You did not hear his voice. He's concerned." She stretched a leg out. "Is the man I told you about meeting him?"

Iris's man was not the sort of guy to pay friendly visits. Exactly the opposite. "Yes," Stefan said. "The man who does dirty work. I need to call him. It may be this works out even better than I hoped. You and Cici stay put. Listen for anything Sara Hamed says about their travel plans."

"They extended their diving tour in the harbor," Iris said. "A full day now."

"Good. Keep listening. You are being paid for it."

The line went dead. Iris slid the phone into her pocket and stood. "I'm cold," she said to Cici. "Stay here while I go for a walk."

"What did he say?" Cici asked around her gum.

Iris shook her head. "Nothing important." She left before Cici could get another question out. As she walked, she turned her face up to a cold sun, though the chill in her bones wasn't only from sitting on a park bench this early winter morning. No, there was more to it, but she didn't want to think too hard on this arrangement. It was a job, nothing more. A longer job than most. Normally she tailed people for the Cana family, at most spending a few hours on a target, no more. Never long enough to hear their thoughts, learn their hopes, to humanize them. Now she knew why. Harry Fox was no longer just some anonymous Morello man she followed around. He was a guy who had just found his mother. A guy who, Iris could tell, had hopes for this Sara Hamed girl. A lucky girl who didn't seem to realize what she had.

Iris stopped at an intersection. Two people stood in front of her. Both had canes. One had silver wisps of hair sticking out from beneath a shawl covering their head. The other was bald, with a head that sparkled in the sunlight, as smooth as polished marble. The couple held hands as they crossed the street, one cautious step at a time.

Iris turned to walk in a different direction.

Chapter 17

Brooklyn

The car's obnoxiously powerful engine roared as Harry fired it up, tires squealing as he laid a line of rubber on the street before easing off the gas. A 1970 Chevelle SS 454 wasn't designed for Brooklyn streets. Only a fool would drive the beastly vehicle in such tight quarters. And a fool the previous owner had been. First, when he'd painted his car lime green. Then when he'd attacked Harry Fox in his house. A mistake he would never make again, thanks to Joey Morello. Who had also found poetic justice in giving the fool's car to Harry. At least Joey had painted it, covering over the virulent lime green with a pleasing shade of red.

Heads turned and one or two middle fingers rose as the shiny muscle car raced through Harry's neighborhood. Harry rarely drove, making his efforts to tame the touchy gas pedal a challenge for the first few blocks. It didn't help that, as he raced along, he called his mom's phone over and over without result. "Come on, answer it." He dialed again, treating the solid red light blocking his path as a suggestion instead of a law. Car horns blared but he made it through unscathed. "Answer the phone."

Maybe she was in the subway. Service was spotty underground, so for all he knew she was zipping past beneath his feet. Unless she didn't take the subway. Some people were funny like that. They never used the underground trains. Rich people, mostly. He whipped around a corner before it hit him. *I have no idea if my mom uses the subway.* He dialed again. What else didn't he know about her?

"Good morning."

"Mom, where are you?" His words tumbled out. "Is anyone around you? Look—right now. Who's there?"

"Slow down, my dear. What has gotten in to you?"

"Tell me where you are."

"Walking to a coffee shop."

"Are you alone?"

"As alone as you can be in Brooklyn."

He slammed on the brakes, skidding to a halt in the middle of the street and setting off another chorus of angry honking. "You're already here?"

"I took the subway over earlier."

"And didn't tell me?"

"Do you recall who is the child and who is the parent? Harry, what's going on with you? Where are you going?"

"Go to the coffee shop and stay there. And tell me which one."

"Why would I do that? I'm grabbing a coffee and coming to see you."

"Trust me, Mom. I have a bad feeling. You need to be somewhere safe."

"I am safe. I'm on the sidewalk."

"That's not safe. I'm serious. Go to the coffee shop and stay there."

She sighed. "If you insist."

Only after she gave him the address and promised to stay put did he hang up. Running another red light, he gunned it as much as a car could be gunned in Brooklyn traffic. Ten minutes passed at a glacial pace as he retraced half his route before the coffee shop came into view. One tire may have ended up on the curb when he parked and jumped out. Then again, it may not have—he dashed away too fast to check, bumped into a man and knocked his camo Yankees cap off as he raced toward the shop. "Sorry," he called over a shoulder.

One instant before he barged through the front door Harry slowed to a walk, took a breath and forced his thudding heart to slow. This was nuts. Probably. But if he was right, that meant danger lurked, likely nearby. That changed everything. He lifted his collar, lowered his head and stepped through the door. Harry did his best impersonation of the invisible man as he slipped through the door and took up a post in the corner, wrapping himself in the shadows.

He didn't look for his mom. First, he scanned the room, looking for any familiar faces on the off chance whoever was after him, if anybody even was, had used someone local, a person Harry recognized. It was a terrible plan and bore no fruit. Strangers filled the coffee shop. No faces he knew, save one. The last person he focused on in the entire place. His mom didn't see him even though her eyes traveled past the corner he'd claimed as his own. Dani Fox sat at a table, takeout cup in front of her, leaning back and watching everyone else. The sun reflected off her watch. Harry stopped watching her and once again scanned the strangers in the room, watching for a head turning, a covert phone call, a hasty departure. No one caught his eye.

He tried to shield himself behind a potted plant that looked healthier than most New Yorkers. Taller than some too, himself included. He sent a text to his mom, aware the phone could be compromised. *That, or you're nuttier than squirrel turds.* They'd either have a good laugh at his expense or be in awe of his paranoia.

His mom pulled her phone out, checked the screen and frowned before gathering her drink and standing. Harry didn't watch her walk out. Once more, he watched everybody else. Who took an interest in the middle-aged woman now leaving? Whose gaze lingered too long on her? People chatted, sipped coffee, read books. No one gave Dani Fox a second look as she walked within a foot of the shadows enshrouding Harry before going outside. He counted to ten, scanned the room again, then followed her out.

"Mom."

Dani stopped and turned. "Harry." A warm smile bloomed. "Whatever has gotten into you?"

He stepped with purpose to her side and took an arm. "I'll explain in a minute. Let's go to this park over here, okay?"

He didn't give her a chance to respond. Instead, he led her several blocks away to a neighborhood park. Two weeks ago he'd have been worried the Cana family might show up in this part of Brooklyn. Those guys he could spot. Now, however, he had no idea who to look for.

He ignored her questioning look until they stood in front of a bench. "This will do," he said. The park was smaller than he would have liked, joggers and pedestrians well-represented on the paths. Even as he spoke, a pair of spandex-clad women ran past at a speed approaching walking. He pulled his mother off the paved path onto the brown grass.

"Do for what?" Dani asked. "Harry, you need to tell me what's happening."

"Hold on." He powered off his cell phone and buried it deep in a pocket. "It's hard to explain."

"Try."

"You're going to think I'm crazy."

"I married your father, remember? I'll be fine."

"I found a sticker on my window."

She didn't interrupt as he told her everything. The sticker, the feeling in his gut, his request to Nora to check it out for him. The whole story took barely a minute. It sounded even more nuts saying it out loud.

"Did Nora identify the sticker?"

"Not ye—Darn." He dug the phone out and powered it back on. "I can't keep this off or I'll never know."

Dani narrowed her eyes at the phone. "Do you—"

"—Shh." He put a finger to his lips. "I don't know," he said softly. "Just being cautious." The phone buzzed with an incoming call before Dani could respond. "It's Nora. Hang on."

She started talking before he could say a word. "You were right."

That chill in his gut turned arctic. "What?"

"The sticker," Nora said. "My guy said it's a listening device. The little wires inside it are transmitters. They can pick up conversations based on vibrations in the glass caused by your voice. It's a bug, Harry. You were right."

The sky seemed to darken. A couple walking by them had shadows on their faces. Or maybe it was all in his head. "What else can you tell me about it?" he asked.

"It's fairly new technology, and it's expensive. Someone's going to a lot of trouble to listen to you."

"Guess I'm not crazy."

"Not this time. You want me to come over?"

"I can handle it," he said. "I'll call you back."

He clicked off and fired a text message to Sara, telling her to stay in the house and not say a word until he returned. Harry slipped the phone into his pocket. "Mom, sit down."

She joined him on the bench. "What's happening?" Dani asked. "You look nervous."

"I am nervous. I have to tell you something. Don't lose your cool."

Her face suggested mild amusement. "I will try."

"My house is being bugged. I don't know for how long or who's doing it, but someone wants to know what I've been saying."

Dani blinked. "Excuse me?" He repeated himself, his eyes everywhere but on her as he spoke. This time Dani seemed to bite. "Are you certain?" she asked.

"Nora just confirmed it. The bug on my window is new and expensive."

"Who would want to do that?"

Harry's jaw tightened. "Only one person I can think of. And he's bad news."

"Who is it?"

"I'll tell you after we get out of here." He touched her arm. "Come on. I parked down the street."

"No." Dani took hold of his hand with a surprising strength. "I'm not leaving until you tell me what's going on. All of it."

There are certain orders a son cannot disobey. "I think one of Altin Cana's men is still trying to get me," Harry said. "He nearly killed me in Greece last month. My bet is he's trying to finish the job now and steal my amulet, or maybe try to figure out what Antony and Cleopatra hid so that he can get it for himself. He's likely desperate, certainly armed. He's dangerous, Mom. This isn't a joke."

The strength in Dani's grip faded. "Impossible."

"Not in my world, Mom."

Every few seconds another person passed, some walking, others running. Harry tried without success to scan each face. There were too many of them. "Come on." Harry tugged on her arm.

Dani didn't move. "Where can we go?"

He looked over his shoulder. "My place. I'll figure something out after that."

"Shouldn't we have Nora help us? Or contact the police? You have proof someone is eavesdropping on you. That's a crime. At least I believe it is."

"It'll take too long. The cops are too slow. Plus, did you forget who I am?" He tapped his chest. "Certain authorities know I'm tied to the Morello family. They'll put my case at the bottom of the pile and keep it there."

"You're part of Nora's team." Her eyes narrowed. "And your stepfather is an assistant district attorney. You aren't the only person with connections in this town, good or bad. I'll call him right now."

Stepfather. The word hit him like fist to the face. "No."

Dani already had her phone out. "What do you mean, no?"

The air grew thick, harder to take in. His skin tingled as the hair rose on his neck. "I'll handle it. I can't run to Nora or…or *Gary* every time I need help. This is my world, not theirs." The words came faster. "Why do you think they asked me to help bring Altin Cana down? Because they couldn't. I'm the one who did it, which means I'm going to handle this. Wait for them and you're likely to end up dead."

The words were out before he could stop them. Driven by a gale-force wind of feelings that had been locked away for decades. He looked up, ran a hand through his hair, then looked at his mom. She sat almost calmly, watching him, a gentle smile on her face. "I'll take care of it, I promise," he told her. His eyes flitted to a man entering the park, his face shielded by a baseball cap.

"I know you will."

Her words grabbed him by the eyeballs. "What?"

"I said, I know you will." Dani Fox put a hand on his cheek. "If you want to handle this, so be it. You're more like Fred than you'll ever realize."

The sentiment should have made the breath catch in his chest. It should have made him reach over and hug her, hold her tightly so she knew how much it meant. It should have pulled every emotional string inside him. Instead, it did nothing.

Because the man mere feet away from his mother had a baseball cap on. A camo Yankees cap. He was reaching into his pocket as his steps quickened.

"Don't move." Harry took the coffee from his mom's hand. She managed not to react. He flicked the lid off with a thumb as the man closed in, four steps away, now three, his hand coming out of the pocket with a black metal device in it. Two steps. A gun. No, a *taser*. One step. The man's hand angled the device at Dani and blue light arced toward the skin on her neck.

Harry threw the coffee at the light. It exploded. One second, camo cap was trying to tase Dani Fox; the next, a lightning bolt erupted between them. Metal flashed in the blaze of light as a knife came out of camo cap's other pocket and flashed toward Harry's side. Harry chopped his arm down and knocked the weapon aside. He shoved his mother in the other direction. "Get out of here," he yelled as camo cap stumbled to one side. "Run!"

Harry grabbed camo cap's shoulder as the man moved past him, latching onto the back of the man's jacket and using his legs to drive the man forward, faster and faster until camo cap lost his balance and Harry planted him face-first in the grass. The guy was quick enough to get a hand free and brace himself against the fall. Camo's head snapped back and caught Harry flush in the nose as they fell. Lights erupted across Harry's vision and his grip on camo loosened. Camo cap twisted free of

Harry's embrace and rolled away. Harry hit the ground and rolled in the other direction. The knife—where was it?

He tumbled sideways into the stone bench, his ribs screaming in protest, then scrambled around to see camo cap coming at him again, with his knife leading the way. Harry vaulted himself off the ground as the blade zipped past close enough shave the hairs from his chin before it clattered off the bench with a dull *ding*. He grabbed hold of camo cap's wrist and twisted hard enough to snap it. The guy moved with him, taking the force out of Harry's attack so his wrist only bent. Bent enough for the knife to fall free. Harry shouted in triumph and grabbed for it.

A fist slammed into his chin to snap his mouth closed, knocking him back. Harry blinked away a headful of stars and lost his grip on the assailant, his foot catching on the bench to send him sprawling into the grass. But camo cap didn't reach for the knife. He came for Harry, lifting his arm, ready to drop a sharp elbow on Harry's face. His teeth gleamed in the sun as he growled, rushing in hard enough to shatter bones.

A rock hit camo cap's head, snapping it back and stopping him in his tracks. Harry spun away, caught sight of Dani Fox reloading with another projectile in hand, then darted toward where the knife had fallen. Metal flashed on the ground. *Got it.* He scooped up the blade and straightened again, brandishing the weapon as camo cap raised an arm against the second incoming rock. The knife grabbed his attention. Camo cap froze and Harry ran at him. Camo turned, tangled his feet and went down in a heap.

Harry was on him in an instant, kicking the man's legs out from beneath him as he tried to stand. "Who are you?" Harry shouted, brandishing the knife. He barely noticed the screams coming from the growing crowd of people around him.

Camo cap didn't answer. He struggled to his feet and tried once more to run. Harry knocked him back down and grabbed a fistful of the guy's jacket. "Who are you?" Still the man struggled, so Harry socked him in the gut. The guy crumpled. Harry threw the knife toward a row of bushes and grabbed another handful of jacket.

"Get off me," camo cap shouted, all harsh consonants in a gravelly accent. A Balkan accent.

"You're Albanian. Stefan sent you, didn't he?" The man didn't answer so Harry raised a fist, the one that used to have a knife. "Answer me!"

"Yes," the man shouted. "Stefan."

"Why?" Harry looked around. Too many people were here. He looked back down to shout one more time. Camo cap's fist met Harry's nose halfway.

Harry fell back, grabbing his bloody nose as the world spun. Camo cap leapt up and raced for the park exit. Cursing his own stupidity, Harry gained his feet and gave chase. Camo cap made it to the sidewalk, racing back toward the coffee shop, dodging between pedestrians as Harry accelerated and closed the gap, pushing his way through the wake of angry people. A skateboarding teenager nearly ran Harry over, his wheels screeching as he swerved.

Garbage cans flew as camo cap turned down a narrow alley, Harry close behind. Their footsteps echoed like gunfire off the buildings. Harry reached out, his fingers clipping the man's jacket. Harry shifted into a gear he didn't know he possessed and reached out as they came to the end of the alley, missing the man's jacket but getting a handful of shoe to send camo cap spinning out of control, tumbling and falling out of the alleyway, across the sidewalk and into the street.

Harry stumbled to one knee. Camo cap hit the ground, then began to scramble up again up as a horn blared. He looked toward it.

A bus smashed him flat. Tires screeched, people screamed, and Harry sprinted the last few steps to the curb. He ran to the front of the bus and looked down at what used to be camo cap on the pavement. His hat had disappeared, along with most of his face. Harry knelt beside the body.

"Call an ambulance!" he shouted over a shoulder. Panicked bystanders babbled and flailed at their phones. "Hurry!" Harry cried out, his hands going not to the man's chest to give aid, but instead to his pockets. CPR wasn't going to help this guy. Harry pulled a wallet, a cell phone and a folded envelope from camo cap's various pockets before a few brave citizens came to Harry's side to help. *Time to go.*

Harry got to his feet, turned and walked away. Nobody followed him. He looked over his shoulder once to make sure before ducking into the alleyway he'd chased camo cap down mere moments ago, breaking into a jog only when the noise from this unfortunate accident faded behind him. He emerged onto the street ahead and ran headlong into his mom.

"Harry." She grabbed his arm. "Are you injured?"

He never broke stride. "Time to leave," he said, spinning her around and towing her along in his wake. "I'm fine. Can't say as much for the other guy."

"What happened?" Her words tumbled out, breathless. "Where is he?"

"Later. Keep moving."

He checked every face until they made it to his car. His mom kept moving even after he stopped. "This is me," he said as the doors unlocked.

Dani pointed at the vehicle. "This is your car?"

"Low-key, I know. Get in."

Only after they were several blocks away did Harry start talking again. "He's dead. The guy who tried to tase you." Harry had to lean closer to catch Dani's words.

"Did you kill him?"

"Nope. A bus took care of it for me." He offered a quick recap of the chase. "The guy had it coming."

"Harry, a man just died."

"A man sent to abduct you and kill me. Don't feel sorry for him."

"How can you know that?"

"You mean other than the taser and knife?" Harry reached into his pocket and pulled out the dead man's wallet. "I took this from his body. Not that I needed it. Did you hear his accent? Albanian. Trust me, I've heard it enough in my life to know for sure." He slid the wallet back into his pocket.

"He is tied to the Cana family?"

"Maybe. Maybe not. Could just be a goon for hire. There are plenty of them in the city." A thought hit him. Far too late. "Are you okay?"

The engine rumbled in the ensuing silence. He glanced over to find Dani Fox sitting with her hands folded in her lap, eyes on the windshield, mouth a tight line. She didn't respond. He nearly asked again, then thought better of it. Several stoplights passed and the neighborhood changed. Still nothing.

"No."

Her sharp word caught him off guard. "What's wrong?" Harry asked. It was the only thing he could think of.

"I just witnessed my son being attacked, then discovered the man who did it died horrifically on a city street."

He nearly pointed out that there were far more horrific ways to die. He'd seen a few of them. "But we're alive. He's not. That's a good thing."

"*Good?*" Now Dani found her voice. "You're lucky to be alive. That man tried to kill you."

Harry accelerated. "It's not the first time."

"Harry, this must stop. You cannot continue to live this way. I can't stand the thought of you in danger. Losing you now…again…would be a living nightmare."

"Sort of like losing your mom before you ever knew her." Dani had nothing to say to that. Harry slowed for a stop sign. "I'm sorry. I didn't mean that. Believe me, I know how you're feeling."

"I would take it back if I could."

"We can't change the past. It's not like I'll hold it against you." At least he'd try not to.

"No, Harry. Don't you see?" She turned to face him. "I made a mistake. This is my fault. If I hadn't agreed to your father's plan, none of this would be happening. Please, don't continue the cycle your parents started. It will not end well."

"You're right."

Dani started in her seat. "You agree?"

"Not like you think. You're right this won't end well if I don't do something about it. There's a man out there with a grudge. Stefan Rudovic won't stop until he's finished what he started over a year ago. I helped take down the Cana family. I'm responsible for destroying everything he worked for."

"You only played a small part."

"He won't care. I represent everything Stefan can't have or didn't achieve. Stability. Success. The Brooklyn gangster dream. He blames me and he has nothing to lose."

"Where is he now?"

"Europe is my guess. Far away from anyone Altin Cana can pay to kill him."

"Then let him stay there."

"That's not how it works, Mom. He'll never let this go. Why do you think Dad made you disappear? People like Stefan Rudovic don't forget. I can't run from this." He managed to keep most of the bitterness from his voice. "Hiding isn't the answer."

"We did it to protect you."

"Now it's my turn. This is my world, Mom. Not yours. The only way you're safe is if I take the fight to Stefan." Harry tapped the metal disc under his shirt. "He's been interested in the amulet and every other artifact I chase for a long time. He wants what I have, what I'm chasing. I'm going to figure out what all this means and show him the only way this ends well for him is if he disappears forever. I can't let him hurt you."

"Don't worry about me. It's you who need to stay safe."

"This isn't up for discussion." He turned into the small driveway by his home. "Call Gary. Tell him to come pick you up. Right now."

Nothing around them drew his attention as they hurried inside. Sara sat at a table, laptop in front of her, scribbling in a notebook. She looked up as Dani and Harry walked in. Harry shot every deadbolt and lock on the door, then pressed a finger to his lips before going to the window, where he found the sticker still in place. He opened the window, reached out and ripped it off. He crumpled it into a tiny ball, then carried it into the bathroom and flushed it down the toilet. After several more flushes just to make sure, he strode back out into the living room.

"We can talk now." Harry went to the corner of the room. To the loaded shotgun Sara had only recently stopped hovering beside as though it were magnetized and she were coated in metal.

"Why did you text me to stay here and be quiet?" Sara asked.

Harry ignored her and grabbed the gun. "You know how to use one of these?" he asked his mother.

Dani's eyes did not widen. Instead, she put her hand out. "For the record, I think this is unnecessary." She took the weapon without another word, and with a move Harry could only describe as practiced, checked that the safety was on and that shells were in the chamber and magazine tube. "Gary insisted I learn how to handle weapons safely. I may not enjoy firearms, but I am proficient in their use."

Harry had to search for his voice. "Right," he eventually said. "Call Mr. Surprisingly Prepared and have him pick you up right now. If anyone shows up before he gets here that you don't like, shoot them."

Sara planted herself between Harry and Dani. "Excuse me. Tell me what's going on right now."

Harry looked out the window as a pair of women exited the park, one pushing a baby stroller. Hardly the sort to be spying on him. "Someone tried to kidnap my mom and kill me just now. I'm pretty sure Stefan Rudovic hired him, and he also had somebody plant that sticker on my window. It was a listening device."

"Your house is bugged?" Sara asked.

"*Was* bugged. Now it's just my house again." Harry closed the window blinds, then pulled the dead man's personal effects from his pocket and set them on the table. "I took these off the dead guy."

Sara shook her head. "He's *dead?*"

"Don't look at me like that. I didn't kill him. The bus did." He recounted the morning's excitement. "Gary is coming to pick up my mom. You and I are getting ready to go to Alexandria. We have to finish this or Stefan won't ever stop. I'll start packing."

Sara went back to the table. Dani grabbed her arm as she passed.

Harry saw that her other hand kept hold of the shotgun. "This is not the prudent course."

"You have a lot to learn about your son." Sara patted Dani's hand. "Forethought can elude him at times."

"Then promise me you won't leave him alone."

Sara's hand paused in the air above Dani's. "We are careful," she said quickly.

Harry went and double-checked the locks on the front door. "Call Gary," he told Dani again as he made his way to the stairs. "Tell him you two need a vacation. Somewhere outside the city."

"Actually, you've just ensured he won't be able to take a vacation for some time," Dani said. "He's likely to sleep at the office a few nights this week."

"Then tell him to have cops watch your place day and night. I'm sure he'll call in a few favors once he learns a man tried to kidnap you."

"And how will I explain that this man is now in the morgue?"

Harry stopped at the foot of the stairs. "Call it good fortune." He flashed a grin. "Or bad, if you're the dead guy. Now call Gary and get him moving. Sara and I have history to uncover."

Chapter 18

Alexandria, Egypt

Harry shot up in his seat as the plane touched down. Barely twenty-four hours after a man had tried to kill him in New York, he and Sara were on Egyptian soil. Harry rubbed his eyes, stretching in the first-class Turkish Airlines seat that was roomier than some New York City bathrooms. He lifted the window cover to find dazzling sunlight on the other side. He slammed it shut.

Harry didn't have to worry about finding his way through Alexandria's chaotic three-story airport. Sara did it for him, letting him trail in her wake as she bullied, dodged, barged and barreled through a sea of travelers speaking a babel of languages from around the world. One minute he was stepping off the jetway, the next he was in the rear seat of a taxi hurtling toward downtown Alexandria. The sand, the bright sunlight reflecting off every visible glass or metal surface, the dusty people. Everything he remembered from past trips to Egypt surrounded him. Every part familiar save one.

"It's cold."

"It's winter in Egypt," Sara said. "And it's not cold. It's seventy degrees. That's twice what it was in Brooklyn."

"Guess I'm used to this place being an oven."

"Don't worry. The harbor will be warm."

A few moments later, a soft tune reached his ears. Harry didn't look over at the source. Instead, he closed his eyes and listened. It was the first time Sara had hummed to herself since being kidnapped.

"Did Rose Leroux get back to you?" she said suddenly, breaking the spell.

Harry's eyes snapped open. "Darn. I forgot to turn my phone on." He dug in his pocket and found the device. He'd been hesitant when Sara first suggested he ask Rose to dig further into the story behind Stefan Rudovic's safe deposit box. Partly because of what he thought he might learn.

Her suggestion had been beautiful in its logic. "If you can tell when the box was last accessed, you'll have a better idea of when Stefan obtained the documents," she explained, meaning the papers describing two of Archimedes' most infamous inventions, papers Fred Fox may or may not have been trying to obtain when he made the fateful trip to Rome. Sara reasoned that if Harry could narrow down when Stefan had obtained them, he might be able to use that timeline to identify *where* he'd got them. Black-market antiquities trafficking could be a small business, despite covering the entire globe. People knew the players. People like Rose Leroux. Figure out who had the documents before Stefan, and Harry might have a new lead on what had happened to his dad. A long shot, but it wasn't like he had any other leads.

His phone buzzed. "She did." Harry scanned the message. "The box was last accessed not much more than a year ago. Right after my dad's murder." Harry slumped back in his seat. "Stefan could have gotten them after my dad died. Whoever had them might have been trying to sell them to Dad, and when he died, they sold them to Stefan. Or maybe Stefan stole them from someone. Or maybe it has nothing at all to do with my dad." He dropped the phone into his lap. "Some help that was."

"Don't frown." Sara touched his knee. "All knowledge has value. Now you know those documents have only been in that box for a year. It doesn't help now. In the future, who knows? It may be important."

She was right and he knew it. That didn't mean he told her so. Harry rubbed his face, a day-old beard rustling under his fingers. That was the problem with getting your hopes up. The world inevitably let you down.

"Cheer up." Sara pointed ahead. "There's our hotel. And see that shiny blue stuff? That's the harbor. We have a mystery to solve."

Her voice pulled him out of the grip of despair faster than any relic ever would. Despite knowing better, he let his hopes rise. Was the old Sara back?

Ten minutes after the taxi dropped them at the hotel's front door Harry was lying on the bed, promising Sara he only wanted to close his eyes for a minute. Several hours later he awoke to Sara shouting that they needed to move *right now* and how did he let her fall asleep beside him and this is all his fault.

A whirlwind half hour later Harry found himself on a bench facing the harbor, their guide having been found waiting outside the hotel—good thing they paid ahead—and after Sara blamed Harry for the mishap, the guide had ferried them to the diving operation's offices at the water's edge. There, they had a front-row view of kayaks, speedboats, fishing trawlers and all manner of vessels churning through the harbor. The guide, a local named Hamdy, went from fake happy to actually engaging when he learned both of his American tourist customers spoke fluent Arabic. That almost changed when Sara took control, however.

"This is where we want to dive." Sara indicated a map she'd prepared. "I marked the site with an *X*."

"I know all the best spots," Hamdy said. "You do not need a map. You have me."

Sara wasn't having it. "This is where we'll be diving."

Hamdy took the paper from her. "Is this a treasure map?"

"Perhaps." Sara flashed her best smile. It worked. "Will you take us there?"

Hamdy frowned. "I know these ruins. They are dangerous." He tapped the *X* Sara had identified as what remained of a collapsed room. "I do not recommend you go inside. You may become trapped if you are not experienced."

"Good thing we know what we're doing." Sara flashed Harry a look. One he knew well. *Don't say a word.*

"I thought you were novice divers?"

"You're remembering someone else," Sara said. "We can handle it."

Harry zipped up his wetsuit with authority. "She's right, Hamdy. We're ready."

Hamdy peered at Harry as he would at an unwelcome relative on his doorstep. "The water can be deadly, my friends."

Harry reached over and clapped Hamdy's shoulder. "Then it's a good thing we have the best guide in Alexandria with us." Harry pulled back. "You are the best, aren't you?"

"No man knows the harbor better than me." Hamdy thumped his chest. "You are safe with Hamdy." His rictus grin would have scared off marauding Vikings. It stayed plastered to his face as he watched Harry struggling with his air tanks. "Do you need assistance?"

"Nope." Harry nearly tore a tendon, but he managed to heave the air tanks over a shoulder. The darn things were *heavy*. "I'm ready."

Hamdy pointed to the water. "Time to dive," he said, loud enough to wake the dead.

The trio clomped onto Hamdy's boat, stowed their equipment, and were soon scything through the water toward Sara's chosen spot. Hamdy slowed as they passed another diving boat, waving at a man on board who could have been his twin brother. "That is the second-best diving guide. You are lucky you did not hire him. He is terrible."

"What's down there?" Sara asked.

"The lighthouse." Hamdy gestured toward the nearby shore where the lighthouse used to stand. "A wonder of the world. The remains fell across the harbor, and the water pushed them around. This is the largest collection of the stones in the harbor."

Harry shielded his eyes against the sun, squinting into the middle distance. "I don't see anybody near our spot."

"It is not a popular site. The ruins could trap a diver who does not have experience." Hamdy didn't say anything further. He looked at them expressionlessly. "It is a good thing you have it."

"It looks like a collapsed room," Sara said. "I want to go inside.

There's writing on the wall."

Hamdy frowned. "I have never gone inside. The visibility is low. Which also makes it dangerous." The craft slowed as they approached their destination, Hamdy bringing them to a gentle halt on the calm waters and lowering the anchor. The deck rolled gently beneath Harry's feet as he zipped up his top, shrugged into his air tanks and strapped on the ungainly fins. Sara did the same, and once Hamdy double-checked everything was as it should be and hoisted the red-and-white diver's flag to indicate a dive in progress, the trio plopped their backsides onto the edge of the boat. They went through the agreed-upon hand signals to be used underwater in case their radios went out. Once they were all on the same page, three thumbs went up, and Harry leaned back into the warm embrace of Alexandria's harbor.

It was as close as he'd ever get to traveling into another world. One second, he could hear seabirds and the lap of waves against the boat, see the blue sky above him; the next, everything was distorted under the water's surface and he weighed practically nothing. Oh, and he was moving like a man on the moon. That's the part he never enjoyed. A guy who stayed alive by wit and speed never liked sacrificing either. He couldn't outrun anyone down here, and it wasn't as though he spent a lot of time swimming in Brooklyn. This was a different world, and now Harry Fox was definitely nowhere near the top of the food chain.

Floating near the surface, he could see far enough to figure out what was really close and what wasn't, but the further they descended, he knew, the murkier it would get. Visibility could be limited to a few feet once they reached the bottom, twenty-five feet down. Unless the water decided it wanted to be clear today. In that case, things would get easier.

Hamdy made a circle with thumb and forefinger. The sign for *okay*. Then his voice filled Harry's head like some sort of omniscient being. "Is everything good?" Hamdy asked.

Harry and Sara both flashed the same sign to indicate they were. "Are your headsets working?" Hamdy asked.

"I'm good," Harry said.

"Same here," Sara followed.

"Good. Follow me to the bottom." Hamdy turned a thumb down, indicating it was time to descend. Leaning forward, Harry let the weight of his tanks slowly pull him to the bottom, avoiding the signals from his brain telling him to kick toward the surface. A sea of opaque blue stretched in all directions. Harry glanced up, the clear sky already murky through the water, then looked down. A few seconds of gentle descent later and the harbor bottom came into view, a white carpet of silky sand that came alive like the night sky when Harry flicked on his headlamp.

Hamdy pointed two fingers at his mask. *Look.* "Do you see it?" he asked, as he indicated a spot near his feet. Harry moved himself closer to the bottom, to what looked for all the world like a black rock, a dark splotch on the pristine floor. He floated down, reaching out to touch the pitted surface. Hamdy gestured for him to circle around to the other side. Harry did and found a goddess waiting.

"It's Isis," Harry said. The Egyptian goddess of healing and magic. One of the most influential goddesses in Egyptian belief. Her unique crown, shaped like a throne and still recognizable if a bit weathered, left no doubt. A fantastic piece half-buried on the harbor bottom.

"There are other artifacts all around us," Hamdy said as he pointed in other directions, to other lumps that were most likely different gods and goddesses keeping watch over the fish.

Harry jumped when a hand latched onto his arm. Sara tugged him toward her, pointing into the distance. A hazy outline waited ahead. "That's the room we need to check out," she said. "Come on."

The outline became clear as the three divers moved toward what looked like nothing so much as a massive shoebox half-buried in the sand with the lid off. As they swam closer, the shoebox turned into a room—the collapsed room Sara had identified, with Greek writing on the wall. She pointed to one side as they moved. Cerberus lay to their starboard side. Three canine heads with teeth as long as Harry's finger glared as he passed. The plinth on which Cerberus had stood for centuries came into view next, red-veined marble attached to the base. The images he'd seen online were coming to life now in terrifying detail.

"The room is just ahead." Sara kicked until she led the way, Harry behind her and Hamdy at the rear. "Hamdy, do you think anyone else will come to this site while we're here?" she asked.

"No. This location is dangerous, and there are many other places to dive with more artifacts to see. Other guides do not want to come here because of the danger. We should be alone today."

A statue hung out of the open shoebox, a depiction of Cleopatra as a goddess, its base still connected to a piece of the distinctive marble that had led them to this spot. Her head jutted out from the interior at an angle. Harry nearly gasped. This was a fantastic relic that, had it been logistically feasible and financially viable to bring to the surface, would have been a welcome addition to any museum.

Sara swam up and ignored her.

"Here's the writing." Sara pointed to the dun-colored surface behind Cleopatra. "Look at these walls." Sara indicated a cross-section of the intact structure. "This isn't a single piece," she said. "It's composed of blocks, cemented together. I can't believe it's intact."

"We Egyptians have strong cement," Hamdy said. "Even two thousand years ago."

Hamdy was right to beat his chest about his people's cementing prowess. The walls had survived not only an earthquake and a subsequent collapse into the sea, but more than a thousand years underwater. Which made Harry only slightly less afraid for his life as he floated outside the shoebox of a room, albeit a shoebox over ten feet long on either side and twice as deep.

"Can you read the writing on the walls?" he asked Sara.

She removed a rubber brush from her belt. "I need to clean this off." She leaned closer. "Actually, these are quite clear. There is only a bit of dirt and mud on here. The current must have cleaned this part of the wall."

"You should not touch the artifacts," Hamdy said. "At least that is what I am supposed to tell you."

"I'm an Egyptologist," Sara said. "I promise I know what I'm doing."

Hamdy shrugged and gave them the look of a man who had already received his payment and a sizable tip before leaving shore. Sara and Harry had offered a story about Sara conducting research, none of it yet verified. Any qualms Hamdy had regarding their intent had been quieted with the influx of cash.

Silt muddied the water as Sara's brush went to work, forcing them to wait for a minute until it cleared enough to see through after she finished. A small number of the Greek words inscribed on the wall made sense to Harry. Quite a larger number did not.

"What's it say?" he asked. "I see Cleopatra's name."

Her finger trailed under each word as she ignored him and studied the wall. Harry looked behind them to find Hamdy not even interested in the wall. Something on the far side of the room had his attention. Harry opened his mouth to ask their guide what it was.

Sara's voice cut him off. "Incredible."

He whipped his head around, bubbles filling his vision. "What?" Harry asked.

"Listen to this." Sara began reading the inscription aloud.

> *My two lights followed the golden discs to this temple.*
> *As Shu and Tefnet,*
> *look past the one who is your Osiris*
> *to find the path to enlightenment.*

Sara latched onto his arm and pulled him close before he could react. "This is it."

Harry was too busy scrambling through what he recalled of Egyptian deities to comprehend. "What's 'it'?"

"Where the amulets sent us. This is what we're supposed to find. Shu and Tefnut are twins."

"Like Cleopatra Selene II and Alexander Helios. Does that matter?"

"Look at the second part." She touched the Greek letters spelling out

Osiris. "Osiris isn't related to Shu or Tefnut, but he *does* have a sibling. A sister."

"...*who is your Osiris,*" Harry said. "Shu and Tefnet are twins, same as Cleopatra's twins. Her *two lights,* who have *golden discs* we followed. Cleopatra built this temple, which means these walls carry her message. Cleopatra is talking about the two amulets her twins have. And *your Osiris* means we need to look at the twins' brother."

"Because Osiris is a brother too," Sara said. "It's a bit of a stretch, but it makes sense. The Egyptian gods had incredibly involved family dynamics. I think Cleopatra is telling us to look to the brother of her twin children. Caesarion."

Harry looked deeper into the gloomy room. "Is he mentioned anywhere on these walls?"

"Hold on one second." Sara pointed at Harry's chest. "Nicely done. Interpreting this riddle."

"Not sure why I brought you along now."

"Then I'll let you figure out where to find an image of Caesarion."

Harry rolled his eyes. "How am I supposed to know what he looks like?"

"Perhaps you could consult an Egyptologist. If you can find one on the harbor floor whom you haven't yet offended."

He grumbled. "Any guidance would be most welcome."

She turned back to the wall as Hamdy propelled himself in behind her, closer to the wall, where he nearly pressed his mask to the stone as Sara began to speak. "Look at the inscription on the wall. There's a space after the word for *enlightenment.* It's unusual, and I suspect it's calling attention to the symbol that comes next. A symbol, not a word."

"Looks like a Greek word to me." Harry squinted. "*Caesarion.*"

"Not exactly. See this line running around it? That's called a cartouche, and it's indicative of royalty. But this one is a bit odd. The line around his name isn't only oblong as most cartouches are. This one has a tail on one side."

"This line at the top?" Harry pointed at what looked like a leopard's tail hanging down from one upper edge of the oblong circle.

"It's a *pschent*. It's a double crown worn by Egyptian rulers. Including Caesarion."

Harry knew a thing or two about Egyptian symbols. "I thought they wore crowns that came to a point. Sort of like an upside-down vase."

"You're smarter than you look," Sara said. "Rulers from various time periods wore different crowns for different occasions. The crown you're referring to is called the *hedjet*, which was common centuries before Caesarion's rule."

"If they have all these crowns, how can you know we're looking for the *pschent* version?"

She pushed past him and aimed her headlamp into the gloomy depths of the submerged room. "That's why."

A statue appeared in the murkiness. Eight feet tall, carved in the shape of a full-grown man with biceps to match, the image of an Egyptian in full ornamental headdress leaned against one wall holding a scepter in one hand. The statue of a god on earth, a pharaoh, though to Harry's untrained eye it could have been any of them.

"That's Caesarion?" he asked.

Sara swam to his side. "You can tell by the head ornamentation and the staff he's holding. The symbol on top represents Cleopatra's lineage, and the headdress tells me it's Caesarion."

Hamdy's voice interrupted them. "Ms. Sara, did you clean any other part of the walls in here?"

Harry and Sara both looked back at Hamdy, who was now working his way slowly along the room walls. "No," she said. "Why?"

"I am not certain," Hamdy said. "Only that it appears these walls have been cleaned."

"I didn't do it," she said. "I thought nobody else would come in here?"

"They would not," Hamdy said. "It is too dangerous. It is most likely that the currents cleaned the wall. I would know if anyone came here. The guides like to talk."

"Then I'll take all the help the water will provide," Sara said. "Come on."

Harry swam with her to Caesarion's statue. "Look at that," he said. "The base has marble attached to it. Red-veined marble. This statue came from the same room as everything else we're checking."

"Which makes it easier for Antony and Cleopatra to keep their message contained. If their twins knew to find this room, they would be able to keep anything they found a secret. Even from their guards and attendants."

"It also would have been easier for Antony and Cleopatra to make sure no one else knew," Harry said. "If they only had to hide information in a single room, they could do it themselves."

"At least as much as any god on earth did work for themselves." Sara leaned around the statue. "Look at the headdress. See anything familiar?"

Harry aimed his headlamp at the rear of Caesarion's head. "Looks like a handle on a drinking pitcher to me."

"The word is *pschent*."

Bubbles surrounded Harry's face as his breathing quickened. "You were right. That's why his name had a strange cartouche around it on the wall—to tell the twins to look at this statue of their brother." He reached for the statue, then stopped. "Why?"

"Think back to what we've found before. Messages hidden in plain sight, where the only way to find them is to know you should be looking in the first place."

"Why change their methods now? I bet this statue *is* the message. And the *pschent* crown is part of it. The back end of it, this tail part. But how?" He kicked closer to the headdress. Green slime covered most of it. "You know what else this looks like? An actual handle."

"Do you think you can twist it?" Sara asked.

He reached for the tail. "One way to find out." Harry's hand stopped inches away from it. "This is weird."

"What is?" Sara asked.

"All the gunk on here is gone."

"Gunk?"

"The green slime. The seaweed. I don't know what it is." He angled his headlamp. "Almost like someone wiped it off."

"Hamdy thinks the currents may be involved," Sara said. "Here, I can try."

He lifted an arm to stay her. "I'm more than just brains, you know. I got it."

She grumbled through the static as he reached for the tail. Harry gripped the pitted stone with one hand, bracing his other hand on the statue for leverage before he tightened his hold on the tail and pulled. "It won't move," he said. "I need a better grip."

He let go of the handle and began circling the statue when his headset erupted.

"Do not move!" Hamdy's voice pierced his ears.

"Why not?" Harry turned toward their guide. The beam of Hamdy's headlamp washed over Harry, and out of the corner of his eye he saw a spark of light flash. Hamdy was scything through the water toward them like a missile.

"Stop!" their guide shouted.

Harry flinched, his arm swinging at the same time Hamdy smashed into him. A bolt of lightning arced through the darkness. Harry flew back, Hamdy shrieked, and a dark cloud bloomed in the water.

"It hit me!" Hamdy cried. He grabbed his shoulder. "My airline. It hit the tube."

Bubbles exploded in the room. Only when Hamdy kicked toward the exit did Harry see a spear sticking out of the ground near his feet. A modern spear, shiny and long and deadly. He looked back, above and past Caesarion's head. A spear gun had been strapped to the ceiling, with a cord running from its trigger to the statue. A cord Harry had tripped when his arm swung around, which fired the spear that sliced Hamdy's shoulder and severed the tube bringing air from his tanks to his mouth. Air that now spewed uninhibited into the water to create a cloud of bubbles trailing in Hamdy's wake.

"I must surface," Hamdy gasped. "Follow me." He vanished upward through the bubbles, flashing out of sight and heading to the surface.

Harry turned to find Sara hadn't moved. "We need to help him," she said.

Light flashed once more and the world shook. A pressure wave smacked Harry like a linebacker, rattling him from toes to skull, and the water around them rumbled with the noise of ancient stones falling. A crack appeared in the wall behind Caesarion.

"That was an explosion," Sara yelled. "To the surface."

"Not without this message." Harry pushed aside a piece of falling stone and grabbed Caesarion's headdress, pulling on the hanging tail with all his strength. A tail that, he now realized, was clear of debris because someone else had already been here, pulled the headdress tail and left a spear gun behind for the next visitor. Then they'd rigged an explosive device for good measure. Which was now bringing the room down on Harry's head.

"It's moving." The stone tail came toward him as he pulled, twisting it around like a crank until the tail pointed to the ceiling. A ceiling actively collapsing on them. He twisted as another shard of rock zipped past his eyes. Harry waved his hand to clear the bubbles as silt reduced his vision to mere feet in any direction. "Nothing happened," he said. "It didn't do anything."

"It opened this." Sara kicked toward the top of Caesarion's scepter, which now stood open like a flip-cap. "There's a hidden panel."

Another falling rock clipped him, sending Harry spinning in a circle. "Grab whatever's in there and let's go," he said. "I can hardly see."

Debris filled the water. "I can't," she said. "It's a message carved into the stone." She grunted as a rock hit her. "Shield me so I can read it."

He would have fallen off his chair had he been sitting on one. *Shield me?* More like *Be a human pincushion so the rock shards don't slice me open.* He cursed the entirety of Egyptian civilization as he went against every instinct and kicked above her, peering through the murky water to try and knock aside any rocks before they smashed her.

He got the first one. Then missed the second. It landed a direct hit on his face mask. Cracks snaked through the glass. "My mask is breaking."

She didn't reply as the stone walls boomed like cannons firing, cracks turning to chasms as the entire room started to disintegrate. The noise rumbled in his chest, his face mask spiderwebbing as another rock hit it and knocked his headlamp askew. The world closed in, dirt and silt and broken stone clouding what little he could see until Sara was nearly lost from view.

"Got it!" Sara grabbed his arm and kicked toward the exit. "I know what—"

Static filled his ears. "Sara?" He shouted her name again as she began writhing beside him. Bubbles exploded to momentarily clear the water in front of him, and through the expanding cracks in his face mask every diver's nightmare came to life. Sara's airline had been cut, compressed air spewing into the water in an uncontrolled eruption. She couldn't breathe.

Harry grabbed one of her flailing arms, wrenched it behind her back and kicked forward. With his other hand he pulled at her tanks and kept kicking until she finally got the idea and slipped free from the now-useless metal canisters. He could barely see a foot ahead, the concussions of rock against rock sending shock waves through the water and rattling his bones as the room collapsed. Harry took one last breath, pulled the regulator from his mouth and pressed it into Sara's hand, still kicking and pulling her to safety. He felt her hand grasp it, then felt Sara kicking with him as he kept hold of her arm, shooting them forward. A rock banged against his air tanks, its weight knocking him down below Sara and dragging her with him. He kept hold of her arm so she didn't lose air, then resumed kicking ahead. The dirty water cleared for an instant to reveal blue ahead, clearer water and a path to the surface.

Then, behind them, there was a dense boom as a bomb detonated and the remains of the room collapsed. Harry never saw the rock that hit him. One instant he was kicking toward freedom; the next, white light filled his vision as a god's fist struck his head and the world went dark.

Chapter 19

Dendera, Egypt

Blue light pierced his eyes when Harry blinked. A screeching voice thundered in his ears, and when he blinked again, a crunching blow rattled his brain and sent him spinning.

"Wake up." The screeching continued. "Harry, wake up."

Hands grabbed his shoulders and tried to shake his head loose. "Get off." Harry waved ineffectually at his tormentor. Light like searing acid assaulted his eyeballs. He lifted an arm to shield them. "Get off me," he growled. "Let me go."

The hands released him. His head thunked off the ground. Ground that bobbed up and down. He tried to sit up. He failed. "Oh, my head." Harry touched the back of his scalp and found a billiard ball had taken up residence under his hair. "That hurts."

"Then don't touch it," ordered the screeching voice, which now sounded an awful lot like Sara. The woman leaning over top of him looked like her as well. "You're lucky to be alive," Sara said. "That rock nearly took your head off."

"Good thing my big brain deflected it."

"If you mean that petrified lump between your ears, then I agree. Now sit up."

"You told me to keep still."

"Want to know what was inside Caesarion's statue or not?"

The pain in his head vanished for an instant as he sat up. Then it returned with a vengeance. "Hang on." Harry pressed a hand to his forehead. "Okay," he said a moment later. "What did you find?"

"A message."

Harry's eyes shot open. "Wait. Where's Hamdy?" The guide was nowhere to be seen.

"Back here, my friend." Hamdy's voice sounded from behind Harry. He turned, slowly, and found their guide sitting on the gunwale. One hand kept pressure on his shoulder, holding a rag against it. A rag stained red. "It takes more than a spear to stop Hamdy." The irrepressible Egyptian's teeth flashed in the sunlight. Then he grimaced. "Who set the trap?"

Hamdy was no dummy.

"I think I know who it was," Harry said. "The same man who I suspect bugged my house and tried to have my mother kidnapped. And kill me in the bargain."

"You did not tell me this earlier." Hamdy frowned. "I would have charged more."

"I didn't think he would come here ahead of us. I didn't think he'd come here at all." Now he turned to Sara. "It has to be Stefan. That's the only person who could have known to come here. I'm so stupid. The guy had my house bugged. He heard everything we said, and I never once figured he'd follow Cleopatra's path."

"I will not ask why you both mention those names," Hamdy said. "Cleopatra. Antony. I do not want to know if you seek their treasures. But I hope you know the best silence is paid for."

Harry couldn't even argue. "I do, and don't worry. You'll get a nice bonus." Harry aimed a finger at Hamdy's chest. "If you can keep your mouth shut."

"Hamdy is very good at not talking."

"Glad we understand each other." He looked back to Sara. "Are you okay? That felt like a bomb went off down there."

Hamdy jumped in. "It was much less than a bomb."

Harry had exactly no experience with underwater explosions. "A grenade? It couldn't have been too big or it would have killed us."

"No, a grenade would have killed you," Hamdy countered. "What you experienced just now was a pressure wave. Explosions underwater take much longer to disperse than those in the air. The water does not compress as easily, which means the force will concentrate on pockets of air if it can. Pockets like your lungs."

"So what caused it?" Sara asked.

"A controlled explosion. They require less material, which makes the device easy to conceal, and the smaller amounts are easier to obtain. It may have been dynamite."

"Placed to kill us with either the blast itself or the debris from the falling room," Sara said.

Harry ran a hand through his wet hair and switched back to English. "I must have tripped some kind of switch by the statue that set off the spear gun. I'm sorry, Hamdy. It's my fault you got shot."

"It is nothing." Hamdy patted his arm. "A lucky shot."

Harry didn't ask for whom. "What did you find down there?" he asked Sara.

"One moment." Hamdy turned, looking at every boat around them. "This man, the one who set the trap. Do you believe he is still here?"

Sara answered. "No. I'm almost certain he's gone."

Hamdy wasn't buying it so easily. "Why?"

"The message I found." She turned to Harry. "That's what was hidden in the statue. A message. One I could tell had already been opened, and not long ago. The algae covering it had been scraped off."

"What kind of hidden message would Stefan have left behind?" Harry asked. "He could have taken it with him and we'd never find it."

"He wouldn't have been able to take a tablet hidden inside the statue. It's part of Caesarion, attached to him. When you twisted the headdress, a panel opened on the scepter. The carving on top of his statue flipped open to reveal a message carved into the stone. I read it before the room collapsed." She closed her eyes and recited the hidden words.

Seek Hathor's favor in her home.
Follow only the message of Ra to locate Thoth's power.

Her eyes opened. "That's everything."

Harry glanced at Hamdy. The guide didn't blink. "What does it mean?" Harry asked.

"Together?" Sara shook her head. "Nothing I can comprehend, though if we take each section separately I may have an idea. Start with Hathor. She was a sky deity in ancient Egypt and the symbolic mother of all pharaohs."

"She lived in the sky?" Harry asked.

"In the story, yes. Which is irrelevant here because all major deities required earthly places of worship, even if they did live among the stars. Hathor was no exception. Her principal temple in Egypt wasn't merely a shrine. It was the centerpiece of a temple complex, a massive arrangement of religious structures protected by an enclosed wall. A place called Dendera."

Harry had long ago learned to trust his gut. Recently he'd learned to trust Sara's as well, so he didn't ask questions, merely motioning for her to go on.

"Ra is another deity. An important one who represents the sun. Depending on which interpretation of the myth you read, Ra is also Hathor's father, husband or son." She held up a hand. "Don't worry about that part."

"I don't judge."

She ignored him. "Your sarcasm is not needed. What we do need is to know how we can follow the message of Ra." Sara's lips tightened. "I'm still working on that part."

"What about Thoth? I assume he's related to the other two in some way."

"Thoth is a wide-ranging deity. He is the god of the moon, wisdom, science and several other expansive subjects. Magic is one. He is not, to my knowledge related to Hathor or Ra."

"Glad to hear it. Sounds like we need to narrow down which power they're talking about. I'd choose magic if I had a say."

"I suspect your answer is waiting."

"Hang on." Harry stood, growled at himself, but managed to keep his balance on the gently bobbing craft. "You already figured all this out from two sentences?"

"You were sleeping while I thought. It took me a few minutes."

"Nice work." He looked to the shore. He glared at all the boats around them. None seemed ready to attack. "Now what?"

"I should think the answer is obvious," Sara said, but instead of explaining, she fired a question back at him. "What do you think we should do?"

The sharp pain in his head was morphing to a dull ache. He didn't have time for this. "I think we should consult an Egyptologist. One who gives answers, not more questions."

"Excellent idea. The answer is we go to Dendera. From there, we follow Ra's message, whatever that may be, and locate Thoth's power."

Something in her voice made the pain subside. He pointed at her chest. "You know where Dendera is."

"Along with millions of others, yes. The Dendera Temple Complex is one of the best-preserved sites from ancient Egypt. It contains Roman chapels, Egyptian temples, incredible gates and one of the most impressive defense walls of the time. It is an incredible place to visit, and I cannot wait to get back."

"You're worth every penny," he said. "Maybe I'll even pay you next time."

"If we can get off this boat and to an airport, we can fly to Luxor in an hour. From there it's a thirty-minute drive to Dendera."

The thought of flying brought his headache back with a vengeance. "Can't we drive?"

"If you want to sit in a car for the next ten hours, yes."

"Airport it is." Harry looked to their guide. "Hamdy, how fast can you get us back to shore? That's where your money is, by the way."

Hamdy stood without a word, moved to the cockpit and fired the engine. "Hold on, my friends." He pushed the throttle forward and their boat zipped off, juking through other craft on a borderline-reckless charge for dry land. A few close calls later Hamdy pulled up to his dock, Harry threw a line toward the waiting dockhand and they were secure.

"Would you like a ride to the airport?" Hamdy asked.

"You a taxi driver too?" Harry asked.

"No, but my cousin is. The best rates in Alexandria."

Sara had her phone out. "If he can get us there in an hour we can make the next flight."

"He will do it."

Hamdy made a call and by the time Harry had their equipment on the shore Hamdy's cousin had pulled up.

Harry touched Hamdy's bandaged shoulder. "I'm sorry about this," Harry said. "Thanks for saving my life down there."

Hamdy clapped a hand on each of Harry's shoulders as though the spear wound had never happened. "You are a good man, Mr. Fox. Be cautious in Dendera. The man named Stefan already tried to kill you once. He will do it again."

Harry promised their guide he would before climbing into the back of the cab. Hamdy's cousin raced to their hotel, where Harry grabbed their bags and settled the bill in record time before an electrifying ride to the airport saw them deposited at the entrance with minutes to spare. The first-class seat—courtesy of Nora Doyle's expense account—wrapped Harry in a soft leather embrace, and before he knew what happened they were touching down in Luxor.

"I got us a car," Sara said as they taxied to the gate. "How's your head?"

He touched it. "Cold. Did you turn the air on?"

"I put an ice pack on it for you while you slept. It should help with the swelling."

It actually had. He felt almost human again by the time he buckled up in the passenger seat of the rental next to Sara. Then she hit the gas, and all he could do was hang on as she made a sincere effort to break every traffic law in Egypt while covering the forty miles from Luxor to Dendera in record time. In her defense, all the other motorists drove like deranged New York cabbies as well. Harry finally took a breath when they skidded to a halt in front of a row of waving palm trees.

"We still have several hours of daylight," Sara said. "Plenty of time to investigate the site."

He got out of the car and shielded his eyes. "This place is huge." At least a dozen structures rose before him, built of light sandstone and dusty marble. Massive walls the height of two men ran intermittently around the entire complex, with a towering temple building fronted by decorated columns and a deadly-looking gate in front of it taking center stage. What looked to be a necropolis sat to one side, suggesting crypts and other subterranean rooms waited below. Then he noted the satellite buildings surrounding the main campus. "Where do we even start?"

"This complex covers over forty thousand square meters," Sara said as she closed her door. "That's a little more than ten acres, for the metrically challenged among us. As to where we begin, I say the main entrance." She pointed ahead. "That large gate."

A soft breeze rustled the palm trees behind him as Harry stepped out of the car. A football field-sized walkway led directly to the tallest structure in Dendera: the remnants of a forty-foot-tall stone entrance. Detailed reliefs were carved on one side of the entrance, while the other façade had collapsed to reveal the structural stonework underneath. A watchful sphinx stood guard on either side, surveying visitors as they entered through the modern metal gate that had been erected between the entrance pillars.

"I think the guard is asleep." Harry nodded at a uniformed man sitting in a chair in the entrance's shade, arms crossed. The guy's chin might as well have been glued to his chest.

"It's hot out here," Sara said. "I don't blame him."

"Too hot for many visitors." He could count on both hands the number of people in sight, guard included. "Is the big building Hathor's temple?" he asked, and Sara said it was.

The front gate's narrow entrance framed a much larger structure, one with brilliant carvings covering the front and royal imagery on each of its six towering columns. An indelibly American monument popped into Harry's head. "This looks like the Lincoln Memorial."

"It does. Which is logical, given the Lincoln Memorial is a neoclassical temple."

His knowledge of architectural influences wouldn't fill a thimble. "Oh."

Sara failed to suppress a smirk. "Neoclassical architectural styles are inspired in part by Renaissance and Baroque architecture, which in turn took inspiration from the classical architectural styles of ancient Rome and Greece."

The connection sparked. "So I should say the Lincoln Memorial looks like this temple."

"There is hope for you yet. If you want to understand where you are going, look to where you came from." She walked around the car and put her arm through his. "Act like a tourist. We wouldn't want the guard to suspect we're up to no good."

Harry didn't budge when she started walking. "Hold on." He pulled his sunglasses from his collar and slipped them on. "We're not safe."

Sara's grip on his arm tightened. "What do you see?"

"Nothing, which doesn't make me feel any better. Stefan overheard us talking about Alexandria harbor. He left a trap to kill us after he found Cleopatra's message. That's the second time he's tried to kill me this week. I have to assume he figured out what the message meant and knows to come here."

"It's possible. I made the Dendera temple connection from my studies. It would likely take a layperson some time, but they could certainly come to the same conclusion." She leaned closer to his chest. "Would you recognize him? Everyone is wearing sunglasses and hats."

"He tried to slice me apart with a trident. You don't forget a guy who does that." Harry reached into his pocket and touched the warm ceramic of his trusty knuckledusters. "Don't worry, I'll keep my eyes open. If I tell you to run, do it."

A pause. "I'm not leaving you."

His head whipped around and he looked at her. Words raced to the tip of his tongue. They remained there. "Then stay alert. He could be anywhere." He began to walk, pulling her along with him, leaving the unspoken thought behind. They'd deal with that after they got out of here in one piece.

Long shadows trailed behind them as they approached the front entrance. A guard sporting a floppy hat perked up at the sound of their footsteps. His head drooped again when they stopped in front of the entrance pillar to look at the carvings. Sara stepped off the stone walkway and onto the gravel. "This is the gate of Domitian and Trajan. These carvings are dedicated to the two Roman emperors. Both reigned around a century after Cleopatra died."

"Which means we can skip this part."

"You would think," Sara said. She fell silent for a minute. Harry kept his head moving as she studied the carvings. Nobody caught his eye, mainly because nobody was around. Unless Stefan had a rifle and was hiding in the distant, craggy hills. No, he couldn't have found a rifle around here. Guns were strictly controlled in Egypt. No way Stefan could get his hands on a rifle. Harry nearly laughed at himself, then stopped. Just like he couldn't have procured dynamite in Alexandria.

"Anything?" he asked Sara. Being out in the open meant he could see everyone. It also meant they could see him.

"No. All of these inscriptions came well after Cleopatra died. Anything that was here beforehand was erased to honor Domitian or Trajan. We can go inside."

The floppy-hatted guard took their money with barely a word, his chin finding his chest once more by the time Harry and Sara passed beneath the arches.

"What about those?" Harry asked, looking up as they entered. "The carvings on the underside of this entrance."

Sara shook her head. "More Roman tributes. They didn't take half-measures when it came to honoring themselves. There would only be room for Romans on this entrance. Anything else had to go." She pointed to the other buildings ahead. "We're lucky they didn't re-do the entire place to feed their egos." The entire rear portion of the gate sported etchings and carvings. It took her even less time to confirm they carried the same messages as they'd seen on the front. "More about Domitian and Trajan. We need to listen to Antony and Cleopatra. *Seek Hathor's favor in her home.* That means the Temple of Hathor. Come on."

The security guard's head popped up as they turned to go. He studied them from beneath the brim of the overly floppy hat, then went back to resting. Harry moved to catch up with Sara, who had already launched into another lecture regarding the structure in front of them. "What was that?" he asked.

"I said a temple has been in this location for over three thousand years. The structure we're looking at now dates to around fifty years before the birth of Christ."

Harry stopped walking. "During Cleopatra's lifetime."

Sara didn't stop. "Keep up. And you're correct. This temple was rebuilt while she was the queen of Egypt. She could have it built any way she liked. Including"—and here Sara touched her lips theatrically—"to contain a hidden message."

The hairs rose on his neck. But once again, nothing caught his eye when he looked around. No distant flashes of sunlight off a rifle scope. No Albanian gangsters creeping up from behind to take them out. The only change of note was that the security guard had been struck by inspiration and had managed to get out of his chair, and was now standing with a phone pressed to his ear. Maybe his boss was calling and telling him to get to work. Either way, nothing to explain the wave of alarm. *Easy, Harry. Stefan's not here. Not yet, at least.*

"What's wrong?"

He turned to find Sara peering at him, lines on her forehead. "Nothing," he said quickly. "Just had a funny feeling is all."

Now Sara did stop walking. "Why?"

He scanned the temple grounds again. "I don't know. Just jumpy. Forget about it." He headed for the temple, forcing the uneasy thoughts from his head. Stay vigilant, not paranoid. Sara had enough to deal with already. She seemed to be getting out of her funk and back to normal. Getting her worked up over nothing would only hurt their cause. And his.

A small knot of tourists walked out of the temple's main hallway. Sara hesitated. Harry did not. "We're good," he said. "Even Stefan can't disguise himself as an Asian woman." He pointed at one of the gigantic pillars that fronted the temple. "Looks Egyptian to me."

A switch turned inside her, and Sara the nervous explorer vanished as quickly as she'd appeared. "There are twenty-four columns in the main entrance," she said confidently. "Each is decorated with traditional Egyptian imagery. This front portion is called the Great Vestibule. We need to check the ceiling."

"What about the exterior walls?"

"I believe Antony and Cleopatra would have put the message inside. That way it's protected from weather, and their children would also have privacy."

The stone ceiling looked down on them from five stories in the air as they passed through the front entrance. Shafts of falling sunlight cut through the air, sand and dust hanging suspended in them. Harry craned his neck. "It's blue."

"That's the other reason I think it's inside," Sara said. "This temple is beautiful. Antony and Cleopatra wouldn't go to all this trouble to hide their message on a dusty exterior wall."

Vivid blue the color of a tropical sea turned the relief-filled ceiling into a brilliant sky. Hundreds of images covered the ceiling, a throng of Egyptian gods and pharaohs, each one a testament to Cleopatra's greatness. Too many to identify, in fact.

"What does it say?" Harry waved a hand to encompass the entire ceiling. "Or mean?"

"A lot." Sara craned her neck, taking in the figures far above her. "Most of it relates to Cleopatra or Hathor, specifically her purview of certain human activities as the goddess of love, fertility, music or dancing." Sara pointed at various images as she spoke. "Incredible, and also very standard for Egyptian temples. I don't think what we're looking for is on this ceiling."

"What about the columns?" Even more glyphs and carvings covered the interior columns in the open-air front hall.

"More of the same. This room is meant to inspire awe and admiration for the people who built it and the deities they honor." One hand went on a hip. "Plus, it's simply too much to look through. If we have no luck in other rooms we can inspect this more closely. Let's keep moving."

The temple was built like a rectangle, stretching far back beyond the front entrance hall in a straight line to the rear wall. Various shrines and sanctuaries branched off on either side as they walked. Spotlights ran along either side at ground level to send dark shadows stretching toward the ceiling and leaving most of the carvings on the walls in a murky semi-dark. Their footsteps echoed off the stonework, bouncing up to the ceiling and back down the hallway as though it were a gigantic cave. Harry's throat went dry after only a few breaths of the dusty air.

"There are thousands of carvings here." He pointed up one wall to where it virtually disappeared in the gloom overhead. "How can we be sure we don't miss anything?"

Sara didn't seem worried in the least. "Remember, Antony and Cleopatra wanted this to be found. By their children, no less. They wouldn't make the message inaccessible or dangerous."

"You mean dangerous like making someone climb a statue outside Luxor Temple?" he said, referring to a mishap on one of her previous adventures while following Cleopatra's trail.

"That was only dangerous because I slipped."

Harry angled his head. "You're starting to sound like someone."

"Who is that?"

"Me."

"Then we're both in trouble." Sara pointed to an opening ahead. "I think I know where to look. All this time we've followed their lead. The last message told us to *seek Hathor's favor*. How do you seek a god's favor?"

"Typically through prayer."

"Which is often done at a shrine. Such as this one." She stopped in front of an opening big enough to drive a semi-trailer through. "This is Hathor's shrine inside her temple. People seeking her favor came here to pray or leave offerings."

Harry opened his mouth. Sara raised a hand, cutting him off. "Do you hear that?"

He turned an ear toward the entrance. A muffled voice sounded, metallic and tinny. "It's Arabic," Harry said. "Can you make it out?"

"The temple is closing in thirty minutes. Hurry up." She dragged him into a gargantuan side room cloaked in shadows. Again the only light came from floor-level lights that did little to bring the walls into view.

"How did anyone ever see in here before electric lights?" Harry asked.

"Torches." Sara pointed at a number of circular openings running up and down the walls. "I wouldn't want to be the priest who had to light all of them. Fall off your ladder from the very top and it won't end well."

Torch holes ran at least forty feet high in vertical rows around the room, tucked between endless rows of imagery and hieroglyphs. "I don't see any Greek writing in here." Harry went to the closest wall, peering toward the ceiling. "None over here."

"You're looking in the wrong place."

He spun around to find Sara pointing at the room's centerpiece. A thirty-foot-high statue dominated the center wall. A slender goddess, wearing what he'd call a red party dress with two straps at the top. In one hand she carried a staff. A massive red circle sat atop her head, balanced between a pair of horns. "Is that Hathor?" Harry asked. Sara said it was. "What's on her head?"

"Cow horns with a sun disk between them."

Harry raised an eyebrow. "Oh."

"Hathor is often pictured this way. When she's not depicted as a cow or lioness."

"I'd choose the lioness."

"Egyptians considered cows and bulls the holiest of all animals. Bulls are strong, representing masculinity. And cows provide life-sustaining milk, which represents motherhood or nurturing. Do not turn your nose up at being drawn as a bovine."

"I'll remember that next time I draw your portrait."

"It will be the last mistake you make. Now, if you're finished, we have a message to decode."

"There must be a thousand pictures and glyphs in this room. Where do we start?"

Her hands found her hips again. "I have no idea."

A face popped into his head. One he found coming to mind more and more when trouble arrived. His father. *What would you do, Dad?* The answer, as usual, was easy. "Start with what you know."

"What?"

"That's where we start," Harry said. "With what we know."

"That sounds like something your father would have said."

Harry nodded solemnly. "It is. He told me if I ever felt lost in the field, take a deep breath and start with what I know. Trust myself to figure it out. That's why I read all those books. Or you do, in this case. Use your knowledge and have faith."

"When did you become a religious man?"

"I never doubt myself. It's everyone else I'm worried about."

"Then where do we begin?"

His gaze went to Hathor. *Seek Hathor's favor in her home. Follow only the message of Ra to locate Thoth's power.* "You're certain the Caesarion statue didn't have anything else to say?"

"Quite."

"Good. We're seeking Hathor's favor right now. We came to her shrine, which is in her home, namely this temple. Next comes Ra. The sun god, the guy who created life. At the very top of the food chain." Harry studied the walls. "One problem. I don't see him anywhere. His head looks like a falcon, correct?"

"Very good. And no, I don't see him either."

"What else can you tell me about Ra?"

Sara put on her lecturing voice and dove in. "Ra ruled the sky, earth and underworld. He created a number of other deities, none of whom I see here. He was the god of the sun, which made it his duty to carry the sun across the sky each day to bring light to the world."

Harry kept his eyes moving as she spoke. "Plenty of sun carvings in here."

"At different times Ra was fused with other gods, most prominently Amun. They became Amun-Ra, the king of the gods who is often depicted as a man with red eyes and a lion's head, with a solar disk surrounding his head."

"Symbols." Harry snapped his fingers. "That's what we need. Symbols. This room is filled with them. Antony and Cleopatra have used symbols to hide a message in plain sight. They could easily do it in here."

"Except there are hundreds of options," Sara said. "Which one do we want?"

"One tied to Ra."

"That is quite an extensive list. And also not definitively related to *the message of Ra*. Wouldn't a phrase or word be more likely?"

"Not for us. That's logical, sure, but what have we found so far? Symbols that only mean something if you know to look for it. I bet Cleopatra used the same process. The message she talks about can be a picture or glyph, something people would never suspect has a double meaning unless—"

"—they know to look for it." Sara's voice softened. "It makes sense. In that case, we should look—"

"Quiet." Harry put a hand over her mouth. *What was that noise?* Faint, at the edge of hearing, the sound of something clicking on a stone floor had caught his ear. Something like a foot, one trying to move noiselessly in what was basically an echo chamber. He turned one ear toward the entrance to their rear. *Click.*

Sara's eyes widened. Harry took his hand off her mouth and took a long step toward the main hallway. He turned around and made a circle motion with his hand. *Keep talking.*

Her voice returned. "A double meaning unless they knew to look for it."

He gave her a thumbs-up and kept going. Gently, on his toes. Sara kept talking to hide any noise he made as he moved. She started describing the statue in great detail, mundane observations that had nothing to do with their search and everything to do with keeping his progress hidden. Several large steps brought him near the entrance. He raised a hand to quiet her. Sara fell silent. He counted to three, then jumped around the front wall and into the hallway, feet spread and fists clenched.

Nothing. The hallway was empty. No lurking Albanians, no armed gangsters ready to punch Harry's ticket. He lingered for a moment, eyes narrowed at the dark corners stretching ahead of him. Far too many dark corners.

"What is it?" Sara's voice rang out from inside the shrine. "Are you okay?"

He gave one particularly dark corner a long stare. Nothing stared back. "It's nothing," he said, walking back into the shrine. "I'm hearing things."

"I heard it too."

"This place is huge. The acoustics are messing with us." He said it with conviction. Then his gaze jerked back to the hallway. "We're fine."

"If you're certain," she said hesitantly. "This temple is remote. There's one guard. We're basically on our own."

Harry reached into his pocket. The knuckledusters hadn't vanished. "Then we'd better keep moving. You were telling me about symbols for Ra."

"Which could be the *message* Cleopatra mentioned. Ra had a falcon's head. Do you see any of those in here?"

A full minute passed as they each inspected the walls. "Nothing here," Harry said.

"Nothing on my side either."

"Give me a couple more options. Maybe it wasn't that obvious. Hiding their message with a more obscure symbol or reference would be more secure."

"Ra is also associated with a ram, a phoenix, or a serpent." She hesitated. "And cats, bulls, or beetles. It's quite the list, now that I——"

Harry cut her off as a spark flashed in his memory. "Say that again. The last part."

She touched her chest. "About cats, bulls or beetles?"

"Beetles. By beetles you mean *scarabs*. Right?"

"Scarabs." Her hands went to her mouth. "Oh my goodness. I never made the connection. Scarabs are how they concealed their message pointing us to the double-headed eagle necklace." Scarab medallions Mark Antony and Cleopatra commissioned to celebrate a military triumph. Medallions which also concealed a message from the pair. A message on the path to this temple.

"Scarabs also represent resurrection or rebirth. Which is what the sun did every day. Is that why they represent Ra?"

"That's exactly right."

"Scarabs are a symbol of Ra. They were also used earlier on this trail to conceal a message. So, what if Antony and Cleopatra didn't use scarabs only once, as gifts? What if they used them again?"

"It's possible." Sara considered it a moment longer. "Probable, even. So it seems we need to look for scarabs on these walls."

Harry didn't even turn to look when he pointed. "Look beside Hathor. On this side."

Sara ran to the foot of Hathor's statue. "Why this side?" She took another step and stumbled. "Ouch." Sara bent down to retrieve the stone she'd kicked, one hidden in the shadows. She looked at it for a moment, then up at the stone figure. "This fell off the statue. It needs to be repaired." Absently, she shoved it in her pocket.

Harry pointed at a row of images on the wall staring at Sara. "Look in front of you."

She seemed to notice the trio of engravings for the first time. Three in a row, each at ground level. "This first one is Ra," Sara said, bending closer. "This next one has the head of an ibis bird. It's Thoth. The last one is Cleopatra."

"Don't forget the big lady in the middle. Hathor."

"Ra, Thoth, Cleopatra and Hathor." She repeated them again, softly this time. A bolt of electricity jolted her body. "Of course. All three gods are in Cleopatra's message in Alexandria."

"I'm not sure about you, but to me that's a strong hint we're in the right place."

"Agreed." Sara lifted a hand to indicate the wall in front of her. "This is where she wants us to be. But what are we looking for?"

"What do you see beside Hathor's head? That top line of writing. A bit hard to make out, but if you squint you can read it."

She narrowed her eyes. "*We visit the gods to honor our Queen. Long live the Queen of Egypt, glory to her reign, selected by the gods to her place beside them. We follow the Queen with Amun-Ra's ferocious power. His guardians guide her toward knowledge as is his duty.*" She turned to Harry, scrunched her eyes up and sneezed. "It's dusty in here. What about that line has your eye? It's fairly standard, a tribute to Cleopatra and an acknowledgment of her obligation as the pharaoh to guide her people."

"It's not the glyphs that caught my eye. It's what's beside them. What are those pictures in front of certain words?"

"Scarabs." The word came out breathlessly, then her excitement vanished. "Which can be decorative in nature. They aren't meant to be read, which can be confusing, but ornamentation in the form of sacred objects is used on occasion."

"I don't think it's decorative. I think it's intentional. Those scarabs are markers."

"Indicating we should look to those words?"

"I think so. Read each word preceded by a scarab, one at a time."

The words came slowly at first. "*Visit the selected place follow Amun-Ra's ferocious guardians...*" She stepped back from the wall. "That makes sense.

Harry, it's not gibberish. I know what—"

"Don't stop now," he said. "Keep going."

"Right." She pointed at the images as she continued translating. "…*toward his duty start for sixty rods to find Thoth's power below seek his mystery to reveal power with golden discs.*"

Sara touched her chest. "That's it. Incredible. The message makes sense. It's logical."

Harry pulled his phone out. "Say it again. I need to write it down. We can't stay here all night."

She read the scarab-marked words again, Harry dictating them into his phone. "This is in case we miss anything," he said as he took pictures of the text from different angles. "Got it." He put the phone away. "Now, what the heck does that mean?"

"The *selected place*. That means 'the most selected of places.' It refers to an Egyptian religious site."

Egyptian. "We're already in the right country?"

"We're only one hundred kilometers away from it." Harry asked where *it* was. "Karnak," she said. "There's a site there that's been standing for almost four thousand years."

He was getting good at distance conversions. "One hundred kilometers is about sixty miles. We can be there in an hour." The long shadows and thickening dark in the hallway caught his eye. "Which won't be in time to see the place tonight. We'll be lucky if the guards don't arrest us for loitering."

"Wait," Sara said as he started to walk out. "There's more to the message. Cleopatra wants us to *follow Amun-Ra's ferocious guardians.* I know what she means."

Harry stopped near the exit, curiosity overcoming the voice in his head shouting at him to collect Sara and get out. "I'm listening."

"Sphinxes. Ferocious guardians are sphinxes."

He looked around the room and spotted twenty of the creatures in seconds. "How will we know which ones to follow? Egyptians put sphinxes on everything."

"You probably don't know. You weren't there."

"Know what about where?"

"Karnak is next to Luxor Temple. The sites used to be connected by a three-kilometer road called the Avenue of Sphinxes. Ring a bell?"

"Why didn't you say so? That's where you found the underground chamber. The one beneath that sphinx statue you had to *dispatch*. The one with red eyes." Several months earlier Sara had traveled alone to Luxor Temple on Cleopatra's path and ended up in a tight spot. The trip had taken her to incredible heights and frightening depths, to say the least.

"It's also where I nearly died, in case you forgot. And yes, the avenue is lined with hundreds of sphinxes. Perhaps more than one of them contains a message from Cleopatra." She hesitated. "Though I could do without the underground chambers again."

"In that case, you're hired." He stuck a hand out. "Come on. We can figure out the rest of the message on our way. I'd prefer not to spend the night in an Egyptian jail for trespassing. These guards don't mess around." He looked uneasily into the hallway but found it empty. "And I think we're the last ones here."

Sara gave one last, long look at the wall before jogging to catch up with him. Their footsteps echoed in the silent passageway as they hurried toward the front exit. Entrances to side rooms loomed as black holes on either side, the ceiling above a dark sky with no stars. A coolness had crept into the air since they entered, enough to raise gooseflesh on Harry's arms as they moved. At least that's what he told himself. Too bad it didn't explain the hair on his neck rising as well. *Take it easy. There's no one here but us. And there are guards to keep watch.* He looked around and ahead. The guards seemed to have vanished into thin air. As though Osiris had whisked them away to join him in the underworld.

Hurried footsteps sounded as Sara quickened her pace. "I didn't realize it was so late," she said as she caught up to him. "It is too quiet."

He didn't respond, increasing his pace. The first gigantic, dark side entrance lay just ahead, and without realizing it he veered toward the hallway's center, away from the emptiness. Not that Osiris was waiting or anything. That was crazy. "What else do you know about the message?" he asked. Better to hear voices than these echoing steps.

"What? Oh, the message. Yes. Well, I believe *his duty* refers to—"

"Stop."

A hard voice sliced the temple air. Sara's hand locked onto his arm as Harry skidded to a halt. It was either that or run smack into the stone statue that had come to life and stepped out of a dark doorway mere feet ahead. A stone statue wearing a temple guard uniform.

Arms bigger than Harry's legs hung at his sides. "What are you doing here?" the guard asked.

He's speaking in English. Harry squared his chest. "We're leaving. I'm sorry if we stayed too late."

"No. You will come with us."

Us? Footsteps sounded from behind them. Harry turned to find another man approaching from their rear, all beard and dusty clothes and hairy forearms. Not as big as the guard, but he didn't have to be. Not with the knife in his hand.

"I'm an Egyptian citizen." Sara took a step toward the uniformed guard. "We have violated no laws. We're leaving."

The bearded man with the knife laughed, his voice scraped raw by a million cigarettes. "You are going nowhere. Tell me what you read on the walls."

"You tell me," Sara fired back. "Clearly you were listening."

The unfriendly smile on his face vanished. "You are lucky, girl. I could not hear. Now you will live, if you tell me what you learned." He raised the knife so the blade caught a ray of dying sunlight and flashed with a fiery spark. "Unless you do not tell me. Then I will make you talk."

Sara turned back to the security guard. "Help us. Call for backup on your radio. This man is threatening us all."

The guard lifted his radio from the clip on his belt. He held it out, twisted a knob, and an electronic *pop* told them the radio was now off. "This? It does not work. Start talking."

Sara glared at the men. Harry watched her. She wasn't afraid, didn't shrink in on herself or hide behind him. No, Sara turned so the guy behind her couldn't see her hand. Or the rock now clasped in it, the broken chunk of Hathor's statue. Sara's eyebrows rose a fraction. Harry got the message. He slipped a hand into his pocket and grabbed the knuckledusters.

Sara lifted three fingers on her other hand. Harry nodded. *Two. One. Zero.*

Sara turned to the guard. "You can have it." The man's head tilted and his eyes narrowed. She stepped closer, digging in her pocket as though searching for something. "It will explain every—"

Her fist flashed in the dark. The guard never saw it coming until Hathor's rock smashed between his eyes and a spray of dark liquid filled the air. He might have dropped straight down. Harry went for the bearded man with the knife.

The guy dodged and stabbed as Harry feinted, stopping short so the knife never reached his stomach. Harry chopped a hand down on the man's extended arm and threw a jab. The chop connected, the jab whiffed past him. Harry saw the man's other fist coming with a roundhouse. He bent backwards to avoid it, but not quite far enough: his assailant's fist clipped his head. A fist hard enough to make his world spin for an instant.

Harry shook the stars out of his vision, grabbed the man's knife arm and twisted, pulling him close. Harry whipped his head backwards and then shot it forward again, his forehead connecting with bearded man's nose. Cartilage cracked, the man grunted, yet still he held the knife. Harry looked up to find the guard down on one knee, struggling to regain his feet, and Sara lifting Hathor's rock to finish the job. She lifted it high, and then suddenly her body jerked and Sara collapsed, gasping, as the guard's fist connected with her gut. Harry twisted the bearded man's arm and the guy screamed, dropping the knife. Harry booted it aside and darted toward Sara.

He had taken only two steps when a meaty hand latched onto his collar, yanking him backwards. His feet flew out from under him and, arms windmilling, he collided with bearded man. Harry headbutted the man, ducked a wild haymaker and landed a shot to the guy's chin with his reinforced fist. Bearded guy went down.

Harry spun to find Sara escaping from the guard's grasp. The guard lunged to grab her, got a hand on her foot and sent her sprawling.

The air shifted behind him. Bearded guy was back on his feet, coming at Harry with the knife out. Harry twisted sideways, the knife whistling past. He grabbed the assailant's arm and threw bearded guy at the beefy guard. The two thugs collided with a gristly thump. The guard's eyes widened, his mouth falling open. Bearded man backed off to reveal the knife handle sticking out of his partner's chest.

The guard looked up at bearded man. His mouth stayed open as he fell, hitting the ground with a thunderous crash. Directly on top of Sara.

Harry grabbed the bearded man's shirt, pulling him back at the same time his reinforced fist flew straight for the guy's chin. Ceramic hit bone and this time the man's eyes rolled up in his head as he dropped.

Sara's muffled curses filled the air as she extricated herself from beneath the guard. Harry reached over and lifted one thick arm to help her get free.

"My wrist!" Sara grabbed at her left arm. "That bastard broke my wrist." She clutched the injured arm to her chest, her jaw tight.

"Hold it still." Harry knelt by the unconscious bearded man. "Maybe I can figure out who this guy was."

"He didn't just want the message," she said. "He wanted to kill us."

"Stefan sent him." A search of the unconscious man's pockets revealed a cell phone, a wad of Egyptian pounds and nothing else. No identification, and nothing remotely tied to an Albanian gangster.

Harry finished checking the man's pockets and stood. "You think he had this guy listen to us to see what he could hear?" Harry grabbed the bearded guy's phone, using the man's thumb to unlock it. He then disabled the password and pulled up the recent call log. "There are only two calls in the history, one incoming from earlier today and one outgoing." Harry looked up. "Ten minutes ago."

"When we discovered the scarabs concealed a message." She grimaced. "You think he called Stefan."

Harry pocketed the phone. "We'll worry about that later. We have to move."

"Stefan could be headed to Karnak right now."

"Where he'll get stuck trying to figure out what comes next." Harry put a hand on Sara's back and guided her toward the exit. "He's not a trained Egyptologist. He doesn't know this country like you do. I wouldn't bet on him figuring it out any time soon. Which is good, because we're going to the hospital. And I'm staying with you." Massive pillars passed on either side as they hurried into the front courtyard. "Antony and Cleopatra can wait."

"Are you certain?" she asked hesitantly. "I can handle a broken wrist myself."

"I'm certain." His tone brooked no disagreement. "I made the wrong choice before. I'm not doing it again."

A thin smile emerged through the pain. "It appears I really can count on you."

Chapter 20

Hospital near Dendera

Monitors beeped with reassuring monotony. The scent of industrial-strength cleaning agents hovered in the air. Harry shifted in the rock-hard plastic chair beside Sara's cot, careful to avoid the intravenous lines snaking across her body. The emergency room doctor had quickly determined Sara's wrist was indeed fractured. Surgery would be required to insert several pins to help the broken bones heal, and through a stroke of good timing the orthopedic specialist had been on duty and available to perform the procedure tonight, which would see her released with a cast the next day.

Sara signed the last of a seemingly endless stream of paperwork required by the hospital bookkeepers.

"That is the last one," a unit nurse said to her in Arabic. "The anesthesia team will be in shortly."

Sara stared glumly at her arm. "I can't believe this. We were so close."

"Don't worry." Harry realized he was reaching for the amulet around his neck. His hand quickly fell back to his lap.

"I saw that."

He made a motion to say *Saw what?* and lifted his eyebrows.

"The amulet," Sara said. "You're thinking about the trail. About Karnak."

"Perhaps I am. You feel like taking me through your thoughts before the operation? We have time."

"I do." A flash of life came into her eyes. "I've been thinking. Read your notes back to me."

Harry pulled up the message translation on his phone. "*Visit the selected place follow Amun-Ra's ferocious guardians toward his duty start for sixty rods to find Thoth's power below seek his mystery to reveal power with golden discs.*"

"That's what I recall it saying. Karnak was known as 'the most selected of places' in ancient Egypt, and it's connected to Luxor Temple by the Avenue of Sphinxes. Sphinxes are Amun-Ra's guardians, and there's little doubt they are ferocious."

Harry had been thinking about the message as well. "Amun-Ra is a solar god. One of his roles was carrying the sun across the sky each day in his chariot."

Sara raised an eyebrow. "Well done. That was his *duty*. Which started each day when the sun rose above the horizon. Where did that occur?"

Relic hunters without a keen sense of direction didn't last long. "In the eastern sky. I'd guess the message is telling us to go east from the Karnak end of the sphinx road."

"I agree."

Harry rubbed his chin. "Any chance you can tell me how long a rod is? I hope we're not talking about miles here."

"The Egyptian rod is equivalent to approximately fifty meters. If we're correct, Cleopatra wants you to travel three thousand meters beyond the end of the Avenue of Sphinxes at Karnak in an eastern direction."

"You've been to Karnak." He paused. "Haven't you?"

"I'm an Egyptologist *from* Egypt. Yes, I've visited the site."

"What's three thousand meters east of Karnak if you go from the end of the sphinx road?"

"Three thousand meters is slightly under two miles." She closed her eyes. Beeping counted the seconds for quite some time until she opened them again. "Nothing."

"Nothing? I thought Karnak and Luxor Temple were beside the city of Luxor."

"They are. Karnak is north of Luxor. Both hug the Nile, like most

Egyptian cities. Travel any distance away from water and there is nothing but desert. Which is well within sight of the city, and near the outer edges of civilization, but it is desert nonetheless."

Harry recalled the last time he drove between Egyptian cities. Civilization to start, then nothing but endless desert as far as he could see, interspersed with the occasional pyramid or ruins until the next city appeared on the horizon. The Nile breathed life into Egypt. "That's good."

"Most of the desert has never truly been explored," Sara said. "Why venture so far from the water only to find more sand?"

"Which tells me there's a good chance nobody's ever taken a close look at the desert two miles outside Karnak."

Now they knew roughly where to look, and evidence suggested Cleopatra had chosen her hiding spot wisely, that maybe whatever she'd left was still there. Which left him with an even more intriguing question. "What the heck are we looking for?"

"*Thoth's power below.*" Sara lifted her wounded arm and grimaced. "Ouch. This hurts."

"You ever break a bone before?"

"Only one ankle, a collarbone, two ribs and one finger. No, two fingers."

Harry couldn't think of a single thing to say.

A glimmer of a smile crossed her face. "The fingers were from kickboxing. The ribs were from a bicycle accident, and the other happened when I fell while mountaineering."

Harry rallied. "A man trying to kidnap you, working with a man trying to kill me. Don't sell the situation short." He quickly looked away. *Nice work, dummy. Keep bringing up all the bad stuff.* A surefire way to scare her back to Germany for good.

"If you put it that way, then I suppose this is quite the badge of honor." She waved her arm around and once again immediately regretted it. "Ouch."

Harry winced in sympathy. "If the desert is empty, I assume we need to look underground."

"Logical. No cliffs, mountains or water to conceal anything. *Thoth's power* will be located beneath your feet."

"Any idea what it is?"

"Thoth is typically depicted as a man with the head of either an ibis or a baboon. Any sign of those is an indicator of the correct path. He's the god of the moon, writing, science and magic, among other subjects."

"Maybe it's a magic lamp."

"That particular folktale dates to the eighth century. Over eight hundred years after Cleopatra died. But if you find it, save some wishes for me."

"My money would be on writing or science," Harry said. "Cleopatra was an educated woman. What did she value? Knowledge, because knowledge brings power. And beauty, in a harsh world."

Sara lifted an eyebrow. "Well said."

"What sort of scientific knowledge do you hide under the desert?"

"Something you believe is consequential enough to save your children when you are no longer there to protect them." Sara shrugged. "Or perhaps I'm biased because I know how their war ends. It could be Antony and Cleopatra had other reasons for leaving this trail. The only one we know with certainty is that this is meant for the twins."

"Is Thoth tied to any specific mysteries?"

"None I can recall."

"At least the golden discs part is clear." Harry touched the amulet around his neck. "We need these. Good thing you brought Nora's."

Sara reached under her shirt with her good arm and lifted the second golden amulet out into the light. "You mean good thing you convinced me."

It had taken some doing, but Harry never went against his gut, and before they left New York his gut had told him Nora's amulet would come in handy. How, he couldn't exactly say, but he'd learned to heed that inner voice. "Every once in a while I get something right." He leaned in and gently rubbed the golden disc. "Which means you have to get better so we can get to Karnak."

She blinked. "What do you mean?"

Harry gestured to encompass the entire room. "Better. Your wrist. You know. Better."

"You can't wait for me."

"Can't wait for you? Of course I'm waiting for you. We're in this together. You'll be better in a week."

"You don't have a week. We're losing this race. You can't stop now."

"I said I'm waiting, and going out in the field with a broken wrist is crazy. We have no idea what we'll face." Harry aimed an authoritative finger at her chest. "You've only done this a few times, and think about what you've seen already. Collapsing caverns, burning oil, unstable bridges." He figured that was a good place to stop. "I'm not leaving you here."

The lines framing the corners of her eyes softened. She blinked once, then pulled a loose strand of hair behind one ear. "Harry, you aren't leaving me. You're *listening* to me. I want you to go."

What was in that I.V. bag? "I'm not leaving." He spoke clearly, his voice even. "I'm staying. Here. With you."

Sara shook her head once. "No."

"I thought you were on the team again. Ready to finish what we started." His shoulders slumped. "Don't you want to come?"

"I would give anything to come with you. Anything." Now she took his hand, her fingers warm on his. Her face hardened and her words seemed to punch straight through him. "But this is what you've been searching for, Harry. To discover what *these* mean." She let go of his hand and touched her amulet first, then his. She took his hand again. "I don't believe in destiny, but if there is such a thing, this is yours. You've come too far to let it slip away. You're Harry Fox. This is what you do. Find Cleopatra's message."

His fingers tightened around hers. "You have to realize something. You're smarter than anyone I've ever met. Way too smart for a guy like me. This is our chase, not mine. I didn't come all this way just to lose you again." His gaze dropped to the bedsheet on her cot. "I'm not leaving." One corner of his mouth turned up. "I can miss hints with the best of them."

"Let me spell it out for you." She lifted her good hand from his and then let it pause in midair. "Actually, you're a reader. You can see for yourself. Here." Sara dug in her belongings and came out with her phone, which she aimed at her face to unlock. "Open my email," she instructed.

Sara had never asked him to do that. His internal alarm bells clanged madly. "Why?"

"I need you to send a message for me." She touched her wounded wrist. "I'd do it myself if I could."

The silent alarm became deafening. "Who should I send it to?"

"Check the drafts folder. The first one."

He navigated to the proper section and found a single message in draft status. Addressed to a name he didn't recognize. "Who is Laurel de Voogt?"

"The curator of the Anthropology Division at the American Museum of Natural History."

He looked at the actual message. His stomach dropped. "No way." Two sentences later, he tore his eyes from the screen. "You're kidding."

"I am most certainly not kidding." She pointed at her phone. "Read it."

He looked back at the screen. Harry rubbed his eyes, the inner alarm silenced. "'Dear Dr. de Voogt, I am pleased to inform you I accept your offer. I look forward to beginning the next phase of my career as the staff Egyptologist and Curator-in-Charge of Asian and African Ethnology.'" His voice trailed off as he tried to process what it meant. "Are you serious? I didn't think you wanted the job after what happened in Norway."

"I didn't." She pointed a finger at his chest. "Now I do. Because of you. Send the email to Dr. de Voogt."

"Because of me? I nearly got you killed."

"Yes, and I have not yet forgiven you for that. Not entirely." Her words came faster now, though with a softness he thought she had lost in Norway. "Being kidnapped made me question everything. What was I doing? Why was I here? How could I possibly think this is what I wanted?"

"Because it's awesome," he said without thinking.

"Be quiet," she admonished. "I doubted myself, and for the past few weeks I've been questioning everything. The sorts of questions that aren't answered at once. I thought I had everything I wanted in Germany." Sara leaned back from him and lifted a shoulder. "Turns out I was wrong. Now I realize Germany was the beginning. A stop on the path. A path I intend to follow to the end."

His beleaguered mind finally shifted into gear and caught up. "A path to Brooklyn?"

"If you don't make me change my mind. I still haven't officially accepted the job."

Harry tapped the phone screen. "Too late now. It's official."

"Then I'm committed. Now show me you are too." She pulled the leather strap holding Nora's amulet over her head. "Take this. Go to Karnak. Solve this mystery. Then tell me all about it when you come back."

He didn't move, didn't blink. The sterile air cooled his suddenly warm skin. Harry closed his fingers around the second amulet, and as his tongue wasn't currently up to forming words, he nodded.

"I'll take that as a yes." Sara crossed the one good arm over her chest. She looked down at his pants pocket. "Your phone hasn't stopped buzzing for the past minute."

"My what?" He shook his head, realized his leg was rattling. "Who the heck is calling me?" He kept a tight hold on Nora's amulet as he pulled the device out. "It's Rose Leroux."

"Is that bad?"

"Hard to tell." He pulled the flimsy curtain surrounding Sara's makeshift bed closed as he connected the call. "Rose, it's Harry. What's going on?"

"Stefan's safe deposit box was accessed only a single time." Rose rattled off the date, then waited. "Does the date mean anything to you?" she finally asked.

Harry closed his eyes. "Help me out. I'm in the middle of something else right now."

"It is not more important than this." Rose repeated the date. "The date is two days after your father's murder."

The possibility crashed into his head. "Stefan took the Archimedes documents from whoever killed my dad." Silence filled the air, broken only by the incessant beeping of various machines attached to Sara.

"What is that noise?" Rose asked. "Where are you?"

"In an Egyptian hospital with Sara. Her wrist is broken."

"How did that happen?" Rose asked.

"Long story," Harry said. "I'll tell you later. Back to the artifact. If Stefan acquired it two days after my dad died, he must have purchased or stolen it from whoever murdered him."

"I agree." The discreet sound of metal rasping on metal rattled in his ear, then burning tobacco crackled and Rose exhaled with a sound of pleasure. "If the Archimedes artifact is what Fred was after in Rome. It's possible this is all a coincidence."

"It's what my dad went after. It has to be." Stefan knew the artifact in his safe deposit box was tied to Fred. That's why he had given Rose the access code—to send a message Harry couldn't ignore. It looked like Stefan would get what he wanted.

"I appreciate you telling me," Harry said.

"I know what violence lives inside Stefan. Life has not been kind to him. Which is no excuse," Rose said quickly. "I still hope he can change."

"The deposit box is bait," Harry said. "If he can tell me anything about who killed my father, I have to go."

"Look at Dr. Hamed before you leave, and consider this. One Fox man is already dead because of this relic. Do not become the second."

"I won't." Harry clicked off, set his phone down and reached into his pocket. "There's one more call I have to make." The phone he'd pulled from their assailant's pocket came out. "Whoever hired those two guys called this phone. Agreed?"

"It would make sense," Sara said.

"Which means I have his number, and suggests he likely wasn't at Karnak. If he had been, you'd think he would have come after us himself. I say we don't keep him waiting for his call any longer. I want to know why we're so dangerous. What makes him so worried about us that he hires men to kill us?"

"Perhaps an offer of a truce is in order."

Harry pulled up the call log. "Something tells me this isn't the sort of guy who's interested in peace."

He tapped the screen, calling the single number listed. Harry put it on speaker and soft beeping filled the air. The call rang again, then a third time. The fourth ring made it only halfway before a hard, gravelly voice answered. "Is it done?"

Harry's breath evaporated. Sara covered her mouth. They both knew that voice. *Stefan Rudovic.*

"Is it done?" Stefan asked again.

Harry licked dry lips. "No."

Silence. A soft crackling was the only indication Stefan hadn't hung up.

Harry went on. "It's not done. We're alive, Stefan. I got your message from the bank deposit box. Where did you get those sheets?"

"Get what?"

"The artifact." Harry went all in now, outlining everything he knew. "That's what my dad was after in Rome. The papers ended up in your New York safe deposit box two days after he was murdered in Rome, which means you know who had them. Tell me their name." No response. "It's why you gave Rose the security code. To get me here. So what is it you want, Stefan? Do you want the amulets? The information we found at Karnak? You always want something. Tell me what it is. Maybe we can make a deal."

"You have no idea what you are talking about."

"I'm talking about my dad's murder. You're lucky I'm willing to negotiate."

Stefan's words were bony dice rattling across a stone floor. "Is that meant to frighten me?"

"It's meant to give you a chance to have a new life. Your old one is gone. You already get to spend the rest of your life running from Altin Cana's retribution. You want to worry about me as well?"

"You have nothing I want."

"What about the truth about my amulet? Does that sound good?" Sara nearly exploded off the bed at that, only settling down when he mouthed *I'm lying*.

"The amulet is a trinket. Keep it. Sell it for all I care. I already know where this path leads, and I am ahead of you. How? My man overheard you and your woman in Dendera."

Harry didn't bite. "You still have to figure out what Cleopatra's message means." He couldn't resist a dig. "You were always second-rate. I'm not worried."

"Second-rate? Perhaps I am, but you—you are nothing, Harry Fox. Propped up by your father and Vincent Morello. Handed everything. That is all you are—a man with no talent. Without them, you are nothing. Run back to your new owner, to Joey Morello. Put a flower on his father's grave from me."

Harry didn't rise to the bait. "You can have whatever's in Karnak. Tell me who sold you the artifacts in that deposit box. That's who I want to find. Not you. Not anymore."

"You want the answer? Find me. Then we talk." The line went dead.

Harry turned back to Sara, jamming the phone into his pocket.

"He wants the amulets," Sara said. "It's what he's always wanted, because he knows they're valuable, but has no idea how valuable they truly are. That's why he mentioned your father and Vincent Morello. To make you mad."

"It worked."

Sara reached out her good arm and took his hand. "You can't let it.

Emotion has no place in the field. Your father told you that."

"That's why I'm going to Karnak."

"You are?" Sara shook her head quickly. "Right. I'm glad you finally listened."

"I'm not going because I'm angry. I'm going because he wants whatever Antony and Cleopatra left behind. Get that, and then he'll come running to me, ready to talk."

Sara's mouth tightened. "You'll be careful." It wasn't a question.

"I'm always careful."

"No, you're not, which is what worries me." She let go of his hand. "But it also makes you Harry Fox."

"I'll be back." He held the second amulet in front of her. "I have to give this back to you. It'll make quite the statement at your new job." His voice darkened. "When we have *Thoth's power*, Stefan will tell me what I need to know. Who sold him the artifacts. And maybe I'll figure out who killed my dad."

Chapter 21

Karnak

Dawn's first light broke on the horizon as Harry turned the key in the ignition of his rental car and headed for Karnak. Leaving last night would have been better, but his body had been having none of it and left him no choice. A wave of exhaustion had hit him after Sara was taken to surgery, and the next thing he knew after she had been wheeled away was a nurse shaking him awake in the empty bed he'd commandeered on the other side of Sara's hospital room. Thankfully, the nurse hadn't woken him until she needed the bed for another patient early in the morning. She had placed a finger over her lips and pointed across the room to where Sara lay in her own bed once again, her arm heavily bandaged, fast asleep. Harry thanked the nurse profusely before giving Sara a soft kiss on the forehead as he tiptoed out. The newest curator at the American Museum of Natural History didn't move, zonked out from painkillers and whatever else they put in you to fix a busted wrist.

The normally hour-long drive took him barely half that and likely put their rental car one trip away from the scrapyard. Harry never took the gas pedal off the floor as he raced from Dendera to Karnak, pulling into a dusty parking area along the western edge of the site before it opened for the day. Not that he would have any trouble getting into the site before then, he thought, looking around in amazement. The government could post a hundred guards and they would only be able to cover a small portion of the exterior entrances. This place was *gigantic*.

The vast, open complex consisted of four main sites, though only the area known as the Precinct of Amun-Ra was open to the public. Harry stepped out of his vehicle, looking over one shoulder to a modern village nestled between the complex and the Nile as he put on a backpack containing a few items that could prove useful, depending on what lay ahead. Beyond the village, a mile distant to the south, the city of Luxor was coming to life, along with the world-famous Luxor Temple outside of which Sara had nearly met her doom a few months earlier while uncovering one of Cleopatra's hidden messages.

Harry patted one pocket as he walked toward an opening in the thick walls, a baseball cap shielding his face from the sun. The warm ceramic of his knuckledusters against his skin soothed his worried soul. Yet when he looked over his other shoulder to the west, nothing but empty sand waited. Sloping hills in the desert impeded his view, really nothing more than sand piled atop dirt baked to stone. If Stefan was out here, he was keeping to the shadows.

But the desert was where he had to go. Where Antony and Cleopatra had hidden *Thoth's power*. A place where the only thing he could see was sand. A place nobody in their right mind would want to explore. His lip curled up. Exactly the sort of place to hide a secret.

Scampering footsteps sounded behind him. Harry spun around as someone grabbed his pantleg and pulled on it. He flinched, then frowned. A child had hold of his pant leg, small fingers clinging to the fabric as the boy showed bright teeth. About the only clean part of him. The word that came to mind was *urchin*.

"Guide? Want guide?" the boy chattered excitedly in rough English, then switched to Arabic. "*Murshid Siahiun?*" he asked. "Tour guide?"

Harry responded in the boy's native tongue. "*La, la.*" No, no.

The boy switched back to English. "Guide? I be your guide."

"No, I'm good." Harry pulled an American bill from his pocket, a twenty. "Here you go." He left the kid wide-eyed, staring at the wealth clasped in his hands.

Harry pulled out his phone and consulted a map of Karnak. The wall encircling this site ran for hundreds of yards in either direction, with signs in front of it at intervals directing visitors toward the main gate. With only the western section of the site open to public access, he could enter through the main gate and sneak his way to where the Avenue of Sphinxes abutted Karnak's exterior wall, or he could stay outside the walls and venture toward the closed southern entrance. He considered. The last guard he'd come across had tried to kill him. Outside it was.

Karnak sat further off the Nile than Luxor, which allowed modern civilization to develop in the crucial space between Karnak and the waters. Densely packed urban housing abutted a dirt road in front of the temple walls, stone and concrete buildings crammed together with no respect for any sort of building or fire code. Clotheslines hung with laundry filled the narrow spaces between two-story structures. Some of the buildings had holes in their roofs, which allowed Harry to peer through the broken windows and see blue sky above. A few of those same broken windows framed anxious faces, peering down at the man walking through what might generously have been called their yard. Eyes darted away or relaxed as they took stock of him. For once, his Pakistani heritage helped him blend in.

He hugged the shade of a hardy palm tree. The sun had barely risen and already sweat beaded on his forehead. He jumped when a dog barked from the shadows. *I'm not bothering you, buddy. Don't bite me.* His footsteps quickened, keeping the dirt road to his left and the local homesites to his right until the Karnak wall ended at a ninety-degree angle. He stopped.

He could turn left and continue to follow the temple wall. Several hundred yards ahead, the wall jutted out from its straight line and turned ninety degrees before disappearing into the rubble of several collapsed statues. He had two choices. Clamber over the fallen stones and bricks until he reached the closed southern entrance and risk running into a guard, or venture into the heart of this ragged urban village until he found a way onto the Avenue of Sphinxes ahead. An image of the guard popped into his head again, this time with a knife handle sticking out of his chest.

Village it was. Harry headed for an alley with fewer shadows than the others and plunged into the village, one eye on the sky to keep a sense of direction. The narrow streets and tight quarters made the buildings seem to lean over him the moment he walked into their shadows, blocking out most of the sky overhead, their windows like empty eyes looking down on this foreign interloper. It didn't help that a new group of ragged children raced across his path every few steps. The kid he'd paid off earlier did not reappear. Harry could have used his help right about now. At least he'd have some street credit with the little guy.

Harry navigated the mazelike thoroughfares. He made a few false starts until he found a way ahead. People on the way either stepped back into their doorways or turned away as he walked by, murmured Arabic words that never quite reached his ears. His intermittent glimpses of the sky nearly vanished completely now under the crisscrossing clotheslines. Twice, he had to hurdle burned-out barrels discarded in the middle of the street. Dusty scooters with chains running through the wheels leaned against pock-marked walls. One more turn. Harry skirted a rusted bicycle frame and slipped between a pair of incongruently vibrant green trees to find the Avenue of Sphinxes in front of him.

Rectangular stone platforms stood at attention on either side of the ancient thoroughfare. All that remained of the regal sphinxes that had once sat atop them were a few decrepit haunches or collections of stones heaped on top of the platforms in haphazard fashion, broken Legos waiting to be put back together. Nothing like what Sara had described during her earlier adventure near Luxor Temple, where a refurbishment of the long avenue connecting the towns had restored the road to its former glory. Clearly the money had run out before the restorers made it to this side. Harry shielded his eyes against the sun and looked south toward Luxor.

Children's high-pitched voices rang out from behind him. Harry looked back and children scattered into the shadows. He touched the amulet around his neck without thinking. The weight of the second amulet, tucked in a back pocket, offered reassurance, as did the one under his shirt. They had to bring luck, he reasoned, here in their homeland, perhaps not far from where they'd been crafted. The question was, what kind?

He shook his head. What had his dad said? *You make your own luck.* Harry pulled out his phone and used the compass app to verify that the expanse of hilly, blinding emptiness in front of him lay to the east. Leaving the cool shade behind, he set off down a gentle slope leading to the avenue, passing between two empty sphinx platforms and onto the stone walkway. To one side lay the ancient southern entrance to Karnak, currently closed to the public. Thick metal bars made it clear nobody would be going in or out that way for some time. To the other side, the Avenue of Sphinxes extended for over a mile until it ran smack into Luxor Temple. Seventy years spent restoring the path hadn't included adding any sort of cover, and with the sun only getting hotter, he couldn't see anybody within a mile of him.

Now, how to get into the desert. He looked back over a shoulder. He squinted. *It could work.*

The village alleys and shadows didn't seem so tight when he retraced his route. Children who had been following him from a safe distance gained confidence, coming closer, whispering and pointing at him. He stopped in the middle of the road, looking at the front door of a building he'd passed earlier that looked a bit less likely to fall down than most. A building he'd passed earlier. Two scooters were chained to the front of it. He stood there and waited. It didn't take long for the first child to come closer.

"*Man yaeish huna?*" Harry asked him.

The kid jumped at Harry's words, but didn't run away. Harry pointed at the house and repeated his question in Arabic. "*Man yaeish huna?*" Who lives here?

A second child emerged from the shadows behind him, younger and even skinnier than the first. "'*afeal,*" she said. *I do.*

Harry bent down on one knee. What he hoped was a reassuring grin met her wide eyes as he spoke slowly in Arabic. "Does the scooter belong to your parents?" he asked. The girl nodded. "Are they inside?"

"Mother is inside. Father is paradise."

"I would like to talk to your mother. I will give you a present if you get her." He pulled a dollar bill from his pocket. "Here."

Her mouth opened, she edged forward, and the little girl stared at the dollar with a look that bent his heart in half. "Please tell your mother I would like to talk to her." He nodded toward the front door.

The girl took the money and dashed up the steps and through the flimsy door. The other children huddled in the shadows whispering and pointing at him, though none approached. Good thing, because he was out of singles. It seemed his gesture had been accepted, for the door opened and a woman who looked hardly old enough to vote walked out. A soft-colored hijab covered her hair, while the flowing robe wrapped around her slender frame was clean, if well-worn. She held his gaze as Harry approached, stopping a respectful distance short of her front door. He kept his voice low.

"Hello." Again he spoke in Arabic. "My name is Harry. Thank you for speaking with me."

"I am Menna." She touched her chest, then the head of the little girl at her side. "This is Engy." Menna nudged her daughter forward. "Go on," she prompted. "Tell him."

Harry took another step forward and knelt to Engy's level. "What do you want to tell me, Engy?"

"Thank you," Engy said. "You are very kind."

"You're welcome. You're a very polite young lady."

The giggle his words elicited might have been good or bad. Not like he could tell. "She is shy at first," Menna said. "But she is learning."

"She's doing just fine," Harry said. "May I speak with you?"

Menna's response was guarded. "What is it?"

Harry pointed to the chained scooters. "Are those yours?"

"Yes."

"I would like to borrow one," Harry said. "I'll pay. Only for the day. I'll return it before the sun sets." He pointed east. "I have to go into the desert. Too far to walk."

Menna gave him a look he could only describe as calculating. "The desert is dangerous."

"That's why I would like to borrow it." He put a hand on his pocket. "How much will you pay?"

He thought of an amount, then added half again. "One hundred fifty dollars for one day."

Menna didn't hesitate. "Five hundred."

Harry nearly stepped back. "That's outrageous."

He couldn't see it, but he swore she smiled. "Do you see any other vehicles for rent?"

"Two hundred," Harry countered.

"Four hundred ninety-nine."

Harry grinned to himself. He could play this game. Numbers ping-ponged back and forth until the price was agreed upon.

"Three hundred," Harry said. The scooter wasn't worth half that, but she had him over a barrel and knew it.

Menna frowned. "Agreed. You will bring it back today?"

"I promise. I'm going two miles into the desert."

"There is nothing out there," Meena said. "Why do you wish to go and see nothing?"

"There's more out there than you can see."

Menna shrugged. Harry handed the cash over. It disappeared into the folds of her robe. "The petrol tank is full. May Allah watch over you."

"Thank you." Harry looked to Engy. "Be good, little one. I will see you soon."

Menna produced a key from her robe. When she handed it to him, she looked at his face, searching his eyes. Then she stepped past him with rapid movements before another key came out of her robe. "We will be here," Menna said as she unlocked the chain securing both scooters to her home. "Tonight, for when you return it."

Harry maneuvered the scooter into the street, put the key in the ignition and turned it. A thundercloud of black smoke belched from the tailpipe, though after the first hiccup the engine rumbled smoothly. It certainly sounded as though this machine had been cared for, at least well enough for him to get two miles into the desert and back, but in truth Harry couldn't tell whether that whirling part was a fan belt or a flux capacitor, so he hopped aboard and hoped for the best. It wasn't like he had other options.

He touched the throttle.

"Wait," Menna shouted over the engine. "Take these." She handed him two bottles of water, which he put into his pack.

"Thank you," Harry said.

Menna leaned close, the engine noise muffling her words. Her mouth opened again and she hung close to him for a breath, her eyes on his. Then she looked left and right. "Be careful," she finally said. "It is not safe."

A cold streak zapped through his body. "What's not?"

Menna tried to speak without moving her lips. "People are not who they seem." That was all she offered before stepping back, her mouth closed.

Harry held her gaze for a long beat, then motored off without another word, her warning ringing in his ears. *It is not safe.* Something had moved her to offer a warning, and it wasn't the desert she feared. A person had frightened her.

Chapter 22

Harry drove between buildings and emerged into the searing desert sunlight. He stopped when he reached the sloping ridge leading down to the Avenue of Sphinxes, looking left and right. No one in sight. Nothing but ancient ruins on either side and sandy hills ahead. He twisted the throttle. The bike's oversized tires handled the hill with ease, the machine juddering as he crossed the ancient roadway and drove toward Karnak, toward the last sphinx on the road. Or what was left of it. A single rear paw remained on the rectangular pedestal, with a pile of broken rock alongside it.

A pair of binoculars came out of his pack. Several hundred yards of desert scrub lay in front of him, and beyond that, sandy hills. The air shimmered as heat rose from the baked earth to distort a blue sky above. The mounds of sand weren't massive, no more than twenty feet high. He needed to get atop the first one to see what waited. Probably more sand. Two miles of it, at least. Harry stowed the binoculars, opened a GPS app on his phone to track his distance, and took off.

Sand assaulted him, the minuscule grains scraped his face and burned his eyes when he raced ahead. Harry quickly found out this scooter did two things very well. It handled desert terrain, and it rattled his backside like an earthquake. A few miles of this and he'd need a chiropractor if he made it back to Brooklyn. Harry gritted his teeth. Not *if.* When.

Hardy desert vegetation gave way to sand washed smooth by wind and time until he reached the base of the first hill, leaning forward when the front tire lifted to pull him up the sloping mound at speed. An explosion of blue sky appeared when he crested the hill. The scooter twisted slightly to one side when he braked and put a foot down, half his boot disappearing into the soft sand. Harry put a hand up to shield his eyes and looked ahead.

Dunes stretched out one after another for miles. A repeated rise and fall of sandy mounds reached to the horizon. More hills were visible in the distance to either side, an endless brown land with no sign of habitation. Some fifty miles distant the Red Sea waited, civilization on its shores, but for now he faced a seemingly endless expanse of inhospitable terrain. The sand looked hot enough to melt rubber.

It's only two miles. His phone revealed he'd made it a quarter mile. Harry touched the throttle, though his hand stayed on it, not turning. He spun and looked back.

Nothing. Then why had a chill just run up his spine? He shook his head and turned the throttle. On he went, up and down and the same again, until he made it ten hills farther into the desert. A check of his phone revealed another quarter mile to go. Sweat was pouring off him in rivers. He cracked one of the water bottles Menna had given him and chugged it in a single go. Good thing he'd brought his own canteen as well.

He gunned the engine and resumed his journey. When he went up what should have been the last mound, Harry found a long stretch of almost flat desert at the top instead of a sloped peak, extending for a hundred yards or so and forming a plateau surrounded by a slight edge. His phone confirmed the two-mile mark lay fifty feet ahead. He hit his mark, then cut the engine. Once his back stopped shouting he pulled an old friend from his pack. An extendable, flexible stick Sara had introduced him to while they were searching for a Viking burial mound. Flexible so it bent instead of breaking. Extendable because you could telescope it out, stick it deep into soft ground to see if anything solid lay beneath, hidden from sight, and then close it neatly back up again. Poke around long enough where there should be something and eventually you'd hit it with the stick.

He set his pack down, found the spot the phone said was precisely two miles from the Avenue of Sphinxes, extended the stick and jammed it into the sand. A foot down it stopped moving. About right for this area of desert, where the sand tended to have a depth of around twelve inches before you found hard earth. He pulled the stick out, took a step forward, then stuck it into the sand again. Another hit about a foot down. *This could take a while.*

A grid atop the ridge formed in his mind's eye, each section the length of a single stride in any direction. Step forward, use the stick, then move and do it again. The topography suggested the hard ground underneath should be at a consistent depth across the plateau. Find a spot that didn't follow the mold and then the fun started. Except digging out here in this oven would not be fun.

He moved west to east in a straight line until he reached the far edge. His phone said that this spot was a bit more than two miles, but these directions deserved a bit of leeway. At the plateau's edge he took a step to the south, turned to face west and started again. Back and forth, west to east then east to west. It was the work of an hour to cover half the search area. An hour under the merciless sun as Amun-Ra shepherded the fiery orb across the sky in his chariot. Menna's second water bottle and half of Harry's reserves later his steps grew heavier, the shirt on his back drying in the heat as quickly as he sweated through it.

Harry turned back toward the city, and began again, his stick going up and down with each step. Not quite halfway back he paused, kicking a hole in the sand to mark his spot before heading to his parked scooter and drinking greedily from the canteen. He wiped a hand across his brow, smearing gritty sand against his skin. Out came his binoculars for another check of the city. Traffic around Karnak had grown busy, tiny people in his lenses moving about the roads. A mile to the south Luxor was doing a brisk business despite the midday heat. If nothing turned up soon he'd have to head back for more water. Wait too long to hydrate and he'd never make it back.

He walked back toward the hole he'd made. A welcome gust of wind kicked up to catch the brim of his hat and fling it to one side. He reached for it, ducking and missing once as it tumbled away. One of his fingers finally snagged it as he pounced, loosing a string of four-letter words into the searing-hot air. He tried to jam the hat on his head with his free hand, misfired, and in a petulant fit rammed the stick hard into the sand, parking it so he could use both hands.

The pliable stick folded nearly in two. Electricity crackled through his body, lighting every nerve. He pulled the stick out. Another jab. Same result. He stepped to one side and tried again. This time the stick went down as usual. Harry dropped to his knees and began digging in the sand with two hands, scooping handfuls and flinging them into the air. On the third his fingernails nearly came off as he scraped hard ground. Dry dirt hardened to concrete over the centuries. Ground too shallow for this plateau. Now he scraped and brushed, hands whirling to reveal a rock-hard slab of earth right below the sand. He kept brushing, his breath coming fast until he realized. This ground was too hard, too flat. He gasped—and sucked in a mouthful of sand, coughing and hacking to wake the dead until it cleared. The ground was *wrong*. Another brush with his hand revealed the truth. It wasn't dirt. This was *stone*, and he'd just found an edge. An unnaturally straight edge.

Quick digging revealed a square piece of stone, perhaps four feet on each side. A line cut in the stone ran around the outer edge a few inches down from the top surface, giving the impression this wasn't one piece of rock, but two, one laid atop the other. His fingers wriggled into the opening. He squatted low, pushing against hard dirt and grainy sand until his grip was solid. Arms locked tight, he tried to stand and lift the stone. His tendons shouted, ready to snap as he pulled, his shoulders burning hot as he loosed a scream to the skies.

The stone shifted a few inches. Harry let go and fell back, gasping for breath. He stared at the rock, then scrambled to his knees and leaned over it again. Sweat stung his eyes as he peered at the rock, his nose inches from it. The top portion had separated from the bottom and was now sitting at an angle. *It's a lid.* The top piece had been laid over the bottom like a lid on a box. Harry's exertions had been just enough to lift the top part so it hung askew. A tiny sliver of darkness was visible now between the top and bottom portions. He put his hand close to the dark opening, then stopped. Images of sharp teeth or claws ripping his fingers came to mind. Slowly now, inch by inch, he edged his hand closer to the darkness.

Cool air leaked out. He grabbed a flashlight from his pack and aimed the beam into the narrow opening, leaning closer. His light revealed more stone, cut at an angle. He muttered a choice word before it hit him. *Stair.* That's a stair right in front of my face.

He put the flashlight away, gripped the stone lid and got down into a sprinter's stance until his feet found purchase in the dirt. Harry leveraged his entire body and pushed. Arms outstretched, feet scraping the dirt, he went nearly parallel to the desert floor as he heaved against the stone. The lid began sliding, revealing one step, then two, until momentum took over and the square lid slid sideways and fell to the dirt.

Dust filled the air as he scrambled to his feet and gazed down. A black square had opened in the desert, and a chasm yawned below him. Steps led into the darkness, descending in a straight line. Harry licked dry lips. *We found it.* He and Sara had unraveled Cleopatra's mystery, following the path she had woven so long ago to this anonymous sand dune.

He pulled his phone out, snapped a picture of the stairway to nothing and sent it to her with a caption of three words. *We found it.*

The backpack went back over his shoulders. Harry stood above the yawning darkness. These steps were *steep.* He squared his shoulders, took one last look at Karnak in the distance, and didn't move. His gut told him to be wary. Or was it the memory of Menna's opaque warning? Harry pulled the binoculars out and scanned in every direction. Nothing seemed amiss. Only a group of kids standing above the Avenue of Sphinxes looking his way. He adjusted the magnification and focused on one kid in particular. It was the ragged, smiling urchin who'd offered to be his guide.

He lowered the glasses. *They're just kids, Harry. Take it easy.* He stuffed the glasses back into his pack and began descending the stairs. *They're just kids.* Too busy trying to stay alive to bother anyone.

His worry vanished along with the sun as he went further into the gloom, flicking his flashlight on to reveal carved stone steps caked with dust leading into the ground. Walls of stone to either side roughly aligned with the width of this hill, yet twenty steps down the staircase showed no sign of ending as the side walls vanished and pillars appeared in their place. He'd traveled below ground level now, under the base of the hill and into the desert floor.

He shone his flashlight beam at the pillars. The round columns of cut stone marched away into the distant dark, supporting a ceiling which stretched for nearly a hundred yards, and only when Harry reached the last step could he get a true scope of the interior. The sweat coating his chest and neck turned to ice as his light played over distant walls. Antony and Cleopatra had saved their best for last.

Chapter 23

An Egyptian temple encircled him. The towering stone columns, each made of circular stones set one atop another, rose seven stories high. Stones the size of compact cars formed walls on both sides, far enough away that his flashlight beam barely touched them. Two statues twenty feet high stood guard ahead, one on either side of a passageway cut out of the far wall. A passageway tall enough for the statues to walk through, if they were so inclined. He turned and aimed his light overhead, following the ceiling from its origins at the steps he'd just descended to where it began to slope sharply down towards the far wall, nearly two stories over his head. That was the other side of the hill, what he'd have walked down if he kept going into the desert.

An entire temple had been built into the desert floor.

Harry stepped away from the staircase and turned. A sheer wall rose behind him. One with no doorways or openings. This was the front side of the hill he'd climbed on his scooter earlier. A thought sneaking around the edges of his mind chattered for attention as he studied the wall. Harry closed his eyes and let it come to him. Something was off. He opened his eyes. "No hieroglyphs."

The walls were smooth and unmarked. What Egyptian temple didn't have hieroglyphs? Facing ahead once more, Harry knelt and ran his fingers over the smooth stones underfoot, cut to fit together perfectly. He touched every block within reach. None moved, so he stood and took a tentative step forward. The floor held, but there were many ways to spring a trap.

One more step and then another produced nothing. Slowly, then with a confidence he didn't totally feel, Harry moved down the passage. Shadows shrank back from the beam of light guiding him, the still air harsh in his throat. Harry stopped at the entrance and gasped despite himself.

Dozens of statues filled the room ahead, lined along either side. He swung his flashlight beam up towards the far wall of the room, revealing another door at the far end. At least one more room waited ahead, then. But first, he had to get through this one and the army of statues standing guard.

An international army. Amun-Ra, Osiris and Isis stood together on one side of the chamber, along with a representation of Cleopatra as a deity; he'd seen plenty of these in Dendera. Beyond this Egyptian entourage was a Roman contingent, with Mars, Venus and Apollo. A male statue behind them looked an awful lot like Mark Antony with a beard, likely meant to show him as Jupiter. Harry almost chuckled at the ego of it all.

He turned and examined the statues on the opposite side of the room. No Egyptian or Roman gods to be found here. The first grouping appeared to be all Greek. Mighty Zeus holding a thunderbolt. Aphrodite, goddess of love. The hard-partying Dionysus in the second row, and Harry suppressed a shudder at the sight of Poseidon clutching a trident. More Greek gods stood behind the others. There were several he recognized but couldn't name. Mesopotamian and Persian deities, judging from their attire.

Plenty of gods, but no artifacts, tablets or other relics waited ahead. Nothing to tell him whether the path was safe. He stayed put, listening to the nagging feeling in his gut. This was wrong, all of it. Every other message on this trail had been protected in some fashion to stop anyone other than Antony and Cleopatra's twin children. Yet now it seemed he had reached the end of their journey and nothing stood in his way. Something was very wrong.

His footsteps echoed as he set off once more down the open aisle.

Nothing happened. He veered toward the closest statue. The biggest one, as well. Cleopatra, in the guise of Isis. One arm at her side, the other holding a scepter, Cleopatra sported an ornate ceremonial headdress big enough to crush Harry flat. The statue's arm appeared solid, not hinged in any fashion. In fact, the statue looked to be carved from a single marble block. No hidden chambers or moving parts to slice him in half.

A quick inspection of the other statues found them much the same. He pulled a lighter from his backpack and lit every second torch mounted on the side walls, leaving the others for later in case his search took longer than anticipated. The second doorway lay ahead. His pocket buzzed as he approached it. A text message from Rose Leroux. He tried to open it, but the connection down here wasn't great, so it didn't load. Apparently she'd sent him a picture. It would have to wait. He stepped to the threshold of the next room. He put the phone away and stared.

Three pillars stood in front of him, each one taller than the last as he looked from left to right. The lowest column was in front of Harry, sitting in the middle of the room with a short staircase leading up to a flat, rectangular platform. To one side of the first platform was a second platform, which was the same size as the first but ten feet higher. There should have been a longer set of stairs leading up to it, but there was not. Beyond this second column was an even higher third column. Again, there was no staircase connecting it to the second column. He swung his flashlight beam around, searching, and then paused it on something that stuck out from the edge of the top platform: a set of stairs, raised like a drawbridge to prevent access. He swung his beam down to the edge of the second platform and found another retracted set of steps there.

He stepped closer and shone his flashlight up, training it over the two raised staircases. He needed to figure out a way to lower them so that he could climb up to the second and third levels. The platforms were too high to merely jump up and grab, while the smooth stone that comprised them offered no handholds for climbing. Even if he did have climbing gear, which he did not, there was nowhere to attach a piton. And forget jumping the gap between pillars. The distance was too great, and if falling to the floor didn't kill him, the Harry-sized spikes below each set of stairs would.

Kneeling, he inspected the floor at his feet, then directed his flashlight beam along the stones leading to the first platform. All unremarkable. Life-sized statues of armed Egyptian soldiers lined the room on both sides. The floor beneath each row of figures was made of dark stone, while the path between the guards was a mix of light and dark stones. Pressure sensitive? Possibly. But which ones? Only one way to find out, a way Harry wasn't interested in trying. Not with those stone soldiers armed to the teeth.

Each Egyptian soldier held either a bow and arrow or two swords. Not stone weapons. Real ones. Metal swords with edges that looked capable of slicing through bone. Wooden bows notched with metal-headed arrows under full draw. The statues with swords had hinged arms, which would allow the raised weapons to chop downward. There were enough armed figures here to discourage any attempt at sneaking through—or back, assuming an intruder was lucky enough to make it to the platform and the treasure it presumably held. Harry looked uneasily from the figures to the platforms to the doorway behind him. He was dead meat if even one of those things came to life.

Which left one choice. Move forward. The light stones seemed to be the key. He stepped into the room, taking care not to stand on a dark stone. His weight went cautiously onto the closest lighter stone. No swords swung or arrows flew, so he moved ahead onto another lighter stone. One of the soldiers farther down the line had lost his sword arm sometime in the distant past. The fallen appendage lay in front of him on the floor, sword still in hand. His phone vibrated. It might be Sara. He removed the device from his pocket to find another message from Rose Leroux. Harry opened it. Four words greeted him. *Do you recognize it?*

She must be talking about the picture she'd sent. He held the phone as high as he could, trying to strengthen the signal, and waited for the photo to load. He pulled the phone back down to face level, impatient. The caption beneath it appeared first. He frowned. *This was also in the bank box.* Nothing appeared for a breath. He held the phone back up again. A sharp pain arced across his back, so he slipped the heavy backpack off and set it on the floor. Still the picture didn't load. Biting back a curse and shoving the phone into his pocket, he looked around the room, following his flashlight beam. Torches lined the walls in here as well. He squinted. Was that a string hanging below them? It was. A string of some kind connected each torch, running the perimeter of the room. It could let a person light every torch from where they stood without having to walk among these stone warriors.

He tucked the flashlight into his waistband, pulled his lighter from a pocket and touched it to the nearest torch. Dry material crackled and sparked before it caught in a flash, light blooming as flames took hold. A beat later the string caught, and, with a series of muted bangs, flame sizzled from one torch to the next. In seconds the utter darkness vanished as torchlight bathed the room.

The Egyptian soldiers came into clear view now. Clear, terrifying view, their weapons gleaming and unforgiving eyes staring. Harry shook his head. *They're statues.* Don't get jumpy now. Not with that three-story deathtrap to climb. He began to move closer to it, and a line of text carved across the first steps came into view. Written in Greek, the language of Cleopatra. A list of three names.

"Athena, Minerva, Thoth." Three gods from three different cultures. Greek, Roman and Egyptian. What did it mean?

His phone vibrated and Harry grabbed it out of his pocket. The photo had loaded, at last. Harry looked at it, and everything changed.

He went still, the room forgotten as a black cloud filled his head. The memory of the night his entire life had changed. A night in Rome.

Harry turned and ran. Out of the torchlight, past the statues and toward the first long staircase, faster and faster toward the sunlight above, dialing Rose's number as he went and then pressing the phone to his ear. It rang when his foot hit the first stair. Her voice came through halfway up. "Rose." His words tumbled out breathlessly. "That was in the deposit box?"

"It was," she said. "Where are you?"

"Still in Egypt." He was nearly outside. "I recognize it." Sunlight pierced his eyes, blinding after the buried temple's underworld gloom. "It's his."

"Are you certain?" Rose asked.

Harry's response was lost in a roar. A mechanical rumble filled the air, accompanied by a billowing cloud of sand. He stepped backwards and nearly tumbled back into the open hole as a four-wheel-drive vehicle burst over the edge of the plateau and raced directly toward him, its wheels churning. Harry rolled, scrambling for the entrance before the vehicle crushed him. He slid down the stairs to safety, stopped and turned on the open staircase, and looked back up into the piercing light. The engine rattled to a stop as the rider killed the ignition, and a shadow appeared overhead to block out the sun. The shadow aimed a pistol at Harry. *Snick.*

"You have been busy."

Chapter 24

Harry bolted back up the stairs. He didn't think, didn't do anything except growl as he ran on a mission to destroy the armed man standing outside. Harry made it halfway out before something collided with the side of his skull and sent him staggering away. He gained his feet and spun around to face the intruder once more, taking another step before the ground in front of him erupted as a bullet slammed into it.

"Stop." Stefan Rudovic leveled a pistol at Harry's chest. "What did you find?"

Tinny noise came from the phone still clutched in Harry's hand. He stuck it in his pocket. "You did it."

Stefan blinked. "Did what?"

"The watch." Harry forced himself to spit the words out. "Rose found a watch in the deposit box."

"I see."

"It was his watch. His only one." Harry leveled a finger at Stefan. "A Rolex Submariner. My mom gave it to him at their wedding. He wore it everywhere. It has blood on it."

Stefan glanced away.

"You're the only person who ever accessed that deposit box. You only used it one time. My dad went to Rome to find the Archimedes text. That text ended up in your deposit box two days after he died. I thought you bought it from the person who killed him. But you didn't buy it. You took it. You killed my dad and took his watch."

"It was an accident."

"What happened?"

"A deal went bad."

Harry scoffed. "He would never make a deal with you."

The gun came back up. "Because I am not good enough?" Stefan spat at the ground. "Your father was nothing without Vincent Morello."

"You have no idea what happened between my dad and Vincent." Harry's hands tightened to fists. "My dad saved his life."

"I did not follow your father. I learned of a deal. The deal with the artifacts Rose found in the bank box. I followed the seller to Rome."

"So you could steal the artifacts?" Harry asked. Stefan nodded. "Who was the seller?"

"A nobody who did not realize what he had."

"Nobody who gets their hands on an Archimedes manuscript is smalltime."

"This man was a fool."

"Was he Italian?" Harry asked. "It happened in Rome."

"No," Stefan said. "He was from elsewhere in Europe. The man was so dumb he asked for advice on where to meet. One person told another person, and later that person told me. That is how I knew where to go."

"The Stadio Olimpico," Harry said. "Largest soccer stadium in the city. Italy played Russia that night."

"A smart place to meet."

"They found a bloody Russian team shirt near my father's body. Were you wearing it?"

Stefan hesitated. "Yes." His eyes narrowed. "Tell me what is down the steps."

"Go and see for yourself."

The gun waved. "You will move, or I will shoot you."

"Good luck not getting yourself killed down there. Besides, if you were gonna shoot me you'd have done it by now. What happened in Rome?"

Stefan's face somehow got uglier. "You will be sorry." He took a step back and switched the gun to his other hand. "I followed the other man toward the stadium. There were Russians and Italians everywhere."

"Their fans always look for trouble," Harry said. "A chump like you would fit right in."

Stefan pointed at the steps behind Harry. "What is that?"

Harry looked over his shoulder. "What is what?" He looked back. "There's nothing ther—"

Stefan's fist clattered off his jaw. Lights flashed across Harry's vision as he went down on one knee, hands on the dirt for balance. Harry massaged his jaw as he stood.

"I followed the seller to a café near the stadium," Stefan said. "I did not know who he was meeting. He sat at a table outside the café. I waited, then approached the seller's table. He thought I was the buyer."

"Until you tried to steal the artifact."

"The seller fought back. We struggled, then your father appeared." Stefan's eyes flicked away. "He tried to intervene. I pulled out my knife. To frighten, not to kill. We struggled and I tripped. I fell into your father." Stefan paused. "It was an accident."

"He'd be alive if you hadn't tried to steal the artifact. You went there with a knife. You're the reason he's dead."

"I did not intend to hurt him. Everyone ran after it happened."

"You took the time to steal my father's watch."

"The watch?" Stefan shrugged. "It was a nice watch. I am sorry I stole it."

"You left him on the street."

Stefan's face hardened. "He died before I knew what happened. I checked his pulse. I did not mean to kill him." The Albanian waved his gun at Harry. "How many have died because of you?"

Harry stood back, arms crossed on his chest. "I'm not helping you. Go ahead and wave that gun around all you want."

"You will help me."

Harry laughed. "You going to shoot me if I don't? You'll never understand Cleopatra's message without me."

"That is why you will help me." Stefan lowered the gun. "Not because I will shoot you. Because I will find the girl if you do not. She is in a hospital right now?" Harry's face must have betrayed him. "I will find her," Stefan said. "Not tomorrow or the next week, then one day in the future, I will shoot her. Unless you help me."

"All you'll do is shoot me when we're done."

Stefan shook his head. "No. This ends today."

A gust of wind blew sand across Harry's face. When it settled, he caught a glimpse of Luxor and Karnak in the distance.

"I'm going to solve this." Harry turned and walked to the staircase. "Either shoot me in the back or follow me."

Harry made it down the steps, then turned to find Stefan paused halfway down.

"What is this place?" Stefan asked.

"Antony and Cleopatra's hidden temple." Harry turned back to the path and moved toward the doorway ahead. "Hurry up."

Hurried footsteps smacked on the stairs and then followed Harry.

"Stop," Stefan ordered. "I go first." Harry paused, then stepped aside, putting his hands out in an invitation. Stefan stood closer to him, yet far enough away Harry couldn't reach the gun. "What is in there?"

"Statues. Gods, mostly. Egyptian, Roman, Greek, Persian, a few Mesopotamians. Cleopatra and Antony are here too." Harry aimed his flashlight around the room and Stefan followed his gaze. Satisfied, he gestured for Harry to start walking again.

"I'm not sure why they're here," Harry called over his shoulder. "The good stuff comes next."

Stefan kept pace as Harry strode to the final chamber. "Stop," Harry said at the threshold.

"This floor worries me," Harry said. He flicked his light off and set it down. "The center aisle is a different color stone. I wouldn't step anywhere else if I were you."

"How did you light the torches?" Stefan looked everywhere but at Harry, the gun now at his side, his eyes wide.

"A fuse connects them so they all catch." He bit back a smile. It sounded like this was Stefan's first hidden temple. Harry pointed to either side. "Those Egyptian soldiers have real weapons. Make a wrong move and I bet arrows start flying and swords start swinging."

"They move?"

Yep, definitely his first temple. "I've seen it before. Now stop being surprised and listen. There are pillars ahead—see the three levels?" Stefan nodded. "Those steps that can connect each level are pulled up like drawbridges. I think each level is a test. Pass the test and the steps lower so you can get to the next level."

"What if you fail?"

"No second chances." Harry pointed at the short staircase leading to the first pillar. "That says *Athena, Minerva, Thoth.* Three deities. One Greek, one Roman, one Egyptian." The names had been lurking in his thoughts. Alongside a nascent plan for revenge, he'd been mulling over the trio of gods. All hailed from different civilizations, had been created thousands of miles apart, yet, he now realized a common thread united each.

Harry turned to Stefan. "Do those names mean anything to you?" he asked.

Lines creased Stefan's forehead. "Athena and Minerva are female. Thoth is male."

"You have to do better than that if you want to survive." The gun leveled at Harry's face. "Or you could ask me." He stepped out of the line of fire and stared pointedly at the gun until Stefan lowered it. "Each deity represents a number of disciplines or virtues to their people. Greeks associated Athena with wisdom and warfare. Romans later adopted Athena, calling her Minerva and tying her to wisdom and war." He recalled the first two, as well as a laundry list of other ideas and disciplines. Sara would be helpful right now. "Thoth is an Egyptian moon god." Harry paused. "He's also the god of wisdom."

"All three gods tie to wisdom," Stefan said.

"I think it sends a message about how to survive this test." He tapped the side of his head. "Brains, not brawn. That gun won't help us."

Stefan stared down at the pistol and then back up at Harry, his eyes narrowed. "What if you are wrong?"

"You have any ideas?" A scowl came Harry's way. "Didn't think so."

The flickering torchlight cast long shadows across the temple as Harry moved toward the set of stairs leading to the first platform. He kept his eyes on the ground, careful not to stray off the center pathway of light-colored stones the color of dusty khaki pants. The ground didn't shift and no arrows flew. He made it to the stairs in front of the shortest column and paused, looking up at the taller column beside it, and up again to the tallest column beyond that one. Three columns of increasing height side-by-side. Too smooth to climb, too far apart to leap between them. He shook his head. Worry about the first column. The rest could wait. He walked up the steps to the flat level on top of it and stopped.

A mythical creature stood at the rear of the pillar. Female, cloaked in a long form-fitting robe. Harry could almost hear the noise of her writhing hair, feel the power emanating from this cursed creature who had once been a beautiful maiden. Versions of Medusa's story described her as a young woman, or as one of the three monstrous Gorgon sisters. No matter the legend, Medusa had been cursed as none before her, a woman who laid waste to anyone unlucky enough to be caught in her gaze.

"Medusa." Harry whispered it to himself.

"What?" Stefan called out from the stairs.

"It's Medusa. Snakes for hair, eyes turn you to stone. That Medusa." Stefan said something but Harry wasn't listening. He studied the Greek words inscribed on the base of Medusa's statue.

Only the symbol of he who violated Medusa will allow passage to what you seek.

"There's a message here," Harry called out. He read it aloud once, then again. "It's a test of knowledge. Antony and Cleopatra did this before." No harm in sharing anything now. It helped him think, and right now he needed to survive this temple. Then he could worry about surviving Stefan. "This path was left for their twin children."

"Antony and Cleopatra left a trail for their children?" Stefan asked. "Why?"

"That's what we're here to find out. Messages or markers we found earlier were written so that only those children—Cleopatra Selene II or Alexander Helios—could follow. The twins received classical educations far beyond the reach of average citizens. They would be well-versed in history, mathematics, religion, you name it. Hiding information by cloaking it in a veil of secrecy, decipherable only to someone with a classical education, was another safety measure to ensure only the proper people followed this trail."

"What does the inscription mean?"

Harry caught sight of a short stone pillar directly behind Medusa's statue. Waist-high, the top was flat and angled so Harry could see three images carved on the surface. He stepped over and ran a finger over them. "There's a pillar back here with three shapes on it." He touched one. "There's a Greek word above them." He read it. "It says *choose*."

Harry looked to one side, then the other. Medusa sat far enough back that the shadows almost obscured her. Now that his eyes had adjusted to the light he could make out holes cut into the temple's rear wall mere feet from the statue. Metal glinted inside each. "There are holes in the wall back here," Harry said. "Holes with spikes in them. Choose the wrong shape and these spikes fire out." Simple, yet ingenious. Because the pillar was tucked behind Medusa, he couldn't choose a Greek word to lower the next staircase without exposing himself to the spikes. "These are buttons," Harry said. "I bet I have to press the right one, and then that drawbridge staircase lowers so I can get to the next level."

"Choose one."

"Why don't you come up here and pick?"

"You choose first, then if you are wrong, I will try."

Harry grumbled, but the thought of Stefan going after Sara kept it short. The stale, dusty air choked his throat as he stared at the pillar. "Three images on this pillar. A sword, a shield and a trident." *Another trident.* He hated those things. "One of these symbolizes the person who *violated* Medusa."

"Tell me what you know about Medusa."

Harry shot Stefan a look. The gun came up in response. "Medusa's myth evolved over time. Originally she was one of three sisters, creatures called Gorgons. She was the only mortal sister. The myth changed over time to represent Medusa as a beautiful woman in the temple of Athena. She angered Athena, who turned her into a monster. Both versions end with Perseus cutting her head off."

"Which is the symbol of Perseus?"

"It depends." Harry touched each button as he spoke. "Perseus couldn't look at Medusa. Do that and he turns to stone. He used his shield as a mirror to watch her reflection so he could get close to her. Close enough to cut her head off with his sword."

"Choose the sword."

"But what if they mean the shield, which allowed Perseus to kill her?" Harry rubbed his chin. "Although every image I've seen of him slaying Medusa shows Perseus holding a sword."

"Then choose the sword."

"Hold on." He ran through the myth in his head once more, and it clicked. "It's not the sword. Or the shield."

"It is not the trident. You said Perseus carried a sword and a shield. No trident."

"Perseus didn't violate Medusa."

"He killed her."

"That's not the same thing. In the Roman version Medusa begins the story as a beautiful girl in Athena's temple. So beautiful that when Poseidon visited Athena's temple he assaulted her. Athena punished Medusa by turning her hair into snakes." Harry pointed to a button. "The twins would know Poseidon violated Medusa long before Perseus entered the picture. It's the trident."

Harry gritted his teeth, sent a hopeful prayer to any gods in the area and smashed the trident button. It dropped into the platform without hesitation.

The walls rumbled. Harry turned, jumped around Medusa and dove for safety as the ground rattled and ancient gears turned.

Chapter 25

BOOM. The floor rattled as he landed. Harry bounced, tumbling and twisting to avoid spikes that didn't come. He slid to a halt as a cloud of dust enveloped him.

"It worked," Stefan shouted.

Gritty sand made Harry's eyes burn. He got slowly to his feet, waving at the dusty cloud until it dissipated enough to reveal the staircase had crashed down into place, inviting him up to the second level.

"Never doubted it." Harry brushed the worst of the dust from his clothes.

Stefan mumbled something in Albanian and motioned to the stairs with his gun. "Up."

"You too scared to go first?" Stefan shoved Harry toward the steps. "Easy. I'm going." Harry passed the statue and stopped by one of the walls surrounding it, leaning close to peer into a hole. He reached in to touch the metallic tip of a spike inside. Still sharp. Still deadly. He backed off, a bead of blood on his fingertip.

"You might want to stay back," Harry said as he climbed the stairs. "I have no idea what's up here."

"If you try to run, I shoot."

"Yeah, yeah, I know." Stefan and his pistol vanished from Harry's thoughts as he ascended to the second pillar. Tiny clouds of powdered stone and sand floated down from the ceiling. The crash of the staircase falling into place had rocked the entire chamber. Harry looked carefully around him. No arrows were imbedded in any walls; the army of statues below had held their fire. He climbed the stairs to the second level and stopped, staring at his feet. An inscription ran beneath them.

"Facilis descensus Auerno:
noctes atque dies patet atri ianua Ditis."

"What?"

Harry jumped. Stefan had come up behind him. "It's Latin," Harry said. "A quote from the Aeneid." Stefan didn't react. "By Virgil," Harry continued. "It's the story of Aeneas, a Trojan who escaped Troy when the Greeks overran it. Eventually Aeneas's descendants became the Romans, including Julius Caesar." Still nothing from Stefan. "It's a myth. Roman propaganda, really. The question is why refer to it here."

Stefan pointed past Harry's shoulder. "Is that why?"

"It looks like a family tree," Harry said. "Or a map. What's that at the top?"

A series of lines had been cut into the floor. All straight, of different lengths and branching off from the lowest point in what resembled an inverted genealogical tree. Latin words were carved into the floor at each juncture where two lines met. A stone pole stuck out of the ground at the bottom near the Latin inscription Harry had recited. It could have been a staff, one that reached to Harry's chest. A square block on top of it had Latin written across the face. Harry ran his finger along the block as he translated. *"Aeneas.* He's the protagonist."

Stefan pointed at the step where the inscription was written. "Does this say more about him?"

Harry shook his head. "It's a quote from the book. *The gates of hell are open night and day; smooth the descent, and easy is the way.* Most people think it's about how easily people can lose their moral compass." Harry tapped the phrase. "Today, anybody with an interest in Roman history can access the internet to read Virgil's work. That wasn't the case in Antony and Cleopatra's time. Only the elite would recognize this quote from the Aeneid. It's another safeguard to prevent any unwanted visitors from making it up there." He pointed to the third level, still high enough to be out of view. "Medusa is a Greek myth. She came first, just as the Greek goddess of wisdom was listed first. Athena, then Minerva, the Roman goddess of wisdom." He indicated the quote. "This is in Latin. So are the words on this platform. Romans spoke Latin. We've proved our Greek wisdom. Now to prove our Roman wisdom." Again he rubbed the stubble on his chin. "Can you read Latin?"

"Why would I do that?"

"To double-check my translations." The stability of the platform's surface didn't worry him. Even so, the breath caught in his throat when he took a step out. It held. What had his interest were the channels cut into the floor to form a big upside-down family tree. The pole with *Aeneas* cut into it sat in the closest channel. Harry pulled out his phone to snap a picture of the interior. A message on the screen caught his eye. *Call lost.*

"Put the phone away."

"I need light to see inside." Harry slipped the phone in his pocket and pulled out his flashlight. "Chill out."

Stefan grumbled, but backed off. Harry leaned over the channel, moving the light this way and that to get a better look. "There are gears under the floor. I can't tell what they do." He stood up and pointed to the staff. "You know what I think this is? It's a joystick. Look at the Latin words on the floor." He indicated the closest one. "That says Lotos, and the one next to it says Aenea. I can only push this stick forward so far, then I have to choose a direction. Both directions have two choices at the next intersection. I think they're locations from the Aeneid." He read several more. "Not just the Aeneid. Some of these places aren't in that story."

Why the overlap between stories? Other place names from the tales caught his eye. "This starting position is labeled *Troy,*" Harry said. "The Aeneid storyline starts with Aeneas escaping Troy as it falls to the Greeks." He pulled his hand back and turned to Stefan. "Virgil wrote the Aeneid as a founding myth of Rome. He tied Romans back to the Trojan people in order to claim direct lineage from Troy to the leaders of his time as a way to legitimize the Roman emperors. It's hard to argue your emperor isn't the right person for the job if his ancestors were great heroes. Even if he became emperor by killing the competition."

Harry indicated the platform again. "I think this combines the two stories."

"Why would they do that?"

"The first half of the Aeneid is based on the Odyssey, while the second half is based on the Iliad." Stefan shot him a questioning look. "There are lots of similarities between the stories. For some reason Cleopatra only chose location names from the Odyssey for her test. I think we have to recreate Aeneas's journey to prove not only that we know the story, but to show how the Romans tie to the legend of Troy."

Stefan couldn't have cared less. "Where did he go next?"

"I haven't read the story in years. Let's see… First, Aeneas gets out of Troy before the Greeks kill him. He takes a boat and founds a new city." Harry laughed. "A city he names after himself. *Aenea.*" Harry opened his eyes. "And that is one of the next choices."

He bent to examine the ruts in the stone again. The stick could only go forward in its current channel until it hit a T-intersection. From there Harry had to turn left or right. Right to *Lotos.* Left to *Aenea.* "It's Aenea," Harry said. "I'm sure of it. *Lotos* is Latin for Lotus. It's also an island where Odysseus went after leaving Troy."

Stefan moved back off the platform, halfway down the steps. "What happens if you are wrong?"

"Probably nothing good." Harry turned to the rear wall. "If I had to guess, I bet those holes contain spears. Make a wrong move and I'm in trouble." He could jump for safety. He might survive the fall. He definitely wouldn't survive landing on the spikes all around. "Here we go."

He leaned on the stick, and there was a high-pitched grinding sound of stone against stone. It moved forward in fits and starts until he reached the intersection. The floor held fast. "Watch out," Harry called to Stefan as he leaned into it, pushing the stick to the left until he reached the next intersection, where it slammed to a halt. He went still.

Stone gears clanked beneath his feet. The platform vibrated. Harry looked over his shoulder to find Stefan at the bottom of the stairs. "Told you."

"Just keep going," Stefan said.

More clanking ensued, the sound of ancient cogs moving after two thousand years of inactivity. "I bet it adjusts after every move," Harry said. "To let me continue if I choose correctly."

The staff now stood at *Aenea*, one of the first stops on their hero's journey.

"After founding a city for himself," Harry explained, "Aeneas tried to create another city, a new version of Troy. Which is a problem for us, because neither of the next two choices is Troy."

"What are the choices?"

From Aenea Harry could only push the joystick one way. This brought him to another T-intersection, when he again had to choose left or right. Right led to *Etna*, left to *Lamos*. "The whole second coming of Troy didn't work out. Disease wiped out many of Aeneas's men. The survivors sailed off and quickly ran into harpies." The ever-present lines on Stefan's forehead deepened. "Harpies are half-bird, half-person creatures who stole their food in the story. The Trojans escaped." Harry tapped a finger on the stick, thinking. "Next came something about a spear. Or was it a shield?"

"This is not the time to forget."

"I'm the one risking my neck. You're hanging back on the steps." Stefan shook his gun. "Yeah, your gun." *Wait until that changes, buddy.* Harry had no idea how he'd change the situation, but he was working on it. His chance would come. "Aeneas and his men kept moving," he went on, and suddenly a memory sparked. "Eventually they came across a guy Odysseus had left behind. Odysseus is the protagonist in the *Odyssey*." His eyes closed. "I think it was in Sicily. Near a mountain called Etna." His eyes flew open. "That's it. The story is a myth but that location is real." He backtracked and started through the Odyssey again. "He ran into the Lotus cyclops, then the cannibals. On *Lamos*. That's the island where Odysseus ran into cannibals. It's Etna for sure."

He almost hesitated. His mind said to make sure, to double-check. Fail here and your worries—and probably your life—would be over. The fear could cripple anyone. He pushed the thought aside. Trusting his instincts got him this far. No time to stop now.

Another right turn as Harry pushed the stick until it locked into the *Etna* location. Gears whirred, the floor rumbled, and Harry held onto the stick tightly. Stefan scampered even further back down the stairs until the grinding and scraping settled. "It worked."

Harry glared at him. "Stop running away. You're missing the show." If Stefan stayed nearby, maybe the shaking floor would throw him off and Harry could make his move. "We're through Aenea and Etna. Next I remember Aeneas's father died and then they were shipwrecked." Something else had happened there. What was it? "Oh. Then the lady shows up. Queen Dido."

Stefan edged closer. "Is that next?"

Harry examined the floor. "Her name isn't here. These are all place names. It's *Carthage* or *Messina*." He wracked his brain. "Where is Messina? Carthage is well known, though. It was a major trading hub, and the Romans laid siege to it for a few years. Which has nothing to do with these stories."

"What about the woman?" Stefan said. "There is always a woman in the myths. Who was she?"

"Queen Dido. Aeneas fell in love with her. She ended up killing herself later after Aeneas abandoned her." His mind sent up a warning flare. "Hang on." Harry aimed a finger at Stefan. "They fell in love in the city she founded and ruled. Carthage."

Stefan waved at the stick. "Push it to Carthage."

"Not until I remember what Messina is."

Messina. No land he knew of, no mountain or famous battle. No historical figures, either. "It's not a city or country," he said aloud. "I don't remember any kings or queens with that name." In his mind's eye Harry pictured the journey of Aeneas as if on a map, moving from port to port through the Mediterranean Sea. Harry drew in a breath. "Water. It's on water. The Strait of Messina. Where sirens lured sailors to their deaths by singing. Odysseus had his men put beeswax in their ears so they couldn't hear the songs, and then lash him to the mast. That's how they made it past. And Messina does appear in the Odyssey, but Aeneas never went there."

He pushed the stick and it clanked into place at *Carthage*. The platform rumbled as expected. "Two choices left. The next one is between *Pallantium* and *Ogygia*. I know this one. Aeneas had a major battle at Pallantium against a king named Turnus. It's not Ogygia, because that's where Odysseus washed ashore after Zeus killed his crew as punishment for stealing the sun god's cows."

Harry didn't give Stefan a chance to ask questions before pushing the stick to Pallantium. Clanks, groans, floor shaking. All of it familiar now. After a few moments, the mechanical adjustments ended and Harry was down to his last decision.

"Almost there," he said. For the first time, he was close enough to read the words of his final choice. He looked first to one and then the other, and then stepped back. "Those aren't names. They're pictures."

That finally drew Stefan onto the platform. He didn't walk straight to Harry, instead following the route Harry had already traversed, all straight lines from point to point until he made it to Pallantium. He looked down at the drawings.

"They look like two plants," Stefan said.

The carvings were two separate images cut in exquisite detail. "One is a cluster of grapes. The other is an olive tree." The thick, gnarled trunk with bushy foliage on its branches even had a few tiny olives hanging from it. "The Aeneid ends with a battle in Italy, near the town of Latium, where Aeneas kills King Turnus, then returns to his home island of Ithaca in Greece. Which of these images is Roman?" He didn't wait for Stefan to answer. "The answer is obvious. Olives. Italy has produced some of the world's finest olive oil for centuries. In ancient times it was one of Rome's biggest crops. Grapes, on the other hand, are used to make wine, and Greece is one of the oldest wine-producing regions in the world."

The steps to the third pillar loomed ahead as Harry pushed the stick toward the olive tree. He glanced over his shoulder to find Stefan moving back to the first set of stairs, the gun now in his waistband. Harry looked away before Stefan turned around.

The stick resisted slightly. Harry leaned into it, stone scraped on stone, and the stick moved ahead until with a final shove it settled into the slot by the olive tree.

His vision blurred as gears churned beneath him. Nothing like before. Harry didn't stop to think before his legs took over, one foot racing after the other as he ran for the closest edge. He blinked and the platform split in two. One second he was running for the edge; the next, his feet were in midair with no ground below him. His arms wheeled, reaching for the half of the platform floor that was now rapidly tilting out of reach. One hand caught a channel in the stone floor and he latched on, the swinging floor taking him with it as it shot down before smashing against the interior wall of the platform pillar. His brain rattled and the skies exploded, but Harry held fast.

A great gush of hot air blew across him as torrents of fire burst from every hole in the wall, gathering in an inferno to incinerate anyone still near the pillar. Harry looked up as Stefan flew through the air, launched by the closing staircase. Stefan screamed in a language Harry didn't understand before gravity pulled him down.

With a grunt, Stefan crashed headlong into Harry, a direct hit. Harry's grip on the rough stone channel loosened and he began to drop. Stefan's fingers scrabbled for purchase as he slid past. Harry stuck an arm out and pressed Stefan against the stone, giving the Albanian enough time to get a hand into one of the channels. Stefan latched on an instant before Harry's grip gave out. Stone ripped skin from his nose as Harry skidded down the now vertical platform toward blackness below.

Chapter 26

"Got you!"

Stefan caught Harry's shirt collar in an iron grip and ripped him out of the air. Harry hung, twisting slightly over the abyss, as flames roared around them, bright enough to light the hollow pillar and reveal another surprise from Cleopatra. More sharpened metal spikes waiting to impale them.

"Hang on," Harry shouted. "Pull me back toward the wall so I can grab it." It took every bit of self-control not to thrash about. Do that and Stefan would lose his grip.

"Stand on my foot!" Stefan shouted.

Stefan's leg went rigid, holding steady long enough for Harry to get a foothold and use the bigger man's shoe as a balance point to push himself over to the vertical platform floor and the fingers of one hand found a channel, and with a mighty effort he swung his other arm up and parked that hand beside the first. Holding tight to the wall like a spider, Harry pressed his face against the stone and closed his eyes for a moment.

"I'm good!" he yelled, then nearly fell as Stefan let go of his shirt. Only when he had a foot jammed in a lower channel did it seem possible they'd get out of this. He looked up at the raging torrent of fire, then pressed his face against the wall again and gulped air so hot it scalded his lungs, an endless—

The firestorm stopped. Harry had no time to blink before there was an ominous rumble of stone gears grinding together, and he began rising. No, not him. The floor was moving, lifting itself back up to where it had been before the collapse. Harry pressed himself against the stone, dug in with his fingers and held on. The roaring and rumbling continued for what seemed an eternity. All Harry knew was the sharp ache of raw skin on stone until a final *boom* sounded and they were lying on a solid stone floor once more. He closed his eyes, waiting.

Harry opened one eye. *Stefan was moving.* "Stop," Harry shouted. "Don't move."

The Albanian froze. "Why not?"

"I don't know what might set this trap off again. Keep still." Slowly, carefully, Harry pushed himself upright to gain his feet. He rose, looking through air that shimmered with the smoky remnants of the recent inferno. Black scorch marks adorned the wall behind them. "Hear that?" Harry asked, listening uneasily. "Sounds like liquid sloshing behind the wall. The fuel for those flamethrowers must be reloading. The traps are resetting."

They both jumped as stone ground on stone once more and the first staircase rose back into a vertical position. In short order the platforms had returned to their original state. The only indication anyone had come through was in the black streaks across the stone walls. The Aeneas joystick had returned to the starting position, ready for the next contestant.

"The first level has reset," Stefan said. He casually withdrew the gun and held it by his side. "Does that matter?"

"Beats me," Harry said. "Only thing I know is we're not getting back over to the first pillar."

"Why not?"

"You think I can jump that far?" Harry indicated the spike-lined pit beneath the nearly twenty-foot gap. "No chance. I doubt you can either."

"We may not be able to safely pass each level if we do not start at the beginning."

He had a point. "Well, we can't get off this pillar without landing on spikes." They were surrounded on all sides. "You have a better idea than trying this one again?"

"You failed on this one."

Another good point. Harry thought for a moment. "I remembered something when we were hanging over those spikes. Aeneas went to a place called Latium at the end of his story. It's an Italian region known for producing grapes, not olives. One of only a few regions in Italy like it. Odysseus made it to Ithaca at the end of the Odyssey. Ithaca is an island that produces olives. The final choice was intentionally confusing. I went too fast and messed up."

"Now we know the right answer." Stefan pointed to the first platform. "If you cannot jump that far, I will throw you." Harry took a step back. "No, no. Like this," Stefan said. He went to one knee and joined his hands together. "Step on my hands and I will throw you. It is not far. You are little."

Harry puffed his chest out. "Not that little."

"You are little. I am strong. I will throw you."

"What's to stop you from throwing me onto the spikes?"

"I would shoot you now if I wanted to kill you. I cannot solve the challenges. You can." Stefan's eyes narrowed. "I saved your life. I could have let you fall."

This was more sense than Stefan had made in his entire life. Harry eyed the gap. "Maybe it will work if we just start on this level."

"Do you believe that?"

Harry did not. "Fine. Go to the edge. I need a running start." Trusting Stefan was foolish, but the Albanian could be correct about needing to start all over again and it wasn't like he had any other options.

Harry ran, Stefan threw him, and seconds later Harry crashed onto the first pillar. Brain rattling, jaw snapping, he landed with inches to spare in a bone-crunching heap atop the first pillar.

"Get up." Stefan's voice carried across the gap. "You made it."

"Yeah, I know." His elbow shouted as he pushed himself up. A knee joined the chorus. "Next time I'm throwing you."

"What?"

"Nothing." He hobbled to the buttons and mashed the trident. Gears whirred and the first set of steps lowered, allowing Harry to rejoin Stefan on the second platform as the sound of liquid moving around behind the wall of flames finally abated. He didn't hesitate to push Aeneas's joystick through the Aeneid journey again, this time choosing the grapes at the end.

New gears rumbled as the final set of stairs lowered from the third and tallest column. Harry watched Stefan out of the corner of his eye as the Albanian studied the staircase. He did not notice Harry slip one hand into a pocket. The pocket hiding his knuckledusters.

Harry gestured to the steps. "Go ahead."

Stefan shook his head. "You first. I will stay here."

Harry eyed him a beat longer. "Sure you want to miss seeing it first?" What he truly meant was *Sure you don't want to give me a free shot at the back of your head?* His fist on its own might stun the bigger man momentarily. His fist with the dusters on top would knock him down for the count.

Stefan flicked the barrel of his gun up the stairs and edged back. "Go."

Harry shrugged. "Suit yourself." This third set of stairs stretched across the largest gap, as wide as the first platform some thirty feet below. The chasm beneath was filled with the requisite spikes to make certain anyone falling from the top pillar wouldn't merely break their neck, but be impaled as well for good measure. He quickened his pace. The third platform came more clearly into view with each step until he gained the top level and stood on the edge, dusty air coating his throat. A dry tongue ran over parched lips. "Of course."

Stefan called out from below. "What is it?"

"Come up and see for yourself." Harry marched ahead without waiting. No need to worry about the floor this time. The final test waited in the platform's middle. A personalized test meant for two specific people. "It's a quiz only two people could answer. Cleopatra Selene II and Alexander Helios. The twins."

A new world stood in front of him. A world imagined by Antony and Cleopatra to ensure their continued rule for generations to come. In the end, it had doomed them all.

"These are lands Antony and Cleopatra distributed to their children,"

Harry said as Stefan came up beside him. "The Donations of Alexandria."

The stone pillar stood not much taller than Harry. Three columns were marked on the front, with initials at the tops of the left and right ones. "AH and CSII are the twins' initials," Harry said. He glanced at the blank stone pillars on either side of the front one, each ten feet wide and nearly as tall. Channels running along the floor made it clear that the two hunks of rock had the capacity to come together with a resounding *crunch*.

"The buttons have words above them," Stefan said.

Indeed they did. A series of what Stefan called "buttons," but what Harry would call markers, ran vertically down the center column. Perhaps sliders was a better name than markers, for each one sat in a horizontal channel carved into the stone pillar. "We're supposed to move each slider into the correct column. Look—they can go left or right."

"Do you know the answers?"

Harry's lips parted. "I think so." The Latin names of countries long since erased were written above each slider in the middle column. Move the slider to the name of the correct twin to pass the test. What happened if he got the answers right was a mystery. What happened if he made an incorrect choice? That was obvious. The two pillars on either side would smash him flat.

He pushed that thought away. "This list is off. There are too many place names." A far-too-brief chat on the topic with Sara back in New York zipped fleetingly through his head. "Some of these places were awarded to Cleopatra's other children." The Egyptian monarch had three children with Antony and one with Julius Caesar. Now he couldn't recall which kid had received what land.

"Start with the ones you do remember."

Sound advice from a cold-blooded killer. "Want to help me?"

Stefan inspected the ground. "No. These two stones will come together if you are wrong. I am not standing there."

"Then maybe I don't want to either. I'll leave and you can figure this out." The gun waved again, this time with a bit more vigor, as Stefan backed out of range. "I figured you'd do that." Harry turned to the main pillar. Figure this out without getting smashed in the process. Then deal with Stefan. Again he licked his dry lips. It was the only plan he had, except soon he'd run out of chances and Stefan would actually use that gun.

Where to start? His dad would say "At the beginning, so you don't miss anything," so Harry decided that was what he'd do, taking Stefan along for the ride. "Antony and Cleopatra orchestrated the Donations after Antony lost a war to the Parthian Empire. They needed to show strength, to remind the Roman Republic who were the two strongest leaders, so they put on a big show and divvied up several nations among their kids."

One nation immediately grabbed his eye. "Libya went to their daughter. I'm sure of it." He didn't tell Stefan it was because the mention of Libya brought to mind the scene from *Back to the Future* where Doc Brown tricks Libyan terrorists by giving them a bomb filled not with plutonium, but with old pinball machine parts. The sliding knob under *Libya* moved easily when he pushed it toward Cleopatra Selene II's column, grinding over until it locked into place. A muted, hollow *boom* issued forth from beneath his feet. The ground quivered slightly. "One down," Harry said.

There was a roar of crashing stone and Harry spun around as the stairs leading from the second platform rose, the drawbridge retracting to maroon them on this island of nations. Stefan skidded to a halt within arm's reach of Harry.

"Why did you do that?" he demanded, chest heaving.

"You think I knew that would happen? I just moved the knob."

"How many others must you move?" Stefan couldn't take his eyes from the stairs. The gun hung forgotten at his side. "We could die."

Harry's reinforced hand clenched into a fist. "I'm not sure." He edged closer. *One more step.* Stefan's back was to him, his attention elsewhere. Harry's arm tensed and he stepped forward.

"Keep going." Stefan darted closer to the steps. He leaned over to inspect them, then turned back to Harry. "What is next?" he asked. The gun stayed at his side.

Harry grimaced. *Next time.* "There are nine total countries. Including *Egypt*, which doesn't make sense. Cleopatra was the queen of Egypt. She wouldn't give it to one of the twins. I think that went to Caesarion. He would rule alongside his mother." Harry tapped the knob below *Egypt*. "This one doesn't go to either twin. It needs to stay put." Which brought up another problem. "Not all of these countries should be moved. I have to leave them in place if they weren't awarded to one of the twin children."

"Move the ones you are certain about," Stefan said. "Perhaps that will be enough."

It was their only play. "I'm pretty sure *Armenia* went to Alexander Helios." Stick with your gut, he told himself, and slid the knob over. Another quiet *boom*, another tremor below his feet. No pillars smashed him. "Cleopatra Selene received two countries in total. Alexander received three." It started coming to him. "Caesarion was officially presented as the true son of Julius Caesar, which meant he would rule alongside his mother. The youngest child was named Ptolemy Philadelphus. How many are left?" He counted nations in his head and on the pillar. "Nine total countries. We moved two correctly so far, which leaves seven. If Ptolemy got three and Caesarion one, that leaves five to be moved."

"You must move three more correctly."

"Thanks for doing the math." Harry studied the pillar, willing his thoughts to take shape. "*Cyrenaica*. That went to Cleopatra Selene II. It was her only other country." He reached out, then hesitated. "Or was it *Cilicia*? I know it was a country with the same first letter as her name. Both choices begin with *C*."

"Leave it," Stefan said. "What about the others?"

"*Media, Parthia, Phoenicia.*" He snapped his fingers. "Ptolemy received *Phoenicia*. I'm sure of it. The first letter thing again." He left that slider knob in place. "*Syria* and *Phoenicia* are staying put because they were awarded to Ptolemy. Same with *Egypt*, which went to Caesarion. That leaves five choices, two that start with a *C*. I know Alexander Helios didn't get either of those, and I'm sure he received three countries in total." Harry grinned. "Process of elimination means *Media* and *Parthia* are his." Those slider knobs rammed home to the accompaniment of more grinding stone gears, none of which brought the two crushing pillars together. "Almost there."

Only two buttons left. *Cyrenaica* and *Cilicia*. One went to Cleopatra Selene II. The other stayed put. But which one? Harry rubbed the back of his neck. "I'm not certain. I can't remember."

"You made it this far," Stefan said. "Think. You know the answer."

"I just told you I don't," Harry snapped.

"You do. Look at what you have done so far." Stefan pointed to the stone testing pillar. "Those are all correct. You will get this one too."

"*Cyrenaica* is part of what's now called Libya. *Cilicia* was part of Turkey. The Romans had issues with pirates in the area. Libya is on Egypt's western border. Turkey is north across the Mediterranean Sea. Cleopatra Selene's other territory is *Libya*. Antony and Cleopatra wouldn't have her govern two nations a thousand miles apart. They were too strategic to weaken her that way. Her other nation must be *Cyrenaica*."

He knew it was right. Knew it in his soul, knew it with the certainty of a relic hunter who'd stayed alive this long by beating the odds when it counted. Harry flexed his fingers in the knuckleduster, kept that hand out of view and reached for the final sliding knob. The instant before it slid over an image came to mind. His father, lifting the golden amulet over his neck and handing it to Harry for safekeeping. Until he returned from Rome. A short trip, nothing to worry about. The last thing Fred Fox would ever give his son.

The knob flashed over. Stefan made a sharp noise behind Harry, the sound of a man ready to jump. Harry didn't even blink. The ground began to shake, the vibrations starting at his toes and running up to his eyeballs, making the temple walls flit back and forth as he took a step back on the unsteady ground and a massive *thud* rattled his brain. Harry spun and nearly fell over.

The staircase bounced as it crashed down to reconnect the second and third levels. Stefan stumbled at the impact, arms pinwheeling for balance as he staggered precariously close to the edge, off-balance and...

Movement on the pillar caught Harry's eye an instant before he charged Stefan, fists balled and ready to shove, accelerating to close the gap as Stefan's mouth opened and he bent back and forth, catching and losing his balance then catching it again as Harry came for him. Harry dipped low, ready to explode forward and shove Stefan over the edge to the spikes below.

Stefan regained his balance and fired. The shot buzzed past Harry's ear. He ducked, twisting instinctively, throwing his weight to the side and skidding down on one knee. Stefan fired again, this shot going wide as Harry backed up, leapt to his feet and dashed for the closest pillar. His mind whirled. He needed to hide and regroup or jump off the edge or do *something* besides getting shot and dying on this godforsaken pillar in a—

The ground by his foot exploded. Harry hit the brakes, the pillar still out of reach as Stefan shouted, "Stop running." Another shot, this one by his other foot. Harry stopped running.

"Turn around." Harry did as ordered. "You are too slow," Stefan said. "And you are no longer useful."

"What about the next test?"

A flicker of doubt crossed Stefan's face. "Next test?"

Harry touched the pillar on which he had assigned cities to each twin. "Antony and Cleopatra aren't finished with us yet. Look."

The cities with their sliding knobs had disappeared, opening like a cupboard door to reveal a new feature that had been hidden underneath the city test. A flat surface with two circular indentations cut into it. Carvings again. *Those are familiar.* Harry's eyes opened wide and he made the only play he had. He told the truth. "I know what those are."

"The circles?" Harry nodded. "Tell me."

"You're going to shoot me once I do."

"I will shoot you if you don't." Stefan grumbled in Albanian. "Tell me what they are and solve this. If you do, I will let you leave."

"So you can hunt me down later? No thanks."

Stefan narrowed his eyes. "I do not want to look over my shoulder forever. I want to find this treasure, and I want to disappear. Forever." A thundercloud crossed his face. "My old life is over. I need the treasure to live. Give me the answer and you can go."

"You think I trust you?"

The gun came up. Stefan meant business this time. "Do it or I shoot you, then I find the woman."

Which ended this discussion. "Fine." Harry didn't believe for a second that Stefan would let him go. He turned and walked slowly toward the pillar. "Come here and I'll show you."

"I will stay here."

So much for getting Stefan close. Get off this pillar and he might have a chance. Harry eyed the temple below, the walkway that right now resembled nothing so much as a shooting gallery. "It's a lock," Harry said. He pulled his mother's amulet from his pocket. "Which takes two keys to open." He lifted his father's amulet from around his neck. "These."

The decorations had given it away because they were familiar. It had taken him a second to place the images. How did he know them? *The amulets.* Each image inside the circles was a reverse of the ones on his parents' amulets. These amulets had set him on the path to this hidden temple. It seemed they would now lead him to the treasure.

His father's amulet went on the right, his mother's on the left. Face first, they slotted in perfectly, the grooved edges locking into the openings. "They must turn," he said, and twisted. The two golden discs rotated under his hands, turning a full circle until they stopped with a gentle *click*.

A sound like a hundred creaky doors opening filled the temple. Harry stepped back, pulling the amulets out as he moved to get a look at the ground below. A flash of movement beyond the tall entranceway drew both men to the pillar's edge. They stood only a few feet apart, gazing into a room that was not as it seemed.

Stefan spoke first. "The statues are moving."

Harry nodded wordlessly. The statues they'd passed in the middle room weren't statues at all. They were hollow, every single one of them actually a container with hinges on one side. The front of each one had swung open like a door to reveal the interior. The doors that had swung open in Stefan and Harry's direction now blocked Harry from seeing what was inside. The doors on the other side did not.

"There's something in them," Harry said. He squinted, unable to make out the contents clearly. "I can't see it."

"It is the treasure." Stefan's voice was nearly in Harry's ear. Stefan brought his gun up and stepped back before Harry could react.

"So much for letting me live." Harry edged away, eyeing the drop that awaited him if he jumped. Thirty feet down onto metal spikes. "Keep the treasure. Leave me and Sara alone."

"I will leave her alone. You?" Stefan shrugged. "It is only business."

Gunshots filled the air. Harry ducked as bullets whizzed past, then stared at Stefan, who stared back at him in bewilderment. The bullets had come from *down below*. He dropped to the ground as more shots rang out and stared over the lip of the platform.

Sara Hamed stood in the entrance, a gun in her hand, blasting away at Stefan.

Chapter 27

"Don't come in here!" Harry shouted down to Sara as he hit the deck. "The floor isn't safe."

Sara glanced down but kept firing, her wild shots driving Stefan back across the platform, the barrage flying wide but close enough to scare him. He returned fire, but Sara stood her ground, holding the gun in both hands now and working the trigger. Rock shattered and shards filled the air before Stefan stopped bumbling backwards, widened his stance and took aim, closing one eye and sighting along the barrel.

Harry charged and didn't stop. Stefan squeezed off a single shot before Harry barreled into him with a lowered shoulder, blasting the bigger man off his feet and sending him hurtling toward the abyss below. A scream filled the air as Harry accelerated, never stopping or looking at the falling Albanian. He flew down the stairs, gaining speed as he crossed the second pillar and descended to the first level before leaping over the final set of steps on a direct line for Sara. Sara, who stood clutching her arm in the middle of the stone floor triggers. "Did he hit you?" he asked, jumping between darker stones to reach her.

"I'm fine." Sara cradled her good arm with the bad one, which he only now realized had a cast on it. "He only nicked me." A red line ran across her forearm. "I'm fine."

Harry looked for the pistol she'd dropped and cursed. It was a distance away, by the stone soldiers. "Don't step on the dark stones," he said. "Follow me."

He made it one step before a bullet cracked off a stone ahead. Harry grabbed Sara's shoulder and went still.

"Stop." Stefan's voice filled the temple. "Do not move."

Stefan, last seen falling into the spiked pit, was now moving quickly down the stairs toward them. One bullet aimed at any of the dark stones around them could set off the army of stone guards and send arrows flying.

Sara realized the danger as well. "We can't run," she said.

Harry barely had time to breathe before Stefan was on them, moving deftly across the light-colored stones. He stopped five feet away, his gun on Harry, his eyes gleaming in the torchlight. "You came for him," Stefan said to Sara. "Your mistake. I would have let you live."

"It's not too late," Sara said. "We can all get out of here alive."

"It *is* too late. This is a business. There cannot be loose ends."

"Keep whatever is in those." Sara waved a hand over her shoulder toward the now-open statues. "We've had enough of this chase."

Stefan shook his head. "No. This ends now."

Harry turned to Sara. He looked past her shoulder to one of the statues beside them. He blinked. "Wait." Harry lifted a hand. "Take these. They're worth a fortune." Hands moving slowly, he pulled the two amulets from his pockets, where he'd shoved them after pulling them from their keyholes. "Two amulets for two lives. After this, we never see each other again."

Stefan did not lower his gun. "Here," Harry said, edging closer. "They're yours."

Greed must have blinded Stefan for a moment, as Harry leaned forward, holding out his palm. Maybe it was torchlight flashing off the gold, or maybe it was Harry's impending demise. Stefan hesitated. Harry lobbed one amulet through the air, sending the golden disc floating toward Stefan. He looked up and reached out to grab it. Stefan never saw Harry fire the second amulet at the floor.

Directly onto a large dark stone.

Harry grabbed Sara and dove to one side as Stefan shouted and fired. The amulet clattered against its target, a direct hit, and the stone grated as it dropped into the floor. Rock ground on rock, stone gears turned and the army attacked. Bows twanged and swords sliced the air in a deadly barrage two thousand years in the making. No place in the chamber was safe. No place except beside the stone soldier with a broken sword arm, where Harry and Sara landed after he tackled her to the ground. Her screams filled the air as he shut his eyes tight and pressed her to the floor, the *swish* and *thwack* of arrows surrounding them in a hailstorm of destruction.

The tumult passed in moments. One second, Harry was crushing Sara to the floor, squeezing them both against the statue's base as he waited to be shot. The next, everything went quiet. Harry opened his eyes. The only movement was Sara turning her head, her torso moving slightly with each breath.

"Is it over?"

Harry lifted his head a fraction. He bumped it against an arrow that had lodged inches from his head. "I think so." He glanced around cautiously. "Nothing's moving."

"Then get off me. I can't breathe."

He stood, crushing Sara only a bit more as he levered himself upright and helped her to her feet. They stood side by side, staring at what remained of Stefan. "He'll be down here for a while," Harry said.

"He brought it on himself," Sara said. "You told him to let us go."

Harry looked away from the carnage, toward the two golden discs on the ground. Carefully, he navigated the minefield of embedded arrows to retrieve them. He did not turn to look at Stefan again.

"How did you find me?" Harry asked as he put his father's amulet around his neck. The other he gave to Sara.

Sara slipped the amulet over her head and tucked it out of sight. "Rose Leroux called me." Her eyes narrowed. "She told me to call Omar. Remember Joey's friend who helped me in Luxor? He picked me up at the hospital and brought me here."

"Where is he?"

"Waiting by the entrance in case Stefan got past us. I told him to make certain Stefan didn't get away."

"Nice thinking."

"Hope for the best. Prepare for the worst." She aimed a finger at his chest. "You have some explaining to do about Rose Leroux. I thought she was a 'business associate.'"

Harry shrugged. "That's mostly true."

Sara fixed him with a look that said this wasn't the end of the discussion before her eyes wandered around the room. "What is this place?"

"Antony and Cleopatra's final test." He pointed to each pillar in turn, explaining how he had passed the three tests of knowledge. "The three names told me it would be about knowledge."

Her lips pursed. "How did you know the Aeneid so well?"

He shrugged. "I like to read. You know that."

"More than I gave you credit for." Now she pointed at the third pillar. "But the Donations of Alexandria? I'm not sure I could recall each of them."

"Remember when we talked about it? I guess it stuck. Then our amulets turned out to be the keys." He pointed behind her. "They opened those."

Sara whirled around. "Opened what?"

"The statues. They were—"

"Closed when I walked in." She grabbed his arm, dragging him behind her as she skirted fallen arrows, avoiding the darker stones for good measure. Seconds later she hit the brakes so fast he ran into her. She turned back and looked at him. "How did you know we'd survive the attack? The arrows and swords. None hit us."

"I noticed one soldier's sword arm had fallen off when I came in here. I knew none of the other swords could get to us if we went to it and kept down."

Fire flashed in her eyes. "What about the arrows?"

Harry studied the walls first. The ceiling second. "I wasn't sure about those." He shrugged. "Want to see what's in those statues?"

Sara gave him a shove, then marched past the last few arrows and into the center temple chamber. She stopped again, and this time Harry stopped beside her. Sara's words came softly when she spoke. "These aren't only statues. These are containers."

Harry explained to her that when he'd turned the amulets in the slots atop the last pillar, they had acted as keys, causing each statue in the chamber to swing open to reveal that the statues were actually hollow. Together they stepped forward to look. Inside each were rows of shelves, and on the shelves, scrolls. Lots and lots of scrolls, each one stuffed into its own small slot.

"These are Egyptian statues," Harry said, then turned to indicate the rest of them. "There are others from different cultures. Greeks, Roman, Persian, and I think Mesopotamian. Perhaps more."

Sara wasn't listening. She had a scroll in her hand and was carefully examining it. "This one is about Egyptian building techniques. It details how pyramids were constructed." She put the scroll back, then removed another and unrolled it, her eyes flitting back and forth as she read. "It's poetry. Ancient Egyptian poetry." Sara carefully returned the scroll and then gazed around her, awestruck. "What *is* this place?"

The front part of Cleopatra's statue opened further under Harry's touch. "Maybe Cleopatra will tell us." He pointed to an inscription on the inside.

"Koine Greek. Her first language." Sara put her finger under the words as she translated. "*Knowledge lights a dark world. Follow this light, my children. Use it in your rule. The Mouseion will guide you.*"

"What a *Mouseion*?" Harry asked. He pulled open the door beside him, this one on another Egyptian statue. "Do you know?" he prompted her. Harry looked back to find her staring inside Cleopatra's statue, one hand still in the air. Her finger hovered beneath the mysterious word. "What's wrong?"

"The *Mouseion*." Sara repeated the word breathlessly. "Harry, do you know what this is?"

He'd made that part pretty clear. "No."

"Ptolemy founded it. With his son, Ptolemy II."

A bell dinged in Harry's head. "Wait, you mean Ptolemy as in Ptolemaic dynasty?"

She nodded. "Cleopatra's dynasty. She was the last of his line to rule Egypt. The dynasty ended with her death."

"Is that why she created this place? If every one of these statues is filled with scrolls, we're talking at least a couple thousand of them."

He might as well have been a ghost. "It isn't lost." Sara lifted a hand to her mouth. "She gave it to her children. So they would rule with wisdom."

"Why would they need to know how to build a pyramid?" Harry asked. "They had people for that."

Sara moved over to another grouping of statues, Greek this time. She reached into Dionysus and grabbed a scroll. "It's a mathematical treatise." She gasped. "By Eratosthenes."

Harry came over to her side and examined the statue. No writing on it, inside or out. "Who's Eratosthenes?" She ignored him and pored over the scroll. "Sara, start talking." He put a hand on each of her shoulders. "What is this place?"

She brushed him off. "Put this back." The mathematical scroll landed in his hands as she raced toward one of the statues he suspected was Persian and pulled it open. A square piece of thick paper came out. "There's artwork in this one," she said before returning the paper. "And more texts." Next she went to what could have been a Mesopotamian god. "A story." She held another scroll out as though he could read it. "It's a story I've never read." The scroll went back inside, and Sara finally looked at him. "This was supposed to have been lost. Burned in a fire, or destroyed through war and neglect. But it's not. It's *right here.*"

A memory popped up. One from long ago, perhaps from a class in high school, or a lecture in college. *Burned in a fire.* His head slowly twisted around. Different cultures. Scrolls. Knowledge to light a dark world. "This is a library."

She walked toward him. "Not *a* library." Sara took one of his hands in hers. "*The* library. The Library of Alexandria."

"No way." The memory crystallized. "I thought it burned down."

"It did. At least, that's what history said." She lifted her other hand to encompass the temple chamber. "Cleopatra must have made copies of the contents before the fire. She knew what it contained."

"Knowledge from across human history."

"Not merely knowledge. Power. Cleopatra understood that knowledge is power." Sara's hands tightened on his. "This is the greatest collection of information from the ancient world. Lost forever. And you found it."

Harry pulled her close. "No. We found it."

Epilogue

The lock on Harry's front door turned. He looked up from the kitchen sink. "Is that you?"

"Are you expecting another woman?" Sara Hamed shouldered the door open, then used her foot to kick it shut behind her. Stacks of paperwork filled her arms. "I hope you ordered food. I'm starving." She dumped the paperwork on Harry's dining table and let her bag drop to the floor. "And thirsty."

Harry rinsed the last of the soap suds off his forearms. A single smear of paint remained on one knuckle. He ignored it. "You're speaking my language," Harry said, turning to her. He reached into the fridge, grabbed a couple of beer bottles and popped the caps off. He took a long pull on one and handed her the other. "How was the subway?"

"Uneventful." Sara drank deeply. "Delicious. Thank you."

They tapped bottles and sat at his table. "Dare I ask how many news reporters called today?"

"You dare not. Thank goodness the museum provided an administrative assistant for my role. I'd never get off the phone."

That's what happened when you made the most incredible archaeological discovery in a hundred years. The first-hand copies from the Library of Alexandria had taken the world by storm. Her find had landed on the front page—below the fold, though—of daily newspapers across the globe. It was, as more than one paper stated, a revelation.

The Egyptian government's initial news conference had been a frenzy, with precious few details offered beyond a summary of the find. Even Sara couldn't guess what might be revealed next. Another Homeric poem? A new mathematical treatise? The world demanded answers while the Egyptian government kept mum. One fact that did come out almost immediately, however, was the identity of the intrepid Egyptologist who discovered the site. Along with the name of her guide.

Sara and Harry's lives would never be the same. The American Museum of Natural History's newest curator had become the face of the museum overnight. Her new boss was thrilled, mainly because money couldn't buy the sort of publicity her discovery brought. People thought he was a genius for bringing her aboard. The man did little to dissuade them.

"I've been invited to a fundraiser with the mayor this weekend." Sara rolled her eyes. "Nora will be there."

"I should ask for your autographs." Harry ducked when a napkin whizzed past his face. "At least you'll have a friend there."

"My invitation is a plus-one. I'm inviting you."

The bottle stopped halfway to his mouth. "You're joking."

She took a drink. "Yes, I am. A world-famous adventurer like you will certainly receive his own invitation."

Though Sara's star now burned brightly, Harry Fox was also becoming renowned. The adventurous guide, an intrepid explorer who had teamed with an Egyptologist to recover part of humanity's gilded past. At least that's what the stories said. Harry didn't speak with any reporters after the story broke, which added to the allure. Not because he wanted to be pursued, but because the less people knew about him, the better. His cozy relationship with an alleged organized crime boss wasn't the sort of thing Joey Morello wanted to become public.

"Use some of that new salary to buy a necklace for the event," Harry said.

Sara tipped her bottle toward his chest. "I was rather hoping you'd let me borrow yours."

Harry reached for the amulet tucked under his shirt. "You want to wear it?"

"Is that a no?"

Of course it was a no. His lips parted. They closed. Why was it a no? Because it was his father's amulet. Because the amulet was a connection to Fred Fox, the last thing Fred had given him. The amulet had been a driving purpose in his life since Fred's murder. A hundred reasons jumped to mind.

Harry pulled the metal chain over his neck. The golden disc was warm from his skin. "It's a yes. You'll look more lovely than ever."

"Thank you." Sara sipped her beer. "You may continue to flatter me now."

He chuckled, then changed the subject. "I'm on a roll with renovations at my new office."

"When are the painters finishing?"

"Tomorrow. I helped them today. If everything stays on schedule we'll finish next week."

"Joey's friends work quickly."

Sara didn't know the half of it. A month ago the building had been a smoking ruin after an alleged gas leak exploded—a gas leak Harry knew had been caused by Altin Cana. That this former pizza parlor would soon reopen was nothing short of a miracle. The sort of miracle construction workers controlled by the Morello crime family worked when Joey Morello told them to do it. If they'd been rebuilding a mere pizza parlor the job would already be complete. However, Joey Morello had bigger plans. Ones nobody expected, least of all Harry.

"It was generous of him to give you the building," Sara said. "On top of paying for the renovations."

Harry nodded. He'd never seen it coming. Joey had sprung the news on him a day after he returned from Egypt. Harry had been at home, lounging on the couch, a Yankees game on the television. He shot off the couch when his doorbell rang, eyes turning toward the shotgun within arm's reach. It took him a second to remember Stefan Rudovic and all the other Cana thugs were no longer a threat.

"Joey?" Harry spotted his boss through the peephole and opened it wide. "Something wrong?"

"Invite me in for a drink," Joey said. He turned to his bodyguard, Mack, the big guy standing below on the sidewalk. "Want to wait in the car?"

"Sure thing, boss." Mack winked at Harry. "Glad you're back in one piece, Aladdin. The girls was gettin' worried."

Harry flung a good-natured insult in Italian at the bodyguard, then nearly bit his tongue when Joey walked in and wrapped him in an embrace, complete with back thumping and a bone-crushing squeeze. Harry's bones and muscles and pretty much everything else needed rest right now, not abuse. "Good to see you, Joey."

"Good to see you too." Joey helped himself to a bottle of beer from the fridge, bringing one for Harry as well. "We need to talk."

Harry's cap popped off and he went still. "Oh."

"Nothing bad. Sit down. It's about the pizza parlor."

"Is it back up and running already?"

Joey shook his head. "It's not going to be a pizza parlor this time." He set his bottle on the table. "I want you to have it."

Harry nearly choked. "Me?"

"Sara is becoming known in the city. News of what you two did in Egypt is getting around." That was an understatement. "I owe you. You saved me."

Harry waved a hand. "You're my friend, Joey."

"I'm not the *capo dei capi* without you. The other families elected me after Altin Cana went down because you made it happen that way. I owe you." Joey raised a hand, palm toward Harry. "No arguments. I'm giving you the old pizza parlor and having it remodeled."

Harry lifted an eyebrow. "Into what?"

Joey looked over Harry's shoulder, into the past. "My father told me something your father told him. Not long before he died."

Harry's bottle made no sound when he set it down. His elbows found the table top.

"Fred told my father he knew his academic career would never come back after what he'd been accused of." Joey lifted a finger. "Falsely accused of. But Fred knew his world had changed, and he could never go back. He told my father that he wanted to make sure you had choices about your own future."

"He never said anything to me."

Joey grinned. "Our fathers weren't the type to talk about this stuff. But he could see how much you liked the relic-hunting business. Heck, we all can."

"That obvious, huh?" Harry grinned.

"Yeah, it is. You're good at it too. The best. Fred told my father he could see you loved it and he thought you might have a future in it. A legitimate future."

Harry smelled trouble now. "You guys are legit." A pause. "Mostly."

"I know who I am." Joey tapped the table with a finger. "I said the world's changing, so the Morellos are too. I'm expanding our operations."

"Taking over the Cana turf."

"That's not what I mean. The future isn't in controlling more physical turf. It's in diversification. We're moving to a new business model."

At times Harry forgot Joey had a degree in finance. "How does it involve me?"

"I'll get to that in a second. Online gambling is our first move. The local numbers racket is a dying business. Same with the card games and bookies. Why wager with us when you can get all the action you want on your phone? The market is exploding, and I want a piece of it. Same with prescription drugs. You know how much a single vial of insulin costs in the States? Ninety-eight bucks."

"Seems pricey."

"You can get the same vial for twelve bucks in Canada. I don't know how many people in this part of Brooklyn are diabetic, but it's a lot. If people can buy their insulin from a guy they trust—that's me—at a fraction of the cost, I'm printing money. I'm also investing in wind energy and on Wall Street. A few of the guys I went to school with can use the sort of money I provide to invest and no one looks too closely at where it came from."

"You're going to need more accountants to handle the new business."

"Not just accountants." Joey winked. "I need bankers." His voice lowered. "I'm opening a bank. It's not as hard as you'd think. All you need is enough capital, clean capital, and a skilled manager. Small, boutique banks are filling underserved niches in the market, and if I do it right, I can make a killing. I can also use the bank to fund our new enterprises. Control the money going in and the money going out. Full cycle oversight."

The district attorney would certainly have his hands full. "Sounds awesome," Harry said. "How does the pizza parlor fit in?"

Joey lifted his hands, putting them together before pulling them apart as he spoke. "I'm thinking an antiquities business. A dealership. Exclusive, the kind rich people come to when they're scouting a new artifact for their mansion in the Hamptons. What do you say?"

"Joey, I can't. It's too much."

"It's not too much, and I'm ordering you to accept. The last order I'll ever give you. This was a gift from my father to yours. They're not here, so now it's from me to you. You get the building, and you get my promise that you never have to work 'special projects' for me again." Joey shrugged. "Unless you want to."

Over the rest of their beers, Harry argued and Joey shot him down every time. Harry eventually accepted the gift. He would be his own man, forging his own path, and while he was no criminal, he could never let go of the thrill of chasing relics. His partnership with Nora Doyle's team provided the perfect setup. Work for Nora when he wanted, and otherwise work for himself. If Joey got involved and Harry ended up making money for the Morello family to the bargain, so be it. Choices. Exactly what his dad wanted for him.

Harry pushed the memory aside as he pulled out his phone and turned to Sara. "The new sign is coming soon." An image of the custom storefront sign he'd commissioned was in his email. He opened it and handed the phone to Sara. "What do you think?"

Sara knew every last detail about Harry and what he'd done, including who Rose Leroux was and how she'd found Sara's phone number in time to warn her about Harry's predicament. Rose had heard just enough before the connection was lost during Harry's confrontation with Stefan to realize Harry needed backup, and the only option was Sara. Well, Sara and an old friend. Rose had also found Omar's number and had Joey contact him. After their escapades in Luxor earlier that year, Omar felt a responsibility for Sara. He had dropped everything to get her released from the hospital and drive her into the desert. Omar had also handled the disposal of Stefan's body before the Egyptian authorities arrived. Monumental archaeological discoveries went over better without arrow-pierced bodies to get in the way of the story.

"It's beautiful," Sara said as she inspected the sign. "Your father would have loved it."

Harry agreed. He hadn't needed to think too hard about what to call his antiquities gallery. "I like it too." He took the phone back and glanced at the understated storefront signage. *Fox and Son.* "I figure my pieces will do the talking."

"Will the amulets be for sale?" Sara asked.

"No chance. However, word is a few previously unknown scrolls will be coming to market. For discerning buyers only."

He'd snagged a couple of the scrolls from Antony and Cleopatra's temple before the authorities arrived. Sara had put up a fight, but not as much as she would have a few months earlier. It seemed she had decided to pick her battles.

Harry traced a circle on the tabletop with his finger. "You still going to keep me in the loop if you get any tips about relics in the wild?"

She finished her beer. "Yes. I'd rather you find them than some unscrupulous treasure hunter. Which, for the record, you are not."

"I knew I liked you."

Harry's doorbell rang for the second time that evening. "Come in," he shouted at the door, which opened to reveal Dani Fox on his porch. "Hi, Mom."

"I hope I'm not interrupting." Dani closed the door behind her, then went to Sara. "How are you, dear?"

"Exhausted. Wonderful," Sara said, getting to her feet and embracing her warmly. "People have mistaken me for someone important."

"Not everyone upends the history books." Dani turned to Harry, who stood and put an arm around her shoulders. "And not everyone is forced to deal with such inhospitable characters as my son. Will you offer your mother a seat?"

"You're a riot, Mom." He pulled a chair out for her. "Everything okay?"

"Why wouldn't it be?"

"You never said why you wanted to stop by tonight."

"Can't I come to visit you?"

He frowned. "You're up to something."

Sara stood. "Speaking of parents, I need to call mine. They want to know when they can come see my new place." Sara had leased an apartment near her office. It was also near the subway, which meant she could be at Harry's place after work in half an hour. If she were so inclined. "Excuse me."

"Want to see the new sign?" Harry asked as Sara pulled out her phone and headed out back. "It's coming this week."

A warmth spread across Dani's face when he showed her. Almost enough to hide the sadness underneath. "It's lovely," Dani said. "Your father would approve."

"I hope so. I can't get my money back." He put his phone away. "So what's up?"

Dani removed a manila folder from her purse and laid it on the table. She did not open it. "Harry, will you be working with Nora's team?"

His mom had grown used to not knowing about what her husband

and daughter did at work. Now she was adding her son to that category. She also apparently sensed there were questions to ask Harry and questions not to ask. "As needed," he said. "My field experience can be an asset."

"I see. And the new business?"

"That will be my focus. Relic deals, the occasional recovery. Other stuff." He didn't go into detail. Mainly because he wasn't sure what those details could be.

"You will be careful."

"I'm always careful, Mom."

"I read the letters Fred received warning him not to investigate his false arrest. Do you remember the one containing an odd phrase?"

"It said *the night brings advice*. That's a French way of saying *sleep on it*. Whoever wrote that isn't a native English speaker. But it's all conjecture. Which is sometimes all you have."

"You sound like your father." Dani patted his arm. "It is an educated guess, but a guess nonetheless. We had no way to prove whether our guess was correct."

Harry's ear perked up. "Had?"

"Good catch. It occurred to me that this stamp could help us." She pointed to the envelope. "The stamps on these letters don't have adhesive on the back the way stamps do now. They were coated with glue, and adhered only after moisture was applied. Moisture, perhaps, from the sender's tongue."

Harry's stomach started to tingle. "Whoever wrote these may have licked the stamps. You can test for DNA."

"Exactly." Dani Fox leaned closer. "Guess what the laboratory found on the back of each?"

"Saliva."

"Not merely saliva. The same specimen of saliva on each. The test results produced an entire profile."

"What did it say?"

"A profile of the DNA indicates a male, almost certainly with dark eyes, whose ancestors came from in or around France."

The air went out of his chest. "I guess that's helpful."

"I asked a friend of mine who works in international law enforcement to check the DNA for any matches in U.S. or other criminal databases. The search did not find any matches, but one stamp had a single strand of hair underneath it. A test revealed this strand of hair matched the profile of the person who licked the stamps. It belonged to a direct male relative of theirs. The most likely reason is the person whose hair I found was in close proximity to the person who licked and applied the stamp around the time it was sent." Dani crossed her forearms on the table. She leaned closer, and when she spoke, her voice scarcely reached his ears. "The person whose hair was found has an arrest record in France. The nature of the offense means his DNA is on file with the local authorities."

Dani opened the manila folder. She turned it so Harry could see the picture it contained. "This is Theo Lloris. His hair was under the stamp."

"He can't be any older than me. How could he be the guy who was threatening Dad?"

"It wasn't Theo who sent the letters. His father sent them." Dani lifted a different image from inside the folder and set it in front of Harry. "This is Olivier Lloris. Theo's father." Dani's finger smacked the middle of Olivier's forehead. "Olivier Lloris co-founded a company that provides tires to Boeing, Peugeot and Renault."

"Tires for airplanes and cars?"

"Yes." Dani studied Olivier's picture a moment longer. "Olivier Lloris's past is a well-kept secret. Very few know the truth about him. Olivier Lloris was born in one of France's least desirable *banlieues*. From there, little is known about how he escaped the housing projects and became a wealthy businessman. Legend has it that Olivier is a gifted painter. Talented enough to create works in the style of successful artists from the turn of the century. Works that—allegedly—have been passed off as newly found pieces and sold to collectors for handsome sums."

"How much are we talking about here?" Harry asked.

"Enough for Olivier to purchase half of a small tire company fifty years ago. He purchased the other half after he and his co-owner went on a fishing trip. Only Olivier made it back to shore alive."

"Convenient."

Dani lifted her eyebrows. "To say the least. Olivier is also believed to own one of the world's largest private collections of cultural artifacts and relics, which he acquired largely through the black market."

"He's an artifacts trafficker." Harry smacked the table. "Magnus Dahl wasn't the only collector paying the men who framed Dad. Olivier Lloris must also have had them on his payroll—either to steal Magnus's artifact from under his nose or to find something else. Dad could have had the cops keep digging into the case, and it could have led to Olivier Lloris."

"Which is why your father never found me or told you the truth. To protect both of us."

Harry lifted the photo of Olivier. The man looked Gallic in every way: light blue eyes around a nose that had been broken more than once peered back at Harry with a calculating look. "He could still come after us."

"Why would he do that?"

"Because of the article in the historical journal that cleared Dad's name. If this guy finds out Nora Doyle is my sister and Gary Doyle is your husband, you think he'll let it go?" Dani didn't even try to argue. "No chance," Harry said. "Guys like this don't leave loose ends. That's why I'm going after him." He lifted a hand to stay her protests. "Not directly. Not even right now. I'll do it my way."

"You promised me you would be careful."

"I'm always careful."

She closed her eyes. "What will you do?"

Harry set the photo down. "Find a relic he can't resist."

THE END

Author's Note

The Library of Alexandria symbolizes one of humanity's great achievements—the dissemination of knowledge to all who seek it through the selfless efforts of true heroes. I personally feel the same can be said about any library in the world, though this one just happens to have a better story behind it. Where to begin? At the beginning is often best.

The initial idea for a great library in Alexandria was likely presented to a man those who have read Harry's prior adventures will recognize. Ptolemy I Soter, king of the Ptolemaic kingdom and pharaoh of Ptolemaic Egypt, as well as the successor of Alexander the Great. Not to mention the nine-times-great grandfather of Cleopatra, the last ruler of his line some two hundred fifty years after Ptolemy's death.

Ptolemy's son Ptolemy II founded the library after his father's death, somewhere around 260 B.C. Estimates of the library's contents range from forty thousand to four hundred thousand scrolls. It was regarded as the capital of knowledge and learning in the ancient world, a place of almost mythical proportions to which scholars traveled from around the globe. Those who studied at the "Great Library" included Callimachus of Greece, who created the world's first library catalogue (not surprising), Eratosthenes of Cyrene, who accurately calculated the earth's circumference, and Hero of Alexandria, who in addition to having a world-class name invented the first steam engine.

However, the common belief that the library burned in a massive fire which destroyed the contents is inaccurate. In truth the library experienced a sustained decline over hundreds of years, in no small part due to shifting political views which forced many notable scholars to find new places in which to conduct research. Part of the library was accidentally burned by Julius Caesar during the course of his civil war in 48 B.C., but this proved temporary as the damaged portions were soon rebuilt.

Egypt's subjugation by Rome following Antony and Cleopatra's defeat at the Battle of Alexandria in 30 B.C. was the first domino in a long series which saw the library shrink due to a lack of support and funding. Official membership ceased around 260 A.D., and history does not offer a concrete date as to when the library officially vanished, nor what became of the contents. All we know for certain is that if any vestiges of the once-great institution existed in 297 A.D., whatever those were would have been destroyed during Emperor Diocletian's siege of Alexandria in that year.

Regardless of its true story, the Library of Alexandria lives on today in story, a metaphorical shining beacon of intellectual progress and humankind's better nature still illuminating our lives over two thousand years later. It's also a fantastic "treasure" to find at the end of Harry's winding path, one which all started with a mysterious amulet several adventures ago. Though Harry has recovered quite the impressive list of relics, unearthing a different sort of treasure delivers what I hope is a unique take on the topic—my way of implying that not all treasure is made of gold or gems (though this one is certainly valuable as well!).

Harry begins this adventure nearly getting himself killed inside a Cana family warehouse. He quickly spots a bust of Alexander the Great's father, Philip of Macedon (*Chapter 1*), an artifact which exists only in this story. However, the inspiration for such a piece—along with a host of other relics to come—springs from the real-life story of artifacts belonging to one Michael Steinhardt, a hedge fund manager and disgraced artifacts collector who used his fortune to amass a museum-worthy collection of historical relics, many procured through decidedly less-than-legal means. His is a fascinating story if you wish to read it, one which shows the fiction on these pages is not quite as fictional as you may think.

In addition to burning down part of the Library of Alexandria, Julius

Caesar truly did own a villa called Horti Caesaris (*Chapter 2*) where Cleopatra and their young son Caesarion stayed when they visited Rome. It is also true that the location of Caesarion's grave remains a mystery, not surprising given he was most likely murdered on the orders of Octavion. Regardless, his was a violent end in a time when such a fate was not uncommon for those who sat on a throne of any sort. Moving from fact to myth, the hound Cerberus (*Chapter 2*) is the mythical Hound of Hades who guards the underworld in Greek mythology. His master Hades is the Greek god of the dead and king of the underworld. Hades received this supposed prize after he and his brothers Zeus and Poseidon vanquished their father's generation of gods, known as the Titans. Not the best deal, if you ask me, but I can attest that Greek myth makes for fascinating, if grisly, reading.

There is no painting on any dome in the ruins of Caesar's villa (*Chapter 5*). The ruins of Caesar's tomb truly are in Rome, and can be visited at the Forum near the Temple of Vesta. As with much of Roman history, the reason for building this temple to Caesar was more selfish than anything else. The Roman Senate deified Caesar shortly after his murder, but not to be outdone—or miss a chance to ride the enormous public support for Caesar—Octavian, Antony and Marcus Lepidus decreed a temple honoring the murdered leader would be erected. Ostensibly they did this to honor Caesar, though one can't help but think this was as much for the reflected glory to shine their way as it was for their fallen compatriot.

As the dome painting is not real, neither is the replica I mention in Cleopatra's palace, currently underwater off the coast of Alexandria (*Chapter 5*). The ruins of her palace are real and can be visited on a diving excursion in the waters beside that ancient city. An earthquake did actually send her palace to its watery resting place. As for hidden messages and explosive traps for unwary visitors, I cannot say with certainty those don't exist.

Archimedes is considered one of history's most accomplished and able scientists, as well as the top mathematician of his time. His scientific proficiency extended to the pair of inventions mentioned in his fictitious documents found in Stefan's safe deposit box. Archimedes' claw (*Chapter 15*) was a defensive weapon supposedly designed to defend Syracuse, the ancient city of his birth and a city with a significant harbor and bay to defend. The giant claw acted like a crane perched on the city walls, one with a grappling hook attached to the end which could drop onto attacking ships, catch them on its sharp ends, and lift the ship out of the water before dropping it back down. If this didn't sink the ship, it would in all likelihood have incapacitated the vessel and stranded any invaders on the water. Modern tests and recreations have confirmed the device could have existed and worked as intended.

On a more modern note, when Harry and Dani Fox are attacked near the coffee shop in Brooklyn, the assailant tries to use a taser on Dani. Harry throws coffee on the active taser, causing it to explode. In the real world this likely wouldn't happen, though the liquid would probably short the taser, or at least stop it from activating while it was wet.

The Gate of Domitian and Trajan Harry and Sara pass through at Dendera (*Chapter 19*) is real. If you are ever in Egypt and visit the complex, you'll find that the temple is rectangular in shape, as described, but the interior does not align with what Harry and Sara found—I changed it to suit the needs of this story.

Karnak and Luxor are again central to Cleopatra's trail, and I'm certain Sara was less than thrilled to return to the site of her near-fatal fall (though she was certainly happy to see Omar again). The Avenue of Sphinxes (*Chapter 21*) is mostly as described, the nearly two-mile-long road connecting the two temples having been renovated over the course of seventy years, with the 1,057 sphinx statues restored to much of their original glory for visitors to enjoy. For the purposes of this story I left certain portions of the renovations incomplete.

As with anything, the world moves on. Harry and Sara dash through history to uncover the Great Library, yet when they return to New York, Sara has a new job and Harry suddenly finds himself running a business. Part of this ties to Joey Morello's foresight, to his vision for what comes next for the Morello family (*Epilogue*). Organized crime is often found at the forefront of business evolution, real-life mobs morphing with the times to maintain a hold on their ill-gotten gains, for such lucrative ventures are not to be discarded easily. The diversification Joey references, moving from loan-sharking and betting operations to more current business ventures is all too real. Today's crime families are involved with online gambling, investments in wind energy and pharmaceuticals, as well as having a stake in Wall Street, the better to diversify their investments. And banking? The mob isn't content to store their laundered money in one any longer, not when it can start its own bank, which allows it to control the interest rates on money loaned to its other operations, and maintain full-cycle oversight of the cash flow. Many a criminal made their fortune in financial services. Sometimes they even get caught—but not as often as they should.

I hope you've enjoyed this final installment of the mystery surrounding Fred Fox's amulet. Harry's world has changed beyond measure over the course of these six novels, starting as a world in which he was lost and floundering, a man in search of answers with little idea where to look. Now some of those answers have been found, but I have a feeling there are new questions on the horizon, new challenges for Harry and those in his orbit, new adventures to enjoy. One thing which will remain the same is how much I enjoy these stories. Thank you for being part of this ride with me. I promise, we're only getting started.

Andrew Clawson
July 2023

Excerpt from *THE THRACIAN IDOL*

Visit Andrew's website for more information and purchase details.

andrewclawson.com

Chapter 1

Corsica

Skin tore from his fingers as Harry Fox dangled thirty feet above jagged rocks. His feet kicked at the sheer cliff face, failing to find purchase while the twisting and turning loosened his grip. One hand latched onto crumbling stone slipped further before he went still, gravity's inexorable grip pulling at him with each ragged breath. The climbing rope around his waist fluttered uselessly on the stiff breeze. He cursed himself. Forget to check one anchor and look what happens.

He could have sworn the piton had been sturdy. Had bet his life on it. Harry closed his eyes. Look how that turned out. One instant he reached for the cliff edge above him, ready to haul himself up and over the edge of precipice, the next his climbing anchor broke loose and he was left dangling by one hand off the side of a cliff, a hand being shredded by jagged rocks, slippery blood making him slide closer and closer to his fate.

Why did that monk get buried up here? Harry pushed the thought aside. First, get on top of the cliff. Then worry about who to blame.

His nose scraped across the vertical rock face. Harry held on, jaw clenched until he stopped moving. Only then did he move his other hand up, fingers crawling over the surface, feeling for any crack or crevice he couldn't see, not with his face pressed against the cliff and feet hanging over nothing but air. On he felt, scraping his fingers up the stone until they snaked into a crevice and locked tight. Fire burned in his shoulders as he took a breath and pulled up, hauling himself closer to the cliff edge with tired arms weakened from a day of climbing. Dusty air filled his nose and lungs as he gulped cool mountain air. No footholds were in reach for his boots to use. Harry shifted his weight to one arm, jammed his fingers as far as they would go—which wasn't very far—into the rock face, and heaved. Up he went, precious vertical inches higher until he reached further onto the plateau above so his forearm lay across the ground, never stopping as he pulled and let his lower hand fall free to shoot up and grab flat ground, pulling and kicking and hauling until with one last push he vaulted up and over the edge, twisting and rolling away from the precipice toward safe ground.

An orange sky looked down on Harry as he lay on his back, chest heaving. Even now, weeks before spring would arrive, the scent of the macchia filled his noise, the wild scrub which covered the island starting to come into bloom to bathe Corsica with the vibrant scents of rosemary, narcissi and too many other wildflowers to count. A uniquely Corsican welcome to this inhospitable cliff three stories above flat ground. A cliff hiding the tomb of a long-forgotten Christian monk. A monk with a secret Harry intended to reveal.

Overextended tendons protested when he got to his feet and tiptoed closer to the edge, leaning over with hesitation to peer at the ground below. Ancient rubble lay strewn across the hillside, the remnants of a staircase carved into it which had long ago fallen. Scorch marks blackened the cliffside he'd ascended, suggesting this forgotten monk had crossed the wrong saint at some point in the afterlife. Harry kicked a loose rock over the edge. It landed with a small, distant *crack*.

He backed up slowly and turned around. Another jagged peak soared above him, the flat plateau he stood on merely a waypoint for anyone wishing to reach the top. Not that anyone had climbed this forlorn peak in years. With nearly five hundred named mountains in the single range stretching across Corsica, this unmemorable peak was hardly on any mountaineering bucket list. Which is exactly what Harry wanted to hear. Three months spent scouring the history books for clues, digging through church archives across France and Germany, never knowing if what he sought lay behind the next wooden door, and all the while it waited for him up here, hidden for centuries. A monk unremarkable in every way, save one.

Abbot Agilulph served in the First Abbey of Aachen in the late eight and early ninth century. An otherwise unremarkable man, Agilulph's life of piety took a dramatic turn when one man read a religious treatise prepared by the humble abbot. The man felt as though God himself spoke through the writings of Agilulph, and this man was so moved he bestowed upon Abbot Agilulph and his entire abbey patronage sufficient to make it a bastion of scholarly learning and discourse in troublesome times. Agilulph became the man's personal clergyman, the holy man to hear his sins and guide his soul. A weighty responsibility Agilulph could never have foreseen. Whose immortal soul did Agilulph care for?

Charlemagne. King of the Frank, Lombards, and later the Holy Roman Emperor. The man often referred to as *The Father of Europe*, a man canonized by an Antipope and to whom many current monarchies across the globe could trace their lineage. Charlemagne changed the course of an entire continent at minimum, and perhaps over half the globe. Dedicated to the arts in a time when others were not, Charlemagne leaned on Agilulph for support and advice as he built an empire, making Agilulph one of the few people outside Charlemagne's family the king trusted with his life. And also, Harry suspected, with much more.

Harry removed a folded sheet of paper from his pocket. He studied the cragged mountainside ahead of him, eyes narrowed. Three months spent searching for the information on this piece of paper took him from Brooklyn to a church in Northern France and a monastery outside Berlin, as well as to several churches and small museums in each country. All based on whispers heard by a woman who knew everyone in the world of black-market antiquities, a world filled with more lies and half-truths than a political debate. What began as a rumor took shape during his journey, Harry finally uncovering the evidence in a musty, dark church basement in a nameless French village, evidence which brought him to this Corsican mountainside, a stone's throw from an ancient village where centuries ago a boy named Agilulph was born.

According to a battered record book Harry reviewed in that nameless French village, Agilulph outlived his benefactor, serving in Aachen's abbey until his death, after which the abbot's body was returned to his home village for burial. Not entirely unusual, but it was a footnote to the mundane entry which caught Harry's eye. The monk whose records memorialized Agilulph's return commented on the number of royal guards who escorted Agilulph's corpse back home. An incredible sight, the monk said, so many guards that the townspeople came out in droves to watch them pass. In addition to the guards, craftsmen accompanied the group into the mountains to bury Agilulph in a secret location high in the hills. None of them spoke a word about why the abbot would be buried in such a place, maintaining secrecy throughout the burial and forbidding the townsfolk from visiting the grave on pain of death. At least, almost none of them spoke about it.

One craftsman felt compelled to unburden his soul in the local village church. Who heard his confession? The monk who recorded this event in the church's ledger, one of the few literate men for miles around. Harry parsed through the Latin entry and discovered the monk had also broken his vows, recounting the craftsman's tale in not only word, but drawing. A drawing Harry now held in his hands. A drawing of an image which Harry believed would not only reveal an incredible secret, but also save his family.

The monk had sketched a face in profile. The face of Charlemagne, a face with large ears, a prominent nose and downturned lips with a laurel crown atop his head. A classic and contemporary image of Charlemagne. One Harry expected to find on the mountainside, if the craftsman from so long ago was to be believed. But where to start?

The paper went back into his pocket as he approached the mountainside. Cold wind kicked up, bringing the scent of the macchia and goosebumps for Harry, who blew warm air into hands scraped raw from his climb. Trickles of blood mixed with the climbing chalk coating his palms. He wiped them on his pants before reaching out to the rock face in front of him. An irregular rock face which undulated in either direction. Plenty of places to conceal a carving on the wall. He leaned back, trying to see around one part of the wall which stuck out further than the others. He leaned back a little further. *That could work.*

The outcropping was deeper than any other. Wide too, and so deep he had to pull out his flashlight to see inside, the rock angled enough to cut off any sunlight trying to sneak through. Lichen and dry moss covered the rocks. He rubbed at the growth, got nowhere and then ripped a handful off. More and more fell away under his hand until a pile of debris lay by his feet. Not that Harry noticed. He was too busy staring at Charlemagne's face.

An identical image to the one in his pocket, carved into the mountainside, tucked away into a crevice big enough to drive a tank through, yet hidden all the same. His breath came faster, the cold dark of this hidden nook turning it to clouds as his hands ran across the mountainside. There must be a way in. A lever, a hidden door, a spring to trip. The craftsman's tale said so. It *must* be here.

Harry shook his head. *Take a breath. Focus.* Think for a second and the answer often presented itself. He looked up. He took a step back. His heart sank. He'd found the door.

This wasn't a mountainside in front of him. It was a massive *boulder*, one brought from parts unknown to cover this section of the mountain. Why? Well, judging from the faint toolmarks surrounding the boulder and the mountain behind it, to mask the entrance to a cave, a cave with something very valuable inside. Why else drag a stone twice Harry's height and equally as wide up here?

To keep people out. Harry couldn't keep a smirk off his face. A good idea, using this hunk of rock. Too bad the people who put it here didn't know about dynamite.

Strict regulations surrounding explosives meant most people in France would be hard-pressed to lay their hands on anything capable of moving a massive boulder. Lucky for Harry he had the kind of connections to bypass governmental restrictions. He went back to the cliff edge, grabbing a trail rope hooked to his backpack below and pulling it three stories up to the plateau he stood atop. Out came several plastic bags of a mixture used by commercial companies to mine, quarry, or otherwise move massive amounts of stone in short order. An evolution of Alfred Nobel's famous explosive, these bags contained ammonium nitrate fuel oil, or ANFO for short.

Stable and deadly, the high explosive wouldn't detonate without a booster explosion, so it posed little danger while strapped to Harry's back. Add in the gel explosive sticks he also had in his bag and it was a different story. He kept the sandwich-baggie-sized ANFO pouches in one hand and the gel sticks in another until he knelt beside the massive boulder and then shoved them as far back as he could, repeating the process on the other side, hiding a tiny battery-powered detonator under each one.

Only after going as far to one side of the plateau as he could did Harry pull out the transmitter and turn on the power. He peered down the mountain for a long minute, searching for any sign of movement. Nobody in sight. Sending out an apology to any wildlife below, he pressed his back to the stone, closed his eyes, and pressed the detonator.

A massive *boom* filled the air. The mountain shook, vibrations rattling his body as Harry pressed himself against the wall and waited for the shaking to end. He'd only used two pounds of the explosive, half of what his contact gave him with a stern warning to "forget my face". Harry was good at that sort of thing. The booming noise faded and the ground stopped shaking. Harry counted to one hundred for good measure before slipping the pack over his back heading to survey his handiwork, picking his way around a debris field mainly comprising small rocks and the occasional pile of dust. He stopped in front of where Charlemagne's face had been revealed beneath a layer of overgrowth.

The boulder had disintegrated. Turned to dust and pebbles. Where once the massive rock stood, only a gaping black hole remained. The entrance to a cave, exactly as the confessing craftsman had said. Harry flicked his flashlight on and aimed it inside, peering through a million tiny flecks of light as dust settled to the ground.

No toolmarks were to be found on the interior. This was a natural cave, repurposed as a monk's tomb. Harry dodged a fallen rock as he took one step in and stopped beneath the entrance. The scratched Latin words in the ancient record book came to mind, the confessions of a craftsman with no idea what his confession revealed. He'd questioned why Charlemagne wanted to bury the monk high inside a mountain cave when the local graveyard was hardly full. Why every man on site had been sworn to secrecy on pain of not only death, but eternal damnation. Fascinating, but not the phrase which made Harry's skin tingle.

Of what need have we for such devious devices in a tomb? The dead cannot walk.

That's what convinced him this mountainside cave was what he sought. A resting place for more than merely a monk with the king's ear. This tomb held a greater secret. A greater treasure.

Musty air filled his lungs as Harry's flashlight beam played over the dusty interior. Warmer than the biting wind outside, the cave had a roughly flat floor leading into darkness, with smooth walls and a rounded roof overhead free of stalactites. Several steps inside brought him clear of the newly fallen rubble, none of which appeared to have come from the inside walls, which was as he'd planned when aiming the blast force outward so it struck the boulder instead of spreading in every direction. The cave structure hadn't been compromised, yet he still paused after a few steps and waited.

Shadows darted across the walls and floor as his light moved around. The dust had settled enough for him to see ahead. His light flashed over the wall, then came back. He stepped closer. "Latin." His word echoed in the still air. "That's Latin."

Letters had been carved into the cave wall at eye level. *CAROLUS MAGNUS.* Charles the Great, one of the names for Agilulph's benefactor. Another was inscribed on the opposite wall in case anyone failed to realize this tomb was entirely about the dead guy inside. *KAROLUS IMPERATOR AUGUSTUS,* the title given to Charlemagne when he was crowned Emperor of the Romans by Pope Leo III in St. Peter's Basilica. The usual sort of bravado from most kings then and now.

Harry pressed on. The hair on his arms rose as he walked, his steps tentative, cautious. He'd seen what happened when you rushed after a relic, so even though nothing about this cave stood out, that's exactly what gave him pause. Nothing in his line of work was this easy. He glanced back as a bird's cry sounded outside the cave entrance. Someone following him? He shook his head. Nobody could have trailed him this far up the mountain unseen. Even if they had, all those rocks he just blasted over the edge of the cliff would have made them think twice about climbing up here.

He turned back, lifted his flashlight higher, and stopped cold. Another cavern loomed ahead. No, not a cavern. A rear alcove, carved out of the stone, barely high enough for a man to walk inside. An additional opening was on either side, both man-made, both dark as night. Harry stopped between the two side caves, with the rear alcove in front of him. The flashlight beam revealed rectangular chunks of rock inside each room, cut stone resting in the center of each, three identical blocks tucked away in this cave hidden on a mountainside. No, not chunks of rock. *Sarcophagi.*

"Three of them," he said in the still air. "To hide the monk. That's what he was talking about."

The craftsman's question came to mind. What sort of *devious devices* did he mean? Harry had a pretty good idea. Which is why he crept toward the rear alcove on the balls of his feet, checking every inch of the floor before he moved. Charlemagne hadn't been satisfied with hiding this monk high up on a mountain behind a massive boulder. He'd hired an entire team of stoneworkers and laborers to erect an additional layer of protection. One meant to keep people like Harry Fox out.

Three identical sarcophagi placed in three identical alcoves. Identical, that is, except for the inscriptions written above the opening to each, a single word for each alcove.

DESIDERATA to the left. *HILDEGARD* straight ahead. *FASTRADA* to the right. Three female names. Three names he recognized. "Those are his wives."

Each of the women listed had been married to Charlemagne. Not a complete list, as the king had upwards of ten wives or concubines, producing nearly twenty children between them. A recipe for disaster when it came time to divide his empire. Interesting, but what did it have to do with a Corsican monk?

"Agilulph was a monk," Harry said to himself. "What does a monk have to do with Charlemagne's wives?" The monk couldn't have taken a wife, so Agilulph wouldn't have been involved with any of them. The monk had come into Charlemagne's life during his early years, having met the young king shortly after he ascended to the throne, which would have been after Charlemagne married his first wife, Desiderata. Did that rule her out?

Patience was a virtue when it came to hunting relics. Unfortunately for Harry, his had just run out. He could stand here all day trying to figure out the connection between a monk and Charlemagne's wives, or he could inspect these alcoves and figure out which one didn't kill him. He moved toward Desiderata's alcove, one cautious step at a time until he stood on the threshold. His light revealed the unmarked tomb and nothing else. No carvings on the walls, no inscriptions on the lid, nothing on the floor to warn him death waited for any who entered. He looked down. He looked up. He squinted against the light. "That's odd."

A pair of lines had been cut into the stone above him. It looked like a doorframe, though one without any sort of door to hold. Harry leaned into the room without crossing the threshold. Nothing of note to be seen. He leaned back and it hit him.

"He's a monk. Monks can marry people. Of course."

Three months of scouring Charlemagne's life taught him more than he ever wished to know about the man. Including who had presided over his marriages. "Agilulph officiated one of the ceremonies." Harry stepped back into the cave. "His marriage to *Hildegard*."

The trusted monk had married Charlemagne and Hildegard the same year Charlemagne's marriage to his first wife had been annulled. That marriage to Desiderata was politically motivated, though what she offered in terms of wealth and power didn't stand up to Hildegard, so Charlemagne did what any ambitious king would do when a new woman came along offering greater influence. He found a friendly church leader and had his marriage annulled. That's when Agilulph entered the picture and joined Charlemagne and his new, richer bride in marriage.

"It's Hildegard. It has to be."

Concern kept his feet glued to the ground. Concern he could be wrong, and concern his haste would get him killed. "One way to check." He ran back to the entrance, picked up several rocks, and came back to Desiderata's tomb. The rocks were roughly the size and shape of baseballs, and Harry Fox had been known to throw a fastball or two in his day. Now all he needed was a target.

Desiderata's sarcophagus hid a trap. It must, the same as Fastrada's had to. Why? This was Agilulph's sarcophagus, and the only woman Agilulph had a connection with was Hildegard, having married her to Charlemagne. Leaning into Desiderata's alcove, but stepping no farther, he scanned the room. Nothing jumped out. The floor was of a uniform color all around, flat rock that was part of the mountain, not man-made. No telltale cuts or openings in the wall in which to hide projectiles, no tripwires or switches meant to trap an unsuspecting intruder. Nothing at all other than the stone sarcophagus.

His light flashed over the stone block. It had a lid resting atop the base, with only a narrow opening between the top and bottom for him to slip his fingers in to raise or lower the lid. Vertical lines decorated the interior of the lip. No, not designs. Harry put one hand on the cave entrance for support and leaned in as far as he could. What in the world?

The vertical lines weren't a design. They were actually small tiles, lined up like dominoes and carefully placed to stand up between the base and lid and running the entire length in either direction. Harry could think of only one reason why anyone would go to the trouble. He stood straight, tossed the rock in his hand up and down, getting a feel for it, then took aim and fired.

His projectile whizzed through the dry air to land a direct hit on the domino-like rocks, spraying them in every direction and sending the rest collapsing in a line in both directions. A rumble sounded before his makeshift baseball landed, the ground shaking. Harry blinked as his nose was nearly sheared off by the gigantic stone door which crashed down from inside the cave wall to hit the floor like a god's fist come down from the heavens.

The rush of air and rumble of ancient stone tumbling was a physical blow, knocking him back before he even thought to leap, throwing him to the ground where he landed in a heap amid thundering echoes. Translucent curtains of dust cascaded from the ceiling, turned to flashing specks in his flashlight beam. Only after the last echoes faded did he get to his feet. A new bounce filled his steps. *I knew it.*

Hildegard it was. A look at the cave mouth found nothing amiss, no bears or intruders on his tail, no authorities arriving with guns drawn. A flash of cold whipped through his body, leaving only a tiny seed of doubt in its wake, one easily ignored. He paused only for a moment at the threshold to Hildegard's alcove. The same little stone dominoes stood between her lid and base, nothing on the floor or walls grabbing his practiced eye. The craftsman wouldn't have left the dominos out of this design, not unless he wanted to give the game away and forewarn any observant intruder as to which alcove was safe and which wasn't.

The seed of doubt returned. Harry stepped over to Fastrada's alcove and found it identical in every way to the prior two, down to the domino traps on the tomb and nothing else of note. Turning back, he eyed the sarcophagus in Hildegard's tomb. The queen's body wouldn't be in there, not unless Charlemagne had it moved from her actual tomb in France. At least he thought it was in France. On Charlemagne himself Harry was pretty clear, but when it came burial locations for the multiple queens involved, things got a bit hazy. It's not as though he could pull out his phone and check online, not in this remote region so far up a mountain.

Running back to town until he had service wasn't an option either. The explosion, or the sound of the ensuing rockslide, could have been heard down there. No, he needed to get in, retrieve what Charlemagne went to such trouble to hide, then go about laying a trap. One designed to catch a man who had destroyed half of Harry's life. A man who would soon discover the Fox family was not to be crossed.

The breath stuck in his throat as he entered Hildegard's cavern. He paused for an instant with one foot inside. Nothing happened. Cool air blew between his lips and Harry went for the tomb. The lid wasn't merely big, it was thick, at least two inches of solid stone. His only bet was to manhandle it open far enough to reach inside. Where he might or might not find a body, but he almost certainly would find something else. An object the craftsman intimated had been left in the cave, though he never said where.

The surprisingly cold stone grated on his fingers. He leaned against the nearest corner, which he could slide over only a few feet to allow him to get inside. He flexed his fingers, bent at the knees, then gritted his teeth. Slow and steady would get this lid off, not slamming into it over and over. Do that and he'd end up with a broken hand, or worse. One hand slipped on the rock and nudged a stone domino off-center, though the small piece didn't fall.

Ancient rocks grated in the walls. The noise rumbled Harry's bones. He didn't think, didn't shout, didn't freeze up. Harry reacted, twisting on a heel and diving for the exit an instant before the first stone domino slipped free, activating Charlemagne's deadly trap as Harry flew through the air. The stone door released with the sound of a falling boulder before it shot down and smashed to the floor with utter finality, clipping the heel of his boot as he landed and rolled clear.

The sound burst in his skull as though a bomb had exploded. Harry lay flat, the ground shaking, heart hammering in his chest as echoes bounced off the walls. How long he stayed down he had no idea, though his chest still thumped as though it would break when he sat up and came nose-to-stone with the door that had nearly sealed him inside for the next thousand years. He blinked. *I was wrong. How?*

It must have been Hildegard. Had to be. Agilulph married her to the king. Who else could be in the correct alcove? He rubbed grit from his face. Fastrada, that's who. The only one left, so unless this was all merely an elaborate trap serving no real purpose, what he sought waited with her.

He fired a half-dozen rocks at the small dominos surrounding her sarcophagus. The stones went flying. The door stayed up. He hurled another few rocks into the chamber for good measure, none of which activated anything, then went for the tomb. The floor didn't fall from beneath his feet. No spears erupted from the walls to slice him. Nothing but a dry footfall sounding inside a small alcove. Harry let out a breath he didn't realize he'd been holding and reached for the tomb lid. A single stone domino remained perched between lid and base. Harry knocked it aside with enthusiasm, flinching as he did. The ceiling didn't collapse, so he did a quick check around the sarcophagus and found nothing of interest. Hands on the lid, legs bent, he pushed against the hunk of stone, slowly at first before pushing harder, leaning into it, boots scraping on the floor as he levered every ounce of strength in his muscles against the gigantic lid.

It moved. Inches at first, enough to startle him, but he kept pushing. Rock ground against rock until it moved again, picking up steam until with a final grunt and shove that nearly sent him tumbling into the open grave the lid slid off and crashed to the ground. He caught himself an instant before his nose smashed into the yellowed teeth of a monk.

Agilulph stared at him from vacant eyeholes. Centuries ago he had possibly been handsome, almost certainly rich from Charlemagne's purse, yet time had taken everything from him except the skeleton which remained. A skeleton clad in what used to be a simple woolen tunic and cowl, both now faded and dry. A single rope encircled his waist, while unremarkable shoes covered the bones of his feet. Harry took it all in with a glance, then reached into the grave. He didn't touch the monk's skeleton or clothes. What he took hold of and lifted from atop his chest was no less ordinary on the surface, yet inside it contained riches beyond measure.

Harry held Agilulph's bible. Not just any bible, but the bible spoken of by a craftsman who poured out his soul to a Corsican monk, a craftsman who never suspected his words would serve as a map for Harry Fox to find a mythical bible. Why did he want it? Vengeance.

Animal skin still smooth even a millennium after it was harvested crackled as he opened the cover. The book represented several months of labor, more if this monk had transcribed and illustrated it himself. Scratched Latin lettering filled the pages, so small as to be nearly unreadable. Harry didn't bother reading any of it. Finding the inside cover blank, he flipped to the rear cover. His eyes widened. *It's true.*

A message covered the page. Not scripture. A personal note. About a peace brokered and an alliance formed. Along with the spoils accompanying the accord.

Harry moved to close the book when a phrase caught his eye. One at the very top. *Eam in dominum suam.* It meant *her home.* Understanding dawned. That was the connection, why the sarcophagus labeled *Fastrada* had been correct. Evidently she had been from this same Corsican town, a native, the same as Agilulph. A fact only those closest to Charlemagne would have known. A perfect way to hide the truth.

He flipped the book shut and slipped it into his backpack. There would be time to review the note in detail later when he prepared his trap. A silent apology to Agilulph for desecrating his tomb, but how sorry could he be for opening a tomb which didn't even have the man's name on it? Charlemagne would likely have claimed he wanted to keep the monk's burial location a secret from the enemies who wanted to unwind an alliance he had built. An object symbolized the accord. An object Charlamagne had gone to great pains to bury. An object Harry could locate using Agilulph's bible.

The cave exit beckoned ahead. Harry put the sarcophagus behind him for good, sparing only a glance at the two sealed doors which could have trapped him inside. Were the tombs empty? Probably. Only Charlemagne and the craftsman knew for certain. Bright light drew him from the dim cave interior, pulling him into the open where he squinted, the light piercing on the open plateau. Harry closed his eyes, lifted his head to the cold sun, and breathed deeply.

"*Non muoverti.*"

Coarse Italian reached his ears. *Don't move.* Harry started, catching himself in time. Having a gun jammed into your neck tended to do that. The gun pressed harder. No message needed this time. *Walk.*

Harry followed orders. He started to turn once, but a harsh command to look ahead stayed that. He could sense the man behind him was tall, taller than Harry, though half the men in the world looked down on him. Two things happened as they approached the plateau's edge. Harry realized his climbing rope had vanished, and voices came from the ground below. Harry was obliged to lean over and look.

Three men stood below. One of them touched his flat cap. "*Ciao.*"

Harry noted their common clothes and dusty shoes. These men looked like a crew of street cleaners, not mountain thieves. He responded to the greeting in Italian. "Is this how you normally introduce yourself?"

Flat cap shrugged. "When the time calls for it." He raised his other hand. Harry couldn't fail to note the pistol it held. "What are you doing up there?" the man asked.

"Exercising," Harry said. "It's a nice day."

"We heard the explosion," flat cap said. "I worried you were injured."

"You followed me up here from the village?" Harry had taken care to check for anyone following him from the rustic town below. He'd seen no sign of a tail. He was clearly out of practice. "Why?"

Flat cap smiled. "The village has ears, my friend. It hears your whispers. Questions about the mountain. About an old monk." His voice dropped. "About a *king*. The sort of whispers that draw attention."

Harry groaned inwardly. Someone at the church must have overhead. Perhaps even the nuns were in cahoots with this guy. "It's nothing," Harry said. "An old legend."

"A legend which causes explosions. What sort of man uses dynamite in the mountains?" Flat cap tapped the side of his head. "A man with secrets to hide. Or, perhaps, secrets to reveal."

A rapid-fire burst of Italian ensued. The man holding Harry at gunpoint revealed three alcoves existed inside the cave. Two were now covered by doors that had slammed shut, while one remained open. A sarcophagus was inside, and they assumed Harry had taken something from it.

"What did you take?" flat cap asked.

"A finger bone. For good luck."

Flat cap grinned. "You are a funny man. Let us see if you are so funny with a bullet in your leg."

"Wait." Harry glanced over his shoulder. The man behind him didn't seem put off by the thought of shooting an unarmed Harry Fox. Far from it. "I found a book. An old bible." He paused. "And another book. I'm not sure what it is."

Flat cap beckoned. "Toss them to me."

"Are you crazy? They could be damaged."

"Toss them or my associate shoots you."

Hard to argue with that. "Find." He looked back at the gunman. "Don't pull the trigger, okay? I'm getting the books."

The man backed up a step. He didn't lower the gun. Harry slipped his backpack off so it hung from one shoulder, reached inside and removed the bible. "I'm giving this one to your buddy," Harry called out. He shoved the bible in the gunman's hands before anyone could argue. The gunman kept his pistol on Harry as he inspected the book.

"What is it?" flat cap called out from below.

As the gunman described what he held, which was in truth an old bible, Harry reached into his pack and rummaged through it for the second book. He seemed to have trouble getting it out, though neither flat cap or the gunman took note, engrossed as they were in discussing the bible. Harry finally removed an object from his bag. One hand stayed closed. The other held the object over the side. "Ready for it?" Harry asked. "Here it comes."

Flat cap had no chance to argue before Harry knelt down, stuck his arm over the edge, and released what he held. Flat cap and his two men below all went for it, the pair huddling around their boss as he reached up and grabbed it. He caught it with the sound of rustling sand. "It is a plastic bag," flat cap said after a moment. "What did you—"

He never finished. Harry pressed the detonator hidden in his hand. Fire erupted, rocks blasted and the trio of Corsican thugs below no longer existed. Harry dropped the detonator as he turned and smashed a fist into the gunman's forearm to send the pistol flying. Harry ducked as a jab brushed his cheek, throwing one of his own in return and missing. The gunman caught Harry with a punch to the gut, doubling Harry over near the cliff edge. He reached for the smaller man.

Exactly as Harry hoped. The blow to his gut didn't truly connect, Harry faking his pain so the gunman came closer. Harry grabbed both the gunman's arms, pulling on them as he bent low and used his body as leverage to flip the man up, over and into the air. The man screamed, Harry turning a moment before the cries abruptly ended abruptly on the rubble below. So much for those thugs.

No other would-be thieves were in sight. Harry scooped the bible up, slid it into his pack and slipped the straps over his shoulders before leaning out to peer at the rocks below. One particularly large chunk stood invitingly close. It's not as though there was any other way off this mountain. Harry grumbled, got down on his backside and grabbed the cliff edge and lowered himself until he couldn't stretch any further. His toes barely scraped the top of the biggest rock below. Harry grinned. *I'm out of here*

Chapter 2

Brooklyn

A soft chime sounded in Harry Fox's office tucked behind the showroom floor. He looked up from the ancient bible on his desk with a frown. *Did she forget something?*

Only it wasn't his last customer, an heiress whose hobbies included stocking her Upper East Side home with museum-worthy pieces meant to impress her wealthy friends. His surveillance system showed a different woman standing outside his door. Someone much more interesting.

"I'm in the back," Harry said into the speaker. A button released the industrial-grade lock on his reinforced front door. "Wipe your shoes when you come in."

The woman in front of his shop flipped him the bird. A grin creased Harry's face when he stood, back cracking as he stretched the knots out. All this adventuring took a toll on a guy.

Sharp *clicks* sounded from the showroom as his visitor approached. Harry's eyes narrowed when she came into view. "You didn't wipe your shoes."

Sara Hamed stopped inside the door. She looked down, stepped inside his office, then wiped her feet on the hardwood floor. "Better?"

"You're the worst."

Sara tossed her handbag on one visitor's chair in front of his desk as she walked around, brushing him out of the way before falling into his desk chair. "My feet are killing me," she said. "I guided three tours of our new acquisitions today. Do you have any idea how long scholars enjoy

287

standing and talking about Egyptian artifacts?"

Harry's eyes remained narrow. "I have an idea."

"Very funny." Her gaze fell to the object atop his desk and she started. "You have it out?"

"I'm trying to understand what Agilulph is saying. At least I was, until you barged in."

Sara leaned over the ancient bible. She did not touch it. "I thought you had a client coming?"

"Come and gone."

"How many pieces did she buy?"

"Enough to keep the lights on for a few months." And to pay the mortgage for several centuries, in truth. Lucky for Harry he didn't have a mortgage on the place. "Apparently word about this place is getting out. A number of her friends have been in touch looking for new trophy pieces."

"Perhaps I can retire soon."

"The museum director would have a heart attack if his favorite curator left after three months."

"He'd manage." Now Sara reached for the bible, gently gripping the front cover and flipping it open. "It's blank."

Harry pulled her arm away. "It's the rear cover." Her mouth opened when the ancient script appeared. "What do you think?"

"Incredible. I can't believe you found it."

"It's what I do."

"Your humility knows no bounds." Her voice was lower when she spoke again. "Is anyone else interested in this artifact?"

What she really meant was *is this going to get you killed.* "Not any longer."

Her arched eyebrow suggested she had thoughts about that. "Tell me what happened. The truth."

He did. At least the highlights, including what happened to the thugs who tried to rob him.

"You should know better than to ask too many questions in a small town," Sara eventually said. "And where did you get the explosives?" He started to respond when she cut him off. "Actually, don't tell me."

One side of his mouth curled up. "I was never really in danger."

Her face made it clear what she thought of that. "Against my better judgement, I trust you. Don't make me regret it."

He knew enough to keep his mouth shut. Instead, he gestured to the rear cover. "Interested in reading a story?"

Sara moved closer to the desk. "Ancient Latin. Agilulph was a monk. He would read and write the language." Her eyes flitted back and forth as she read. "This is Agilulph's recounting of Charlemagne brokering an alliance between his empire and the Abbasid Caliphate. The agreement between Charlemagne and Caliph Harun al-Rashid stopped an ongoing conflict between the two powers and united them against any common enemies. The Abbasid Caliph was one of the few opponents capable of defeating Charlemagne." She looked up at Harry. "Peace with the caliphate allowed Charlemagne to focus his resources on other conquests. It's a major reason he became the *Father of Europe*."

"Keep reading," Harry said. "The agreement wasn't only a couple signatures on a contract. What do kings like to do when they make peace?"

Her gaze returned to the page. "Exchange gifts," she said shortly. "Including an elephant."

"I'm not interested in elephant bones."

Sara read on. "Chess pieces, perfume, a candelabra." She stopped, then looked up. "And a water clock, in which al-Rashid placed the keys to the holy city of Jerusalem. That's what you're after. What you want to use as bait. Charlemagne's clock."

"Pretty hard to find a better lure than the keys to Jerusalem."

Sara didn't blink. "Are you certain this is what you want to do?"

"He destroyed my life. He forced my mother to abandon us. He may not have killed my father, but what he did led my father to be murdered. Yes, I'm certain."

What was in her head, he couldn't say, and right now he wasn't sure he wanted to know. Sara knew all about Olivier Lloris, about how decades ago the French industrialist helped force Harry's father to turn away from his wife and raise their son to believe his mother was dead. Three short months earlier Harry had reunited with his mother, and soon discovered a man he'd never heard of had stolen not only his father, but two decades in which he could have had a mother.

Harry couldn't let that stand. That's why he needed Agilulph's bible. To exact his revenge.

"Perhaps you should let it go."

"I can't."

"Whatever you're planning won't change the past."

"This is about the future. About making sure we live on our terms, not his. Olivier Lloris isn't the kind of guy to let things go. He needs to understand I'm different. Guys like him never hear *no*. It's time he did."

Three months ago Sara left her university teaching role in Germany to accept a position at the American Museum of Natural History. Mainly because it was a massive step forward in her career as an Egyptologist. Another small part was that it brought her to New York. Where Harry happened to live.

She only shook her head. "I won't try to change your mind."

At least she knew that much about him by now. "Thanks." He pointed to the book. "Agilulph mentions several locations. Any of them jump out at you?"

Sara looked back down at the book, then did the oddest thing. She closed it. "Could we do this later? I have an event this evening and need to get going."

Harry almost fell backward. A museum event was more important than this artifact? Than an untold story no one had read for centuries? The Sara Hamed he knew would skip her own wedding for an artifact like this.

He cleared this throat. "Right. Later is fine. Tonight if you're not too tired. Tomorrow works as well."

"I'll call you." A wan smile momentarily crossed her face as she stood. "I know why you're doing this. I might do the same in your situation.

That doesn't make it right. Remember what happened a few months ago. We nearly died in—"

The doorbell chimed. Harry turned to the security monitor and found Joey Morello standing outside his door. "Joey?" Harry frowned. "I didn't expect him."

"I should be going." Sara grabbed her bag and headed for the front door, Harry trailing behind after he released the lock. "I'll inspect the book later."

Every question on Harry's lips stayed there as Joey walked into the shop. His face lit up when he saw who was inside. "Sara, what a surprise." Joey opened his arms for a hug. "It's good to see you."

Any frost in the air dissipated, if only for an instant. "You too, Joey." She returned his embrace. "I was just leaving."

Joey almost stopped himself from glancing at Harry. "Too bad. We need to get together soon. The three of us. I want to hear all about the museum."

"I'd like that." She squeezed Joey's hand before heading outside. Sara didn't turn to look at Harry as she walked out.

Joey lifted an eyebrow after the door closed. "Bad timing?"

Harry pulled his gaze from the closed door. "No." He waved a hand. "Not at all. She's just sorting through some stuff."

"Would that *stuff* be your adventures?"

"I wouldn't call them that. More like a vacation, really."

"Any trip with more than one corpse involved isn't a vacation." Joey inclined his head to the glass display cases surrounding them. "How's business?"

"Steady. I might have to hire someone if word keeps getting around."

"I hear the high-rollers near Park Avenue are learning about this place."

Harry didn't bother asking how Joey knew. A guy like Joey stayed alive by keeping his ears to the ground, and Joey had plenty of people to do that for him. "My only problem is they want more exotic pieces each time. Getting inventory is the biggest challenge."

"Good thing you know your way around an ancient temple." Joey winked. "Speaking of artifacts, did any of my pieces sell?"

"A couple," Harry said. "I'll have the money over next week. Once I finish with the accounting."

"I appreciate it." He rubbed a thumb over the cleft in his chin. "You don't have to sell those for me if you don't want to." A pause. "You know that."

Harry did. A year ago he never would have considered saying no to Joey Morello, least of all because Joey was his boss. You didn't turn down a request from your boss lightly. Certainly not when he was the head of the New York mob. "I know," Harry said. "And I'm happy to do it." He gestured to the showroom. "You gave this place to me. It's the least I can do."

"You earned it," Joey said. "And I'm serious. You ever don't want to move money through here, tell me. I have other places to clean it."

Selling Joey's artifacts wasn't about profit. It was about dirty money. The sort a mob boss made from illegal operations which needed to be laundered. Harry's legitimate business could do that. "How are your other businesses doing?" Harry asked. "The new ones."

"A work in progress," Joey said. "I bought into an online casino and sportsbook. The taxes are ridiculous, but people still love to gamble. My piece of a new wind energy farm near Buffalo is turning a profit already." His face darkened. "The boutique bank is another story. You wouldn't believe how much red tape I'm wading through to get that set up."

Joey hadn't worried about red tape before in his life. Same as his father hadn't. Mob bosses had other things to worry about. Things like staying alive. "I can only imagine," Harry said. "Glad to hear it's all coming together."

Joey smirked. "My father will turn over in his grave when I get my tax bill." Joey waved a hand. "Enough about business. I was passing through the neighborhood so I wanted to drop in, see how you were doing. Corsica can be a tough place. I know some of the guys on that island." His voice took a reproachful tone. "You should have asked for my help."

"And have your friends force me to give them a cut of the profits?" Harry shook his head. "No thanks. The only guy I pay tribute to is you."

Joey wagged a finger. "Not anymore. This is your business, not mine."

"It's out of respect."

Both men chuckled. It was the same line Harry's father had always said when talking about Vincent Morello, Joey's father. Vincent, who gave Fred Fox a second chance at life. "Some things never change," Joey said. "Including you Foxes getting into trouble."

"Like I told Sara, it was no trouble. Hardly worth talking about."

"Humor me."

Harry took a breath before launching into a recap of his adventure, this time leaving nothing out. "I have an idea about where to look for the water clock and keys," Harry finished as they stood in front of his desk. "Agilulph's message suggests several locations."

"What does Sara think?"

"She hasn't had a chance to properly review everything yet."

Joey looked at the book. "Is that because you keep putting yourself in harm's way, or because you're working with a guy like me?"

"Sara loves you."

"I know." Joey winked. "The problem is my professional side. She knows what I do. If Sara's ever going to settle down with a guy, she may not want him to have ties to the mob."

"Settle down?" Harry looked around the office. "Did she say something to you?"

"You can be pretty dense for a smart guy." Joey shook his head. "I know she didn't move into your place yet, but it's definitely on her mind. She didn't move here for the food." He pointed at the book. "Or the issue could be your quest to find Charlemagne's relics. No girl wants to be with a guy who's trying to get himself killed."

"It's not about me. It's about protecting my family." A beat passed. "And her."

Joey held a hand up, palm out. "I'm not arguing. I'd do the same thing. You can't let this Olivier chump get away with what he did. Not to mention guys like that won't let a weakness go. He finds out you're an artifact hunter like your father, maybe he thinks it's an opportunity to add to his collection by using you." One of Joey's fingers pointed at Harry's chest. "There aren't many guys with your skillset running around."

"The only relic he's getting from me is a live grenade. Without the pin."

"That's the Harry Fox I know. If I can do anything to help, ask. I have acquaintances in France. I bet a few of them know people who know Olivier Lloris."

"I appreciate it, Joey. And I will." Harry's phone buzzed in his pocket an instant after Joey walked out the door. His heartbeat accelerated when he saw who was calling. "Hello, Rose."

"Harry, my dear. Back for so long without a call?"

The only person in the city more connected than Rose Leroux was the mayor. Maybe. "Forgive me, Rose. It's been a bit hectic."

"You are forgiven." The sound of metal grating on metal came through his phone, followed by the crackle of burning tobacco. Harry could almost smell the cigarette smoke floating from the end of her long-stemmed holder. "What did you find?"

Harry told his story for the third time today, focusing on the artifact. "I'm not looking to sell it," he said. "At least not yet."

"Even a man with his own antiquities shop will come to me eventually. I will be here."

Rose Leroux was the biggest fence in New York. She was right: Harry would need her eventually. She'd moved his relics long before *Fox & Son* antiquities existed. However, Rose could do much more.

"There is another matter I'd like to discuss," Harry said. "One you're well-positioned to assist with." The crackle of burning tobacco was her only response. "Does the name Olivier Lloris mean anything to you?"

Silence ensued. "Perhaps it is best if you tell me why you want to know?" Rose finally said. "For your sake. And mine."

If anyone else said that Harry would think they were afraid. Anyone except Rose. Legend had it the last person to cross her was at the bottom of the Hudson. Harry believed it.

"Olivier was the person blackmailing my father to never contact my mother for two decades. He's the reason my family stayed apart for so long. I need to earn his trust. Then it's time for payback."

"I see." Ice clinked on what was certainly crystal. As far as Harry knew, Rose never drank anything but martinis, no matter the time of day. "In that case, the answer is yes. I am familiar with the name."

"Have you worked with him before?"

"I never reveal the names of my clients. Not even to you."

She'd been in this business before Harry was born. Some habits never went away. "Fair enough," Harry said. "If I wanted to discreetly make him aware that a Frankish bible with ties to Charlemagne is for sale to a discerning buyer, could you make that happen?"

"I will not dignify that with a response."

Of course she could. She was Rose Leroux. "I thought so. Would you do that for me? I'll send you photos of the artifact."

"I will contact the appropriate people. Olivier knows how to contact me if he is interested."

As much a confirmation Rose had worked with the man that Harry would get. "Thanks. I appreciate it."

Now the sound of what might be several olives falling into a martini glass filled his ear. "Harry, are you certain this is wise?"

"No. But I'm doing it anyway."

Rose sighed. "I understand. If Olivier discovers you provide the same service your father once did, he may come after you. Either to force you to retrieve artifacts for him, or to keep you from speaking out about what he did to your father. Possibly to prevent you from exacting vengeance. It does not matter. Either way, I understand."

Nobody could ever accuse Rose of not being perceptive. "I figured you would." He scratched at the stubble on his cheek. "Now why don't you tell me the real reason you're warning me?"

"The warning is for my safety, not yours. Three months ago I made what many would consider to be an ill-advised decision, a decision involving you. The fewer reasons I give people to associate our names, the better."

"Do you regret it?"

"Not at all. I am merely being cautious. In our line of work, caution keeps one alive."

No surprise Rose would still be nervous. Three months ago she helped Harry fabricate evidence to bring down Altin Cana, boss of the Albanian mob in New York and one heck of a dangerous guy. His crime family might no longer exist, but that didn't mean anyone in Rose's professional circles would take kindly to hearing their fence played a role in putting the Cana mob boss in jail. Even if it made financial sense. For the remaining families, business had never been better, and booming business meant more money for Rose Leroux.

"All I need is Olivier's attention," Harry said. "Nothing else. Your name will never come up again unless it's to move the artifacts I have for him."

"I hope my trust in you is not misplaced." Rose took another puff on her cigarette. "It sounds as though you are determined to do this. I will not stop you. However, be aware of who you are facing."

"You've heard more about this guy than just his name."

"Olivier Lloris is a successful French industrialist. No doubt you've heard rumors about how he arrived at his place in life. The untimely death of his former partner. The alleged painting forgeries. He is not a man to trifle with."

"You act like I haven't dealt with his kind before. He's a good painter who faked a couple canvasses and he pushed a guy out of a boat."

"That is exactly why I am warning you. Harry, you deal in antiquities and cultural relics. Unsavory characters abound in your world, some foolish, others deadly." Her voice roughened. "I have traversed the world of fraudulent paintings for years. Trust me when I tell you the people who deal in such goods are more deadly than you realize. Allegedly 'found' paintings attributed to renowned artists can sell for millions of dollars. Such vast sums are more than incentive enough for people to kill."

"Did Olivier kill anyone for a painting?"

"Perhaps. Perhaps not. I have heard stories of people who questioned the validity of works tied to Olivier disappearing. Nothing proven, of course."

"If he's good at what he does, there would be no proof." Harry scratched his chin now. "I appreciate the warning. I'll be careful."

"Thank you." Another pause. "Olivier was born into poverty one of Paris's least desirable *banlieues*. The local elementary school now bears his name, as does the library and at least one health clinic."

"That's what rich people do to make themselves look better."

"It works. I say this only so you understand there are many people who view Olivier as a force for good."

"I'll keep it in mind."

Rose seemed to have made her point. "I will be in touch once we have his attention. Until then, I suggest you consider obtaining more artifacts of interest."

"Why?"

"Olivier Lloris is never satisfied with one relic. He always wants more."

To continue the story, visit Andrew Clawson's website at andrewclawson.com.

GET YOUR COPY OF THE HARRY FOX STORY
THE NAPOLEON CIPHER,
AVAILABLE EXCLUSIVELY FOR MY VIP READER LIST

Sharing the writing journey with my readers is a special privilege. I love connecting with anyone who reads my stories, and one way I accomplish that is through my mailing list. I only send notices of new releases or the occasional special offer related to my novels.

If you sign up for my VIP reader mailing list, I'll send you a copy of *The Napoleon Cipher*, the Harry Fox adventure that's not sold in any store. You can get your copy of this exclusive novel by signing up on my website.

Did you enjoy this story? Let people know

Reviews are the most effective way to get my books noticed. I'm one guy, a small fish in a massive pond. Over time, I hope to change that, and I would love your help. The best thing you could do to help spread the word is leave a review on your platform of choice.

Honest reviews are like gold. If you've enjoyed this book I would be so grateful if you could take a few minutes leaving a review, short or long.

Thank you very much.

About the Author

Andrew Clawson is the author of multiple series, including the Parker Chase and TURN thrillers, as well as the Harry Fox adventures.

You can find him at his website, AndrewClawson.com

or you can connect with him on Instagram at andrew.clawson

on Twitter at @clawsonbooks

on Facebook at facebook.com/AndrewClawsonnovels

and you can always send him an email at:
andrew@andrewclawson.com.

Made in United States
Orlando, FL
30 November 2024

54703759R00173